MW01229668

WILL BE DONE

A Kingdom Fantasy Novel

Jim Doran

Copyright © 2023 Jim Doran

All rights reserved

The characters and events portrayed in this book are fictitious. Any similarity to real persons, living or dead, is coincidental and not intended by the author.

No part of this book may be reproduced, or stored in a retrieval system, or transmitted in any form or by any means, electronic, mechanical, photocopying, recording, or otherwise, without express written permission of the publisher.

ISBN-13: 978-0-9601017-7-1 (digital)
ISBN-13: 978-0-9601017-6-4: (paperback)

Cover design by: Daniel Johnson
Printed in the United States of America

This book is largely about siblings, so this one is for the sibs:
Sherry and Tom Doran
Jayne and John Doran
Judy and Joe Malecke
Tricia and Bill Wittenberg

QUOTES

"Music makes me forget myself, my true condition. It carries me off into another state of being one that isn't my own...Can it really be allowable for anyone who feels like it to hypnotize another person, or many other persons, and then do what he likes with them?"
  - Leo Tolstoy, *The Kreutzer Sonata*

"I became the kind of parent my mother was to me."
  - Maya Angelou

CONTENTS

MAP

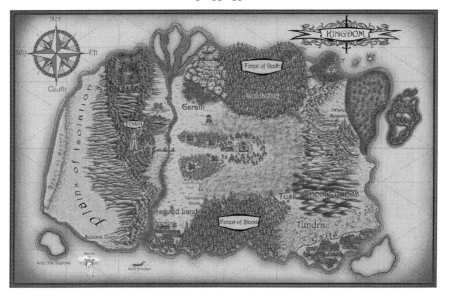

WORLDS

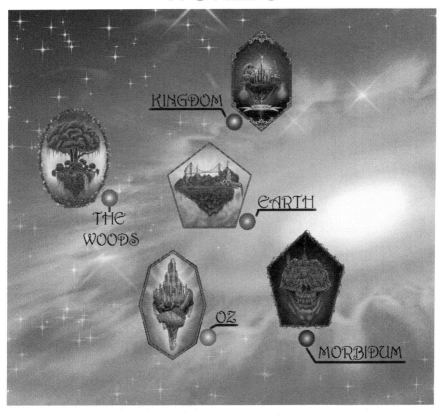

CAST OF CHARACTERS

Earth Citizens:
Harold Saturn - Earth author and data scientist, aka **Hero**.
Sondra Saturn - Earth author and chemist, aka **Sanders**.
Fitzie Saturn - Six-year-old son of Sondra and Harold.
Alice - Descendent of Wonderland Alice, Traveler. Fairy tale: *Alice in Wonderland*.
Sylvia Swonewith - Earth politician and former social worker.

Kingdom Royals:
Penta Emily Corden - Kingdom queen, eldest, teleporter. Fairy tale: *The Maiden without Hands*.
Beauty Corden - Kingdom queen, adopted daughter of Penta, aka **Shaina**. Fairy tale: *Beauty and the Beast*.

Helga Helvys - Kingdom queen, second oldest, warrior, cures curses. Fairy tale: *The Marsh King's Daughter*.
Danforth Tyreeph - Kingdom prince, bard, former Earth resident, married to Helga.

Valencia Arkenson - Kingdom queen, third oldest, match girl, luckiest. Fairy tale: *The Little Match Girl*.
Graddock Elston - Kingdom rogue, adventurer, married to Valencia.

Cinderella Hartstone Jolly - Kingdom queen, fourth oldest, events organizer, charmer aka **Radiance**. Fairy tale: *Cinderella*.
Roger Jolly - Kingdom prince, married to Cinderella.
Cuthbert John Jolly - Kingdom prince and son of Cinderella and Roger, aka **Cutlass John**.
Snow Valencia Jolly - Kingdom princess and daughter of

Cinderella and Roger, aka **Snowy Vallee**.

Snow White Whisper - Kingdom queen, deceased, cannot be harmed by weapons, aka **Coal**. Fairy tale: *Snow White and the Seven Dwarfs* and *Snow-White and Rose-Red*.

<u>Kingdom Citizens</u>:
Celeste Constellation - Kingdom pixie and royal spellcaster.
Planet Constellation - Kingdom pixie, deceased, sister to Celeste, parallel to Sondra Saturn.
Grr - Kingdom suitor to Princess Beauty. Fairy tale: *Beauty and the Beast*.
Lyken - Once huntsman to Snow White, doorman to the queens. Fairy tale: *Snow White and the Seven Dwarfs*.
T Pennilane - Kingdom selkie, Cinderella's best friend.
Turducken - Powerful elf mage. Planet's friend.
Big Mac - Servant at the royal palace under the queens. Later, bartender at the Inn of Five.
Wysdel - Resistance fighter.
Raquel - Twelve-year-old human girl. Trapped maiden.
Sinope - Nineteen-year-old sprite. Raquel's sister.
Mangiafuoca - Human woman. Owns toy shop in Tusk.

<u>Non-native Citizens of Kingdom</u>:
Lenore Marstings - Lives in the Forest of Blood. Were-raven. Resistance fighter.
Julia - Lives in the Forest of Death. Leader of forest tribe. Resistance fighter.

TIMELINE

A brief timeline of the events that came before *Will Be Done.*

In Kingdom Come Time

981 - 986: The five queens of Kingdom are born

995: Valencia learns how to sell matches (Story: "Aeron's Choice" in *Kingdom's Advent*)

996: Cinderella meets Roger at a wishing well. (Story: "Oh, Well" in *Kingdom's Advent*)

998: Penta becomes owner of the Inn of Five

999: Cinderella attends the festival and meets Roger as "the mysterious maiden."

1000: *Kingdom Come* - A Kingdom fantasy novel

1000: Cinderella marries Roger Jolly (Story: "Fitting" in *Kingdom's Ascension*)

1002: Radiance's Retreat is built

1003: *On Earth, As It Is* - A Kingdom fantasy novel

1004: Penta adopts Beauty (Story: "Shaina and Grr" in *Kingdom's Ascension*)

1004: Harold and Sondra Saturn are married

1005: Helga marries Danforth (Story: "A Fairytale Wedding" in *Kingdom's Ascension*)

1006: *Deliver Us* - A Kingdom Fantasy Novel

1006: Sylvia Swonewith is elected mayor

1007: Fitzwilliam Saturn is born

1007: Valencia and Graddock are married

1009: Sinope and Raquel's mother is killed (Story: "The Green-Haired Abductor").

1012: *Will Be Done* - A Kingdom Fantasy Novel

01 - KINGDOM CAN'T

Harold

Not every day does Alice of Wonderland show up at your house and invite you on an adventure. But today was unlike any other day.

Alice stood on my doorstep, waiting for me to invite her inside. Not the eleven-year-old girl from the novel, this Alice was thirtyish years old, had light-red hair, lived in Minnesota, and was a good friend of the family. Descended from a long line of Alices, this version bore the same name as her mother and grandmother before her, a lineage traceable all the way back to Lewis Carroll's book.

A light drizzle coated Alice's hair. "May I come in, Harold?"

I stepped aside. "Of course. I'm just surprised to see you. Trouble?"

Alice held up two fingers. "That's the second reason I'm here. Important one, but I need to see Sondra first. Is she home?"

I gestured for her to enter the living room of our colonial. Alice paused before proceeding, for we both heard someone approaching the staircase across from the front door. My wife, Sondra Saturn, descended the stairs, laundry basket against her hip, and stopped at the bottom. Alice turned to her and stepped forward, tears forming in her eyes. "Sondra, I'm so sorry to hear about your mother."

Now on the bottom step, Sondra dropped the basket, sending it tumbling to the floor and spilling its contents. Though she was standing on the ground, the taller Alice was eye level with my wife. Sondra's eyes squeezed shut as Alice wrapped her arms around her thin frame, and her tears flowed down her cheeks as freely as they had for the past two weeks.

Sondra responded in a cracked voice. "Alice."

Alice spoke over her shoulder. "I was on a mission during the funeral or I would've come."

Sondra sniffed. "It's okay."

They held each other for a long moment, and then Sondra moved back. Removing her glasses, then wiping her eyes, my wife said, "I appreciate it, but I can tell you didn't come here just for me."

Alice held her friend at arm's length. "You'd be surprised." She sighed and looked down. "But you're right. I have something important to ask of you, and it involves Bree. But first, we'll visit for a bit."

Sondra blinked away her tears. "Bree? My horse?"

I snorted at the word "horse," and Sondra squinted at me. "He *is* a horse."

"You're stretching the definition, honey." I offered to take Alice's coat after she removed it. "Bree's a hobbyhorse."

Sondra picked up the scattered clothing and restored the items to the laundry basket. "Bree becomes a real horse when we need him to and allows us to Travel to different worlds. On the other hand, Alice's looking glass allows her to go to different worlds, but it's still a mirror, Harold. Speaking of which, where have you been, Alice?"

Alice picked up a stray towel and handed it to Sondra. "Wonderland, ironically. But also Oz."

"Now that's Traveling with a capital 'T.'" I hung up Alice's coat.

I pointed to the back room of the house where we often visited with guests. "Why don't you come in, take a seat in there, and explain what's going on?"

Alice stepped through our messy living room. Our six-year-old son's toys were scattered around chairs. I almost called for Fitzie to come and pick them up, but he'd want to visit with "Auntie Alice" first, so I refrained.

The back room we kept relatively tidy for adults with a wall-mounted television and skylights. In one corner was a gold-framed painting of the cover of my first book, *Kingdom Come*, depicting the five queens of the world of Kingdom holding pennants. The painting caught Alice's eye. "You moved this from your library."

"Yes." I rubbed my chin. "More light in here."

"He uses it to steer the conversation to his novels." Sondra changed her expression to a blank, wide-eyed stare and spoke in a high voice. "Oh, Harold. How do you write so many books?" She responded with inaccurate mimicry of my own vocal tone. "I actually live the adventures I write, you know. Ha ha."

Alice turned sharply to me. "You say that? My Guild of Travelers won't be happy if you even suggest your Travels to a fairytale world are real."

I waved a hand. "No one ever believes me."

Shrugging, Alice chose a brown leather loveseat and settled herself within view of the painting. Sondra plopped down in our wingtip chair in arm's reach of the loveseat. "Harold, why don't you make us some tea?"

And there it had come. Sondra's cue for me to exit and

allow her and Alice to discuss Sondra's mother's funeral. I had sat and listened to Sondra discuss her feelings when her mother passed, but together women create a kind of magic more powerful than any spell I have ever seen cast in Kingdom. By talking, women touch each other's souls. This is what my wife wanted and needed, and Alice was more than happy to oblige.

Retiring to the kitchen, I put on tea for Alice and Sondra. The tea was some variant of Earl Grey that promised more oxidants and nutrients than any common tea could deliver. Waiting for it to steep, I turned on the stove's fan, allowing our visitor and my wife to have a private conversation.

When I returned with the tea, I placed it next to the side table adjacent to the love seat. The second cup went to Sondra who was brushing tears out of her eyes. I set the kettle down on a low, rectangular table with a cloth towel to protect the surface. The table was in the center of the room, easily accessible for someone to pour another tea. I sat down on a beige couch across from Sondra.

My wife spoke, her voice heavy with tears. "My mom's death wasn't the only reason you came, right?"

Folding my hands, I gazed at Alice expectantly. Alice sipped her tea and placed it on her coaster. "The Guild has an emergency. I don't have to talk about it if this is a bad time." Alice set her hand on Sondra's.

Sondra squeezed Alice's hand. "No, I'd like to hear more."

Alice leaned forward, her look severe. "If you say so. As of a couple days ago, Travelers cannot enter or exit Kingdom."

I tilted my head as if I'd heard a sour note in an orchestra. "What?"

Kingdom. The land of fairy tales come to life, incredible creatures, and legendary queens. Closed? How can you close off an entire world?

"Our normal ways to Travel from here to there no longer work for Kingdom. As if all usual paths are closed. Every other world—Wonderland, Oz, Astage, Morbidum, the rest—are open." Alice used finger quotes around the word open. "No one is having any trouble reaching them. But Kingdom? Nothing we do works."

Sondra set her cup on her saucer. "Your looking glass won't allow you to go there?"

"No. I hit the glass when I've attempted it."

Sondra brushed back her black bangs. "Is that why you're here, Alice? To ask me to ride to Kingdom on my boy Bree?"

"Yes. All our totems haven't worked, but we're hoping yours might. Bree comes alive when Traveling. That's rare and might make a difference."

Narrowing her eyes, Sondra said, "If it works, no one takes Bree away from me. Is that clear?"

"The Guild only hopes to make contact with our members who are stuck there." Alice patted Sondra's hand. "The organization will be in your debt if you succeed."

"The Guild." I growled the words. "I don't like your little clandestine group of Travelers who make up rules about visiting other worlds."

"Too many unlicensed Travelers have spoiled other worlds, Harold, when they introduced something that doesn't belong there. Think of a foreign organism invading a location without a predator."

"But the rules, Alice—"

"Harold, what would happen if someone brought a semi-automatic to Kingdom? Disaster, that's what. This is the Guild's purpose." Alice picked at a piece of lint on her capris, clearly uncomfortable with the debate. "The point is, if you could find a way there, the Guild would relax the rules for you two and feel that they owe you one."

"I'll get Bree." Sondra stood and left the room.

Alice nodded to where she left. She lowered her voice. "How do you think she's handling her mom's death?"

I bit my lip. "Not well. It was sudden. She reconciled

with her sister, Karen, which is a good thing, but Karen's not her mom."

Before we could talk more, Sondra returned with her hobbyhorse, Bree. Bree is a long stick like a broom handle with a plush, brown head. She mounted the toy and stroked the stick horse's fabric mane. "Hey, Bree. Wake up. Time to go to Kingdom"

Squaring her shoulders, my wife rocked the horse and bounced up and down...

...and nothing happened.

Sondra shook the handle of the horse. "Come on, Bree. Let's go."

After five minutes of unsuccessfully trying to kickstart her totem, Sondra gave up. I also gave it a whirl, unsuccessfully. Bree had only worked once for me, though.

Alice picked up her tea and looked at the bottom as if reading the dregs. "You can't Travel there, either. Kingdom is shut off from the outside."

"Has this ever happened before?" I handed Bree back to Sondra.

"No, it hasn't." Alice twirled the teacup in her hands while staring at us. "The queens of Kingdom would never shut down access even if they knew how to do it. The Guild and I are afraid someone powerful has cast a spell to keep outsiders away. And someone with such extensive magic must have ill intentions for our friends there."

The three of us looked at the painting of the five queens on the wall. What was going on there right now?

Later that night, I checked on our son, Fitzie, at bedtime. He was long past tucking in, yet my rambunctious son would occasionally not be sleeping but playing on his gaming system or reading a comic out of my old comic book collection. Tonight, Fitzie's tousled, chestnut-brown hair

—inherited from me—and his hazel eyes—inherited from Sondra—peeked out from under his covers.

I reached for the light switch. "See you tomorrow, kiddo."

Before I could shut off the light, Fitzie lowered his covers that depicted the Marvel Knights past his chest. "Aunt Alice was here. And someone moved Bree."

Leave it to a first grader to notice such a detail. "Right. Alice wanted to see Mom's stick horse."

Fitzie scooted up. "Why? So she could go to Kingdom?"

I knew where this was heading. No use trying to cut this conversation short, so I stepped into the room. "Though Bree only works for Mom, we still don't want you touching him. He's not a toy." Well, he was a toy, but…

"So Mom was going to Kingdom?"

I moved next to the bed. "We talked about experiments, right? This was only an experiment."

Fitzie looked to his left where a map of Kingdom hung on the wall. "Where do you think she'd end up? In the Hills of Despair with the giants? Or in the Forest of Blood with the tardalings?"

"Tardalongs, Fitzie. Hopefully not with them. Those wolfy-things can make their eyes like spotlights and freeze you in place." I formed my hands into claws and put them near my eyes. "Now good night."

"Do all creatures exist in Kingdom?"

No way I was exiting this tucking-in quickly. "Why do I think you're trying to stay up past your bedtime?"

Fitzie blinked with an innocent face, and I slumped my shoulders. He knew I loved talking about Kingdom at length, having had three adventures there. "Any creature exists in Kingdom that's ever been in a fairy tale and a few more. What happens there inspires people here on Earth to write their stories. Like from a vision. Only a few of us have actually gone there."

Fitzie scratched his ear. "And statues of you and Mom

are there. And one of Mom as a pixie?"

I shook my head. "No, the pixie statue is of Planet, the pixie who looked and acted like Mom in Kingdom. I met her before I met your mother. She's the one who died, Fitzie."

Fitzie nodded his understanding. "But Mom can become a pixie in Kingdom."

"Yes."

"And you and Mom are friends with the queens of Kingdom?"

Here he went! "I'm saying good night, Fitzie."

"Wait. Wait. Five sisters." He held up five fingers and lowered one at each name. "Penta is the oldest and the wisest. Helga is the one who kicks butt. Valencia is the Little Match Girl. She doesn't die in Kingdom as she does in Earth's fairy tale. And then come the two easy ones—Cinderella and Snow White."

At his mention of Snow White, I lowered my eyelids slightly. "Snow White's dead, Fitzie. No, the fifth queen is Penta's adopted daughter, Beauty. But one thing's for sure..."

I leaned down and embraced my son. "Snow White was the best hugger across two worlds. Now, good night, son. I'll see you in the morning."

Fitzie squirmed, but I held him tight. Five years had passed since I had last been in Kingdom. We'd hear news from Alice now and then. But between raising Fitzie and our jobs, Sondra and I hadn't had a chance to visit. And given the news Alice brought us today, I might never go there again.

With that depressing thought, I left Fitzie's room.

02 - A BACK DOOR

Harold

Seven months then passed. Seven months of keeping in touch with Alice, of her consulting with Glinda of Oz, of her debating whether to consult with dark magicians in other worlds. Every attempt the Guild made failed, and I worried more and more about the people I loved in the fairytale world.

One autumn day, I emerged from my library to see Sondra perched on a ladder putting up black streamers over the doorway into our back room. A few sheets of paper of Fitzie's drawings, including one of a city named Exile with zombies roaming around, decorated the walls. A plump, plush ghost sat on our end table holding a sign declaring Halloween was coming again.

Without looking at me, Sondra called over her shoulder,

"Would you mind sewing Fitzie's Batman costume? He wants to reuse it this year."

"Why? Stupid outfit is too small for him."

Sondra heard the growl in my undertone and turned around. "Who put the pea under your forty mattresses this morning?"

"Twenty mattresses. Where's the sewing hatbox?"

Sondra came down off the ladder, chore unfinished. "Right where you left it last. What's up with you?"

I didn't respond.

Sondra folded her arms. "Another rejection?"

I glared at her.

"I'll take that as a yes," she said. "You'll be accepted. Don't worry."

I turned and marched toward the laundry room. "What if I don't? What then?" I muttered.

Surprisingly, Sondra followed. And heard me. "Then we'll do what we discussed. You'll publish Kingdom's short stories independently. No shame in that."

I entered the narrow laundry room while Sondra loitered outside. Opening the cabinets, I searched for the hatbox where we kept all the needles and thread. No dice. "I know that, but I'll always question..."

Sondra tilted her head. "Question what?"

I slammed shut a cabinet and placed my hands on the washing machine. "Was I good enough?"

"You published three novels, Harold. Of course, you are."

I took a deep breath. "Yvonne was my champion. You know what happened when she left the publisher after my second novel."

Sondra put her hand on her hip. "They were rude not to return your calls."

"And they didn't renew my contract."

I looked down at the drain in the floor. Sondra knew, but I couldn't say it to her face. She reached over and nudged my chin up then pointed to a far cabinet. "The hatbox is up there. So you've shopped your latest collection around. Someone will either pick it up, or we'll publish it without them."

I looked her in the eyes. "What if it's not good enough? What if everything that was good about my last novels was because of Yvonne."

In a movie after a husband confesses his innermost fears, the wife of that character will usually cross the room and embrace her spouse, reassuring him with kind words. Not my wife. Sondra plucked a rolled-up sock from a laundry basket on the floor and beaned me with it. "Of course, it's good enough. I read it, and I think it's great."

I picked up the sock. "You're my wife. You're obligated to say that."

"No, I'm not." Sondra reached into the laundry basket and threw another sock at me. "If it sucks, I'll tell you. I've said before that your horror novel about the scarecrow stinks. These stories don't." She tossed a third sock my way.

"Stop throwing socks at me!"

"Then stop being such a jackass." With her foot, Sondra slid the laundry basket closer to me. "What the hell is the matter with you?"

Retrieving the socks, I tossed them back into the laundry basket then turned to the cabinet. "A ghost guided me to Kingdom the first time when I united the fairytale queens. Ever since then, the people there believe that I'm some heroic figure. What if I'm not? What if I'm an average person who got lucky, the same as with the book contract?"

Sondra wouldn't give me an inch. "You are a lucky guy. You married me, didn't you?"

"Sondra—"

At the same moment, our phones sounded an incoming text message. My phone dinged, but Sondra's made a bubbling sound. Given that she's a chemist, she naturally chose a ringtone befitting her profession. We both retrieved our cells and read a message from our mutual friend, Sylvia Swonewith.

11

She had also been to Kingdom in the past and was a good friend of Snow White before the queen died. Sylvia had told us Alice reached out to everyone who had ever been to Kingdom in hope they could figure out a way back.

The text read, "Hi. I'm in my car outside with Alice. Are you home?"

"Is Sylvia now Alice's personal chauffeur?" I asked.

Sondra's thumbs clicked over the display on her phone. "Sylvia made Alice promise to include her if she had news about Kingdom. I'm not sure why Alice didn't call us instead, though."

I opened a cabinet and retrieved the hatbox while Sondra proceeded to the front room.

After my wife opened the door, I heard car doors slam and an indistinct conversation. When I rounded the corner, I stopped short before bumping into our visitors. Alice was dressed in a red jacket with black slacks and stylish knee-high boots, a manila folder under her arm. Next to her stood six-foot Sylvia. Sylvia had full, dark hair and an elongated face. She nodded to me politely when I appeared.

I skipped traditional greetings. "Is Kingdom open again?"

Alice shook her head and grimaced. Maybe her presence here wasn't about Kingdom at all but another Traveling destination.

Sondra patted Alice's shoulder. "Come in and sit."

With the sun shining down through our skylight in our back room, Sylvia and Alice took their seats while Sondra put on tea. As excited as I was, I couldn't start without Sondra so I asked my visitors how they were doing. Sylvia responded that she had decided to not seek re-election as mayor of a small town near us. Without my prompting, she described the smear campaign with a subtle anti-Semitic message run against her in the first election. She had squeezed by, but the episode had taken an emotional toll on her.

"They were lies, Sylvia," said Alice. "You don't have to

take that."

"I love to govern, but I can't stand the politics, as it turns out," mourned Sylvia. "Too many jerks in this world and not enough mispacha to go around."

I crossed my arms. "You would've made a wonderful second-term mayor."

"Thank you, but my public service life is behind me now. I want to take my parents' inheritance and do charity work for a while. I'm going to help young, abused women find safe shelter."

After I explained Fitzie was at my folks for the weekend, Sondra entered and poured out three cups of tea. She handed me a soda from the refrigerator, and then she settled in the wingtip chair near the television. "So what's going on?"

Alice set her teacup gently on the coaster. "Everything I say next is in the strictest confidence. If the home office found out I was talking to you, they would remove me from the Guild immediately. I would be banned from Traveling, the first Alice in my family history to be so."

I sipped my soda. "Understood."

Alice placed the manila folder on the table. "The Travelers have been working on the Kingdom conundrum, but nothing in the archives has helped. This is unprecedented. But I have access to information they don't—my parents' files."

"Your parents are Travelers?" asked Sondra.

"My mother, Alice, and my father, Clem, are both high-ranking Travelers. Throughout their assignments, they've filed their reports, but they've also kept private notes away from the Travelers Guild. They never meant for me to read them."

I opened the hatbox at my feet and took out a needle and thread. I was going to sew Fitzie's costume while I listened, but I couldn't help but interrupt. "Why not?"

"Parents don't want to show their children their dirty, little secrets. My parents had to suppress information at times, shatter people's dreams, or other nasty bits of business. Let me explain. You know about the Traveler's Guild, but unregistered Travelers exist like Dorothy Gale and Jack Sawyer. We keep a close eye on them. The ones who create chaos...well...better I don't say what exactly happens to them. We have people surveying the internet every minute of every day looking for rumors about Traveling. Nearly every time, these curious posts about other worlds peter out."

"What happens when they don't?" I asked.

"They discover something, and sometimes, they Travel. If someone is interested in Traveling and happens to gain knowledge, we monitor the situation closely."

My eyes narrowed. "The operation sounds like Big Brother."

"We don't always interfere," said Alice. "When we sense events are unfolding naturally, we back off. Sometimes we're part of the plan, sometimes not."

Sylvia rubbed together her lily-white hands. "What did you find out?"

Alice referred to the folder. "When my family and I helped fifteen-year-old Penta return to Earth after she was sent here against her will, they received a new task. This folder has information on a man named Joseph Macquin. My parents were assigned to monitor Joseph as he started inquiring about Traveling. While we've kept the other worlds a secret from non-Guild members, Joseph somehow figured out they exist. Likely, he discovered it from a Traveler with a big mouth."

My fingers tapped the side of the chair. "Can he take us to Kingdom?"

Alice shook her head. "Joseph was fascinated with Traveling, particularly to Kingdom. He researched it in his late teens. He wrote a blog my parents deleted multiple times, comparing off-world Traveling to Jules Verne's *Around the World in Eighty Days*. Then he disappeared nine years ago. Fortunately, my parents retained notes on him that aren't in the Guild archives."

I moved a needle in and out of the Batman costume. "He

found a way to Travel without a totem."

"Yes, and my parents suppressed it."

"A back door to Kingdom!" Sondra exclaimed.

Alice grinned. "You could call it that. Joseph's website had his research on back doors. He purchased a totem illegally and Traveled to a few worlds but didn't discover a way to Kingdom. In my parents' next entry, they say Joseph disappeared from Earth, and the Guild expected he found a way there. They sent my parents to retrieve him."

Alice paused and took a sip of tea. Sondra nearly jumped out of her seat. "Don't stop now! Did they find him?"

Alice set down her cup. "No. When they returned, the Guild instructed them to ruin his reputation. My parents aren't bad people, but they followed instructions. In rebellion, though, they kept some of their findings from the Guild. In particular, how Macquin Traveled to Kingdom."

"Did they write it down?" I asked.

"In detail." Alice opened the folder, and flipped a few pages. "The instructions say to Travel to a particular world and then shimmy through a log that Joseph had marked. The log is a totem. When you exit the other end of the log, you should land at the Circle of Counsel in Kingdom."

Finally, a lead. My foot was bouncing up and down. "What world did he go to?"

Alice sat back. "And there's the problem. The connecting world is protected. Travelers aren't allowed to go there. The Guild won't even try this route."

Sylvia reached for her teacup. "But this is an emergency. Surely, the Guild can make an exception."

Alice said, "Have you heard of the butterfly effect? Guild members do not travel through time, but we do travel through worlds that inspire writers in the past and future."

Sylvia peered over her teacup. "I'm not familiar with the butterfly effect. And what do writers have to do with this?"

"I've forgotten you haven't Traveled to anywhere but Kingdom, Sylvia." Alice sat back. "You likely think all the fairy tales that ever could be written have been. But think of other worlds. The events there inspire artists, especially authors, to write them down as stories here on Earth. Over time, we've categorized them into literary genres or one author's work. For example, Shakespeare had a connection with the world called Astage. Nearly all his plays are history there."

"A Shakespeare world." Sondra rocked back and forth. "But he's dead. How do you change the outcome of his stories?"

"An unlicensed Traveler once went to Astage and interacted with characters there." Alice licked her lips. "This rippled into one of the characters taking a different course of action. Now we have the tragedy *Macbeth* instead of the comedy *Mcduff*. The Traveler, though he lived in the present, was able to change the world and inspire Shakespeare to write a different play."

I shook my head. "That's crazy! As you said, we don't time travel."

"No, but it still happens. In less than a second, Shakespeare's *Othello* becomes *Iago*. When Travelers return, they realize it. The Guild has managed to undo many of the changes. Not easy work."

"I'm surprised you let anyone Travel, then." I snipped off the thread I had been using to sew.

"Most worlds are fairly resilient, but certain ones exist that are extremely susceptible to changes by Travelers." Alice rubbed her hands. "The more delicate worlds are categorized as restricted. This is the reason I'm bringing the matter to you."

We sat back, now understanding the seriousness of the problem. Alice continued, "The Guild would never let you Travel to the intermediate world Joseph went to. It's a known world, but it's so classified I can't even tell you its name."

Sondra threw her hands in the air. "So how do we get there?"

"Not 'we.'" Alice looked into her lap. "If I'm caught there, the Guild will make sure you never see me again. Harold, Sondra, you have to promise me you'll go as quickly as you can directly to Kingdom. Do not linger in the protected world."

I made a mock show of crossing my heart. "Of course."

Sylvia patted her legs. "I promise as well. My friends are in Kingdom. I'm unemployed and have yet to start my charity work, so no one will miss me here."

"One more promise," said Alice. "If you Travel there, the Guild will trace it back to me and my family. Will you look for Joseph Macquin while you're there? If you locate him, you'd be doing a service to the Guild. That way I might be able to smooth things over when they come down on me."

I wasn't fond of doing the Guild's dirty work, but her request was reasonable. "We promise."

"Alright." Alice ran her finger along a page in the folder on her lap. "I can whisper the world's name to Bree. You have to be extra careful, though. Avoid all contact with anyone if you can. We often have a change of clothes for arriving Travelers. You won't have that. You have to do your utmost to find this log quickly. According to this, it's about five hundred yards west of the entry point to the world."

"Five hundred yards?" I put the sewing kit back in the hatbox. "That's a short walk. No problem."

Sondra stood. "I'll fetch Bree."

The Woods

03 - SCHERZANDO

Sondra

I called my sister, Karen, who immediately agreed to drive ten hours to watch Fitzie. Karen and I had had our rough patches, but that was done for now with my mom's passing. She and I communicated nearly every day over social media, keeping each other informed of our routine lives. Funny how events change over the course of a few months.

"I'll take great care of Fitzie at your home," Karen said on the phone. "Don't worry."

"If he's with you, I won't, Karen."

"I'm concerned about you leaving and not coming back. I'll pray for you."

I patted Harold's arm. "Eh...I have Harold. He's Kingdom's lucky charm."

Harold frowned at my statement. Oops. I'd poked a sore

spot.

Harold and I retrieved Fitzie and hugged him tightly as we prepared to leave. I tapped my son lightly on the nose. "You listen to your Aunt Karen now."

My sister adored Fitzie so this wouldn't be hard. He grinned. "When will you be back?"

"Soon. Aunt Alice will be here until Aunt Karen arrives."

"You look funny in those clothes." He fingered the tan tunic I was wearing. Fortunately, we had costumes from fantasy conventions Harold had attended. One even fit Sylvia.

"Yes, I won't make the cover of *Vogue*." I kissed him on the head. "I love you."

Minutes later, Sylvia, Harold, and I were seated on the hobbyhorse, ready for our trip. We three barely fit on that horse. I was in front, snuggled up against Bree's neck, and Harold and I were so close it was a good thing we were husband and wife.

Alice whispered the name of the protected world to the plush head on the stick toy, and my horse, Bree, filled out to become a real horse that carried the three of us. His chestnut-colored body expanded into an equine figure, and his wool hair became a dark mane. I loved and trusted my horse the way pet owners love their pets. Bree knew where he was supposed to go, and he clip-clopped about a bit with my hand on his side. Fitzie clapped and whooped, and Alice put a protective arm around him. We wished each other a fond farewell.

I leaned forward like a jockey in a race. "Okay, my boy. Go!"

Bree leapt ahead. His front hooves never landed in our house. An oval, large enough for us to pass through, appeared in the air, and we bounded into it. Bree's hooves landed on grass in the middle of a clearing in a forest. At first, I thought we were back in Kingdom. The air was pure and had that sweet taste to it; the trees were tall and nearly all the same size.

Bree shook his body, alarmed and agitated. I put my hand on the side of his head. "Hey, boy."

He was having none of it. He bucked, and we three flew off his back. I hit the ground awkwardly, but the soil in this world was spongier than Earth's. I felt as if I'd landed in a bed of moss. Bruised, yes, but nothing was broken, thanks to the softness.

Why was Bree acting so oddly? This world felt as peaceful as a nature screensaver. I patted Bree's back. "Bree?"

My horse whinnied, rotated, and took a few steps away. He turned to eye me, and I approached him with my hand low to show him I meant no harm. Instead of nuzzling it, the damn horse jumped, a rift in the air appeared, and he was gone! Through the crack in space, I briefly saw our living room again. I couldn't believe it! My trusted companion had abandoned us here.

"Bree!"

Harold held up a finger to his mouth. "Shush! We don't know what type of world this is. A Tyrannosaurus Rex could come along."

I didn't like losing Bree, and Harold knew it. He gently took my arm. "Bree'll be okay."

"He's our ticket home."

"Let's make it to Kingdom, and then we'll figure out our ride home," Harold said. "We've returned other ways before."

Sylvia rubbed her arms. "Where are we?"

Surrounding us was a multitude of trees—ash, oak, elm. They were gathered in clusters, impossible to become lost in. Birds sang around us, and the sun shone down like a gentle embrace.

We walked west through the forest with Sylvia taking the lead. The day was a perfect summer gift—a day where you walk along a field and you shake a soda bottle, open it, and let it overflow just for the hell of it. That sort of day. As we walked, I found keeping my mind focused on the log difficult. I felt like lying down and staring at the sky. Maybe plucking a blade of grass and putting it between my teeth as I discerned pictures in the clouds.

Wait. I'd never done that before. Why did I think that?

Sylvia turned around. She bounced up and down impatiently. "Why are you two going so slow?"

I saw a similar sentiment on Harold's face. He swaggered as he walked—his eyes had a faraway look.

I scuffed my feet on the grass and suddenly had an urge to walk barefoot. "I feel like staying here. It would be fun, don't you think?"

Sylvia breathed in deep. "Yeah." Her eyes lit up. "I bet they have magic here."

She was right. Magic. But not the spell sort. A different sort of magic. I wanted to skip instead of walking. After all, skipping is far more enjoyable.

Harold reached out to me and slapped my arm. I stuck out my lower lip. "Hey, what did you go and do that for?"

He tittered. "Tag."

Sylvia put a hand to her mouth and giggled. "You're it!"

Tag? Was he serious? We had more important things to do than play tag. We had to find the log because that pointed the way to hidden treasure. Hold on. No, it didn't. We were going to go through the log and arrive at…the other side? I couldn't remember, and it was all Harold's fault for slapping me on the arm! We didn't have time to play tag, or go exploring, or fall asleep in a hammock while counting the birds in the sky. Besides that, I was not GOING TO BE "IT!" I HATED BEING IT!

I'd show him! I swatted at Harold to tag him back, but he jumped away and laughed at me.

"You're it! You're it!" he taunted.

"Grow up!" I shouted at him, but I shook my head. I didn't want to grow up.

Harold stuck out his tongue. "Never! Why should I?"

Sylvia pirouetted around, her hands above her head in a pose like a ballerina's. "I'm graceful."

"Hey! Hey!" I shouted. "We need to go. Something is happening to us, you bunch of boogers!"

"I know you are, but what am I?" retorted Harold.

"You're so immature, Harold the Barrel," I said.

Harold licked his finger and put it in the air. "It's a classic."

I grabbed his ear, and Sylvia's arm and dragged them forward. Harold pulled away. "Great! Now I got cooties!"

"You're such a goober."

Sylvia said, "Let's all lie down and tell a story. I useta do that with my friend Carla. I want to tell a story about a ballerina who turned into a princess."

Harold frowned. "That's a dumb story. I write better ones. My next ones won't be about a bunch of *girls*, though."

Sylvia looked hurt, and her lip trembled. "I like my story. I wanna be a princess."

Wait-a-second. We gotta get to that log. "Come on, you two! It's like the mother tomato said to the baby tomato. Ketchup!"

"Har har!" said Harold. He stepped back. "You'll have to catch me."

"Booger! Don't run away."

Sylvia started dancing in the opposite direction. "Don't be a sourpuss, Sondra. You're acting like my mother."

Mother. I didn't want to be a mother. I wanted to run and play with them. I wanted to chase butterflies, and find secret trails, and mix different sodas and taste the result. I didn't want to be the mother. My mom could be—

And then I remembered.

I flopped to the ground and the tears flowed from my eyes, far easier than in years past. I wailed, and both Sylvia and Harold stopped. They looked at each other.

"What did you say to her?" asked Sylvia.

"Nothing." Harold shrugged. "She's just goofy."

"Mommy!" I cried. "I lost my mommy."

I struggled to catch my breath. "I've tried to be a good girl, but I lost her. I thought I would have her one more day, but I didn't. She died, and I'm completely alone!"

Instantly, Sylvia was on her knees next to me. She

grabbed me and hugged me. "Oh, Sondra." She started crying too.

Even Harold kneeled next to us. Without a word, he put his arms around us.

I hiccupped, trying to catch my breath. "She would've wanted me to be brave. I've tried to be the girl she wanted me to be, but I miss her *so much*. No one understands."

Sylvia squeezed me harder. "I understand."

"How could you?"

Sylvia blinked. "Because I was a social thing-a-ma-jig person before I was a mayor. I hafta understand. I feel bad."

"So do I," said Harold, a tear dripping down his cheek. "She was like my mother, too."

The tears flowed out of me, and as they did, I felt... lighter. More relieved. I found what had happened hard to put into words. Like how you feel after a good hot bath.

We sat and cried a bit more until Harold peered into the distance. "What does that sign mean?"

Sylvia and I turned around, and we saw a wooden sign on a pole sticking up from the ground. The placard of the sign was in the shape of a rectangle. Sylvia bit her lip, concentrating. "I've heard of this place."

The sign read The Hundred Acre Wood.

Harold shook his head. "Oh no! No, no, no!"

The revelation lifted us out of our funk. Sylvia was a mayor, Harold was a data guy, and I worked with chemicals. And we were not where we were supposta be.

Harold broke the silence. "Do you think *they* exist?"

"I'd like to meet them." And suddenly I understood. I knew why this was a protected world. The barriers of adulthood rose in my mind, and I started acting my age. "But we can't. No adults are allowed here. The beauty of those stories is they are undefiled by people our age."

Nodding, Harold said, "Right. Bree started to change too. His animal instinct warned him to leave before he started having pony thoughts."

Sylvia tensed her shoulders. "We can't be seen! At our age, we'd ruin everything."

And then the voice of a young boy calling through the forest cut across the landscape. "I thought I heard voices."

"Hide," I said.

We ducked behind a clump of bushes moments before a pre-school boy with light brown hair entered the clearing. I suddenly thought of Fitzie and how far away I was from him with no way back. My maternal instinct wanted me to go out and give the boy in the clearing a great big hug. He was the symbol of boyhood, not the snotty little pipsqueak types who throw snowballs at your car either. He was the true child, the one and only, and we were ten feet away from him.

Christopher Robin looked around the clearing and then stopped and stared at the bushes between us. He tilted his head, and I thought he could see us. We all held our breaths, but he turned away and skipped off.

We stood, and I touched Sylvia's arm. "We must find the log. Now."

Once we were moving with a purpose, we found the fallen timber. We hurried to it, one side hanging over an edge that dropped two feet. I noticed someone had carved a word on top of it. "Verne."

"This is it," said Harold.

Thanks, Captain Obvious. Joseph might as well have carved, "This is the log you are looking for."

Sylvia went first, and Harold followed. I went last but paused and looked around. What an amazing place this was. We spend so much time and effort keeping Earth clean, and this Shangri-La was virginally spotless. If only I could declutter my mind in the same way. I'd remove all the garbage I've picked up since reading the books of my childhood. If we could return to innocence, the world would be a far better place.

04 - CIRCLING THE CIRCLE OF COUNSEL

Harold

As I exited the log, I took a deep breath and filled my lungs of air untainted by smog. The comforting scents of honeysuckle, lavender, and mint filled my nostrils—all pungent yet pleasant. The sun was setting and the many chirpings, croakings, and whisperings of the night, all uninhibited by technology and man-made machinations, welcomed us back.

Sondra, Sylvia, and I had landed in the middle of an oval of stone chairs known as the Circle of Counsel. Originally, only four stone chairs occupied the plain. Over the years, six more had been added. All species from dwarf to pixie, dragon to giant came together here as a seat of government. They debated current issues then requested the queens to enact new laws.

"We're here!" said my wife. Now that we had made it to Kingdom, we had to take on our "Kingdom" names—Hero for me and Sanders for her. Tradition stated people navigating between worlds received new names, though I think the pixie, Planet, when I had first met her here just made that up. Anyway, Planet had dubbed me "Hero," and Sanders became my wife's name after another adventure. Sylvia hadn't received a Kingdom name yet, though she had Traveled here many times.

Sanders shrugged her shoulders and her pixie wings emerged. Beautiful aqua-green appendages sprouted from her shoulders, capable of giving her flight. She stroked the membrane of her wings. "Let me find my bearings, and then I'll teleport us to the Inn of Five to ask what's been going on."

Sylvia retrieved her glasses from her pocket and put them on. "What's that?"

She indicated the top of one of the thrones where a sign hung. Sanders pointed at the sign and a beam of light, penlight size, split the darkness. Written on the wooden board were the words "Snow White Lives!"

Sanders flew over to the sign and examined it. The placard was etched on a piece of wood and the letters engraved by a knife and colored in with black ink. She turned back to the group. "Hero, I thought she was dead."

In my last novel, witches had cast an aging curse on one of the queens, Snow White. As an elderly lady, she sailed off to die. When I thought my novel was done and I was about to publish it, I received a letter from Penta who had asked me to include some text as an epilogue. The text described a scene with the remaining queens and hinted that Snow White might not actually be dead. In the six years that had passed since, Penta never sent me another letter stating Snow White was alive, so I assumed she was truly dead.

Sylvia crossed her arms. "Three years ago, I discussed

this with Alice. She told me that the living queens of Kingdom fabricated the events in that letter for the people of Earth. The people of Kingdom thought of Snow White as an extraordinary queen, but still human. The people of Earth think of Snow White as a legend, and legends never…" Sylvia's voice cracked. "Die."

I cleared my throat. "That has been my understanding as well. I thought Snow White was dead. So why would someone put up that sign?"

Sylvia looked south to the Forest of Blood. "Are we sure this is Kingdom?"

I breathed in deep as I peered around at the circle of chairs and the woods to the north. I had been here many times before. "Yeah, it is."

Sanders flexed her fingers. "Alrighty-then. Let me teleport us to the inn to dig up info."

Sparkles sprang from her fingertips, and we disappeared. Sanders could cast a few common spells, but her real power came from her imagination. She drew from her knowledge of chemistry and biology, her playfulness, and her experiences on Earth.

With a flash, we dissipated and reappeared about twenty yards away from the Circle of Counsel.

"Sanders, I thought you knew how to cast this spell," I said. "You practiced it with Celeste."

Celeste, pixie and sister to Planet, had visited us on Earth for Fitzie's baptism years ago.

Sanders put a hand on her hip. "Yes, Celeste explained it to me and we practiced. But I have no magic on Earth the way she does, so we had to pretend."

"Pretend? How did you pretend?"

Sanders stiffened. "I sort of did the gestures and chanted, and then hustled into another room."

Sylvia's mouth dropped. I ran a hand through my hair. "I don't think that's the same thing as actually casting it."

"Celeste said I was doing it the right way! Let me try

again."

My wife closed her eyes, and the sparks ignited at her fingers once more. Her shoulders shook, and she raised her hands. With a snap of her fingers, we disappeared a second time.

And reappeared fifty yards away from where we had been standing.

I crossed my arms. "Well, it seems Sanders the Implausible, as you call yourself, needs a little work on her teleportation spell."

"Oh, shut up!"

Always the peacemaker, Sylvia told her, "You need a little more practice, is all. Let's walk to the Inn of Five to ask our questions."

The Inn of Five had been run by one of the queens, Penta, before she ascended. I doubted she would be there now. Too bad as she was the one I'd most like to catch up with.

Before we took a step, however, a raven flew from a nearby tree and landed on the ground in front of us. She then transformed into a dark-haired woman in her late twenties—not a stranger, but a friend from the past, a woman from the Morbidum world who called Kingdom her home now.

"Lenore!" I shouted.

Lenore ran forward and took Sanders' hands. "Greetings! I'm so glad to see you."

"Lenore, what are you doing—?" Sanders began.

"We can't stay here," the dark-haired beauty interrupted. "You've been spotted. I spied a scout scurry off when you arrived. While no more are around, we must leave at once before the soldiers come."

I grasped and squeezed Lenore's hands as she extended them to me. "What do you mean?"

"I'll explain it all when we're safe," she said. "The scout and I were both watching the Circle. He doesn't know who you are, only that you are a threat. For me, you're the hope our small band of resistance fighters need right now."

"Resistance fighters?" I asked. "What do you mean?"

"The queens aren't in power anymore, Hero," she responded. "A king has taken their place. He calls himself King Piper."

"How did that happen?" asked Sanders.

Lenore held up a hand to ward off our questions. "No more. For now, follow me!"

Our old friend turned into a bird and flew south. The three of us followed her out of the clearing and into the grasslands. Nocturnal chitters and the flapping of unseen creatures overhead were the only interruptions to the stillness of the night. The grass brushed against our leggings as we trampled forward, occasionally dodging a picklebush. While I wanted to enjoy the serenity of Kingdom at night, I had too many questions.

Eventually, we approached a ravine. Lenore descended the steep drop-off. After Sylvia, Sanders, and I climbed down, we noticed a door in the wall of the ridge. Lenore landed in front of the entrance and turned into her human form. Opening the door to reveal a small room carved into the ground, she gestured frantically. "Inside."

We entered, and Lenore lit four candles and placed them at a small table. We sat around it, taking up most of the room in this small space. A loamy scent hung in the compartment, and we had to duck under roots in the ceiling. The outside noises were blocked down here.

Lenore sat at the head of the table. "I'm so delighted to see you all. I'd hoped you would come to restore Kingdom again, but right now, you must be confused."

"I'll say!" I scratched my ear.

Lenore reached under the table to a small shelf and retrieved a scroll and a box. "I can explain some of what has happened, but not everything. Lift your elbows so I can unfold a map of Kingdom."

After she unrolled the scroll, Lenore placed the box on a corner to hold an edge down. Opening the container, she retrieved several rag scraps from its contents and held them. "We have to be careful of Piper."

"Who the hell is this Piper dude?" asked Sanders.

"As near as the Resistance can figure, Piper has all of Kingdom convinced our beloved queens never ascended to the throne. No one believes, or knows of, your first adventure here, Hero. If you tell anyone in Kingdom that you found and united five sisters and that they rule together over this land equally, they'd call you a liar."

"But that's what happened," I protested.

"I understand," replied Lenore. "But the story everyone now believes is that Piper appeared from nowhere thirteen years ago and overthrew illegitimate King Shade—the same time when the queens defeated him. Furthermore, they think he has restored Kingdom to its current state of glory."

Sylvia held down a curling edge of the map. "But can't the queens convince the people of the truth?"

Lenore looked at the scraps in her hand. "They could if they could remember themselves. But like the rest of Kingdom, they've lost their memory of becoming queens."

I leaned forward. "What?"

Lenore set down the scraps, and I noticed they were roughly human shaped. "When I realized everyone had forgotten the sister queens, I rushed to the Inn of Five and found Queen Penta with no memory of her past. If you ask Penta, she was adopted and raised by a blacksmith who died a few years ago. She purchased the inn and runs it as a barmaid. It's all true up to the point where you had met her, Hero. She has no memory of her battle with King Shade, her coronation as high queen, or any of her sisters."

I rubbed my temple. "Lenore, why can you remember and no one else can?"

"A few of us remember. Me and my friend Julia in the Forest of Death. The Travelers who were stuck here. We think, because we weren't born in Kingdom, the spell did not work on us."

I shifted on my stool. "So here we go again. Like the first time I was here, we must travel around Kingdom to find the queens and convince them, again, that they belong on the throne."

Lenore held up two fingers. "We face two differences. The first is the legend that five peasant girls would rise and become queens has also been erased from people's minds. That legend helped you convince the sisters they were destined to be queens. This time, they are going to be harder to convince."

Crap. Lenore was right. The first time I was here, once I found the queens, citing the legend had been the key to persuading them.

Lenore held up the rag dolls in her hands. "But don't lose hope. The other difference is I know where most of the queens are."

"You do?" I asked, trying to figure out what the dolls represented.

"Indeed. The movement has been busy recruiting and sending people out looking for the other four. One was easy to find, but the other three much more difficult."

Lenore selected one of the dolls, and Sanders chuckled as she examined it. "That's a doll of Cinderella, isn't it? It's crude but it looks a little like her. Did you steal it in your bird form?"

Lenore pulled back, affronted. "I am no common crow!" She puffed out her chest. "I am a raven. And I found the set of the queen dolls on a trash pile. Some child didn't remember her own queens and threw away her toys."

Lenore was too proud to admit she picked these up as a raven, but as a woman, she was rummaging around in a trash heap? "Where's Cinderella?"

Lenore placed the blonde-haired doll in the forest in the north. "Cinderella goes by her birth name again, Radiance. In her story, she ran away to the Forest of Death and joined a conclave. There she remains. Fortunately, my friend Julia is with her."

"Where are the others?" asked Sylvia.

"We looked in Exile for Valencia, but she had left, and we have not found her yet." Lenore put the smallest doll in a city named Tusk. "But we believe she's here. Tusk is closest to her last known location."

Lenore then selected a rag doll with long, black hair. "This is Beauty, and she lives in Halifax Manor as a lady. The legend has it that Piper saved her from her oppressor, freed her, and established her as the lady of the manor."

"He took credit for Penta's actions, too," I hissed. "She freed Beauty when she adopted her. What about Helga?"

Placing a rag doll on the Marsh of Wishes, Lenore bit her lip. "She may be hard to contact. She has taken holy orders as a Sister of the Beatific Vision. She lives in a convent in the Marsh of Wishes."

Sanders jerked her head. "She's a nun?"

I smirked, picturing the warrior queen in religious garb. "Are you surprised?"

"I suppose not," said Sanders. "She always was the religious type."

"What about Snow White?" Sylvia asked. "Is she living or not?"

"Why would you think that?" Lenore looked at her sharply. "Because of the signs?"

Sylvia picked up a doll with dark hair, holding it tenderly. "What do you know of the signs, Lenore?"

"They are messages to others in the Resistance movement. They don't mean anything to the people who have lost their memories. Someone has told me they are similar to your Earth message of 'Kilroy was here' in some war. They encourage us to keep fighting."

Sylvia cast her eyes downward. "So, she's not alive. You're using her name as a tribute and secret code."

Knowing how sad this news of Snow White made Sylvia, my wife switched the subject. "I hate to rain on everyone's parade but restoring the queens' memories is only half the battle. They're not magical. How are they going to throw a counterspell to Piper's?"

Lenore selected and placed the Penta doll on the Inn of Five. "You're right that they aren't magical, but they have their abilities. Penta can teleport, Cinderella can influence people. Magicians exhaust their essence daily and must wait for a new day to continue spellcasting."

Snorting, Sanders grumbled, "Yeah, tell me about it."

"But the queens have unlimited use of their gifts. And they have sought out and collected powerful magical items now. Wishing stones, holy swords. Save the queens, and together we can save Kingdom."

"They had versatile allies before they ascended as well." Sylvia's eyes lowered. "If only Snow White were alive. She could really help us."

I nodded. "The remaining queens are a force to be reckoned with, though. Spell or no spell."

Sylvia's eyes brightened at my mention of a spell. "Sanders, did Celeste teach you a counterspell or anything that might aid us?"

"A spell so strong it erased everyone's memories in Kingdom? I doubt I have the power to counteract it." Sanders frowned. "I wouldn't know where to start."

"Cheer up, Sanders the Implausible." Lenore's eyes sparkled. "The Resistance knows a countermeasure for the queens' condition. The key to restoring each monarch's memory is the one force more powerful than magic—love. Specifically, true love's kiss."

Sanders rolled her eyes. "That old chestnut."

Lenore frowned, not understanding the reference. "If we can persuade the queens to kiss their husbands, that kiss will break the spell. Not on everyone else, just the queen and her husband. However, the Resistance consulted a mage who is an expert on mesmeric spells. She believes when the last queen kisses her true love, the spell will be broken across Kingdom."

I rubbed my jaw. "We need their husbands then. Where

are they?"

"Cinderella's husband, Roger, is at his home," said Lenore. "Valencia's husband, Graddock, was last seen in the royal city of Town. Grr, Beauty's beau, should be at the manor as a servant. Helga's husband, Danforth, is going to be a problem, though. He and Helga had a falling out, and we think he returned to Earth."

"Fantastic." I leaned back in my chair. "So, Helga is out of luck, and so is Penta because she never had a true love. And since kissing a maiden is essentially the same as asking her hand in marriage here, none of the queens are going to be willing to pucker up for their true loves immediately. They'll be cautious."

"Nonetheless, the Resistance figures if we can turn three of the queens' hearts, we have a fighting chance," said Lenore. "Three queens might be enough to figure out a loophole for Queen Penta."

Sanders looked thoughtful. "We'll cross that bridge when we come to it."

I picked up the Penta doll and examined it. "I want to go to the Inn of Five. If I can urge Penta to become an ally, we'll be far better off. She's a towering presence even if her sisters don't realize they're related."

"And why do you think you can influence her?" asked Sanders.

"Because I'm her best friend. I think I have a way to convince her she's a queen." I straightened my shoulders. "I guess I have to take on the mantle of the hero again."

Lenore grimaced. "Actually, Hero, I think the person most likely to succeed in this quest isn't you."

I reared back. "Why?"

"Clearly, Piper isn't affected by his own spell. Regarding the queens, he has changed everyone's memory to replace what you accomplished with his own exploits. He saved Helga from her curse and convinced her to become a nun. We can't find Valencia, but we found out he had saved her from freezing in Exile as you had done your first time here."

My mouth dropped open. "The scoundrel has taken credit for the things Planet and I did."

"Yes, he has." Lenore released a long, unsteady breath. "And he knows about Planet. Statues of her exist all around Kingdom. Though he's hidden the statues of the queens, the depictions of Planet are too numerous to hide. Paintings of her exist in homes. Small dolls of her are sold in the marketplaces."

Sanders' eyes lit up. "I'd like to see one since I look so much like Planet."

Lenore reached into the container and handed a small rag doll to Sanders. "Planet's quite embedded in the fabric of Kingdom's culture now. Removing her presence wouldn't have been easy. Piper chose another way."

I crossed my arms. "What way?"

"The memory he instilled into everyone was that he met Planet and they did the things the two of you did together. He and Planet rescued Helga, Valencia, and Beauty as well as unseated King Shade. Hero, he also replaced your relationship with Planet with himself."

I was speechless. I had fallen in love with Planet on my first adventure here and would have remained here after that if she hadn't died. "Are you saying—?"

"I'm saying that Piper changed the story and erased everyone's memory of Planet dying. He rules Kingdom with a disguised pixie who calls herself Queen Planet." Lenore looked at Sanders. "You're the spitting image of the queen."

05 - TWO'S COMPANY

Sondra

The Inn of Five tavern provided shelter and overnight lodging to all manner of Kingdom residents. When Hero first came to Kingdom, the Inn of Five was where he had first met Penta. Penta was the owner and barmaid of the inn. She had the colorful history of rejecting the devil's proposal for her hand in marriage by cutting off her hands. Penta had replaced the hands with silver, metallic replicas that she kept covered with white gloves. Magically, they were fully flexible.

"If we enlist Penta on our side, convincing the rest will be easier," Hero said while we made our way through the darkness toward the inn.

Spreading my pixie wings, I took to the air to avoid the rock-strewn road. "How do you figure?"

"Being the eldest, she's the most responsible. Her wisdom combined with her dedication to her tasks makes her the perfect ally."

I love my husband, but he is a little blinded by his friendship with Penta. He overlooks how quickly her anger accelerates to rage while protecting her sisters and her daughter, Beauty.

When we arrived at an intersecting path leading to the inn, Lenore stated she would hang back, far from the view of the tavern. As she was part of the resistance group and known around these parts, Lenore shouldn't be seen with us if we wanted to make a good impression. Our guide also suggested I change my appearance so that people didn't mistake me for the queen. Pixies are naturally magical, but even they have a quota of spells they may cast per day. I still had enough to whip up a quick cantrip, though, while thinking of someone to impersonate. "How do I look?"

Hero furrowed his brow. "You look like Charlie but with glasses."

Charlotte Denril-Lace was an actress and friend of ours and Sylvia's. With her beach-blonde hair, height, and her oval face, she was beautiful in every way I was not. Penta had met her on Earth with Sylvia.

Sylvia covered a smirk. "If I only had a camera."

I tossed my hair back the way an actress might. "Hero, hold my glasses."

Lenore said, "If you convince Penta, bring her here. We call this place 'the crossroads.'"

We agreed and traveled on to our destination. As we entered the inn, we noticed it was crowded with servants and patrons. A large group of men were seated in the center of the room playing cards. Three caninorians, dog-people of Kingdom, stood near the fireplace, howling an ode to ale. Of course, Penta herself stood behind the bar, wiping it down with gusto.

Penta wore a simple barmaid's gray tunic, black skirt, and her distinctive white gloves. Her auburn hair was tied back, and dirt smudged her left cheek.

Sylvia, Hero, and I approached the bar cautiously. Hero cleared his throat. "Penta?"

Penta ceased wiping down the counter. "May I fetch you a mug of something delicious?"

I winced. Penta appeared less confident and more submissive than the woman I had known. She hunched over, seemed placid but not at peace. What had happened to her?

Hero put his hands on the counter. "Do you remember me?"

A man, also behind the counter, stepped next to Penta. She dropped her rag on the counter. Her face was full of questions. "Should I?"

Those in our party looked at each other, and I nudged Hero aside. "Hello, Penta. Do you remember me, or this lady?" I gestured at Sylvia.

She looked at each of us. "I cannot say that I do. Are you the guardians of this man?"

Cool, Penta. Score one for women's rights! Hero tried again. "My name is Hero Saturn. Do you recall that name?"

"No, I cannot say I do."

The man next to Penta asked, "What is this all about?"

Bald, burly, and broad-shouldered, he stared at us. Several tattoos showed on his forearms. With a gray shirt and brown pants, he looked like a bouncer.

My husband remained focused on Penta. "We have information for you."

Too soon. He was moving too fast. I decided to change the subject. "My name is Sondra Saturn, and this is our friend, Sylvia Swonewith."

Penta examined us. "It is a pleasure to meet you, Sanders."

No matter how I introduce myself, everyone always

calls me Sanders in other worlds. "I see that hasn't changed," I muttered.

Hero set his hands on the bar counter. "Can you tell me if you've seen Queen Helga, Queen Beauty, Queen Valencia, or Queen Cinderella?"

Penta's eyes widened and she leaned forward. "Oh, them. Well, the queens are upstairs changing their clothes."

Hero looked hopefully at the stairs, and Penta looked at her companion and laughed. "I will go along with your make-believe story. Whatever your name is, you are a peculiar one. As if we had four queens in Kingdom! And as if those queens would visit a simple inn! Big Mac, have you ever heard such nonsense?"

Big Mac! Some of Kingdom's people have silly names, names that mean something else on Earth. Now "Big Mac" had joined the growing list of names that elicit groans.

The man chuckled but eyed us.

Hero said, "So you've never heard of Helga Helvys, Valencia Arkenson, Beauty Halifax, or Cinderella Jolly?"

Penta folded her arms. "Of course I have heard of the legendary Helga Helvys. She became a nun, I believe. And if you are talking about Lady Shaina Halifax, I know of her too. The other two I do not know."

"I assure you, we've met before," Hero said. "If you'd just accompany us to the crossroads, we can discuss—"

Penta interrupted, "Are you going to pepper me with questions and requests all night, or are you going to buy something to drink and move on?"

Pointing at her gloves, Hero asked, "Silver hands, right? How would I know that? And how did you get them?"

Aha! This was Hero's trump card. Penta's hands were tied to her history when she broke her engagement with the devil. Her hands connected her to her past and would be proof that she was a queen. Excellent idea!

The bartender grunted. "Penta is known for her silver hands because of her unfortunate accident as a child. The magic ax her father bought turned on her. How rude of you to bring it up."

Penta nudged the man and shook her head. "Let us tell them the truth, Big Mac."

Gesturing for us to come in closer, Penta whispered, "Spies are everywhere. They must not find out who I am. Will you promise to watch for them?"

Now we were coming to the heart of the matter. We had a million questions but before we could ask them, she reached out and laid her hand on Sylvia's arm. And with that gesture, Sylvia disappeared into thin air. Cat's piss! I forgot Penta could teleport other people as well as herself.

Hero stepped back, out of Penta's reach. "Where did you send her?"

"The crossroads." The queen used her gloved thumb to point at the front door.

Sweat broke out on Hero's forehead. "Try to remember, Penta. When you were younger, a demon asked you to marry him, but you cut off your hands to resist him. As punishment, he sent you to Earth, where I'm from. You found a way back and became a queen here as a result."

Penta shook her head. "Nonsense. I lost my hands in an accident. Now, I suggest you join your friend I sent out of here before I have Big Mac throw you out."

A voice from the group of men called across the room. "I hardly think that is necessary."

A hooded man stood and flipped down his cowl. He was a broad man with light brown hair in curls down to his shoulders. He had a disarming grin and a mole on his left cheek. His eyes sparkled in the light.

Penta gasped and bowed her head. "King Piper."

I gasped and swooned. "Kris Heavens!"

Yes, Piper was the exact image of a Hollywood actor back on Earth. Kris always played the honorable guy, and the worst the gossip rags could say about him was he didn't give enough to charity. Kris Heavens couldn't have journeyed to

Kingdom. I had seen an interview with him a couple of nights before. That would make him a...

"Parallel." Hero finished my thought.

Yes, a parallel. People who look the same but are born in different worlds. They share some traits with their other-worldly sibling but are different people. Like twins. Planet was my parallel in Kingdom, and Hero and I have met others in our adventures.

Everyone in the tavern was on one knee except Hero and me. The villain had appeared this soon in our adventure? Usually, the Big Bad takes a while to display his face. His face wasn't altogether unpleasant, either, in a lifeguard sort of way. In my imagination, I could picture a swab of suntan lotion on his perfectly formed nose. He flashed a smile at the two of us, and I received a different sort of flash.

Uh, maybe I shouldn't think of him that way. Piper was evil. Truly devious. Had a spell that put you under his power. Yeah, that was it.

Hero put a steadying hand on my arm. "Why are you rocking back and forth?"

The false king regarded Hero curiously. In my disguise, he hardly paid any attention to me. I leaned over to Hero and murmured, "Why is he here? Seems odd."

"The scout must have alerted the troops, and he must have magicked himself here," my husband answered. "He knows if we convince Penta that she's a queen, we are well on our way to completing our first task."

My humble husband wouldn't add that Hero's gift of persuasion is legendary in Kingdom. Some here believe it's supernatural. It's not, of course. He's tried it on me multiple times but can't quite convince me he needs a man cave.

Piper stepped toward us. "I have not had the honor of meeting your companion, but I'm sure you, sir, are far from home. Perhaps, instead of bothering these good people, you should return there."

Occasionally, Hero is true to his nickname. He

straightened his shoulders and glared at Kris, ermmm, Piper. "We're going to restore the true queens."

Piper's eyes narrowed. "There are no true queens!"

The so-called king reached into his jacket and produced a knife. Hero's eyes widened. "That's my knife. The one I had during my first adventure. How did you get it? Have you stolen everything from the time I united the queens of Kingdom?"

Piper rolled the knife's hilt in his hand. "This is my knife. Obviously everything you believe true you stole from *my* life. Guards!"

Two soldiers appeared behind Hero, and another one positioned himself behind me and grabbed my arms.

"Escort him to the crossroads with his friend!" Piper bellowed.

Hero tried a move from the movies and elbowed one soldier while trying to swing his leg and trip the other. The first soldier didn't flinch. The female soldier he tried to trip, barely swayed. He then tried to run but they grabbed his shoulders and locked arms with him.

The false king nodded to the door and the guards dragged Hero away. My guard pulled me. I shrunk into my pixie form and escaped his hold, flitting off. Piper wanted to play at parallels, well he challenged the best parallel person I knew.

Me.

I dropped the Charlie disguise and returned to looking like myself. The room erupted in shouting.

"Queen Planet!" Everyone bowed respectfully.

Huh. A girl could get used to this.

I put my hands on my hips and glared at my "husband," slack-jawed at my appearance. "How dare you arrest your wife and her friends! Now, release him."

I was too late. The other guards weren't paying attention to the commotion I had caused and had hurried Hero out of the inn. I had no ally. Penta stared at me, eyes wide. Oh, if she only remembered.

Unfortunately, Piper caught on quickly. He must have

42

known about Hero and me and assumed I was still on Earth. Clearly, he thought Hero had journeyed here with our friends —Sylvia and Charlie—whom Kingdom residents regarded as champions. If he said I'd disguised myself as the queen, he knew I would ask everyone to cry and see me through their tears. One cannot disguise themselves magically through a veil of tears. Once they saw me as Sanders, and assumed I was Planet, it would strip the villian of his leverage. Score one for being a parallel!

Piper grinned a Kris-Heavens-worthy smile. "Oh, dearest, you little scamp."

I didn't like where he was taking this conversation. I needed time alone with Penta to convince her before our opportunity elapsed. "I would like a moment with the barmaid. I have an important matter to discuss with her."

Piper scowled. "I'm sure you do. Let's discuss this 'matter' together with the maiden, shall we?"

"Me?" Penta turned a ghostly white.

"I really think it would be better—" I began.

"I would hate to declare royal privilege on my loving spouse," Piper said.

I wasn't going to win this one, so he would have to listen in. He'd try to prevent me from speaking, but I had magic. I'd use it on him if I could.

"We can talk in the kitchen." Penta's eyes shifted to a door in the back of the room. "Although it's small and dirty for two people of your stature."

Piper waved his hand. "I was not always a king, as you know. I am most honored to be in your establishment."

My cheeks burned with his false modesty. What a creep.

Penta led the way, and Piper told the guards to stand ready but not follow. Piper also asked Big Mac to join us. I had no idea why.

The four of us entered a narrow kitchen as a cook ran out to tend the bar. We stood in a circle with a counter full of vegetables, fruits, and meats and a counter on the other side of the room with spices and flavorings. Good thing I was the size of a hummingbird, or we wouldn't have had enough room.

Piper crossed his arms, displaying his dimple. A very cute dimple, I may add. In a placating voice, my false hubby said, "Now, Penta, please indulge my *wife* in this tall tale she is about to tell. My gorgeous love does love to spin a yarn."

I wanted to be irritated, but he'd called me gorgeous. I heard it loud and clear and wanted to record that a Kris Heavens look-alike called me gorgeous. Anyway, I put aside my doting fangirl for the moment and turned to Penta. "Please listen to me. You are under a spell, but you don't know it. Some of your memories have been removed and replaced with false ones. I won't say who did this or why, but I need you to trust me and accompany me to reunite you with your family."

"But I do not have any family," protested Penta.

I bobbed in the air impatiently. "Yes, you do. You don't remember the time with your sisters. Please, Penta. Come with me on this quest."

She glanced at the bartender for a moment and took a deep breath. "I suppose Big Mac could look after the inn while I am gone."

Piper scratched his head. "I have heard this story before, my lovely."

He called me lovely, too! Oh, why didn't I have magic to capture these moments so I could replay them.

"As I recall, Penta can regain her memory in some way." Piper put his index finger to his lip and tapped it. "Now, how could she do that?"

Piper knew about how to break the spell because he cast it. Why was he giving this away? Clearly because Penta wasn't attached to anyone.

I gritted my teeth. "She could reclaim her lost memories if she kissed her true love."

Piper beamed, and Penta brightened and grinned. Something was going on. Piper pointed at me. "Indeed, that was the countermeasure. Penta, would you oblige us?"

Oblige us? What was he talking about? "But Penta does not have a true love."

Penta quirked an eyebrow. "Is that so?" She turned and grabbed Big Mac by the collar. And then she kissed him and kept her forehead next to his, smiling. "*He* is my true love."

My mouth hung open. I mean a fly could've flown in and set up a nice hotel to vacation inside and I wouldn't have noticed. She'd kissed him!

I bobbed up and down in the air, gaping at her.

"By royal decree," said Piper. "Penta, send my wife to her friends to let them know her little joke has backfired."

Penta turned to me and reached up as if to turn off a light. "Good-bye."

When she touched me, I disappeared too.

06 - INTERMEZZO 1

Sixteen Years Earlier

Everything was wrong because *he* had won!

Fourteen-year-old Penta sat on the stone ground, rocking back and forth, crying. She had had her father cut off her hands, and now she couldn't use her palms to block out the cacophony of horns, scrapings of the metal insects, and the woodpecker-like—but louder—rhythm of metal pounding rock. And the air! Foul and filthy. She choked on each putrid breath she took. She didn't dare breathe through her nose again. If she did, she would smell the sweat, marsh gas, and urine that made her stomach sour.

One of the beetle-shaped creatures—about the size of a catapult— raced past her. The organism had wheels for feet and moved far faster than she could run! If they caught sight of her, they would certainly consume her. More worrisome were the towers stretching to the sky. Thrice-taller than the castle her father had once shown her, she imagined them toppling on her, for they couldn't remain upright like that for long.

When her demonic adversary had banished her here, she had appeared near a constrained triangle of grass, the only patch in sight. She had crouched behind a small bush in the tiniest patch of lawn but knew it wouldn't keep her safe for long. She could walk from end to end in this so-called field in less than thirty seconds. But the grass and shrub were the only familiar items from Kingdom in this alien place where she found herself.

Every sense signaled her to attend to it. Block out the noise! Remove the fetid scent! Stop tasting the grimy air! Her sight, though, nudged her to explore more. The building next to her touched the sky. The structure was rectangular, white but dirty, yet the tallest construction she had ever seen. Affixed to the top was a blue emblem of a shield. Might knights live in such a framework? Would they help her?

On the other hand, the windows were all shaded, blocking her ability to see inside. Only an evil mind would want to hide in the darkness. What if the residents of this area collected people like her in this building—people who shouldn't be here?

A fortress? A prison?

Penta stretched her neck to look around at the surroundings and caught sight of another shape, and for a moment, her jaw dropped slightly. Could it be? Even in this foreign location, could there be a building that reminded her of home? Those spires...were they the steeples of a cathedral?

Taking a deep breath, Penta stood and ran across the grass to a stone walk, turning in the direction of where she had spied a holy sanctuary. Curiously, the white pathways were smooth and raised above the darkened roads where the giant beetles on the march buzzed in straight lines. Encouraged, she spied other people—only humans, no other species—on the walks across from her, paying her no heed. They seemed unconcerned by the metallic creatures in the road. She blinked multiple times when she examined one of the mammoth insects. Was she seeing things, or did a person sit inside of the creature, holding a wheel? Was this some sort of a carriage?

Penta stepped to the edge of the walk, determined to cross the dark pavement between the wheeled monstrosities. Taking a step onto the lowered stone, she was yanked back onto the stone walkway. She turned, ready to fight her aggressor, but relaxed to see an elderly man, worry lines imprinted on his forehead. He had grabbed her arm to restrain her from going onto the road before one of the noisy carriages raced by.

The old man released her when she looked down at her arm. "*Senorita*, where ya going? *Estas loca*? Gonna get yourself killed?"

The man smiled at her, perhaps a sign of compassion. Maybe this world wasn't as horrible as it first seemed. However, his eyes widened when they spotted where her arms ended.

Covering her stumps under her armpits, Penta nodded toward her objective across the street. "Please, sir. I am endeavoring to make my way to the cathedral."

The old man pointed to a small box painted with a glowing, orange hand. "We must wait to cross."

The sign changed to a white walking figure. Goodness! Would this world ever stop amazing her? Certainly, this world had magic. And if it did, then a powerful mage could throw a spell and send her home!

The old man set a gnarled hand on her shoulder. "Now we cross. Do you want me to take you to Old Saint Mary's?"

She nodded and followed the man across the road to another stone pathway. From there, she could make her way to the church. Turning when she reached the other side, she curtsied to the man. "You have made such a difference to me. I thank you."

The man raised his eyebrows, but before he could reply,

Penta turned and sprinted for her destination. Climbing the steps, she paused before the door. Without hands, how was she to open them? She hooked her thin forearm in the handle, pulled, and the door swung open. The dark coldness and whiff of incense reminded her of home.

Penta entered.

07 - HALIFAX MANOR

Harold

"They kissed?"

"Yes, Hero, they kissed," Sanders answered.

"He kissed her?"

"No, she kissed him."

"And she said what?"

"He is my true love."

Grimacing, I turned away from Sanders, Sylvia, and Lenore in her human form and looked back over my shoulder toward the prairie. The Inn of Five was off in the distance to the south, or in Kingdom-speak, cuuth, but returning there was not an option. We had made fools of ourselves in front of Penta and alerted the evil usurper at the same time.

I swung back around. "Are you sure she said that?"

"I just said so twice." Sanders toed the dirt at the

crossroads, not daring to meet my stare.

"Was it a friendship kiss?" Lenore rubbed her hands together. "In Kingdom, to get around the kiss-means-marriage rule, some press their top lip to the bottom lip of a friend. Children mostly play this game, but adults who aren't quite committed sometimes do the same."

"Two lips touched two lips." Sanders made lips with her fingers and pressed them together in the traditional smooching motion

Lenore shuffled her shoes. "We have heard rumors..."

I turned toward her. "You knew?"

"Rumors, Hero," replied Lenore. "He is not her true love. She would've remembered her past if he was."

I squinted at her. "Are you sure?"

"Positive!" Lenore scowled. "But she kissed him! She must abide by Kingdom's customs now and either marry him or secure his permission to kiss another."

I crossed my arms. "She's under the influence of the spell. The kiss doesn't mean anything."

Lenore said, "She'll disagree with you. When she comes out of it, she'll feel an obligation to marry Big Mac."

"But why?" I pointed in the direction of the Inn of Five. "Clearly, he isn't her true love or she'd realize she was a queen. How come the rest of them are permitted to marry who they want but she isn't?"

"You're angry because she's your friend," said Sanders.

"Damn right!" My cheeks burned with indignation. "Why does she get stuck with a raw deal? I don't even like that guy. His eyes are too close together. He's not even big!"

Lenore shook her shoulders, resembling a bird fluttering its wings. "He was a dustman in the castle for years before Piper appeared. Big Mac showed up at the inn after the spell went into effect and started helping Penta. He's been a good guardian, not that she needs it."

I narrowed my eyes. "I still don't like him."

"I have no doubt he loves her, but Penta is a changed

woman," Lenore continued. "If this had never happened, she wouldn't have kissed him. Of that, I have no doubt. But if they come out of it, she will marry him, and their tale will be a rags-to-riches story for him."

Sanders put a hand on my arm. "Hero, pull yourself together. We've mucked up Penta. We must find the others."

Lenore looked northeast. "I'm not sure why Piper hasn't shown up to throw us in jail yet, but we should keep moving. Fortunately, Halifax Manor isn't too far from here. "

Sanders tugged on my arm. "Let's go, Hero. I know you're itching to return there, but we need allies—the other queens."

I allowed her to pull me forward. I didn't like leaving Penta in that situation. She wouldn't leave me like that, but Sanders' logic was sound. Reuniting the others now that I had screwed up Penta's chance sounded like the right thing to do.

Fortunately, Sanders had enough magic to conjure a small campsite, and guard duty allowed everyone to muster a decent night's sleep. Then for breakfast we had a helping of a blue, dimpled fruit. Walking down the roads of Kingdom after we broke camp reminded me of my first adventure here. Some of the flora and fauna resembled Earth's varieties, but most of it did not. Trees with leaves that were teacup shaped, bushes that pulled up their roots in the middle of the day to chase the sunlight, birds that left a trail of fire in their wake, all welcomed me back. Kingdom wasn't the safest place—far from it—but it could be a wondrous place to visit.

Sanders, Lenore, Sylvia, and I journeyed together north by northwest toward Halifax Manor, home of Queen Beauty. The lush-green countryside and perfumed heather made me grateful to Alice for figuring out how to find our way here. Thinking of Alice, I touched Lenore's elbow. "I meant to ask. Have you heard of a man named Joseph Macquin?"

Lenore squinted as if rolling around the name in her brain. "No, I can't say I have. But perhaps when you convert Beauty, she will know."

"We read about Penta adopting Beauty." Sanders stretched her shoulders. "And giving her the Halifax estate."

Lenore nodded. "Princess at thirteen. Queen at sixteen. She's now eighteen. Energetic, clever, and a touch overzealous, she believes that Piper saved her from Lord Halifax who had her imprisoned in his manor."

"Wait a minute." Sylvia half-raised her hand. "I thought the Beast held her captive in his castle."

"That's Earth's interpretation, but that's not how it went down in Kingdom," I said. "The beast, Grr, was a groundskeeper on the estate. Lord Halifax was the true monster, and he kept an orphaned Beauty, or Shaina, for himself. He planned to marry her under the legal age."

Lenore continued the tale. "Grr escaped the manor and told the queens, and Penta adopted Beauty after throwing Halifax in jail. But in Piper's version, he discovered Lord Halifax's plan and imprisoned him. He bequeathed Halifax Manor to Beauty where she's known as the Duchess of Halifax, Lady Shaina."

"Where is Grr?" asked Sanders.

"On the estate with Beauty. I've flown here and watched them," said Lenore. "The good news is I've seen signs of attraction. Lingering looks, smiles, even some minor flirting."

"Have Beauty and Grr kissed before?" Sylvia asked.

"Queen Beauty hasn't married Grr yet, but they kissed many times before Piper's spell."

I jumped over a line of six-legged rabbits hopping across the trail. "Well, this shouldn't be too hard then."

Sanders rolled her eyes. "Yes, Lenore. Leave it to us to screw it up."

From the position of the sun, I would wager another hour had passed while we progressed down the meandering road. None of the trails in Kingdom were straight. To keep our minds off our failure with Penta, the conversation ranged from the local bestiary to how we'd find our way back home. On this last topic, Sanders heaved a great sigh. "I hope I get to see my little Fitzie's face again."

Those words barely spoken, Sanders grabbed Lenore's sleeve. "I almost forgot. Cinderella has children. What about them? Has she forgotten them too?"

"Yes," answered Lenore. "We found her son and daughter in an orphanage in the royal town. A resistance fighter is looking after them with the queen's other loved ones. Except for Dawn, Helga's daughter. She's missing and we haven't been able to find her, which is very troubling as she's a gliff."

"I hate these Kingdom words I don't understand." Sanders rubbed her forehead. "Now what is a gliff?"

"I thought someone would've written to you about it." Avoiding a puddle in the road, Lenore said, "a gliff is a baby born with wings that don't work. They are helpless beings, never growing in adult intelligence or strength, usually dying young. A Traveler said Earth had a term for children like her but without the wings. Down's syndrome."

Sylvia sucked in a breath. "And you haven't found her."

Lenore shook her head.

I feared what would happen to a lost Down's syndrome child without a parent in Kingdom. "Could Danforth have rescued her?"

Lenore bit her lip. "The rumor was Helga's husband returned to his native world, Earth, before the memory loss spell was cast. The Resistance has no idea how to leave Kingdom to verify it."

As the day wore on, we played a game like license plate where we competed trying to find various beings of Kingdom. While Sylvia was the first to spot a pegasus and a wyvern, I led the pack with a squonk, a kitsune, and a dormadog. Sanders hadn't seen anything first and had distracted me with a kiss to have Lenore call out a tardalong. Clearly, I would've spotted the tardalong first when it turned its spotlight eyes on us.

As the sun was ascending in the sky, I fell back next to Sanders while Lenore and Sylvia walked slightly ahead of us. Last night, and part of today, I reflected on our journey to Kingdom. I had a question for my wife, but I didn't want anyone else to overhear, especially Sylvia. I made a gesture to slow down, and Sanders knitted her brows but agreed.

When our companions were far ahead of us, I lowered my voice. "I wanted to discuss what happened when we were in the world between Earth and Kingdom. The woods."

Sanders pressed her lips together but didn't otherwise react. I could practically feel an iron barrier erect around her. Apparently, she'd anticipated my question.

I licked my lips. "Your mother's death...I had no idea you were still hurting so much. Why didn't you tell me?"

"I don't like my id hanging out there for all to see," replied Sanders.

"Your what?" I asked, thinking I didn't hear her correctly.

"Id. Ego. Superego. Our ids were on display on that last world, and I didn't like it. I suspect I'm like most people."

"But I'm your husband. You can confide in me."

One half of Sanders' mouth turned downward. "I know. I've thought of talking to you. But then I'm afraid I'll start—" She sniffed, but continued, "...crying and won't be able to stop. Deep inside, I think this is something I must figure out myself."

"Grief is not something you figure out. I lived in that state for over a year after my sister died."

Sanders brushed my hand with her fingers. "But your sister had cancer. My mom was here one day, and then she wasn't."

One of the worst nights of my life. Sanders' father called me from the hospital, saying Sanders' mother had collapsed walking in the park. He had sketchy information, but they knew it was her heart and she was in surgery. And by the time we arrived...

"I'm sorry. I miss Mom Saturn, too."

Sanders grabbed my hand. "I feel like a kite with a severed string. I'm adrift in the sky, just waiting for the wind to give out, and then I'll come crashing down, all broken sticks and paper."

"What can I do?" I asked.

"Nothing. I need something to say good-bye. I haven't figured out just what that is yet." Sanders hunched her shoulders. "Don't try to fix it, Hero. I'm not one of your quests."

I laid my hand on her shoulder. "You'll tell me, won't you? If the grief becomes too heavy to bear."

"I'm Sanders the Implausible, Hero. Nothing's too heavy for these pixie shoulders."

I didn't like that answer, but before I could respond, the women ahead laughed at something. Sanders grew pixie-sized, spread her wings, and darted ahead. "Hey, girls, what's up? Don't leave me out of the good times."

Denial? Depression? Who knew what stage of grief she was at.

After another long stretch of walking, we approached an elm with a message carved into it. It stood in a lone field with eight-foot haystacks lined up in rows. We approached the tree, anticipating the message. "Snow White lives." Yup, the resistance movement had been here. For some reason, I didn't find this comforting.

Sylvia picked up her left foot and rubbed the bottom of it. "I wish I could fly like you, Lenore. All this walking is hard on my arches."

Sanders waggled her fingers. "Not a problem. I'll try another teleportation spell."

"Maybe you shouldn't," Lenore observed. "You don't know how far we have to go."

"And you might teleport us into the middle of a

mountain," I added.

Sanders snorted. "Just for that smart-ass, I'm going to do it. Everyone, prepare yourselves."

"I'll fly just in case." Lenore transformed into a raven and shot upward.

"Scaredy-bird," grumbled Sanders. "Here we go."

The land vanished around us and was replaced by a different set of fields. I blinked. She had done it. She had teleported us close to Halifax.

But then I noticed the sun. We were heading north, and it had been a little behind us. Now it was in our view and a little to the right. "We're not facing north anymore."

Sanders gulped. "I just changed our direction. No biggie."

"Let's start walking north again," suggested Sylvia.

Lenore was nowhere around—a bad sign. After journeying for about thirty minutes, our friendly raven bolted in from overhead. She descended and turned into human form as she touched the ground. "Hello."

Sanders looked excited. "How close did I get us to Halifax?"

Lenore gave her a small smile. "You made up the distance to the north—"

Sanders turned around and smirked at me. "See?"

"—And lost it to the west. Sorry, Sanders."

My wife sighed. Sylvia placed a hand on her arm. "You mastered the distance. You'll find your bearings. Just a little more practice."

At that moment, Sylvia reminded me of our friend, Snow White. Sylvia's gentle demeanor exactly mimicked that of the dead queen.

In the afternoon, Lenore asked directions from a brownie, and we trudged through the fields until we reached the Halifax estate. We had to travel through tens of acres of wheat and pear and peach trees to come upon the three-story, partially wooden home of Queen Beauty.

Unlike the abandoned, gloomy castle of the Beast, this manor was warm and inviting, like a woodsy retreat. A crushed-stone path led between topiaries to the front door, an ornate wooden door with brass handles.

In human form, Lenore brushed her hand along a shrub carved in the shape of a young maiden. "Beauty owned this manor before Piper cast his spell. She would retreat here with Grr, reconstructing it to eliminate all traces of Lord Halifax. She's hosted numerous balls here, and it was here that Grr proposed to her.

"Do you know what you're going to say to her, Hero?" asked Sylvia as we made our way up the steps.

"I have an idea."

Transforming herself into the taller and thinner Charlie form, Sanders used the knocker to pound on the door, and a female elf answered. The diminutive butler examined us. "The free rations are handed out at the barn." She pointed to the east. "That way."

I straightened up. "We are here to see Be…Shaina."

"Do you have business with her?"

"We do," replied Sanders.

"We're wandering storytellers," I lied. "We've come to tell a tale to Lady Halifax. Her groundskeeper, Grr, gave us food, and this is our repayment."

The elf grimaced. "One moment."

The butler shut the door, and after a few minutes, she opened it again. "Follow me."

We were escorted into the grand hallway beyond the front door. The foyer itself was compact with doors on all walls and a staircase ascending to the second floor.

The elf waved her hand and the doors into an adjoining music room opened to our left. We entered and spied Beauty playing the piano with a driving, melodic tune sounding from the instrument. She was dressed in a white-and-blue shift with a flowery, sky-blue skirt and black slippers, very comfortable clothes. As we entered and the door shut behind us, Beauty finished with a rolling flourish, her golden replacement hands lifting together into the air. To mimic her mother's fate, witches had cut off her hands when torturing her. She had replaced them with golden replicas.

Beauty spun on the bench, and I have to say she lived up to her name. Brown-skinned, black ringlets cascading down to her shoulders, she regarded us with gentle brown eyes and gave us an inviting smile. She surveyed us all and gestured to various seats in the music room. "Please."

This seemed too easy, but I took the chair closest to her. "We are sorry to bother you."

She waved away the excuse. "Shelfie tells me you are storytellers? I have not heard a good story in some time. Will you tell me one?"

Perfect. I would clap myself on the back if I could. "Absolutely. This story is of a young woman who loved a young man. They were inseparable and complemented each other in the best of ways. But an evil sorcerer was jealous of their love, and he cast a spell on them, removing from them all memory of each other."

Beauty picked up purple gloves sitting on the piano. "What did they do?"

I had her hooked. "Their friends tried to convince them that they loved each other, but neither would believe them. However, one of their friends figured it out. The solution to their problem was true love's kiss. If they kissed, the spell would be broken, and they would be in love again."

"But how did their friends convince them to kiss each other?" Beauty yanked a purple glove over her golden hand. "A kiss is a marital bond with each other. They would not kiss a stranger."

"Despite the spell, true love prevailed. And after they kissed each other, their love for one another returned."

"You better stick to novel writing," murmured Sanders.

Beauty blinked. "Is that all there is to the story? It seems rather brief."

I raised my eyebrows. "I'll tell you a secret. It's a true story."

The doors flung open, and we all leaped up from our chairs. A half-dozen soldiers marched in toward us, weapons ready. Before we could react, they had us surrounded. Lenore eyed the windows for a quick escape, but they were all closed.

Beauty stood and gestured to us. "Here they are, as you predicted."

A bulky man in the lead shouted, "You are under arrest."

A set-up, of course. Piper knew we were in Kingdom now and had guards stationed around all the queens. Crap.

The soldiers grabbed my arms, but I leaned toward Beauty. "Shaina, listen to me. You're the woman and Grr is the man. He's your true love. You must kiss him to remember."

The soldiers had our arms behind our backs and started pushing us out of the music room. Beauty hurried over to the door to cut off our egress from the room. She pointed at me. "You are enemies to the king and queen. You lied about being storytellers, and now you expect me to believe you?" She turned to Lenore. "And you have brought with you a felon. Why should I listen to you?"

"I know the story of how you lost your hands and had to replace them with golden ones."

Beauty glanced at her purple gloves. "I lost them in a hunting accident. I..." she grimaced, eyes shifting as if she had misplaced something.

I tried another tactic. "Do you love Grr?"

"Leave him out of this!"

I jutted my chin to the outside courtyard. "All the topiaries outside are of young women. They're all *you*, aren't they? Though he doesn't even know it, he's expressing his love for you in the way he maintains the estate."

Beauty dropped her arms to her side.

Lenore said, "And the music you were just playing. It's your and Grr's song. The royal musician wrote it specifically for the two of you, and he played it when you started your courtship."

Beauty furrowed her brow. "Impossible. That song has been around for...it has been..."

She faltered and dropped her head. The bulky soldier said, "Excuse me, my lady, but we have orders to escort these reprobates to where the king can have a word with them."

08 - THREE'S A CROWD

Harold

Dazed, Beauty stepped aside, and the soldiers pushed us through the grand foyer. We emerged outside to the late afternoon sunlight. A coach squatted at the end of the courtyard. Four axles and eight wheels, the rectangular platinum-and-copper base looked large enough to seat ten people.

Once Lenore was unhampered, she transformed into a bird and flew away. Surprisingly, the soldiers ignored her but marched the rest of us forward. A soldier in heavy armor standing before the carriage jerked his thumb to the side. "The tall one stays outside. The king would like to speak with this couple."

"Alone!" shouted Piper's voice from inside the carriage.

The soldiers escorted Sanders and me into the ornate vehicle and onto a cushioned bench. Across from us, Piper sat behind a serving table, sipping tea. After the soldiers left, he viewed us over the brim of his teacup. "May I offer you tea?"

Sanders dropped her Charlie disguise. "Are you freaking kidding me?"

"I am not uncultured. In fact, I am not an evil man at all. I could have thrown you in jail back at the inn. Instead, I decided to allow you to see one of the queens. Tell me, did Shaina seem unhappy to you?"

I tensed my shoulders. "Her name is Beauty."

Piper waved the teacup. "Did she seem in distress? Am I holding her in Halifax Manor against her will?"

I didn't answer.

"The queens are blissfully unaware of their past." Piper sipped the tea. "They are all content and perfectly happy."

"I doubt that."

"Tour Kingdom. Find out for yourself. Just don't try to restore their memories." Piper drew a horizontal line in the air. "Do not cross that line."

I shifted uncomfortably.

Piper said, "Allow me to tell you a little about myself, and then I will leave you with a proposition."

I considered upsetting the tea service and bolting out the door, but the soldiers would have us back here in a minute. I'd have to listen to him, but I didn't have to like it. "Whatever it is, the answer is no."

"Now, now, Hero." Piper wagged his finger. "My proposal involves the restoration of the queens' memories. I have faith we can come to an agreement."

Doubt it. I crossed my arms to express my reluctance.

Piper sipped his tea. "I do not hate the former queens. Not at all. They ushered in a golden age, but then they tarnished it. The problem with success is one cannot sustain it for long. The queens, like most monarchs, added rule after rule, law after law, until they became bureaucrats. People had to wait in jail for months before they could stand before a hearing in the royal court. And sometimes, instead of judging justly, the queens abided by a law that did not pertain to the petitioner's situation. Queen Penta nearly lost Queen Beauty by obeying her own laws."

He wasn't wrong, but I wouldn't concede the point. "But she didn't. Penta upheld the law and saved Beauty."

"Grr saved Beauty, not Penta's overreliance on her rules." Piper set down his teacup. "The queens wronged me. Fully admitted it, as well. I helped my town, Haylon, rid itself of vermin, and the mayor and aldermen cheated me. But when I appealed to the queens, they said the ruling would have to be by appointed judges in my quadrant. They assured me the judge would give me justice."

Oh, boy. A wronged villain. The worst kind.

"But before my trial commenced, a tragedy befell the children of Haylon, and the town blamed me. They came to kill me, so thus I received no justice!"

Piper slammed the teacup down on the setting with a resounding crack.

Sanders gripped the padded bench we sat on. "Why do I feel you're not telling the entire story?"

As if noticing her for the first time, Piper turned to my wife. "Sanders the Implausible. 'Tis an honor, you know. I am a great admirer."

Sanders gulped. She had been unusually quiet during this entire exchange, and I was a bit worried. My wife took a deep breath. "Frankly, you remind me of someone whom I admire, too."

Oh, the Kris Heavens connection. I had forgotten he was a parallel. Yes, Kris Heavens was a good actor, but he was not the man before me. "To clarify," I said. "She doesn't admire you but the person you resemble."

Piper gave Sanders a hang-dog face with soft eyes. "Well, that is too bad. As I said, I am not the villain here. I cannot express how much respect I have for you or Planet."

"You leave Planet out of this," I hissed.

Piper sat back. "Hero, you and I are problem solvers. So let us come to an arrangement. I will restore the queens' memories and allow you to return to Earth. No one gets hurt."

"The catch?"

"The queens and their husbands must return with you. I will send a chest of gems and precious metals with you. The queens may live out the rest of their lives, free of the burdens of the crown, on Earth."

I scoffed. "They would never agree to this."

Piper tapped a finger on the side of his nose then pointed at me. "We will not ask them then. As long as you do not reveal to them how to get back to Kingdom, and I will have your word on this, everyone will be happy."

"I'm sorry to inform you, we have no ride to return to Earth." I sat back, smug at the revelation. "We're stuck here for the moment."

The false king waved down the excuse. "I closed this world, so I know how to open it long enough for a Traveler to take you home. Along with the queens."

Sanders shrugged. "I don't understand. You already have the queens where you want them. Why send them to Earth and restore their memories? What's in this for you?"

Piper regarded my wife. "You are. I want you to become Queen Planet and rule with me."

"What!" My response was not a question.

"What?" Hers was.

"The woman impersonating Planet is becoming more and more careless. The power is going to her head, and the people are turning on her. The palace staff hates her, and truthfully, she is starting to annoy me too. But you, dear Sanders, are better than the real thing! Your personality, your charm. You were born to rule, my girl."

Sanders' jaw fell open.

"Absolutely not!" I said. "She's not staying here."

Piper raised an eyebrow. "Does Hero always speak for you, Sanders? I would never do so."

I'd stepped into that one. Fortunately, Sanders laid a hand on my arm to prevent me from putting my size elevens deeper in my mouth. In a steady voice, she answered Piper. "I'm a wife, a mother, and a scientist, and damn good at all three. I love my husband, my son, and my job. And while your offer is charitable, why not just let the queens go to Earth with me and Hero?"

Piper wagged a finger at Sanders. "Because I know *you'd* find a way to return them here."

Oh, this conversation was too much. "You expect me to just abandon my wife?"

"You have Penta." Piper flashed a Kris Heavens-worthy smile. "Everyone knows you are in love with her."

My hand clenched the cushioned seat of the carriage. "I am not... She's only a friend."

Sanders gripped my arm. A warning. "We're going to decline, Piper. And if you attack us in this carriage, I will transform back to make it look as though you killed your queen. Death of your wife is not good for your image, is it?"

Piper leaned toward Sanders. "I like you. A lot. You would be an excellent queen. Instead, you have chosen the harder path. Someone in your party will die because of your foolishness. My pipes played a dirge this morning, and the music is connected to you, Hero. You will bring ruin to one, or several, of the queens if you proceed. I shall allow you to sally forth on your quest, but do not forget I gave you an option at the start."

"You don't know one of the queens will be hurt," I countered.

"Oh, but I do." Piper narrowed his eyes. "Now get out."

Sylvia, Sanders, and I met up with Lenore ten minutes

later as we strolled away from Halifax Manor, pondering what to do next. Sylvia posed the theoretical question, "Did we think it was going to be that easy?" as an attempt to assuage our failure. Yet, no one could deny I was zero for two.

The four of us decided to progress onward instead of trying again with Beauty. Roger Jolly, Cinderella's beau, wasn't too far northward. We trudged across the grassland toward our next destination, the Jolly home, discussing Roger's current situation with Lenore.

Roger was a prince and husband to Queen Cinderella, but because of Piper's spell, he now believed he was a farmer. He lived in the small house where I had first met him just south of the Forest of Death.

After a while, Sanders and I took the lead and let Sylvia and Lenore chat behind us. Sylvia's interest in ornithology and Lenore's other life as a bird made the two a good match. The subject bored me and my wife, and catching each other's eyes, we moved ahead, knowing Lenore would guide us if we strayed from our path.

I squinted at the sun and guessed our distance. The four of us wouldn't reach Roger's farm by foot today as the sun was rapidly setting. We'd have to seek shelter. This only contributed to my foul mood as we sojourned onward.

Human-sized, Sanders bumped me with her shoulder. "You seem unusually quiet."

"I could say the same for you," I replied.

Sanders retrieved her glasses from her pocket and put them on. "I'm just thinking of the audacity of Piper to offer me the throne. He must really be desperate."

"I don't know." I avoided a stone moving by its own accord across the path. "You're an intelligent woman, solid spellcaster, and beloved hero of the people."

Sanders waved her hand. "All true, of course." She smirked at me. "No, I mean the nerve thinking tempting me would be easy when I have a husband and a child. Kingdom's not even my home."

This conversation seemed an appropriate cue for me to switch to her real name. "But, Sondra, you could be queen."

"I don't care, Harold. What's all that worth when the man who truly understands me is a world away. You're the other half of my heart. That idiot certainly wouldn't be. And Fitzie! I'd never see him again. Cat's piss! Piper's an arrogant jerk thinking I'd just walk away from my life and join him."

I remained silent. Sanders turned sharply at me. "Don't tell me if he made you that offer, you'd consider it."

"I don't think he's gay."

Sanders scowled. "You know what I mean. What if Penta were an evil queen and she made the same offer to you?"

I tensed my shoulders at Penta's name. "Is that what this is all about? I don't love Penta, Sanders. No matter what Piper says, I'm not attracted to her."

Sanders reared back. "I never said you were."

"Then why didn't you choose Helga or Valencia for your example?"

"Because Valencia looks like your sister, and if you accepted an offer to couple with her, I'd puke. But mostly because the rest of the queens were married or are engaged, and Penta is the only single one. Are you worried that I think you've got a thing for Penta?"

I wouldn't meet her eyes.

Sanders adjusted her glasses—her gesture before a speech. "Penta is my friend, but she's your special friend. You and she bonded over Planet's death." Sanders put her hand on my cheek. "She loves you, but not like a husband and not like a brother. She loves you like a friend, and that's why seeing her not recognize you hurts so much."

"Yeah."

Sanders patted my cheek. "I'll never be jealous of Penta. I promise."

My wife was right. The side of me that mourns Planet I share with Penta. But I have dozens of quirks and bad habits that Sanders puts up with every day, and still loves me. Sometimes, I think the forbearance of living with your spouse's foibles are the real signs of true love.

When my eyes didn't meet hers, Sanders transformed to pixie size and floated in front of me, moving backward. "Make sure I don't hit a tree, or a large bird doesn't swallow me, okay?"

I nodded.

"Now what's up, sourpuss?"

I avoided her gaze. "What do you mean?"

"This mood isn't about Penta. What's disturbing you so much?"

I shrugged.

"Is it Beauty?"

I kicked a rock out of the way but didn't answer her.

Sanders said, "I wouldn't worry about Beauty. We'll get another crack at her."

Now I locked eyes with her. "What if we don't? What if I had my shot, and I blew it?"

"Come on. You're Hero. You goof up all the time but make it right in the end."

"What if I don't? What if I'm not the guy who's prophesied to bring the queens together this time? I used to be able to gather the queens just like I used to be able to publish a book."

Sanders shook her head and a few golden sprinkles fell to the ground. "Now this is about publishing? You're making too much of a small setback."

Dodging a falling leaf, I said, "Maybe I'm not. Maybe I succeeded before because I was *supposed* to succeed. I had the prophecy on my side. Now, I don't. I used to be able to impress the queens by knowing the end of their stories. They moved past their happily ever after years ago. Now, I don't know how to lure them to our side."

Sanders stretched out her hand and tipped up my chin. "You have friendship, sincerity, and determination on your side. And you have one more thing."

Oh, here it came. "You?"

69

Sanders wrinkled her nose. "Duh. Of course you have me, but I wasn't referring to that. You have the truth. The truth is powerful, Hero, and may be more powerful than magic in this case. Tell me, Piper brainwashed everyone, right?"

"Yes."

Sanders bobbed along backward. "But there's a resistance movement, and a way to restore the queens' memories, also right?"

"Also right."

"Therefore, Piper didn't think of everything, because he doesn't know everything." Sanders scratched her chin. "In Beauty's case, the topiaries and the song she played. We must think of those things that will bring our queens and princes together. The truth always finds a way to be told."

I hadn't thought of it that way.

Sanders hovered centimeters from my face. "Now, cheer up, and let's go get a prince." She kissed me on the nose.

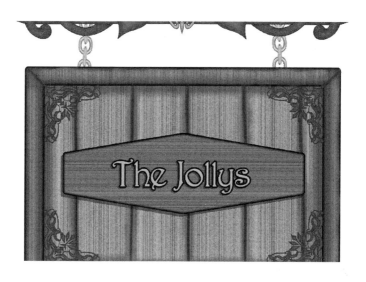

09 - A JOLLY TIME

Harold

We walked until well after the sun set, and then a friendly dryad farmer allowed us to camp out on his property. Hospitality was a staple in Kingdom since the queen's ascension and must have continued during Piper's reign. That night, the four of us discussed the task ahead. Joining this prince and this queen should be simple because, of all the monarchs, the romance between Roger and Cinderella was legendary. They both knew and loved each other before she had become queen. In comparison, Valencia had met Graddock on her way to the throne. They'd be starting over. And Helga and Danforth? Worse, because Danforth wasn't even in this world, and we had no idea how to return to Earth.

The following morning, the farmer filled our satchels

with fruits and vegetables, and we continued our journey. Lenore flew ahead, scouting for soldiers. No sign of Piper or his army. Maybe he was only worried about the queens and not the princes. One could hope.

At about noon, we arrived at Roger Jolly's residence. We approached the same single-room house where I had first met Roger. The wooden exterior had a green-tiled roof matching the olive-colored shutters on the windows. Back then, his residence was surrounded by dirt. Now his yard was alive with a lush garden, verdant plants, and rows of peas, corn, lettuce, and sparkling plants. The air around the house smelled of lavender, grass, and loam. Bees and butterflies fluttered around the garden, nearly glowing in the sunlight. We made our way past all this as we proceeded to the front door.

Sanders held up a finger to keep us from knocking and transformed into her Charlie disguise. We couldn't let Roger think the queen had come for a visit. After we knocked, a voice called out. "Around back!"

We made our way along a rock-strewn path to the back of the house and saw two men working in the garden. I didn't know the man closest to us, but the second man, looking a bit older, was the man of the hour. Roger Jolly.

Roger was slightly over six feet tall with unruly dark hair and a bushy beard. Dressed in brown overalls, he picked raspberries off a bush.

We started to walk toward Roger, but the other man stepped in front of us. Roger moved to the back of the garden, allowing the other worker to intercept us. The man had the same bone structure and similar nose to the prince, which led me to think he was related. He held up his hand. "Greetings. Who are you?"

I nodded to Roger. "We are here to see Mr. Jolly."

"Is that so?" The man looked over his shoulder and then back at us. "For what purpose?"

Sanders smiled pleasantly at him. "Who are you?"

The man, taller than Roger, with gray hair and a

piercing stare answered her. "I am Hollander Jolly. Roger's brother."

Sanders slapped a hand over her mouth, holding back the laughter. She spoke through her fingers. "Please tell me you don't go by Hollie."

These Kingdom names could be something else! I interrupted my wife before she angered Roger's brother. "We are visitors to these parts. We have come from a far land and were last here when King Shade ruled. The garden has grown in that time. May we have a minute with your brother?"

Hollander shifted to stand between us and Roger, "My brother does not like to talk to people. I will be glad to discuss whatever matter you have with him."

Time to put to use Sanders' lecture on the truth. "We need to discuss his past. He knew a certain maiden he met at a wishing well years before the war. This concerns her."

Roger must have heard us because he stopped picking bugs off a plant and straightened up. He started toward us.

Knitting his brow, Hollander asked, "At a well?"

"Soro's Well, to be precise," said Lenore.

Roger put his hand on his brother's shoulder. Dour but resolved, Roger addressed us. "I recall the wishing well. I met a servant girl there nearly every day before I joined the army. She was a true friend."

"Do you recall her name?"

Roger shook his head. "She was a Hartstone. I recall that clearly."

"Radiance Hartstone?" Sanders said. I'm glad she spoke. I almost called her Cinderella. Radiance was Cinderella's name before she changed it. I had explained to her how the Earth story of "Cinderella" had provided us with a positive role model, inspiring Kingdom's Cinderella to adopt the name.

Roger brightened. "Yes, of course. How is Radiance? No harm has come to her I hope?"

I eyed Roger's cottage home. "I hope not either. Can we go inside and talk?"

The brothers exchanged a glance and Hollander answered, "I wish to be present."

I pinched my lower lip. An odd request, certainly, but I'd agree to anything to discuss this topic with Roger.

The brothers led the way into the house, carefully making their way around the garden. The house was a little more decorated than I remembered it from years ago. Then, the one-room dwelling contained a bed and little else. Now, someone had painted it a light purple, the bed was sturdier, and a cabinet of drawers stood in the corner. Against one wall, Roger had a table with two chairs.

I quickly made introductions, and the brothers bowed courteously. Roger offered us the chairs and Sanders shrunk and floated in the air next to us.

I folded my hands. "You remember Radiance Hartstone then?"

"Indeed, when she was twelve years old. I knew her for too little a time."

"Did you ever see her when she was older? Perhaps you went to a festival and met—"

Hollander cut me off. "We are not going to discuss that!"

Roger looked interested at first, but then deferred to his brother and hung his head, saying nothing.

I held up a hand. "Sorry. Did I say something wrong?"

Hollander stood and positioned himself between us and Roger. "We do not speak of that time. If you want to know anything about the festival, you may as well leave."

Sanders bobbed up and down. "Is it because your brother spent all his money chasing a young lady at the festival who lost her shoes?"

Hollander turned on her. "And he nearly died of poverty in this house. When I found him, he had not eaten a morsel of food in days. I had to nurse him to health, despite his protests. I took months trying to interest him in anything again."

"But don't...do you not see how much he loved her?" Sylvia clasped her hands together.

Hollander crossed his arms. "He chased a ghost or a land-bound siren. If I had not been at the festival myself, I would never have believed she existed. She disappeared after my brother ruined his wealth and reputation by fitting that damnable slipper on every woman in the neighborhood."

"Did you try the slipper on the women at the Hartstone's?" I asked.

Roger set his jaw. "I did."

"Including Radiance, though she was only a scullery maid?"

I knew the answer. Cinderella was, in standing, a slave and so she was not summoned when Roger reached the Hartstone residence. Cinderella's spirit was crushed when her true love had ridden away after trying the slipper on her stepsisters.

"I do not recall." Roger trembled. With excitement, perhaps? "Are you implying my maiden was someone I overlooked?"

Time to reveal more truth. "She is no ghost. We know who your mysterious maiden is and where she lives now."

Hollander replied, "And how much will it cost us for you to reveal what you know? Fifty gold? Or will you take my brother away, and rob him?"

Hollander hadn't finished before Roger asked, "You know where she is?"

Sanders flashed a thumbs-up sign.

Hollander turned to his brother. "Do not let them sway you, brother. Think of your garden. The flowers and the bounty are your mistress now. The plants will never leave you. This lost encounter only drains your money and your health."

Roger cowered under Hollander's words. He slouched, his scowl deepening. "I am sorry, but Hollander is right. I cannot embark on any journey seeking the maiden from that night. Without knowing who she is, I will ruin my life and my family's reputation."

The time had come to put the puzzle pieces together for

him. "The maiden is Radiance Hartstone."

Roger laughed. "There is no—"

"'Chance the mysterious maiden at the festival was Radiance?' Is that what you were about to say?"

Roger opened his mouth to speak again, but I interrupted him once more. "You will say that your maiden looked older, but then we'll tell you people dressed up with their hair carefully arranged often do. In return, I'll ask you to think back to the slave girl and your maiden and consider if they could be the same. Could they be, Roger Jolly?"

"How did you know what I was thinking?"

Sylvia rubbed her hands together, peering out the window. Would the false king's guards show up now when we're on the verge of convincing him? I pressed on, determined. "How I know what you were about to say does not matter. What matters is that you believe me. Radiance is your maiden, and she lives not far from here in the Forest of Death."

Lenore spoke quietly. "Radiance is with a friend of ours."

Hollander put a hand on his brother's shoulder. "Roger, stay with me. Do not listen to them and ride off again."

"If they know the truth, Hollander. This is the best information I ever had on the maiden. All who claimed to be her never matched her beauty. But petite Radiance...grown up." Roger stared at a spot in the air away from everyone. "Indeed, she could be the maiden."

"But, Roger—" began Hollander.

"She knew me that night like no other. You recall it as well. We both agreed after the last night of the festival that she must have been someone close."

Hollander clenched his jaw. "Or an enchantress."

Roger shook his head. "Then she would want something. My body, my wealth, my subjugation. No, she wanted nothing."

Hollander turned to us. "Why would you torture him after all these years?"

"We will guarantee his safe return here if we are

wrong." Sylvia stood and struck a pose of authority, every bit in mayor mode. "But we are not wrong!"

Flushed, Hollander swung on us. "Who are you people? Why are you so interested in my brother's affairs?"

We had agreed not to try to convince Roger he was a prince until he had met Cinderella, strategizing his attraction to his maiden would be the best way to have him join us. "We heard this tale about two parted lovers and hoped to reunite them."

Hollander glared at me. "And where did you hear this rumor after all these years? Why would anyone keep this knowledge to themselves and then decide to tell you four?"

Crap. His probing was good. I had to admire how much he desired to protect his younger brother from harm. I had to come up with a fib and I thought of a doozy. "The wishing well the two of you met at. Soro's Well."

"Who told you there?" said Roger.

"The well itself. As you know, the well speaks. We asked it, as a wish, to tell us a tragic story, not believing it would grant us such a boon. The well told us how you met there, how you went off to war and lost your leg, how Radiance cared deeply for you, how her mother's ghost dressed her for the festival, and how you searched for her for months."

Roger stood, addressing Hollander. "If the well spoke to these people and told them Radiance is the mysterious maiden, then she must be the one."

The color drained from Hollander's face. "These people are going to rob you, Roger."

Roger held up his hand. "I will not carry money, and I should be able to overpower two maidens, a pixie, and a flabby man."

Flabby man! True, I had gained a few pounds, but really!

Roger turned to us. "I will go with you. Do not lie to me. If you do, I will repay you with my sword."

Lenore blanched, but I was surprised Sylvia and my wife grinned ear to ear. Roger put a hand on his brother's shoulder.

"I am sorry, Hollander, but I must follow this through even if it will lead to disappointment."

Hollander returned the gesture on Roger's other shoulder. "I will take care of your garden. Come, let us harvest from it for the journey."

Sondra

I'm sure you've heard the saying "as the crow flies" which is a very unscientific way of saying "in a straight line." Why not say it's about two miles if you went in a straight line instead of "as the crow flies?" And what is so special about crows anyway? Do blue jays fly in a zigzag pattern? Do robins become drunk and fly around in circles?

Anyway...

Fortunately, we had a raven. Lenore turned into her winged form, and she flew ahead over the forest to Julia's territory about fifty miles as the *raven* flies. Within sight of the Forest of Death, we spied our friendly raven after four hours. Lenore transformed into her human form and cheerfully announced she had landed in the commune where Cinderella lived. This area, known as Ozark's Territory, was a province unto itself and not part of Kingdom.

Our bird companion had sought out the leader of the commune, her friend Julia. She had forewarned Julia that we were coming to unite Cinderella with Roger.

The Forest of Death. An entangled set of dark woods and briars whose leaves blocked most of the sunlight. The massive tree trunks would slow us down but not stop us. Since this place wasn't as ominous as it sounded, I'd often remarked the queens should rename it The Forest of Getting Burrs in Your Butt.

As we marched toward the line of trees demarking the edge, three identical soldiers appeared in front of us. They were normal in every way except they had no eyes. The "man" in the middle held up his hand, arm outstretched and palm facing us. "Halt. By order of King Piper, you are to turn back."

I leaned toward Lenore. "What's this?"

She frowned. "Piper's golems. Made of clay, but they die the same way as humans."

Roger strode forward, arms up. "With all due respect, we seek only to travel into yonder forest. Certainly, you will allow us to pass."

The soldier beckoned him forward. When Roger stepped within an arm's reach of the creepy soldier, the guard formed a fist and swung it at Roger. Roger dodged the blow by his whiskers.

Roger stumbled backward in surprise. "Uncalled for, sir. I am a peace-loving citizen—"

The golems had drawn their swords and held them up. Roger unsheathed his own weapon and brandished it before the others. "Now come, let us talk—"

The soldiers charged forward, ignoring Roger's attempt to placate them. My blood boiled at the odds and my mind flipped through options as if I were consulting a rolodex, determining which spell to throw.

Turns out the odds weren't in their favor. When Roger readied himself for battle, he extended his sword outward so the golem in the middle couldn't advance. Then, he jumped up, performed a split in midair, simultaneously kicking both left and right guards in the chest. The aggressors on either side fell backward. When he landed on his feet, he charged the central figure who had slashed at him clumsily.

With an elegant thrust, Roger plunged his sword into the central soldier's chest. No blood poured from the wound, but the figure dropped to the dirt. The other two rushed at Roger from the right and left. Our companion released his sword, grabbed two knives from his belt, and flicked them in different directions at the two opponents. The knives buried themselves into their chests, and they—like their leader—collapsed to the ground.

Roger stepped up to the one on the left and toed it. "Lousy golems. Piper's army is full of them. They are cheap, clean, and servile. Also, highly inefficient. Why are they attacking us? I am a good citizen and pay my taxes."

After he retrieved his weapons, Roger waved us forward. "Shall we proceed?"

Squaring his shoulders, he led us toward the tree line until three guards appeared in front of us. The one in the center extended his arm, palm facing us. "Halt."

Roger stopped. "If this keeps up, we shall never get into the forest."

I wiggled my wings. "Leave this to me. I'll teleport us there."

Sylvia paled next to me. "May I choose the soldiers instead?"

"Really, Sylvia. You must have faith. Watch this."

Centering my magic, I teleported us right into the forest. Well, not directly into the forest. Actually, not in the forest at all, but about a hundred yards to the right.

The soldiers spotted us immediately. From there, we engaged in a footrace to the tree line. Lenore and I took to our wings, and Roger, Sylvia, and Hero dashed forward.

I slowed the guards down with a cantrip that actually can trip. My little prankster spell gave us enough time to enter the woods where the sentries stopped before entering. We weren't far from Ozark's Territory. Since the region was considered out of Kingdom, Piper knew better than to follow us there and start a war.

We proceeded at a trot, or in my case a glide, deeper into the forest. When we were sure the golems weren't following us, we stopped and took a breath. Roger asked, "Why would King Piper direct sentries to stop us?"

No one answered him as we trekked forward. The Forest of Death was different from the Forest of Blood. The Forest of Death's trees were spread out further and were taller than those in its cousin to the south. Rumor had it that no one had ever mapped the entire forest and lived to tell the tale. Supposedly, underground creatures lived in the center, waiting for a chance to snatch a weary traveler.

Using a makeshift trail Lenore had scouted, we advanced toward Ozark's Territory. I landed on my feet, allowing my wings to rest. The immense trunks of the trees could give the redwoods a run for their money. The exotic flora in the forest excited the scientist in me, but I'm not much of a botanist. Still, a plant that has silver leaves with a gold trim made me want to snap a photograph.

As we walked, Roger shivered. "I lost my leg in this forest fighting Ozark."

Before he could stop himself, Hero opened his big mouth. "The Malfleurs severed it."

Malfleurs were tree-like beings that had served Ozark when he was alive. I hoped we didn't run into them, but we had larger problems with Hero's slip of the tongue.

Roger turned to Hero and squinted. "How do you know that? We have not met before, have we?"

Avoiding Roger's stare, my husband said, "When we were trying to find your house, someone told us about you."

Roger rubbed his beard. To dismiss the awkward moment, I strolled up beside him. "So, Roger. What are you going to tell Radiance when you see her?"

"I love her." He spoke with conviction and without hesitation. I always liked Roger.

Lenore cleared her throat. "You may want to speak to her a bit before making so bold a statement. Since you overlooked her when you were trying on the slippers, Radiance may need some convincing first."

Roger lifted his chin. "I will speak true, and she will understand my heart. You will see."

Lenore turned to me and rolled her eyes. I grimaced. I hoped he was right.

The Forest of Death

10 - THE FIRST REUNION

Sondra

We proceeded deeper into the Forest of Death, where unlike the bordering region, the sunlight rarely penetrated the sprawling canopy, and the ground was an uneven mixture of gnarled roots and fetid moss. Animal life was abundant here, and six times out of eight I could name the creature in front of us, though the owl with the third eye threw me. The trees inhibited our progress, and despite our efforts, we had to stop before we reached Julia's. Stumbling around in the dark was too dangerous for us to continue onward.

Though eerie wailing broke the silence multiple times during the night, we managed to have a decent rest. Then we set out in the early morning after a quick breakfast of berries and carrots. I had turned into a pixie at one point to fly beside Roger and Sylvia who were strolling along together. Careful not to jostle me, he said, "I have always admired pixies. They are a wonderful species."

Disguised as Charlie, I brushed back one of my blonde locks. "I'm not a true pixie. Not one hundred percent. I was born human."

Stunned, Roger blinked. "I apologize. I assumed because of your appearance and spells."

"Ah, don't worry about it. Some of my favorite people are pixies."

Roger stepped over a hole that was home to some god-knows-what creature. "The pixies saved my life in my battle near this very spot. I am truly grateful that King Piper abolished the trade in pixie scalps. Scalping pixies is a savage profession."

Before the queens came to power, men hunted pixies for their scalps to make them into scarves and muffs. The queens immediately outlawed this disgusting act. I thought I would push Roger a little for information. "I suppose with a pixie on the throne, it was time."

"Indeed. Clearly, Planet's gentler hand may be behind these edicts. 'Tis something we common folk do not see."

"You are anything but common." Sylvia put her hand to her mouth. Oops.

Roger smiled at her. "I thank you for the compliment and return it. You are very pretty, Ms. Swonewith. And yet, the most beautiful woman in the world would still rank second to my fair maiden."

A few hours later we came to a massive oak with a carving on its trunk. At first, I believed this would be a sign or warning, but the words, upon my coming closer, were ones we had read before. "Snow White Lives."

Roger reached out and patted the tree trunk. "Rest assured, friend tree, that King Piper will root this forest of malicious rebels. I fought for King Shade in these woods but learned the hard way he was an unjust king. King Piper, on the other hand, is a magnanimous ruler."

Oh, give me a break. "Is there anyone who does not like King Piper?"

Roger thrust back his shoulders. "No one I know. That pesky resistance movement is doomed. They are nothing but troublemakers and ruffians. King Piper has assured us that he has it well under control."

We glanced at each other. How was Roger going to take the truth when we told him? Hopefully, with his history connected to Cinderella, he would be more open to the actual events.

As the sun started to set in the west, the trees thinned a bit and we arrived at Julia's village. Hers was a large clearing in the otherwise well-populated forest. Her camp was filled with rejected beings from other parts of Kingdom. Many smaller fairies whose magic is less powerful than that of other magical beings, flitted around the dwellings. I spotted dryads, unicorns, and unigards—a black horse with a silver horn. Malfleurs, dead tree bark creatures that wore cloaks and looked like monks, eyed us warily. Whenever he was near the Malfleurs, Roger's hand brushed the hilt of his sword.

Two dryad sentries escorted us into the camp. "Camp" is an understatement as the heart of Ozark's Territory is the size of a neighborhood. Wooden enclosures—many half-spherical in shape—lined the paths, and rope bridges between the tallest trees provided another way to move around. An artist had sculpted faces of the various species living here on a dead tree in the center of the encampment.

Julia emerged from a large hut made entirely of wood and rope. We knew her from a previous adventure. She wore her dark hair longer now, and dressed in a green tunic and brown leggings. Perched on her head was a tiara made of branches and leaves.

She scurried to Lenore and hugged her and then

curtsied to the rest of us. When she came to me, she wrinkled her brow until Lenore told her I was Sanders. The disguise confused her.

Hero eyed her tiara. "You seem to be acclimating to Kingdom well."

Rolling her eyes, Julia adjusted the circlet. "Kingdom is heavenly. At least, it was until this latest business. Sir?" She addressed Roger. "Will you fetch me my robe hanging on that birch across the clearing?"

"Roger Jolly, at your service." He bowed and set out on his chore.

Julia murmured, "He doesn't remember?"

I shook my head.

Roger held out the robe, and Julia received it with a word of gratitude. She turned to one of her companions whose top half was that of a human man and bottom half was a tiger standing upright on two paws. "Rex, please locate Radiance and Pennilane and ask them to wait for me beyond the ridge."

The creature named Rex bowed.

"Thank you, dear."

Julia turned back to us. "Mr. Jolly, can you wait outside while I have a word with my friends inside my hut?"

Roger nodded, peering after Rex as if Cinderella was likely to show up now.

Julia led us into the hut and closed the door, whispering. "One day a little over six months ago, Cinderella and Pennilane wandered into my territory. They claimed they had been here for over seven years and were surprised when I told them they didn't live here. Cinderella insisted on being called Radiance instead of what she calls "that degrading name my sisters called me." When I went to send a message to the royal castle for the queens, my messengers acted as though I were the one who was daft."

"This all happened soon after Piper cast the spell, I assume," said Hero.

"Yes. I thought I was losing my mind until Lenore flew

in a few days later." Julia touched Lenore's shoulder. "Since then, I've kept Cinderella here. She's been pleasant overall but spends a lot of time with Pennilane. The two of them are thick as thieves."

Pennilane. A selkie and Cinderella's best friend. I blew hair away from my eyes. "Does she act like Cinderella?"

"Again, I caution you not to call her that name. I have made the mistake a few times and received a frosty stare. She's a changed woman. Remember, she believes she has spent many years living here. She's hardened some."

Rex stuck his head into the hut. "Miss Julia? Ms. Radiance and Ms. Pennilane are over the ridge, awaiting you and the others."

I was thrilled to meet Radiance again. Each queen has something about her I admire, and with Radiance it's her unconventional manner. If you didn't know she was a queen, you'd never guess it. She eschews most of the stiffness of royalty.

Julia led us out of her dwelling place. "I think it best you four take Roger to them and leave me out of this. If the pairing doesn't work out, I'll still have Radiance's trust, and the Resistance needs to keep her safe."

We motioned for Roger to join us, and Lenore, Sylvia, Hero, and I stealthily ascended a small ridge. At the bottom stood the source of our quest into the forest. Radiance and the taller Pennilane had their backs to us. We carefully made our way down behind them while they turned and spied us coming.

A great warrior, Pennilane looked mostly the same as when I'd seen her before; she was a Brown woman with white whiskers and close-cropped hair. Radiance, a woman in her middle twenties, looked stunning even after spending eight months in the woods. Some women are lucky that way— I'm not. The last time I had met her, she was regal-looking, wearing a gown embroidered with gold. Now, her tangled hair, torn dress, and thin figure told the tale of how she had been surviving these past months. I couldn't spot her rosy cheeks under her dirty face, and her blonde hair was a shade darker.

Upon seeing Roger, Radiance blinked rapidly as if he were a vision. Then she shook her head. Her bright blue eyes narrowed.

When Roger jumped down to the level ground, he dropped to his knees in front of her. Tongue-tied, he didn't say anything. Radiance only continued to shake her head.

Pennilane lifted her spear, but I quickly levitated it upward. "You have no need to attack us. We will not hurt you."

Hero cleared his throat. "Radiance Hartstone."

Radiance ignored my husband. Her eyes were locked on Roger. Her mouth moved a little, trying to form words.

Pennilane stepped between all of us and Radiance. Peering around her friend, Radiance's eyes squinted with rage. I was so taken aback by her expression, I readied a spell without thinking.

Hero held out his hands, palms up, a surrendering pose. "We aren't here to hurt you. We want to talk. Please."

Pennilane held her hand up. "Return the use of my spear."

I said, "Give us your promise you won't attack us first."

Pennilane shook her head, but Radiance put a hand on her shoulder. She straightened up, and the hidden queen within appeared. "We will not hurt you if you promise not to attack us."

Roger stepped back as if she had struck him. "Attack you? I could never do that."

She held up her hand to him, not looking at him but us. "You do not speak. I have nothing to say to you."

"But–"

Hero stepped forward. "Hold up, Roger." He turned and addressed Radiance and Pennilane. "We mean you no harm. You don't know us, admittedly, and I know we sound like we're not from around here. Truth is, we are from far away, but please believe me when I say I know about you."

Radiance's attention darted from Hero to Roger, her eyes resting on Roger more than my husband. "How?"

"I will explain in time. Let's say we were sent here to right a wrong. Your past, Radiance, isn't right."

The queen arched an eyebrow. "How do you mean…not right?"

Hero maintained an even tone. "It wasn't right you were treated as a slave. It wasn't right that you and Roger were separated so young. And I know the pain you suffered watching Roger ride away with your sisters and not coming back for you. That wasn't right either."

Radiance's jaw tightened.

Hero swept his arm around. "You came here, seeking refuge, perhaps starting over. But the truth is you were always meant to be with this man." He pointed at Roger. "We've come to restore him to you. After all this time, he still loves you, Radiance."

She breathed in deeply, and Pennilane stiffened. The selkie murmured something only her partner could hear, and Radiance nodded. Radiance took three steps forward, stopping in front of Roger. She examined him up and down as his eyes glowed with his admiration for her. In a quick motion, she slapped him across the face.

We all started toward them and hesitated as she turned and faced Hero. "I do not love this man. I waited and waited for him, but my heart broke long ago, and I put back the pieces myself. Do you think me a foolish maiden who needs a man in my life to be the person I want to be? Begone from here! I will not tolerate your presence any longer."

Sylvia said, "Cinderella!"

Her eyes glared at Sylvia. "How *dare* you call me that!"

This was turning ugly. Hero struggled to find the words to say to convince Radiance. Unfortunately, Roger spoke first. "You were my maiden at the festival. You were the one I danced with all three nights. You lost your slipper on the last night."

She poked him on the chest with her index finger. "Of

course I was! I was young and a fool! How could I ever have believed you were the one for me, you lubberwort!"

Roger hung his head. "I never stopped looking for you."

"I do not care." Radiance fisted her hands on her hips. "You had your opportunity back at the Hartstones and you did not use it. You *knew* I was there. You tried the slipper on my evil stepsisters but did not give a thought to me. If you had asked for me, you would have realized I was the maiden. You did not once seek me out. Even after I ran away, I dreamed you would come for me. And then one day I realized I did not need you. The younger version of myself believed in romance, but not me. I have grown up, Roger, and do not need true love."

Roger gestured to us. "These good people explained to me that your dead mother gave you the dress for the festival. How could I have guessed you, who were so low in life, could have such a dress?"

Hero winced at the words "so low in life." Radiance's voice was venomous. "Because true love does not seek outer appearances. It seeks the heart."

Roger held out his hands. "And now I offer you mine. I know a lot of time has passed, but you have my devotion. How can I make reparations? I will do anything for you, who saved me from a void of despair."

Radiance hesitated. Roger's confession, so open and honest, clearly made an impact. Yet her resolve remained solidly in place. "You are too late."

Putting his hands behind his back, Hero shuffled closer. "This is a turning point in your life, Radiance. You need to rise above it and make the right decision."

Radiance glared at my husband. "And how do you know what the right decision is for me? This man comes to me to woo me. I will not be won that way. No *reparation* for the injustice done to me is possible."

"I will love you all of my days," said Roger. "I will court you. In time, you will see my intentions were never to hurt you. I will never pursue another. If you forgive me, I will only betroth you."

Radiance leaned forward. "Betroth? I be-loathe you!"

Pennilane said, "Let us leave them, Radiance."

Radiance held up a hand. "Not yet." She indicated Roger. "This one does not interest me, but the others do. They run words together and admit they come from far away. They know about me. Why spend so much energy trying to unite a former slave and a disgraced soldier? I have learned one lesson in my life—no one does a good deed for nothing. I want to know who you are and why you want me to return to my cumberworldian past."

Hero smiled. "Cumberworldian? I know you like new words."

Radiance bit her lip. "This is what I mean by your familiarity with me. How do you know I collect unique words?"

We looked at each other. Lenore said, "We can't tell her. She will never believe us."

Hero sighed. "We don't have a choice."

My husband cleared his throat and told Roger, Radiance, and Pennilane of the queen legend and his former adventure in Kingdom. When he finished with the true queen's part, she stopped him. "This never happened to me."

"It happened. Your memory has been erased."

"By who?"

"King Piper."

Radiance looked shocked. "Our good and fair king would never do such a thing."

"It's all true."

Radiance crossed her arms. "And you can prove it?"

Hero shifted. "You can."

"How?"

He nudged Roger. "You kiss your true love."

Radiance looked puzzled, but only for a moment. She looked over at Roger and shook her head, wagging her finger. "Oh, no! No! No! I refuse to kiss that man!"

"Your memory will come back to you. You'll become a queen again. No, that's not right. You are a queen."

Roger said, "But...she is no queen. And I am certainly not royalty. I cannot marry above my station."

I rubbed my jaw. "Skip to the end, Hero."

Hero side-eyed me then continued. "Radiance, you and your sisters are queens who rule Kingdom with grace and mercy. You made this place a land of peace, not Piper. You married Roger and elevated him to prince."

Radiance laughed. "Oh, this is too much. It is a bedtime story."

"Better," said Hero. "It's a fairy tale. Ask yourself three questions. How do we know you so well if we are strangers? Why is it so important to us that you and Roger fall in love again? And why...why do we care so much about you?"

She cocked an eyebrow. "Why *do* you care so much about me?"

I couldn't keep it in any longer. I rushed up to her and hugged her as she stiffened. "Because you're our friend. Our dear friend who keeps her sisters from being Gloomy Gusses, and who uses ridiculous words at the wrong time, and who truly was the one who abolished seal hunting in honor of her friend, and who makes us all believe in undying romance. You are all of this and more. Believe us."

I awkwardly separated from her and wiped my eyes. She stared at me curiously. "I cannot fall in love again, but I admit, I am interested in this story. Pennilane is my sister in spirit, but to have sisters by blood? And you said I made the law to abolish seal hunting? And I throw festivals and balls as queen." Radiance stared off into the distance. "Yes. I believe I would do all those things."

Hero said, "Will you at least accompany us until we can prove to you this is real?"

Pennilane stepped forward. "No."

Radiance lifted her chin in a regal manner. "I think I will."

91

"But Radiance." Pennilane turned to her. "They will only break your heart again."

Radiance led her away and the two of them had a boisterous "discussion" out of earshot. I so wanted to listen in. We regrouped and invited Roger, who was standing by himself and looking dejected. Sylvia eyed him. "Do you believe us?"

Roger scratched his beard. "I agree this is a far-fetched story, but if it brings me together with Radiance, I will believe it. If you are false, kissing her is not against the law. If you are true…" He arched an eyebrow.

Not completely a believer but convinced enough to kiss her. I'd take that any day. "It's true. The harder part is proving to Radiance that she's really a queen. We made it past step one and convinced her to come with us, but this doesn't mean she's willing to kiss you. What do we have to do to get her to pucker up?"

Sylvia bit her lip, and Hero observed a spot on the ground. Lenore's face brightened. "Oh, I've got it." She looked over her shoulder at the two arguing women. "It's perfect."

11 - RADIANCE'S RETREAT

Harold

The idea to unite Radiance and Roger was purely inspired. Heck, it was a great plan—one worthy of a hero who would unite the queens and save the day. Did it originate from the hero? Or his savvy yet sarcastic wife? No. The suggestion came from Lenore, our guide. Maybe she was the Chosen One.

Lenore eyes shone. "Roger built a chalet for Cinderella on their first wedding anniversary. The home is embedded in the Grok mountains—tiny, given the castles around here. Cinderella loved it and decorated the inside with all her flourishes. The married queens use it to spend time there with their husbands. Cinderella would often disguise herself and go among the population, seeking out a newly married couple. She'd gift them a weekend at the chalet."

Perfect. This building sounded exactly like what we needed. "How far away is it?"

Lenore frowned. "Roger christened it Radiance's Retreat. We'd have to march a few days in this forest, through the fairies' territory and other fae homelands, and then across the river known as River. A week and a half?"

We reflected in silence. A long journey, to be sure. My thoughts were interrupted by Radiance's raised voice.

"But Pennilane, if they wanted to ransom me, could they not have come up with a more plausible story?"

Sounded as if Radiance was winning the argument.

"What about teleporting?" I suggested. "Julia must have some magicians who can cast a teleportation spell."

Lenore shook her head. "In order to teleport, a common spellcaster needs to know the destination. No one in Julia's camp knows about Radiance's Retreat. We're likely to be teleported inside of a mountain if someone attempted it."

"So, we're out of luck teleporting," I remarked.

"Hey, I'm right here." My wife's tone didn't disguise her snark.

Lenore, Sylvia, Roger, and I shifted uneasily, staring down at our shoes. Before I could describe the image of our bodies embedded in rock to my wife, she up held her hands. "Got it."

Lenore frowned. "If Celeste were here, we could do it. She's such an accomplished sorceress that she can teleport anywhere without knowing details about the location."

Sanders bit her lip. "We need Celeste. Maybe we could stop at her house on the way?"

Celeste Constellation was the preeminent spellcaster in Kingdom and my wife's best friend, but she wouldn't know any of us. "We'd spend too much time convincing her to join us."

"We need to be able to teleport, Hero." Sanders sighed. "Kingdom's too large."

"I may have a solution to that," Lenore said. "Julia has magic bird seed, capable of transforming one into a bird. If we're all birds, we might be able to make it in less than a week."

"Except that Cinderella and Pennilane may fly away." I shuffled my feet. "Aside from you, we'll all be getting used to our wings. And we may encounter hunters."

Roger scratched his beard. "If we had a boat, we could make good time."

"Roger, you just reminded me!" Lenore raised her eyebrows. "Julia has a ship. Piper doesn't know it, but her people 'acquired' the *Swan Princess* disguised as pirates. She has it hidden on the north bank of this forest."

I had myself ridden in the *Swan Princess* before. Equipped with magical sails, the ship flew over the water at a tremendous speed. The vessel's only drawback was it couldn't fly over land, but it could easily reach the northern entry into River and then sail south. "Perfect. Though the march north may take some time."

"Rest assured, Hero." Lenore patted me on the shoulder. "Julia has an answer for that, too."

The queen and the selkie were still arguing, but Radiance seemed to be winning. Their voices grew louder as they discussed going with us.

Radiance said, "I cannot help it, Pennilane. You know I have been yearning for a journey outside of Ozark's Territory for months. Something is drawing me to see more of Kingdom, and I am curious about these people."

"They will kidnap you." Pennilane folded her arms. "This will end in your ruin."

Radiance rolled her shoulders. "You know, I am not helpless."

I called for them to join us. Radiance chose the point furthest from Roger while Lenore told them our plan. When Lenore described Radiance's Retreat, Radiance looked sharply at Roger. "You supposedly built this for me?"

For once, I wished the prince would fib and assure her

he did. But of course, Roger had no memory of constructing the chalet. "I do not recall doing so."

Sanders broke in. "But a place like this is exactly something Roger would do for you. It's totally him."

"I admit, I am curious about this building named after me." Radiance mimicked Sanders by adding, "*Totally* curious."

Lenore clasped her hands. "Before we go, I suppose I should tell you a few things about the Retreat. It's not a typical chalet. For one, the building is invisible most of the time. We'll have to conduct a ceremony to make it appear."

"But you know how to make the chalet show itself?" I asked.

"Oh, yes," answered Lenore. "The ritual is very simple. And the second safeguard is the chalet has magic surrounding it that will only allow a couple to enter."

Radiance's eyes narrowed. "You mean...me alone with him?"

"That is the general idea."

Pennilane grabbed her friend's arm. "No. I need to be present to protect you."

"Why?" I asked. Everyone looked surprised at my simple question.

Pennilane gestured to Roger. "Look at him! He's taller and twice Radiance's weight. He could easily press his advantage on her."

I chuckled. No, he couldn't. Radiance was far more powerful than any of us. "You knew about your ability when I met you the first time. I assume you still know what you can do?"

Radiance examined her fingers. "Yes, if I point at someone, I can make their consciences guide their actions. 'Tis near-impossible for them to commit a transgression around me."

Pennilane protested. "But he is a powerful man, Radiance."

"But he would not harm me." Radiance's face softened

slightly. "Despite everything that has happened, this I know about Roger Jolly."

Squaring his shoulders, Roger addressed Pennilane. "Absolutely. I would never *press my advantage* on her. If you want proof, have her use this ability on me. You shall see."

Radiance snapped. "I would never use my ability on you."

Interesting response. "Why not?"

Radiance's mouth moved but no words formed. "I...I am not sure. Perhaps, in the past, I promised myself I would never use my ability on him, but I have no memory of it."

Excitedly, Lenore rocked on the balls of her feet. "This is well-known throughout Kingdom. Before Piper's spell, Radiance's love for Roger was authentic and never a result of pressing *her* advantage."

Wrapping her arms around her body, Radiance looked away. Another point in our favor. While their memories were changed, her beliefs were core to her identity. Those beliefs included Roger's love for Radiance, and her promise to him.

Lenore gestured to the ridge. "Let's return to camp and discuss borrowing the ship with Julia. She has an item that will assist us."

We marched back to Julia who was discussing her daily duties with Rex. The leader of the camp turned to greet us as we approached, and her eyes flitted back and forth between Roger and Radiance. Radiance noticed and grimaced. "You knew, did you not?"

"I told you months ago you were born to rule." Julia frowned. "I've offered for you to take my place, but you decline each time without explanation. Something deep inside of you knows you are not supposed to rule Ozark's Territory. You were meant to rule Kingdom."

Radiance tsked. "Bedtime tales."

Lenore laid out her plan to Julia who shook her head knowingly. While Julia and Lenore discussed details, Radiance stared at Roger. She respected and trusted Julia, and Julia's acknowledgment of everything we said seemed to lower her defenses. She was at least looking at her husband now.

When Lenore mentioned the *Swan Princess*, Julia interrupted her. "Of course, you may borrow it. And you'll want to board immediately, I assume."

Lenore took Julia's hand. "A better friend than you, Julia, I couldn't find."

Julia ducked into her hut and emerged holding a cylindrical object—a spyglass. She handed it to Lenore. "Will you do the honors?"

"I will."

Julia marched over to Radiance. "Pennilane will join you in case you're nervous, but Radiance, you need to discover this for yourself. However, if this fails, and I am certain it won't, you may return here, and we shall speak of it no more ."

Radiance put her hand on Julia's arm. "I admit that I am excited to go on an adventure. But do you really know these people?"

Julia placed her hand over Radiance's. "Know them and trust them. You are in safe hands, Radiance. Now gather with your..." She raised an eyebrow. "Entourage."

Radiance snorted and stood next to Pennilane. Sanders, Sylvia, and I lined up with an open spot beside Radiance. Roger bowed to her. "May I stand next to you?"

Taking a deep breath, she sighed. "Yes."

Roger took his place by her side. "What are you going to do, Lenore?"

"Just hold still. The spyglass belongs to the captain of the *Swan Princess*. Holding it would make me the captain for this voyage, I suppose, but I don't know much about sailing."

"I know how," said Roger.

"Perfect, but not needed. Other than navigation, the ship sails itself." Lenore raised the spyglass to her eye. "Return to the sea!"

And then, the soil-filled smells and darkness of the Forest of Death disappeared. In its place, the salt-tinged scent of water, the waves of water crashing against the shore, and an expansive blue sky filled our senses. We squinted in the abundant sunlight.

Lenore, Roger, Radiance, Pennilane, Sylvia, Sanders, and I stood on the deck of a three-mast, wooden ship. We all wobbled as we gained our sea legs, for the ship was docked in the water. Lenore lowered the glass. "Welcome aboard the *Swan Princess*. Roger, help me set a course. The rest of you, enjoy the view!"

The boat was docked in a hidden inlet at the north end of the Forest of Death. After the course was set, the ship rose into the air and flew just above the water, only breaking the larger waves. Without the resistance of the current, the ship moved faster than any other transport in Kingdom, and I predicted we'd be at Radiance's Retreat in twenty-four hours.

Before everyone split apart to explore the ship, Sanders explained her resemblance to Queen Planet and dropped her disguise. Radiance gasped and Pennilane narrowed her eyes, but everyone accepted my wife's natural looks after a moment of surprise.

Radiance and Pennilane went to the bow and gripped the railing, wind blowing through the queen's blonde locks and her friend's fur-length hair. The selkie's white whiskers were plastered to her head. Roger wandered around the ship, and looked over its edge, tight-lipped. He seemed not to trust the vessel, but ironically, he might have been the one who sailed it the most before he lost his memory. Sanders, Sylvia, Lenore, and I gathered and discussed our next move.

"What happens when we arrive at Radiance Retreat?" asked Sanders. "We wait outside for them?"

A fair question, and I didn't have an answer. "No, we don't have time to waste. When Roger and Radiance are inside, maybe one of us could remain behind while the others search for the next queen?"

Hair whipping around her, Sylvia raised her hand. "I will. Pennilane is so anti-Roger. I will attempt to win her over."

"The rest of us should try to find the next queen," I said. "Lenore, which way is Helga?"

"The opposite direction, I'm afraid. And Valencia is even farther than that."

Sanders adjusted her glasses. "What about the princes? We need them too."

"Right." I tapped the railing of the ship in thought. "We need Graddock, and I have no idea how to reach Danforth."

Lenore said, "I suspect Graddock will be an officer in the king's army. He'll be in Town which is a couple day's journey from Radiance's Retreat."

"Then that's our next destination."

"We are so close to Faerie Forest. Let me go there and see if I can't convince Celeste to join us," Sanders suggested.

Split up at this point? Celeste Constellation was the most powerful magic-wielder in Kingdom, sure. But was seeking her out now wise?

"She's under the spell, Sanders." Lenore brushed some of her black hair from her face. "You won't be able to change her mind."

"If we have her on our side, we can teleport." Sanders rolled her wings. "You all know it. We should try to recruit her."

"She's not going to know who you are," observed Sylvia.

Sanders stuck out her chin. "But she'll know Planet, her sister. I'll pretend to be her. As the queen, I could order her to join us, but I'd rather go to the Constellations as their daughter. I want to win over Celeste."

I took her hand. "I don't like splitting up and leaving you on your own!"

Sanders stepped up to me and patted me on the chest. "I know what you mean. Who will protect you?"

"This isn't funny."

She cupped my chin. "I must try to recruit Celeste. We need to teleport, or we'll be here for weeks. My teleportation is...uh...a work-in-progress."

I didn't like it, but she had her mind made up. "Be careful."

She saluted. "Yes, sir!"

Lenore pressed something into her hand. "This is a magic ring the queens used to communicate with each other and their allies. I purchased it from one of their companions when she lost her memories of the queens. And here is my ring with the same spell." She handed it to me. "You two may use the rings to communicate with each other."

Above the swaying currents and a few startled kelpies, we sailed our way west at a rapid clip. In the late afternoon, we found ourselves north of Faerie Forest. Sanders mumbled something about throwing a locator spell on Celeste. Like a pirate, she spread her wings and jumped on the side of the ship. "Avast mateys! I'll see you in a while."

I leaned forward and pursed my lips. "Please be cautious. If not for me, then for Fitzie."

She pouted as if I had stolen her fun. "Sure. Bring our son into this conversation. I'm only going to the Constellations to see Celeste. What could go wrong?"

"Piper's men could be waiting for you there. Celeste may sense you're an imposter and hand you over."

Sanders tapped me on the shoulder. "Thanks for the vote of confidence, but I've got this, Hero."

I said, "Take care of yourself."

"I will. And you take care of them."

Sanders nodded at Radiance and Roger who were looking on. She pointed at them, then at me and herself, and leaned down and kissed me. She cupped her hands and called to the queen and her prince. "Your turn."

Radiance rolled her eyes but grinned. She had already accepted my wife's playful vibe. For his part, Roger stepped back from Radiance and gazed at her. The expression on his face said he longed to make Sanders' suggestion come true.

Sanders turned and leapt off, floating down to the trees of Faerie Forest. The average-sized tree in this forest came up to our noses, so the woodlands looked more like a model than actual woodlands. Sanders shrunk as she approached the forest and zipped through the trees. In a heartbeat, she was gone.

Radiance left Roger and approached me. "I like your wife. She is a bit of a free spirit. Or should I say, 'she's.' You've inspired me to speak in contractions."

I didn't want to tell her she had been speaking in contractions for years. "She would say you were the fun-loving one."

Radiance smirked. "While I may never end up in love myself, I do enjoy seeing others so much in love. Your concern for her is sweet."

I leaned against the railing. "The king is after her. I'm worried."

The queen said, "I suppose I should not—shouldn't—ask, but why does he want to imprison her?"

"He doesn't. He wants to marry her. It's complicated."

Radiance gasped. "But King Piper is married to Planet. True, your wife looks exactly like Planet, but he wouldn't leave his wife for her twin, would he?"

I pushed away from the railing. "Yeah, that's your *honorable* leader for you. I hope you remember this conversation when you come to your senses. We need you. Now more than ever."

I walked away and left her to her thoughts.

The next morning, Radiance pointed to the trunk of a

tree as we rounded the bend from sea into the outlet of the main river of Kingdom. She said, "This is the third time I've seen the writing 'Snow White Lives' carved into a tree. Who is spoiling our trees? When I get my hands on this Snow White, she'll have a lot to answer for."

The ship skipped over the waves, dodging other boats by going over them to the amazement of the sailors steering those crafts. We proceeded south toward Town as fast as the ship sailed. My prediction of twenty-four hours was close, but I had overestimated the *Swan Princess'* speed. From the sun's position, we disembarked approximately thirty hours later.

We all had to adjust to walking on solid ground again except Roger. I remarked that he had done a good deal of sailing as a prince. "And you say you've been gardening all your life?"

Roger rolled his shoulders. "I did feel comfortable on the ship. It reminded me of...I don't know."

"A lost memory, perhaps?"

Roger set his hand on my shoulder and grinned. "Perhaps. Onward."

Late in the afternoon, we came to the edge of Grok's Teeth. I had never had a chance to explore this corner of Kingdom before, so I enjoyed the beautiful vista as we traveled. Flat plains led up to jagged mountains with snow-capped peaks like the heads of spears pointing at the sky. Lenore came to the base of a steep hill and climbed up the side. When she reached the top, she swung her arms out and we halted. The other side of the hill had a deep gorge that looked dangerous to descend.

A narrow chasm separated our hill from a mountain on the other side. Lenore pointed at the mountain where an enormous, circular alcove made an indentation. The alcove had a diameter of approximately a half-kilometer. From the mountain, a waterfall rained down into a trench around the empty circle, eventually flowing off the side.

"The chalet is on yonder mountain," Lenore said.

I squinted but knew I would see nothing. "You said this place is invisible? And you know of a way to reveal it?"

"Yes. Follow me," said Lenore.

We descended a dirt path and came across a level embankment set into the hill. Someone had carved a small, semicircular lookout point into the soil. The ground was covered with cobblestones, and an ornate bench sat to the side. At the edge of this small platform were two large stone columns.

We gathered at this point, and I peered over the edge. "Getting down looks hazardous, and we'll need gear to climb the other mountain."

Lenore ushered Roger and Radiance between the two columns. "We won't need to climb down. I was part of Valencia's wedding party when she and Graddock came here. They performed the ritual in front of me." Lenore eyed the queen. "You were there, too."

Radiance frowned. "I've never been here before in my life."

Lenore stood between Roger and Radiance, like an officiant at a wedding. "Roger, Radiance? Please join hands."

Radiance grimaced but held out her hands. Roger took them gently.

Lenore swayed, the wind ruffling her shift. "And now you must proclaim your love for each other."

Radiance jerked her head. "What fool came up with that idea?"

Wiping her lips nervously, Lenore said, "Actually, you did. Roger asked you to come up with a ritual, and you said this would be the perfect one."

Shutting her eyes, Radiance spoke in a flat tone. "I love you."

Roger's voice was soft and full of meaning. "I love you."

Radiance's eyes snapped open. Clearly, his proclamation of love struck her in a place she didn't expect. She hesitated before removing her hands and stared into his eyes. Yes! If nothing else, he had knocked a few bricks out of that wall that surrounded her.

After their declaration, a stone bridge formed out of thin air, leading to the plateau. The magic overpass wasn't anything fancy, no railing and rather narrow. But what it led to was completely different. As the bridge formed, the chalet appeared in the large alcove on the side of the mountain. The chalet was a four-story building made from white stone with two turrets and rounded ornamentation at the top. When the sun hit a waterfall rushing down a mountain behind the building, a rainbow formed over the top of the roof. The entrance was shaped like a heart.

I couldn't picture anything more romantic if I tried. "Wow! Sanders is going to regret missing this."

Both Roger and Radiance continued to hold hands, jaws hanging down. They glanced at each other and then back at the beautiful dwelling, speechless.

"The bridge isn't how I remember it, but the chalet is. What do you think?" Lenore asked.

"I don't have words to describe it," breathed Radiance. She blinked, then released Roger's hand.

Pennilane gripped her spear tightly. "I sense a trap. Perhaps this bridge is an illusion, and once Radiance sets foot on it, she will fall to her death."

Lenore strode out onto the bridge. In the center, she jumped up and down. "The bridge is solid but narrower than I recall. I cannot enter the chalet because only a pair of people may cross the threshold."

Radiance tapped her chin. "I admit I didn't think it existed."

As Lenore returned to the platform, I asked, "Could it be then, perhaps, we're telling the truth?"

"Some things make sense. Others do not." Radiance eyed me. "I will stay at the chalet the rest of today and half of tomorrow. If my memory has not come back after an entire day in this place, then I return to Julia. Are we in accord?"

"Two days," I countered.

"A day and a half." Radiance raised her eyebrows. "'Tis my final offer."

I put my hands in the air. "All right. It shouldn't take more than a day and a half anyway."

Pennilane grabbed her friend's shoulder and spun her around, "Radiance, do not enter. The chalet is enchanted to look like a miniature castle, but it may be an illusion. This could be the house of a witch."

Radiance observed the building again. "If it is, the illusion is perfect. It knows exactly what I would like. What a beautiful dwelling!"

Roger held out his hand to escort his beloved across the bridge. Radiance regarded his hand with disdain and proceeded across the bridge herself. Roger turned around and nodded at the chalet. "We shall be inside."

I had united them, but would it last? When the door closed, I mumbled a silent prayer to whatever benevolent deity would listen to me. As I finished, Sylvia and Pennilane began setting up a tent we had lugged from the ship. Lenore joined me.

I looked south. "Did you say it's a three-day journey to Town? If so, we better start now."

"Remember when I said Julia had magic birdseed that would turn you all into birds?" My were-raven companion reached into her pouch. "She let me borrow some."

Lenore removed her hand and opened it. A tiny handful of what looked like yellow seeds lay in her palm. She poured some into my hand. "The journey should take us about a day if we go straight to Town. What do you say, Hero? Are you ready to fly?"

The Constellations

12 - AMONG THE CONSTELLATIONS

Sondra

With a quick locator spell, I was able to find the Constellations' house without asking for directions. Not that I have any problems asking for directions—sometimes I ask for them to strike up a conversation even if I know my way. Faerie Forest, with its pint-sized trees that look huge to a pixie, was a charming place. And the pixies, elves, and brownie neighborhoods all have their different vibes.

I arrived a few hours after leaping off the ship, soon after nightfall. All the houses here are up in the trees, reminding me of brightly colored birdhouses but constructed for intelligent creatures. Some were long and skinny, affixed to a trunk with strong ropes. Others were attached to multiple branches and spread out in a ranch style. The windows were circular and tinted—I wasn't sure they were glass at all, perhaps some magic barrier. All habitats glowed with some aura, and most sparkled.

My plan was simple, if a bit deceitful. First, I'd claim to be Planet to avoid the question of why I looked like her. Once I had their confidence, I'd tell them the truth. Barging in with Piper was a louse would win over nobody.

I landed on the grassy floor at the base of the Constellations' tree. This was Planet's home before she died; entering it claiming to be her made my stomach twist in a knot. These were people I cared about. Tricking them to gain their trust before I told them the truth...well, I knew that wasn't right.

Gritting my teeth, I lifted off the ground to the entrance. I hesitated before their front door, not made of wood but a material like a curtain. The "door" depicted an outer space scene with twinkling stars and comets in motion. I changed back into my form—a mirror image of Planet. I straightened my tunic, tilted my head left and right, and removed my glasses. "Here goes nothing."

I almost knocked but then realized the error in that approach. After all, I lived here, or once did. Queen Planet must live in the palace—though she wasn't Planet at all. Nevertheless, she wouldn't knock. This was confusing!

I entered the Constellations' front room. Planet's da was seated and performing magic on a three-legged stool, repairing one of its legs. An older man with a scruffy face and beard, Da had a slight frame, and his green wings drooped behind. When he saw me, his spell dissipated, and the stool fell to the floor. He stood, mouth hanging open.

Here went nothing. "Da?"

I had hoped for a welcoming reaction, but his expression wasn't one of delight. Da gasped, and then managed to croak, "Celeste!"

The interior doors matched the front door, appearing as little star fields. Celeste stepped through one with a rag wiping a dish in her hand. Her golden hair was pulled back and tied in a ponytail, and her face was paler than usual. When Planet's sister saw me, she dropped the dish. "Planet!"

I wanted more than anything to take Celeste's hand and ask if she remembered me, but I had to play out the ruse. "That's right!"

Da asked, "That's?"

Oh, yes. Cat's piss. "Newest fad. The old running-words-together thing. I'm back."

Celeste snorted, but Da cleared his throat. "Manners."

They both lowered themselves to their knees and bowed. Their servile gesture had to be one of the most embarrassing moments of my life. "Get up! I'm family!"

"But the last time we came to the palace, you told us never to see you again!" exclaimed Da. "We didn't bow then, so we naturally thought—"

Oh! Who was this woman who was impersonating Planet? A right bitch is what I think.

I cleared my throat. "I acted poorly and wanted to come and say I'm sorry."

Da asked "After eight years? You suddenly show up?"

How could I tell them eight years hadn't gone by since their memories told them otherwise. I had last communicated with Celeste a year ago, and had seen Planet's da five years ago. They both knew I was Sanders and knew about Planet's fate.

Celeste's face became solemn. "Not suddenly. She has heard."

My eyes shifted from Celeste to Planet's father and back. "Yes."

I had no idea what they were referring to, but the tone in their voices warned me to proceed with caution. I swallowed while they stared at me, expecting me to say something. I stared back, trying not to give myself away.

Celeste gestured to the star-ridden curtain behind her.

"Do you not want to see her?"

Her? "Of course."

Celeste nodded and walked through one of the star-gated doorways. Following along, I found myself in a narrow hallway with three other curtained doors. As Planet, I had a faint memory of this place. We were in the bedroom passageway. The three other doorways belonged to Planet, Celeste, and their parents. I guessed we were heading for Planet's room, as the "her" they referred to must have been a lodger, or resistance fighter, or someone of note. Celeste, however, strolled into her parents' room.

Bobbing along, I followed and entered a low-lit room with a medium-sized bed and chairs surrounding it. On the other side of the room stood a dresser against a wall. In a corner huddled a small table littered with elixir bottles. And on the bed lay Ma Constellation: pale, drawn, skin pulled tight. Her chest rose with effort.

When the realization hit me, I put my hand to my mouth. Her wings were folded under her and lacked any normal sparkles. Her thinning hair was mussed and spread out over her pillow. Though her eyes were closed, they moved back and forth beneath the eyelids.

Ma Constellation was dying.

Celeste leaned down to her mother. "*She* has returned."

Ma Constellation's eyes opened, and her mouth dropped open in anticipation. I felt sick to my stomach as I approached the bed. Lying to Celeste for a good cause was one thing, but pretending to be her daughter to a dying woman was quite another. Yet I couldn't back out now, so I sat down in a chair and leaned close.

Her voice was brittle as a thin coat of ice. "Planet? Is that you?"

A huge lump formed in my throat. I could only nod.

Celeste turned on her heel. "I will leave you two."

I wish she wouldn't, but I was incapable of speech. I had only met Ma Constellation in person at a party in Kingdom the last time I was here, but I'd felt an immediate bond with her then. Celeste had told me so much about her parents I felt as though I knew them. However, meeting her like this now was too much.

Her trembling hands reached out for mine and I took them. Ma rasped, "I missed you."

Oh God, this was awful. The tears welled up in my eyes, and the waterworks were mirrored in hers. Fortunately, I wasn't disguised because she would've seen right through it. "I missed you, too."

"But you came home."

I couldn't lie. I couldn't say I came for her. I merely nodded.

Planet's mother croaked. "Hard to speak when I first awaken. Tell me, how have you been?"

I licked my lips and closed my eyes. I had to pretend I was Planet. I began. "The palace is wonderful, Ma. Let me tell you about it..."

Two hours later, I emerged from her room. She had fallen asleep fifteen minutes earlier, but I'd held her hand and put my other hand on her face. She'd reacted positively to my touch. Celeste stood in the hallway when I exited. "Back to the palace?" Her voice? Ice.

My eyes shifted to Planet's old room. "Would you mind if I spent the night in my old room?"

Celeste frowned. "We do not have guards here."

"Could you throw a few spells? Your incantations should suffice," I answered.

"Me? You trust me with your life?"

I couldn't tell Celeste what a long day it had been, and I was emotionally spent. "Yes, Celeste. I trust you more than anyone else. Just keep the locator spells away." My eyes drooped. "I need sleep."

She started her spell as I crossed the starry threshold into Planet's room. The Constellations had converted it into a guest room, but pictures of Planet were all framed and on each wall. I noticed they were all from her childhood with the Constellations, and none from when she was a "queen." Interesting. Turning away, I flopped into the bed of feathers and fell asleep seconds later.

The next day, I woke up with a start. Maybe the ghost of Planet pinched me for deceiving her dying mother. I certainly deserved it. I heard voices in the front room. Celeste's high-pitch and Da's sonorous even tone, but also a third.

I exited Planet's room and flew to the front room. When I moved through the curtain of stars, I found Da and Celeste talking to a woman I didn't recognize.

The stranger rotated to me and broke off mid-sentence. Her eyes focused on my own, and her mouth turned down. Was she from the palace coming to call me out? She didn't say anything, instead shifting uncomfortably. I would guess she was in her late twenties, with an overbite and nose like a cauliflower. Her black hair, horribly cut at various random lengths, had some strands braided. Her blue eyes tracked me when I entered. "I can make your meal if you share with me a bit of your food. I am poor and famished, but I work hard."

The family looked at me. Da said to her, "I am sure you recognize Queen Planet." Then to me, "Planet, this is Wysdel."

"I did not know the queen was staying with you. I sought you out because I had heard you were a generous family." Wysdel examined me closely, appearing both nervous and upset at the same time. She swallowed hard and then curtsied, nearly to the floor. "I was passing through Faerie Forest and wondered if this loving family might provide me with a bit to eat."

Celeste said, "Of course we will. I will prepare breakfast."

I looked at Celeste with admiration and she caught the glance. She spoke severely. "What is the matter, Planet? You may be royalty, but work still must be done around here."

"I know...I..." What could I say?

Celeste continued into the kitchen, brushing me with

her shoulder. Da spoke to Wysdel. "You will have to pardon us. Queen Planet has returned to visit us after eight years."

Wysdel nodded to the doorway Celeste proceeded through. "Let me assist Ms. Celeste."

The strange woman left me with Planet's father. I crossed my legs in midair, and he sat down across the room. We locked eyes then both looked away. I cleared my throat. "How long has she been…?"

"About a month," he said. "Will you consider what I wrote you?"

Uh oh. Maybe best just to ask. "And that was?"

Da Constellation frowned. "Allowing Celeste to study at the castle? Certainly not now, but in the future. Keeping us away from you, Planet." He examined his shoes. "We do not understand."

Ooh, that fake Planet! She was going to get an eye-poking from me when I met her. I swallowed the lump in my throat and shifted the topic back to Planet's sister. "Why does Celeste need to study? She graduated with top honors."

"Yes, but she has not practiced. She was top ranked eight years ago when you left, but since then, she's dropped to eighteen in Faerie Forest."

"Impossible," I said. "She's the best magic wielder in Kingdom."

Tears in his eyes, he grunted. "Not since you left."

I took a deep breath. "I can explain, Da. I explained to Ma why I've been gone."

He held up a hand. "If whatever you're going to say was good enough for your Ma, it is good enough for me too, Planet."

Despite this awful false daughter treating them like garbage for what they thought was eight years, Da and Ma still loved Planet. They weren't simply being courteous because I was the queen but their daughter. Yet with how the fake Planet acted, they should've kicked me out of the house. "I'm going to make this right, Da. In a little while, Celeste will be top ranked. I will see to that. Your favorite daughter will be back on top."

He stood up suddenly, knocking over his chair and walked over to the starry doorway leading to the bedrooms. He stopped before going through but didn't face me. "What gave you the impression she was my favorite?"

I gulped. Despite the time I spent lurking in Planet's subconscious and the time I spent with the Constellations, I never knew he favored Planet.

I didn't see him until a late breakfast of sugared scones and a tart tea in the pint-sized kitchen. The four of us ate together. Celeste, Da, and I avoided talking to each other. Wysdel addressed us separately and chatted nervously through the meal. When we were done, Celeste stood. "I will clean up."

"Nonsense, dear," said Wysdel. "You did most of the cooking. I will clean up. Perhaps I could request a word with your sister too? 'Tis not every day you get to meet the queen!"

Celeste put a hand at the base of her neck. "Oh, I am sure the queen is much too busy."

A word with me? If she was one of Piper's little emissaries, I was going to have it out with her. How dare she come here and involve the Constellations? Of course, I was doing the same thing, but I was on the right side.

Wysdel stared at me, and I flinched. Her piercing look was like that of a hawk staring at a field mouse. "I would be happy to," I said. "Celeste, you attend to Ma."

Seemingly surprised, the Constellations left the room while Wysdel gathered the dishes. Once Da and Celeste were out of earshot, Wysdel put the dishes in the tub and scrubbed them, her calloused hands scratching at the remains. "What are you doing here, Sondra?"

My breath caught in my throat. "I'm not Sondra. My name is—"

"I'm? Not I am? You will have do better than that."

115

I admit, she had caught me off-balance, but I am not easily intimidated. My eyes narrowed. "And who the hell are you?"

"Language, Sondra!" She tilted her head toward me. "Resistance movement. Lenore contacted me to help you."

I breathed a sigh of relief. "I was afraid you were one of Piper's stooges. Do you remember the real events of Kingdom?"

"Of course." She placed a plate in a rack to drip dry. "The five queens, the princes. I remember it all. Again, what are you doing here?"

I looked at the doorway to make sure no one was going to enter. "Recruiting Celeste."

"She will not remember."

My wings fluttered nervously. "I have to try."

"And you're going to do that by impersonating Planet?"

This stranger, reprimanding me, should've gotten on my nerves, but her approach was gentle. I trusted her but proceeded with caution. Something I'm not known for. "I admit pretending to be Planet is a terrible idea, but it was the only one I had. Celeste is my best friend. She'll understand why I did this. I didn't know about Ma Constellation."

Wysdel removed another plate from the water. "You must leave them. The quest comes first, and you know it."

"If we had Celeste, we could teleport to any location. Getting around would be so much easier."

Wysdel reached out and took my hand. For a moment, the gesture reminded me of someone else, but I couldn't think of who it might be. "You must be the one who casts the teleportation spell," she said. "We need more magic wielders in the Resistance, and you need practice. We will leave at noon."

"I hate telling them."

Wysdel nodded. "But you must. I am not without compassion, and if you were Planet, I would not press. But you are not Planet, and you have a quest to complete."

I dropped her hand. "Let me try before we go. This sounds dumb, but I need this victory. I need to tell Celeste everything and try to enlist her to help us. If I don't, and we succeed, she'll never forgive me."

Wysdel grabbed a towel. "I will give you two more hours, but no more. We have much to accomplish."

The day was full of sunshine, and Celeste and I sat in the air across from each other above a small mushroom patch with red and green spots on their caps. The light reflected off her golden hair giving her the appearance of an angel. She shifted in her simple brown tunic. Her severe look showed me she was only here because I was a queen and had asked for a private conversation.

I put my fingertips together. Yes, I was queen and she had agreed to it, but she wasn't going to give me an inch. I took a deep breath. "I am going to tell you something. I want you to hear me out, the entire story, and then discuss it. Will you do this for me?"

Celeste narrowed her eyes. "Fine."

I picked a few mushrooms and fiddled with them while telling her the real history of Kingdom, careful to avoid speaking of Planet or Hero, or my role in any of it. I wanted the focus to be on the queens, and how they were under a spell. Celeste looked at me as if I had sprouted antennae and compound eyes. And when I told her she was the court magician, she threw her head back and laughed. "Oh, really. This is too much. What would royalty want with a second-rate pixie?"

I ripped off a mushroom head and tossed it at her. "Stop that. You're the best damn magician in Kingdom. That's why you're the court magician."

Celeste cast a minor fizz spell and hit me with it. My tongue tingled from its effects.

"Let me see if I understand," she said. "The king...the king of Kingdom...has stolen my memory. Me! An ordinary pixie in Faerie Forest. For many years, I have truly been a court magician serving under five queens and three princes. In that time, you and I have become close."

"This will all make sense if we restore your memory."

"And how will we achieve that?"

"Once the queens kiss their princes, everyone in Kingdom will remember the truth."

Celeste huffed. "Why are you doing this, Planet? You ignore us for years, then you come home all humble, acting as if we are close. And now you tell me this ridiculous story."

Time for the truth. This was going to be hard, but I had an idea. "Celeste, cast a locator spell on Piper. Where is he right now?"

She shook her head. "I am sure he's warded from simple spells like mine."

"Throw it, Celeste. Give it your all."

Celeste stood and cast the incantation. Her eyes widened. "You are right. I can push past the counter spells. I have found him, sitting on his throne."

"Good. I was worried he might be somewhere else. Is there a throne next to his? And is someone sitting on it?"

"Yes," Celeste answered both questions.

"Shift the locator spell to Planet. Is it she on the throne, or the imposter like I said?"

Celeste frowned. "No, 'tis not her."

"No 'tis not!" I ripped up more mushrooms from the ground.

"No spell can hide one's identity from someone weeping. I have viewed her through my tears and she is Planet."

"Makeup, not magic, Celeste. When I get my hands on her." I clenched the mushrooms in my hand and turned them into mush.

Celeste regarded me with wide eyes. "Planet, where have you been all this time? Are you in trouble? Are you part of this resistance movement?"

I hung my head. "Celeste, move the locator spell to me."

"Why, you are right here in front of me."

I sighed. "Throw the spell. It will prove what I said."

Celeste did as I asked and gasped. "I must not have spelled it right."

"I'm sure you did it right. Celeste, I'm not Planet."

"But I have seen you through my tears when you were not looking." Celeste examined me from a different angle. "You are not magicked to look like my sister. And you act so much like her."

"But magic doesn't lie. You know that I'm not her."

Celeste put her hand to her chest. "And you say we are friends."

I took her hand, and she looked at it curiously. "The best of friends."

Celeste withdrew her hand and folded her arms.

I sighed. "Not convinced? You threw a spell when you were twelve on the foliage where Planet was going blipsie-doodle and she got a rash. One she had for weeks."

"Who told you that?"

"You did. You know things about me, too, just as secret, but you can't remember it. Regarding my child, I owe a debt I will never be able to repay. For that alone, I'd die for you."

"Who are you?"

"My name is Sanders. If you had your memories, you'd know you and I are close."

I reached across to grab her hands, but she pulled them away. I said, "Try to remember, Celeste. I really need you to try. Please."

Celeste shook her head. "I do not remember you. And this story sounds like claptrap the resistance movement would dream up to discredit our king."

I pointed toward the palace. "You know that isn't Planet on the throne! How credible is your king?"

Leaning away, Celeste said, "I still do not know if I believe you."

Cat's piss. I had to use extreme measures. "Fair enough." I extended my hand, clenched my fist, and then extended my pinkie. "Pinkie swears are serious stuff. You know the consequences if someone breaks one. I will make you a pinkie promise that I'm telling you the truth."

Celeste's eyes went round regarding my little finger. "If you were lying, I could never exact the penalty."

"Cut off all my fingers but the pinkie? I'll do it myself, Celeste. No, don't flinch because I'm not worried. I'm telling you the truth."

Planet's sister made a motion for me to lower my hand. "I will not make you swear it."

"Celeste, what else could I say or do to convince you?"

She reluctantly leaned forward. "Give me some time. This is all too much."

I gently put my hand on her arm, and she didn't move away. Forward progress, I hoped. "Wysdel and I must leave, but I'll come back. I promise."

Later, I met with Da and told him I was leaving. Celeste came in while we were talking and put her hand on his shoulder. Da Constellation didn't show any sign of surprise. I hated that Piper put in his head that Planet was a pompous queen who had abandoned her family. I pressed my lips together, determined to redeem Planet in their eyes.

"I will be back. I promise both of you."

I hugged Da, and he returned it. "Be careful, little Planet."

Ugh. This was awful. "Your daughter loves you, Da."

Imprecisely worded, but the truest thing I had said to him. I turned to Celeste. "Could I have a word outside where Wysdel is waiting?"

We left the house and floated down to the ground. I said, "I'll be back. Please believe in me until then. And be careful."

"Careful?"

"Because Piper knows how powerful you are. And he may try something."

Celeste's eyes widened. "But why? I am only—"

"—the most powerful sorceress in Kingdom," I interrupted. I tapped her on the heart. "And don't you forget it."

Wysdel approached, and I waved to Celeste before she returned to her home. Wysdel and I walked twenty yards away, and then the maiden turned to me. "Teleport us to Town. Lenore has been sending birds to me. The rest of your party are at Radiance Retreat but nearly ready to head for the royal city."

I took Wysdel's rough hand and closed my eyes. I gathered all my magic and focused on a spot outside of town, then we disappeared. When I opened my eyes, I found we were on a beach. "Where are we?"

Wysdel touched her chin and surveyed our surroundings. She put her hand over her eyes to shade the sun and looked at the sea. "At the end of the Beach of Bounty, I believe. I recognize that archipelago in the distance. About a four-day walk to Town."

I sighed. "I knew this was going to be hard."

Wysdel grabbed my hand. "Again."

13 - THE THIRSTY WENCH

Harold

I admit that I hadn't fully lived until I turned into a bird and flew in the air above Grok's Teeth. Planet had lifted me off the ground to travel once and I've floated to the ground in Planet's and Sanders' arms, but nothing compares to spreading your own wings and gliding on air currents. Lenore twilled at me a few times. I thought she was telling me to be careful, but later I figured out that she was laughing. When I laughed, my voice emerged as a melodic birdsong. The wind above and below me, the flexibility and mobility, and the heightened sense of sight and hearing, all added to my utter joy of being a bird.

Lenore and I landed in a patch of land north of

Kingdom's main city known as Town. Within minutes, I had lengthened into my own form again. Lenore wiggled her shoulders to shake off a loose feather. "Sounded to me as if you had a good time."

"Do you have any more?"

She shook her head. "Magic birdseed is hard to come by if you're an outlaw of the crown. Come on, Town isn't far."

Trust me, walking was not comparable to flying. I glanced up at the birds soaring above and wished I were back in the sky with them. That is, until a wyvern came out of nowhere and plucked one from the sky. I gulped and proceeded forward, wondering how I'd avoided a similar fate.

We arrived at Town in the early evening. I had visited the royal city many times before. The familiar two-story, wood and stone buildings, the rushing carts and wagons of the workers and residents, the click of boots on the stone roads, all felt like coming home. The smells of savory stews wafting from windows overpowered the cloying scents of horses and their droppings. The Alpine-framed shops with peaked gables, or the corner stores with thatched roofs made me wish I could visit here for once instead of only passing through.

The crowds were thinning when we arrived, and most of the carts hawking their wares were closing for the night. I noticed a stall selling fur pelts and recognized one that looked like a seal.

My stomach clenched. "Has Piper reinstated hunting selkies?"

"Pixie scalps will be next," said Lenore darkly. "He is slowly undoing the good work of the queens. Let's try the Thirsty Wench tavern first. Graddock is well-known at that establishment."

We traveled through the main thoroughfare of the city under the lamps waiting to be lit for the night. I brushed shoulders with the humans, elves, and trolls of Kingdom. "I've heard of this Thirsty Wench before but have never been there."

Lenore kept pace with me. "Nor I, but its reputation is

infamous. Rumors say the tavern is a sordid, dirty little place where brigands and swindlers go to have fun."

"I cannot believe the queens didn't shut it down."

"I heard that they tried once when they first became queens," said Lenore. "They were unsuccessful. I'm not sure why."

I brushed off a merchant trying to sell me a pineapple-shaped purple fruit. "We need them back. This isn't the same neighborhood as I remember it. It seems…"

"Less inspired."

I eyed a woman pointing at coins which stacked themselves. "Exactly."

After wandering around trying to find the Thirsty Wench, I finally stopped and asked for directions. Yes, I hated doing it, but the lack of street signs forced my hand. The sordid establishment squatted in the northern end of Town—the seedier section. The buildings here were dirtier and some had collapsed, leaving behind only a pile of rubble.

With the sun setting, I couldn't distinguish all the features of the Thirsty Wench. The watering hole had four stories covered in vines with no windows. An iron roof squatted on top like a pillbox hat on a mobster. The only entrance was a large oaken door with cast-iron braces. A replica of a knife sticking out of a wall next to the door held a sign in place that proclaimed its name. Under the placard was a picture of a bottle with a skull inside.

Gazing at the building, Lenore touched her chin. "If we enter together, we're going to draw attention. This place is frequented mostly by men. If you go in alone, they'll mistake you for a customer."

"I may come out on a stretcher."

Lenore reached into her pocket and produced several silver coins. She placed them in my hand. "I have faith in you."

I threw back my shoulders and pushed open the door. As I crossed the threshold, the overpowering smell of smoke clogged my throat and made me cough. Due to the low lighting, I stumbled in, noticing that only large ceramic bowls on stands holding candles provided light in the eating area. In the back of the room, however, a large globe shone down on a stage. I couldn't spy a light source, so I assumed it was magic.

My eyes adjusted to the darkness as torrid smells of garbage and feces assaulted my nose. My stomach turned over and I paused before proceeding. The Inn of Five was spacious, clean, and well-lit. This place was the Inn of Five's evil doppelganger in every way. I stumbled against a table as I made my way in. Having to zigzag around to make it to the bar, I stopped in my tracks when I saw the hanging cage.

Most of the establishment was focused on the cage, and I stared at the figure enclosed inside of it. A short female creature danced in place. She looked vaguely like a pixie but more alien in appearance. Her long face was purple with oval eyes, a sharp nose, and pointed chin. Her dark hair fanned out like a triangle halfway down her back. Her face, not unpleasant, looked haggard. She had extended, triangular-shaped ears with jewelry dangling from the lobes. Her fame consisted of stick-thin arms and a slim waist with proportionate legs in high-heeled shoes. Insect-like, transparent wings completed the picture.

The creature in the cage was dressed as a barmaid, but not like the barmaids at the Inn of Five. Her threadbare top wrapped around her upper body revealing her stomach, and her short skirt didn't reach her knees. I noticed a discarded blouse draped on the floor of the cage. The "barmaid" twisted in a certain way as she reached behind her back and unfastened her top to a roar of approval of the crowd—all men.

How could something like this exist in idyllic Kingdom? Sure, this happens all the time on Earth, but this activity didn't belong here. Part of me was enraged. The creature's expression clearly broadcasted that she was not enjoying this demonstration in the least. But part of me, I hate to admit, was a little curious if the "no touching" Earth policy applied here.

Sanders' voice echoed through my head. "Pig." In my

defense, I wasn't gawking in lust, but surprise. Yet the mere thought of my wife prompted me to ignore the show and obtain the information I needed. If I lingered, my wife wouldn't be angry with me but disappointed, and that was far worse. I marched toward the bar area to ask about Graddock.

I circled around a few men who shouted to get out of their way and made it to the long counter. When I finally found a barmaid—a young elven woman with narrow eyes and a grimace on her face, I was grateful she was fully dressed. I cleared my throat nervously.

Wiping the counter, the barmaid asked, "What'dya want?"

I took half the coins Lenore had given me and slid them toward her. "Information."

She eyed the money suspiciously. "I do not know nothing."

"I am looking for a person. Name's Graddock."

She put her hand on the coins and took them, depositing them into a hidden pocket. "I have never heard of him."

The roar of the crowd behind me crescendoed and died off. The act was over. I held out my hand. "Then give me back my silver."

The elf threw down the rag she had used on the counter. "What silver?"

"Come on."

"Do ya want a drink or not?" The elf produced a mug from under the counter.

"No, just information."

"I could use a shift, Merwynda," piped a voice to my right.

I jumped, not having realized someone was floating next to me. The entertainer in the cage, now reduced to the size of a small bird, bobbed up and down. While her lower body was covered, her upper body remained exposed. I immediately averted my eyes.

Merwynda's eyes narrowed. "What happened?"

"The Burnock gang stole my top again."

I retrieved a handkerchief and handed it to the creature. "Take this to cover yourself."

The elf snorted but lowered herself behind the counter and fumbled around for something. The floating being next to me squeaked a reply. "Thank you."

I leaned over the counter and addressed the barmaid. "Do you know of anyone around here who might know a soldier named Graddock? I won't begrudge you the silver if you give me a lead."

She popped up with a tiny shirt in her hand. Holding it out for her coworker, she asked, "You want to know about Graddock?"

"Yes."

She gestured me closer to her, and I leaned forward. She cupped her hand, about to whisper in my ear. I turned my head and noticed the female creature, now clothed, riveted to our conversation. My attention wasn't on her, but the secret the elf was about to tell me. Instead of speaking, she boxed me on my ear.

I pulled back and covered my ear with my hand. "What the hell!"

Merwynda winked. "Jargog! This man just tried to steal from me!"

A green creature with a protuberant snout and stringy beard appeared beside me. I recognized his species. Ogre. "Who are you?"

I turned away but two others blocked my path. I'm not a big guy so I'm unsure why they surrounded me, but before I could explain what I wanted, they grabbed me. The three ogre bouncers rushed me outside and threw me out of the door. One grabbed a pail just inside the door and doused me with its contents. Out of a sense of proprietary, I won't describe what the bucket contained.

Lenore flew down and transformed, holding her nose.

"Charmed them, did you?"

"Those people are jackasses."

"And proud of it."

We stood outside, regarding the Thirsty Wench. Lenore sighed. "I can approach someone walking out saying I am lost and looking for my brother. Perhaps that will work."

"You aren't going to approach anyone who walks out of that building."

Focused on the door, Lenore grimaced. "I am not naive, Hero. I understand what type of men frequent such an establishment. We had them on Morbidum, my world, as well."

"What if someone snatches you?"

"I'll turn into a bird."

"And what if they hold on and capture you in that form too. No, Lenore, it's too big a chance. We must find Graddock in a different way."

The tiny being from the inn emerged from the door, floating along on her unusual wings. She held out my handkerchief to me in the fading light of this day. "Here, sir, is your handkerchief."

I accepted it and blushed. "Thank you."

The creature remained next to me in the low light, gently swaying in the air. "You seem much too noble to be frequenting the Thirsty Wench. And you use contractions." She examined me quizzically.

Lenore nodded to our new acquaintance. "I'm Lenore. Who are you, dear sprite?"

The sprite quirked an eyebrow. "Dear? A term not usually used by humans with sprites."

Lenore lifted her chin. "I don't believe in the nonsense that sprites are the lowest form of fairy, Miss…?"

The fairy curtsied in the air. "Sinope."

Sinope glanced back and forth between us. "Kindness, contractions, and you believe sprites are equals. Tell me, do you grant quests? Are the two of you knights?"

Before I could answer, Lenore squared her shoulders. "I

am."

That's right. She was knighted by the queens. I had forgotten.

Sinope's oval eyes enlarged, and her purple irises expanded. "I knew you were knights. I have a quest for you. One any honorable knight couldn't pass up."

I shuffled. "In other circumstances, I'd be happy to help you. But we're on an important quest right now, and we can't spare the time."

Sinope rubbed her chin. "I know where Graddock is. If you go on this quest, I will lead you to him."

Lenore and I looked at each other.

Beaming, Sinope asked, "Interested?"

Sinope's Home

14 - SINOPE'S SISTER

Sondra

I examined our surroundings. "Now where are we?"

Wysdel hung her head. "We are in the elven part of Faerie Forest near Garath."

"Is that closer to Town than Wraith's Repast or not?" I asked.

"'Tis at least on the same body of land," said Wysdel.

"Don't rush me. The way you urged me to teleport on Wraith's Repast, you would've thought our lives were in danger!"

"I did it because our lives *were* in danger!"

I reached out and touched the bark of something resembling a fifty-foot eucalyptus tree. "You have to admit that this attempt was better. A vast improvement from the time I landed in Bremen on top of an outhouse. Or the time

I landed near Soro's Well and you scared those trolls half to death. But it wasn't as bad as the time—"

"Sanders! Please, give me a moment." The maiden peered in all directions and then brightened. "We may be near the home of Turducken, the elf. Perhaps you, looking like Planet, can convince him to teleport us. He and Planet were friends when they were little."

I swear my connection to Planet was both a blessing and a curse. I had lived vicariously through her and had experienced her falling in love with Hero. She and I were more than twins for everything she thought wonderful about Hero, I thought the same. Hard to admit now, but I was jealous of Planet finding Hero first. Though I've loved him longer and deeper, certainly spending more time with him, I know a small piece of Hero's heart will always belong to Planet.

Brushing back a lock of hair, I asked, "I'll need to look like Planet, huh? How will I explain why the queen needs his help?"

"You will think of something. Now follow me."

Wysdel's definition of "near" meant a two-hour walk, but we arrived at a small wooden house that extended into a hill. We marched up to the front door, and Wysdel reminded me to drop the Charlie disguise I had been using. After I transformed back, I pounded on the door.

Turducken opened the door, and his eyes grew wide at the sight of me. He instantly fell to his knees. "Queen Planet."

I'm glad my husband wasn't here to see Turducken groveling. When Hero was falling in love with Planet, he falsely believed Turducken was a romantic rival. My insecure husband's initial impression of that elf had soured his opinion of him to this day.

I took the cute elf's hands. "Get up. We know each other too well for that nonsense."

Turducken stiffened. "You were quite clear the last time I met you."

Ugh...that stupid false queen again! "I was wrong to

treat you that way. You're my dear friend. You know that."

Turducken's expression, initially withdrawn, brightened at my words, thinking I was the queen. When I was here before, I had talked and danced with Turducken. If he had his memories restored, he would know me as Sanders. But my true identity, and any memory of Hero, had been suppressed by that stupid spell. Once we lifted this curse, he'd remember me as his friend again.

"Why are you here, my queen?" asked Turducken.

"Call me Planet, Turducken. And I am sorry to say, I have a favor to ask."

The elf smiled. "You know I would do anything for you."

I knew he would. I had just talked to Hero through the communication rings, and he informed me he was in Town, the royal city. "My friend and I—oh, this is Wysdel, by the way. Anyway, my friend and I need to get to Town. Could you spell us there?"

Turducken straightened his shoulders. "Consider it done." He inclined his head at Wysdel. "My lady, 'tis charming to meet you. If you will take my hands."

Turducken held out his hands, and Wysdel and I took them. Wysdel smiled at the elf. "Inside the main gate."

Turducken nodded, and we vanished. In less than a heartbeat, the three of us were standing in the middle of an empty thoroughfare a few yards from a lamplighter busy with his chores. As night was settling in, most of the people had left the streets.

I threw my arms around Turducken. "Thank you, my friend."

Wysdel rubbed her chin after we finished our embrace. "Could you hail Hero on your ring and find his current location?"

I complied. "Calling Mr. Hero. Come in, Mr. Hero."

"Hi, Sanders."

"I am headed your way. Where are you specifically?"

The voice through the ring responded, "Outside a

mapmaker's shop. Maisy's Maps."

Wysdel turned east. "He isn't far. You two go in that alley so no one sees the queen," she commanded. "I shall retrieve Hero." She leaned down and whispered in my ear. "Try to convince him to remain with us. We could use his magic."

I nodded, and Wysdel rushed off. I bit my lip, "I wish I could thank you for helping us out."

The elf waved off my gratitude. "'Tis nothing. Not like that time you and I were chased by the Bee-Maidens of Rox. Who knew their stingers shot magic as well?" He chuckled.

I laughed with him, having no idea what he was talking about. "Yes, you saved me that time."

"You promised me a friendship kiss if we got out of that," said Turducken. "Remember?"

"Oh yes, a friendship kiss." Uh...I recall Lenore talking about it. "Do kids still press their top lips to the other's bottom lip?"

Turducken nodded.

I thought of Planet and how much everyone missed her. Some days, I missed her too, though I had only been connected with her for a short while. Turducken grieved her as well, in his way, and my heart melted a bit. "I never gave you that friendship kiss, did I?"

Turducken snorted. "Planet, you do not think I took you seriously, did you?"

He wouldn't have brought it up if he didn't. I lifted an eyebrow. "Did you?"

Turducken blushed and regarded his feet. Piper's spell may have made Turducken think Planet was alive, but in his core, he still grieved her death. My pretending to be Planet must have opened that old wound. The hole in my heart from my mother's loss was raw, and I realized then so many people had similar holes in their hearts.

I put my hands on Turducken's shoulders. "In a little while, you will remember something about me that will make you sad. You'll think about this conversation when it happens."

Turducken looked puzzled but didn't speak, so I continued. "I'm not the same Planet you remember. You could almost think of me as a different person. But I'm still your friend. And in honor of times past, I'd like to give you that friendship kiss now."

Turducken spoke quietly. "But you are the queen."

"Let's just pretend. Right now, I'm not the queen. Just a friend."

I approached him lip-to-lip then lowered a fraction. Turducken trembled as I grew closer, and I pressed my top lip to his bottom lip, kissing his chin. I pressed into him, kissing his clean-shaven skin when I was rudely interrupted.

"What the hell is going on?"

I pulled back and turned around, wincing. The voice was Hero's.

Hero strode toward me. Behind him were Lenore, Wysdel, and a tiny purple fairy who wasn't a pixie, but I couldn't identify her species. Of the arriving party, the plum-colored creature stared at me with wide eyes then lowered her head in respect. Oh, she must have thought I was the queen.

Hero stopped next to me, glaring at Turducken. "What are you doing?"

I stood, blushing. "It's not what it looks like."

Wysdel rushed up behind Hero and grabbed his shoulder. "She gave him a silly friendship kiss. Kids do it all the time."

Turducken clenched his jaw. "Who is this, Planet?"

Hero pulled away from Wysdel and addressed her. "Butt out. I didn't even catch your name when you found us. This is between me and my—"

No, Hero! You're going to blow it. "Friend! As you know, *Hero*, I am married to King Piper. And whoever I bestow a *friendship* kiss on, I do it as a great honor and honor only."

He stopped, breathing heavily. "Perhaps we can discuss this later, my *queen*." He gritted his teeth.

Turducken narrowed his eyes. "Is this man bothering

you, Planet?"

Oh, how I wanted to say "yes," and have Turducken cast a fizz spell on my envious husband, but of course I didn't respond affirmatively. Oh well, there went our chances of having an accomplished magician join our small band of adventurers. Hero's jealousy and Turducken's pride could not coexist.

I gave Turducken my full attention. "No, he's a dear friend. Just a little overprotective at times. Thank you so much for helping us. Please return home. I have inconvenienced you enough already."

Turducken's eyes shifted between me and Hero. "If you are sure."

"I am sure. Thank you for bringing us here safely. You're my friend. Do not forget it."

Turducken nodded and then disappeared.

I turned to Hero. "Again, we fail to have Turducken join us because of your jealousy. Goodness sakes, Hero. Are you going to yell at me if I kiss my father, too?"

"That's different, and you know it."

"Only you, and you alone, think Turducken is a bad guy."

Hero crossed his arms. "He's a little weasel. Who came up with the two of you having a friendship kiss anyway? Did he ask you to do it?"

I bit my lower lip. "He didn't come up with the concept, Hero. You heard the kids of Kingdom do it. But yeah, he sort of mentioned it."

"Aha!" Hero nearly jumped up in the air. "See? He wanted to kiss my wife. He's been lusting after you since I first met him."

The purple creature blinked. "Wife? But she's King Piper's wife."

I jerked my thumb at the fairy. "Who's this, and how much does she know?"

Hero nodded at Wysdel. "Same question. Suddenly, this

woman appears and tells me she's with you and brings me here in time to see you kissing the elf."

Wysdel raised her hands. "'Tis a good moment to make introductions." She looked worriedly at the purple being. "However, I am not sure we should discuss this in front of her."

The little creature put her hands on her hips. "Because I'm a sprite? Is that why?"

Wysdel shook her head. "No, not at all. We are on a dangerous quest. I am worried about your life."

"Oh, then." The sprite aimed both thumbs back at herself. "I'm Sinope. I work as a revealing dancer at the Thirsty Wench. Hero came in and watched me perform."

Hero turned white, and I stepped toward him. "What is a revealing dancer?"

"I take my clothes off," Sinope said.

Hero put his hands up, warding me from him. "I didn't watch her. I turned away. I swear."

I phrased my next question through clenched teeth. "Are you telling me I just sent home one of the most powerful magicians in Kingdom because of your jealousy, but earlier today you were putting dollars in a sprite's G-string?"

Flustered as he was, Hero seemed to be aflame, cheeks and all. "You know I wouldn't do that, Sondra."

He used my Earth name. We only use our Earth names in Kingdom when we're being completely honest with one another. I took a deep breath. I owed it to Hero to let him explain exactly what he was doing in a fantasy strip joint. But before Hero could justify his actions, Lenore stepped forward.

"He was looking for Graddock. We all know he frequents that tavern, so he gallantly went in himself and asked questions. Sinope knows where he's located."

Sinope floated up to me, head lowered. "My queen, if I may, Mr. Hero gave me a handkerchief to cover myself with when someone stole my shift."

I had to admit that this sounded like Hero. Frown still in place, I said, "I'm not the queen. I only look like her. I'm married to this lug." I reached out and patted Hero's arm.

Hero turned to Wysdel. "And who are you?"

Lenore interrupted before Wysdel could answer. "I will vouch for her. She's part of our...troupe. If you get my meaning."

Wysdel clapped her hands. "Let us be off on our quest, and I will explain." Her eyes shifted to Sinope. "Lenore, will you fly ahead with Sinope to ensure we will encounter no ruffians?"

Lenore shifted into her bird form, and she and Sinope took to the air. We emerged from the alley and marched across the cobblestone street to the main gate entrance of Town, pausing only to allow Wysdel to buy a sword.

When we reached the gates and the two women were out of earshot, Wysdel lowered her voice to a whisper. "The Resistance sent me to Sanders, Hero. I remember the queens and the true past of Kingdom."

Hero scratched his unruly hair. "I'm sorry for being rude, but I had to know."

Wysdel said, "I do not blame you for being suspicious. Piper has spies all over Kingdom, and some have changed their appearance. We must be cautious. But those in power often think sprites are weak creatures so I trust her more than most. Nevertheless, tell me about Sinope."

Hero blushed. "I hardly looked at her in the tavern, but she gave me my handkerchief back."

Wysdel said, "We must be on our guard with her. Piper's moles have infiltrated the Resistance before."

Hero examined Wysdel, and she looked away. "Moles? Isn't that an Earth term? Who are you to this resistance movement?"

Wysdel bit her lip and looked around. "I am but a peasant. I heard the term moles from an Earth Traveler."

Eyeing her, Hero said, "You seem awfully cultured to be a peasant."

Wysdel blanched, and her expression again reminded

me of someone, but I couldn't remember who. The Resistance fighter mouthed "too many" and tugged on her earlobe.

Hero nodded. "Fine. Lenore vouched for you, so I'll trust you."

As we traveled into the surrounding countryside, we remained separated. Lenore and Sinope acted as scouts while Wysdel, Hero, and I trekked along the grassy land leading toward River. We observed Sinope turn south and we followed her while Wysdel relayed several local legends about the area to pass the time. Clearly, she knew a lot about Kingdom, and while I wanted to interrupt several times, I kept silent to invite her to reveal more about herself. While she enjoyed telling stories, she avoided my baited questions about her past.

We arrived at a small farm, and they lent us their barn to sleep in and gave us Kinship Pie. Wysdel explained that the residents around these parts were welcoming and encouraged us to eat the meat dinner. It tasted like a spicy version of Shepherd's Pie, and I was enjoying it until Wysdel told me the meat was from a tardalong.

We stayed the night there. I told the others to sleep, and I would take the first watch, casting a pixie spell to keep myself from falling asleep. Wysdel nodded, and I was amazed she trusted me so entirely that she drifted off immediately. As I watched her sleep, breathing through her large, horse-like nostrils, I thought about her. Many people in Kingdom knew about us but didn't really understand us. We were the mysterious visitors who talked funny and lent a hand in an emergency. This woman didn't treat me in that way. She reminded me of my sister, Karen.

Thinking of my sister reminded me of home. I usually hadn't talked to Karen much as she lived far away. I know staying in touch by way of social media is easy, but she had her life and I had mine. We'd post messages to each other sometimes about what was going on in our lives. That routine was polite and she and I had a decent relationship, much better than when we were growing up, but distance made remaining close difficult.

Karen was my father's girl, perhaps because she was the first. I was my mother's. Growing up, I had many spats with my mother, but we also went through times when she encouraged me. Karen was naturally smarter than me in school, but my mother told me I had more determination. My mother saw great things in me and was the proudest person in the audience when I graduated college with honors in physics. She was my confidante. Taken from me too soon.

I focused my attention away from my mother to the sprite. Given my science degrees, I found Sinope fascinating to observe. I had seen her species wandering around the queens' castle in the past, but never interacted with them nor knew they were called sprites.

In the morning, Sinope and I were the first to arise on Lenore's watch. The three of us complained about flying against wind currents as Hero and Wysdel woke up. Sinope was surprisingly easygoing and enjoyable to talk to. While we gathered supplies for the journey, I thought of a question for the sprite. "Sinope, why do you work at the Thirsty Wench?"

"I have a younger sister who's in my charge. We're stepsisters and she's human, but I would do anything for her."

"Can't you work as a waitress in a tavern?" I asked.

Sinope snorted. "No one would hire a sprite. We're only allowed jobs like the one I have."

Hero put out his hands. "If the queens were back, they would fix this. They'd shut down the Thirsty Wench."

Wysdel and Lenore exchanged a surreptitious look. I asked, "What?"

Wysdel said, "Nothing."

Lenore seemed undeterred by Wysdel's evasiveness. "The use of sprites as revealing dancers happened under the queens' rule as well."

Hero looked stunned. "No way! Why would the queens put up with that?"

Wysdel crossed her arms. "You do not understand, Hero. The queens outlawed pixie scalping and scores of other injustices. Some of the people revolted when they did this. One group even tried to assassinate Cinderella for her stand on seal hunting. The queens know these acts are barbaric, but they removed people's way of life without any replacement. People were unable to feed their children, and they had to make a drastic reduction in their way of living."

"Who are the queens?" asked Sinope.

"I'll explain it all later." Hero scowled. "I thought Kingdom became a better place under their rule."

"A better place is not a perfect place," lectured Wysdel. "Not all the people of Kingdom love the queens. They have been engaged in one war after another. Many call this a golden age, but problems still exist. Every government must face its own trials."

Hero threw his arms up in indignation. That gesture's so cute. I fully supported him too.

Hero said, "Piper says he took over because the queens became bureaucrats. I'm starting to wonder if he has a point."

"It was not that easy, Hero." Wysdel pulled in her shoulders, clearly uncomfortable with this topic. "The queens knew revealing dancing for people who cannot find another way to live is wrong. They passed safety laws. This is not how the queens would want the world, but they made compromises."

Sinope put a hand on her hip. "I get paid, and Merwynda and the trolls enforce strict rules about touching. It isn't so bad."

Hero sighed. "You shouldn't have to do this. Not here. This place is supposed to treat everyone as equals. I was told that when I first came here, but it is like sprites are a lower class than everyone else."

An awkward silence fell until Sinope spoke. "We are."

Hero marched away in anger. I looked around. "I'll talk to him. Where are we going?"

Wysdel said, "I thought Sinope knew where Graddock lived?"

"I do, but first Hero agreed to go on a quest for me," the sprite said.

Wysdel shook her head. "No. We have no time for side quests. We must find and unite the princes and the queens. You will take us directly to Graddock."

Sinope flew up to her face. "No. Hero gave his word to help me out."

I came between them. "Wysdel, if we can get the quest out of the way quickly, everyone will be happy. Fair?"

I expected more of a fight from her, but she softened. "Fair, but it depends on the quest."

Sinope said, "Retrieve your husband and I shall tell you. We are only three hours from our destination."

I flew to Hero who was pacing around outside. Before I could speak, he asked me a question. "How could the queens allow this? They champion women's rights. It just seems... wrong."

I put a hand on Hero's shoulder. "We tend to build up our leaders in our minds, believing them flawless. When we disagree with them, though, we shouldn't lose faith in them. You and I both know the queens, and we know if they decided to allow sprites to bare all, they must have had a long debate. I'm sure they felt uncomfortable with their decision."

"I'm going to talk to them about it," said Hero, his jaw unclenching.

I kissed him on the cheek. "You do that after we break the spell on them. Now, let's go back to the barn. You agreed to a quest, and we have questions."

After we arrived, I decided to defuse some of the tension by changing the subject. "Hero, what was the name of the guy you were asking about?"

He eyed me. "Joseph Macquin."

I surveyed our small group. "We're looking for a Joseph Macquin. Wysdel, ever hear of him?"

"Never." Wysdel shrugged dismissively. "Let us travel. While we walk, Sinope, tell us about this quest."

Sinope hovered before the rest of us as we exited the barn and started on our way. "When I was young, an alchemist took me in after I was abandoned. She was a strict but fair mistress. When I was seven, my guardian added another orphan to her home. The new baby was human, and I took care of her. She became like a sister to me.

"Anyway, as she grew up, she became more and more beautiful. The three of us made a family of a mother and two daughters. My mother was terrified of a rival she said would kidnap and kill us. She locked us away in our home and never let us go outside."

"Sounds bad," said Hero. "Never being able to leave."

Sinope flew under a few low-hanging branches. "Mother realized she couldn't keep me tucked away from the world. I rebelled and she let me roam, but not so with my sister. My mother had a fondness for her, and my sister was more complacent than me. Last year, our mother died unexpectedly, leaving my sister imprisoned by the remnants of my mother's spells. All you must do is free her, and I'll tell you where Graddock is."

I shrunk to pixie size and took to the air. "Sounds easy to me. My magic should be able to cut through any lock."

"It will not be that easy," said Sinope mysteriously.

We continued south and soon encountered an abandoned group of houses, followed by an open field. As we crossed a line of trees, Sinope said, "This is my mother's property. Cover your mouths for a few minutes."

The odor of a mixture of rotten eggs, sour milk, and seaweed flowed between the cracks in my hands and into my nostrils. I gagged, and Hero's eyes watered. I didn't want to take a breath. Sinope flew forward before us, and if she hadn't, I would've turned around and made haste—as they said in

Kingdom—in the other direction. However, we soldiered on, and the smell dissipated as we moved forward. Eventually, it disappeared altogether.

Sinope looked at us over her shoulder. "My mother created that smell to keep people away. The stench surrounds her property in a circle. We are close now."

We walked for less than fifteen minutes and entered a close-knit barrier of trees. We then advanced through the woods until we came to a clearing. When we entered the clearing, Hero and I stopped and both of us gasped at the same time. On the left side of the small field stood a large tower with a single window at the top of it. Hero, gazing upward, addressed Sinope. "Your sister's name isn't Rapunzel, is it?"

"How did you know?"

Radiance's Retreat

15 - ADAGIO

Radiance entered the chalet before Roger and halted in the main room. The chamber was two stories tall with stairs in the center leading up to a suspended crossing walkway on the far side. A fireplace was set against one wall of the room—its opening large enough for Radiance to walk into without ducking. It burst to life as they came in.

The fireplace's blaze radiated a gentle heat as if welcoming Radiance and Roger further inside. After allowing the heat to warm her, Radiance rotated around, taking it all in. An oval-shaped rug depicting the sun, moon, and stars, each with smiling faces, covered most of the floor. Divans and couches, arranged carefully, were interspersed throughout the room. Tucked into the corner of one couch, a pillow had the hand stitched image of a stylish slipper.

Could this really be hers? She adored the colors in the rug. The room appeared comfortable, not showy. The furniture and accents she would choose for her house. Correction. A house her alternate self had lived in with Roger.

Roger's eyes bugged out. "God's heaven!"

Radiance cocked her head. She had never heard him use this expression before, but it seemed exactly right. She wanted a word to respond with, something unique and witty. Instead, "awesome" slipped out.

Radiance ran her hand over her divan. "This chalet cannot belong to you."

Roger put his hands on his hips. "To us, if we are to believe Hero."

Radiance frowned at his response and spied another room through an open doorway off the main chamber. She entered and found this led to a drawing room filled with musical instruments. This area had windows that looked out over the gorge in front of the chalet. Another warm and inviting room with soft couches.

Roger followed her into the room. Radiance examined the furnishings. "Where are the chairs?"

"A house designed for couples to sit together," observed Roger.

Radiance pushed him out of the way to leave the room and ascended the stairs. Roger followed, but they separated on the second floor.

Radiance walked to the end of the hallway toward an alcove that extended out of the side of the chalet. The ceiling and walls of the extension were enclosed in glass. In the final light of the day, she peered down to the backyard and gasped.

A well. A perfect replica of the well where she had first met Roger—Soro's Well. Who built it, and what was it doing here?

Radiance bit her lip. At first, Hero's story of her past seemed absurd. If she had married Roger, she would certainly remember it! But she refused to use her ability on Roger to make him leave. When he had said "God's Heaven," it had rung true in her head, as if she had heard him say it before. And this chalet was practically a monument to them! What had seemed absurd a day ago now appeared possible.

Radiance put her hand on the glass and pictured her and Roger at the well, not as children, but at their current age. He was lifting up a bucket. She was splashing him with water. He folded her in his arms and leaned down, pressing his lips against hers. She drew him closer, wanting to taste his lips, wanting to—

"Radiance!"

Roger's voice carried down the hallway, breaking her daydream. Startled, she touched her lips with two fingers. A kiss that never had been, but the sensation was so very real.

She shook her head and moved down the hallway to where Roger had called for her. He had ascended to the third level, so she scurried up the stairs to a small room at the top.

Roger stood in the center of the room on the third floor, shaking a spent match. Curiously, the room had no windows. Roger had lit two candles in sconces on the wall of this room filled with shadows. He beckoned to her, his face a beaming lighthouse. Unable to help herself, she was excited by his enthusiasm. "What is it?"

He lifted his eyes to a painting on the wall between the candles. Radiance followed his gaze and viewed a portrait of two people, she and Roger, in a loving embrace, looking longingly into each other's eyes. The painted version of Radiance's eyes expressed pure joy.

She gaped at the picture. "I don't believe this."

"If Hero was right and King Piper erased your memory, he would not have known about this place. He could not remove the truth about us."

Radiance tapped her chin with her index finger. "Perhaps Pennilane is right. This place is the home of a witch, and this is all an entire illusion to fool me."

"To what purpose, Radiance?"

"To trick me into falling for you again."

The corners of Roger's mouth turned down. "I would

never trick someone I hold so dear."

Radiance gulped. "Still, this place could be a spell."

Roger put a hand on his stomach. "One thing is not an illusion. I am hungry. I will go downstairs and see if I can find anything in the pantry."

Radiance remained behind, gazing at her younger, happier, and unjaded image. Her years of despair—gone. The painter had caught her smile exactly right.

Snorting, Radiance stomped out of the room and advanced to the other end of the hallway. She checked a few rooms but noticed something missing—no chairs or beds. What a curious chalet. She entered the last room and stared around in wonder. The chamber was adorned with rose-colored tapestries over pink wallpaper. A four-poster bed with light-red pillows sat in its center. Her eyes focused on the bed, the only one on the floor. The frame was in the shape of a heart. Someone had designed it so that the two people resting there had to be close together.

Retreating backward out of the room, Radiance shut the doors, turned, and put her back against the portal. "If you really did design this place, Roger, curse you."

Proceeding downstairs, Radiance went to find Roger on the first floor. She stopped in the main entry hall and pictured herself on a couch in front of the fire with Roger's arms wrapped around her, both of them sipping from the same goblet of wine. The firelight reflected in their eyes.

"No. I refuse to believe it."

She passed through a series of doors into a dining room. Poking her head into an adjoining space, she found Roger in a kitchen, standing in front of a platter of beef and pouring a heavy brown liquid into a gravy boat.

"Where did you find that?"

Roger turned around. "I found potions in this kitchen with instructions. I mixed one and another, poured it on a plate, and beef appeared. The gravy came from another potion. I found a few herbs and spices to mix into the gravy. Dinner will be served momentarily, my dear."

Roger's term of affection came out naturally as if he had referred to her as "my dear" for years. Radiance hadn't noticed his name for her at first, retrieving place settings and returning to the dining room. As she set them down, she realized he had called her "my dear," and she hadn't objected. She stomped her foot in frustration.

He wasn't allowed to refer to her as a "dear" or any such affectionate term! No matter how much she liked it.

And she did like it.

Seated, Radiance watched Roger enter the room with the roast beef. The meat smelled succulent, and her stomach growled loudly. Roger set down the platter and carved the entree, placing a choice selection on her plate. He then cut himself a portion.

Radiance said grace, and they ate. She began with no table talk at first, determined to draw out the awkwardness. Finally, she succumbed and commented, "This is very good."

"Thank the potions."

"The spices bring out the flavor," muttered Radiance.

"Did you just pay me a compliment?"

She swallowed the meat on her fork. "Because I like the work of the chef doesn't mean I love the chef."

They continued, and when she finished, she put down her utensils and set her hands in her lap. Roger placed his utensils on his plate. "What are you waiting for?"

She blushed. "I don't know. For a moment, I thought someone was going to clear it."

Grinning, Roger said, "As if you were a queen."

She picked up her plate and threw her fork and knife on it with a loud clatter. "No, nothing like that."

In the kitchen, she pumped the sink and washed her own setting. When Roger entered, she stepped out of the way. Let him clean his own dishes! She wasn't going to offer. No longer a slave girl, she would let him do his own chores.

As he primed the pump, Radiance put a hand on her

hips. "We have a problem."

He scraped his plate with a knife. "And what is that?"

"The house has only one bedroom, and the bed is unsuitable to our current situation."

Roger quirked an eyebrow. "If you believe Hero, we are married. The bed is ideally suited."

"I don't believe Hero! I want the bedroom for myself along, with the entire third floor."

Roger dipped his dishes in the water. "You want me to sleep down here?"

"I would prefer it, yes," she replied.

Roger set the dish out to dry. "I agree, but 'tis not to my liking."

"Did you honestly think we would share a bed tonight?"

"If we kissed and found that we were married, yes."

Folding her arms, Radiance said, "Here is an idea. You stay here for years and years waiting for me, and after all that time is up, we shall declare our love for each other."

Roger pointed at himself. "I believe Hero. I cannot explain it but ever since he clarified our situation, I have believed we belong together. 'Tis not as if we have been separated for years, but rather a shorter time. If what he said is true, I sought you out shortly after you went to the Forest of Death."

She bit her lip, hoping he wouldn't notice she felt the same way. "In his story, you still did not realize I was the maiden when I lived with my terrible stepmother and stepsisters."

"True, but his story paralleled mine closely. Both tales had a time I sold everything to find you, and failing that, I sat in my house and starved. I nearly died of hunger."

Radiance stepped back and put her fingers on the edge of her chin. "Truly?"

"Yes, in Hero's story, he found me and led me to you." Roger rubbed his beard. "In my memories, my brother found me and convinced me to work. We planted the garden at my house, but the timing is all wrong. I planted that garden six months ago. I have memories of planting it both many years ago as well as six months ago. If what Hero says is true, King Piper replaced my memories, and I came home expecting to find a garden. When I did not find one, I planted it."

"But if you planted it six months ago, the garden would not be mature," she countered. "And you told me you have been harvesting from it."

"I used magic seeds. The garden appeared overnight," explained Roger.

"You are trying to confuse me. You sleep down here tonight, and we will discuss this tomorrow."

Roger slumped. "I see your logic. If we are not married, 'tis a scandal. I do not mind sleeping on a couch, but I would rather you were with me."

Shaking her head, she turned and ran upstairs, eventually reaching the pink room. Radiance examined the door for a lock. No luck. She supposed a chalet for loving couples wouldn't need locked doors. Reflecting, Radiance rubbed her ring finger, empty of any marriage token.

She regarded the bed and imagined herself snugly in his arms. Breathing in quickly, she huffed. "No!"

Her eyes closed. She prayed she'd fall asleep quickly.

Rounding a corner of the hedges surrounding her estate, Shaina stopped in her tracks. "I have found you at last!"

Grr, the Halifax groundskeeper, clipped a tangled bush. He gripped the pruning shears in his gnarled hands. His canine-shaped face beamed on seeing her, and he opened his mouth to reveal his sharp teeth. Stooped, with thick, unruly hair growing out of his neck and arms, he turned to her and lowered his shears. "Lady Halifax."

Shaina stepped up to him, waving as if dismissing a fly. "Dispense with the title. You and I have always been the best of friends, have we not?"

"Indeed."

The other servants called him deformed and crude, but Shaina reprimanded them for this. Grr was a winsome man, unconventional, and loyal to a fault. Certainly, his bloodline contained at least one non-human ancestor, but that wasn't Grr's fault. And Shaina wasn't attracted to what everyone else called proper and perfectly formed. Other women could have their perfectly formed physiques and picture-perfect faces. She lived on the wild side.

Shaina fingered the hedge Grr was cutting. "Not cutting the topiaries into figures today?"

"Just maintenance." His eyes never left hers.

The intruders had pointed out Grr had shaped all the bushes in her form. She had examined the grounds, and while their observation was an exaggeration—some were formed to resemble other animals—she had verified their claim. One, in particular, resembled her strongly, and if she shifted to the left and looked around it, she could see another hedge in the shape of a heart in the line of sight. For two days, she had pondered the storyteller's tale, dismissing and then returning to it.

Shaina licked her lips. "I have noticed many of the shrubs are in the shape of young maidens. Some say they look like me. Was this intentional?"

Grr blinked a few times. "No." He pounded his chest, indicating himself. "Lets mind wander while cutting. Makes the hours go by quicker."

Grr's gesture of referring to himself by pounding his chest instead of saying "I" always endeared him to her. Why hadn't she spent more time with Grr lately? The groundskeeper was a true friend, her only one, from her childhood.

Shaina tilted her head. "They look like me, Grr."

Alarmed, Grr bowed his head. "Did not mean to embarrass you."

"Embarrass me? I clap in response." At this, she clapped

her hands, the sound echoing across the yard.

Shaina continued, "Your topiaries are a work of art. I am sorry the subject does not live up to the representation."

Grr lifted an eyebrow. "The model is perfect as she is."

So honestly given, the compliment filled something she had missed but hadn't known was gone. This conversation, meant to be a quick compliment to Grr, was taking on a new meaning. Why had she ignored her friend for so long? Why had she not seen the topiaries for what they were? She always suspected Grr's affection for her but was surprised at her reaction when said emotions were so evident.

Shaina brushed her cheek playfully. "I can hardly compare to nature's splendor."

He lightly touched her hand. "*Are* nature's splendor."

Shaina sucked in a breath. Heavens, she wanted his touch. She cared little about whether the statement was true or not, she appreciated it coming from him, whom she—

She…what? Was the word "adored" about to follow?

Overwhelmed, Shaina stumbled for words. "I…em…I… That is to say, I wanted to give you a gesture for your hard work. A token of my affection."

She originally intended to kiss him on the top of the head. Shaina was a full head taller than Grr, and a light peck would show her appreciation. She and Grr had kissed each other on the cheek many times before as children. This would recall those earlier, happier times.

But as she lowered her head, she moved to bring her face level with his. Her body turned traitor to her thoughts, but something deeper wouldn't be denied. A thought stole into her mind. She was going to kiss him, right here, in the hedge maze. She was going to break the custom of kissing only your future fiancé. But Grr wouldn't mind giving his permission if she decided to marry another. He was her best friend, after all.

Surprisingly, he seemed ready to kiss her too, and this emboldened Shaina. No, she wasn't a reckless girl, but this seemed *right*. Without giving it another thought, she lightly pressed her lips to his. In seconds, she knew she had done the right thing—all regret washed away. She was with someone she felt affection for; he had worked hard on the topiaries to reflect her grace and style, and she wanted to give him her most treasured gesture.

And he was Grr.

And she was Beauty.

And she was a queen.

Their eyes widened at the same time, but they didn't part. Instead, Beauty closed her eyes and pressed her lips firmly onto his, making up for the lost kisses over the past seven months. The kiss made her blood race and her body tremble with emotions.

When they parted, Grr put his hand on her cheek. "Beauty."

She responded with the same gesture. "I am...I'm Beauty Shaina Corden." She took a trembling breath. "A queen." Awe and reverence sounded in her voice.

Grr nodded.

"My mother is Queen Penta." She blinked rapidly then narrowed her eyes. "We've been bespelled as have the other queens, my aunts."

Grr's eyes narrowed. "Who did this?" He pointed at himself. "Will capture him."

"'Tis the odious king," she spat. "Or the one who calls himself thus. That elf in our house, Shelfie. The king gave me memories of him. False memories."

Grr bared his teeth. "A spy! We march on the palace."

Beauty straightened up. "No, Grr, we can't take Piper on alone. We need an army."

"Army?"

Beauty looked north. "And I know where to raise one."

Sinope's Home

16 - TOWERING PROBLEM

Harold

Rapunzel's tower! Sanders and I had often wondered if other famous fairy tale characters existed in Kingdom. While most were found—Snow White, Cinderella, Beauty, the Little Match Girl—we still hadn't discovered all of them. Occasionally, Sanders and I would muse as to whether Sleeping Beauty or Thumbelina existed in Kingdom. At the top of our list of speculation was Rapunzel, but we always figured she would be easy to find. Look for a large tower.

Sinope pointed to a door at ground level. "Only I can enter. Our mother constructed the tower to keep half-wits and vagabonds from trying to kidnap us."

The tower itself stood seventy feet tall with a surface as smooth as a modern Earth rocket ship. True, it was built of stone, but the stones all melded into each other to form an unbroken surface like glass. The only breaks in the surface were four horizontal, black lines that wrapped around the cylindrical walls. The first line should have provided a handhold, but it was out of reach.

I approached the base and ran my hand down the exterior. "No chance of climbing it."

Sinope furrowed her brow. "Of course, you can't climb it. What kind of protection would that offer?"

Unimpressed, Lenore gazed upward, likely having read Rapunzel on her home world. Wysdel didn't look surprised, an uncommon response in my experience. Whenever I found myself in a fairy tale in Kingdom, the residents often questioned how I knew the story, or why I asked about slippers or poisoned apples. Wysdel stood staring up at the window, tapping her chin.

A young girl surveyed us from one window at the top of the tower while putting her hand on her chest. To be clear, most fairy tale princesses are illustrated as eighteen-to-twenty-year-old women. Rapunzel looked as though she belonged in middle school. One feature I noticed immediately. Her golden, curly hair extended down to her shoulders—no further. What kind of a Rapunzel was this?

Not surprisingly, she was pretty—a clear complexion, small nose, and a rounded chin. She pulled back the sleeve of her brown tunic and waved to Sinope. "You have brought others?"

"It's a rescue, Raquel!"

"Raquel?" I asked. Now I wasn't sure she was Rapunzel at all.

"'Tis the name Mother Gothel gave her," explained Sinope. "Her parents named her Rapunzel. I'm curious how you came to know her by that name."

"'Tis a long story," I said. Truthfully, a short one.

Sanders shook her wings. "No problem. I'll have her down in a minute."

Her wings spread out, and she took off like a missile toward the girl. Sinope called after her to stop, but my determined wife flew like a bullet to its mark, in this case, the window. As she neared it, a force propelled her backward as if a giant invisible hand had swatted her away. She tumbled head over heels back toward the trees. She then sailed over a staff embedded in the soil with a Y-shape at the top. At first, I worried the stick might impale her. Fortunately, my wife recovered before crashing. She crumpled and rolled when she hit the dirt.

I ran to her. "Are you hurt?"

She lifted a hand. "What do you think?"

"I think you're hurt, Sanders. But sometimes you surprise me."

"This time it hurt." She rose to her feet and her wings straightened out. "Yeah, nothing broken."

Sinope flew over to us. "You don't think anyone could've flown her down? Do you think my mother was a dolt?"

I took Sanders' hand to steady her, and we returned to the tower. "Sanders, can you throw that spell where you disconnect your hand and send it up there?"

Sanders brushed back a stray lock of hair. "With the barrier in place, what good would that do?"

I stared upward at the girl in the window. "We're being silly. I can see only one solution to this." I cupped my hands. "Rapunzel, Rapunzel, let down your hair."

The girl blinked, and Sinope asked, "What good is that going to do?"

I eyed the teenager with the furrowed brow. "I was hoping she might just cut her hair, and she could send down a thick braid for us to climb."

Sinope put her hands on her hips. "What? Do you think you could climb her hair?" She threw her head back and laughed.

Ah, yes! Did I mention that Kingdom's stories don't match ours exactly? They are mostly the same with some small differences. I stepped back and examined the tower and spotted something curious. The tower wasn't in the middle of the field—it was to the left. The rest of the field, next to the tower, was taken up by two large circles of stone as if they were foundations of two more towers. While interesting, they didn't inspire any thoughts of how to help the girl down.

No one could climb to her; no one could fly up to her. She didn't have long hair. I considered having her jump and Sanders casting a spell to have her gently float down. This made me nervous. I wasn't going to put a girl in danger.

Sinope scratched her head. "Can you rescue her?"

"I'm thinking."

"What kind of hero are you?" she asked.

"The kind kind." Sanders retrieved her glasses from her pocket and put them on. "The best heroes are always the kindest."

I nearly fainted. My wife didn't compliment me much, and I was touched.

Wysdel sighed. "I am not unsympathetic to her plight, but she is safe up there. We have other quests in Kingdom that require our attention."

I rolled my shoulders. "But without Graddock, we can't proceed to Valencia. We need him."

"Someone else must know where Graddock lives," she murmured.

By distracting me briefly from the problem at hand, Wysdel helped me see a potential solution. Staring at the tower with its three lines, I wondered if my idea would rescue the princess or was just plain crazy. As usual, Sanders was my sounding board. "Sanders, do you think this is a Towers of Hanoi problem?"

My wife's eyes sparkled. "I think you're onto something."

I love that Sanders is a science and math fanatic and

knew exactly what I was talking about. The Towers of Hanoi problem has a base with three dowels on the left, right, and center. The leftmost dowel runs through the center of several discs, each smaller than the disc below it. The resulting shape resembles a tower. The trick is to move the discs from one dowel to another without putting a larger disc on top of a smaller disc. You succeed by moving all the discs in a tower shape to the right.

Rapunzel's tower was the left-most tower. We had to move her tower from left to right in the sections demarcated by the black lines. In the middle of the operation, the very top section would be on the ground. It should be close enough that Rapunzel could safely jump from its window.

As I examined the tower, I was more convinced I was right. "In our world, we could use a crane to move the segments of the tower. Perhaps we can find a friendly dragon here to move them?"

Sanders narrowed her eyes. "Maybe not."

"What do you mean?"

Sanders stepped up to the Y-shaped staff and kept her eyes locked on the tower. Grabbing the pole, she positioned it so that, from her point of view, its sides were around the edges of the top of the tower. "Sinope, warn Rapunzel. I'm not sure what's about to happen."

I have to say that my wife is a creative genius. She has a talent to think of the craziest ideas that work. She held the stick so that the top section of the castle lined up with the edges of the stick. I ran behind her and eyed it. Carefully, she moved the stick to the rightmost empty platform, and the top section of the building separated from the rest of the structure. It drifted to the right and landed on the rightmost circle. Rapunzel hovered in midair for a moment then gently floated down to the next section of the tower, still entrapped within its confines.

Rapunzel's new section didn't have a window, but I was excited. She was closer to the ground now. Sanders bit her lip and again lined up the Y-stick with the second segment of the leftmost tower. She moved her stick to the middle base, and as before, the section of the tower separated and followed her motion. Once again, Rapunzel floated down to the third section. She was almost at the bottom.

The Tower of Hanoi is not a difficult problem if you know you must backtrack to solve it. Sanders moved the rightmost, top piece of the tower on the middle base, then returned to the leftmost section again. She moved it to the right—Rapunzel lightly falling again—and then piled the central section on top of it. Rapunzel now looked out the window close to ground level.

"Rapunzel's at the bottom. I assume you'll move the base now?"

Sanders nodded, moving the last piece on the middle platform, and the entire construction lifted into the air, leaving the young girl standing by herself with no tower on the leftmost area.

I squeezed my wife's shoulder. "You're brilliant."

Sanders beamed. "Why, thank you. Brilliance is my specialty."

As I was saying, my not-so-modest wife had it solved in less than two minutes. When the last piece was moved, Rapunzel stood in the middle of a field and gazed at us through shining eyes. Sinope flew to her and embraced her, laughing. We all approached her but Sanders. Even though Rapunzel was free, the tower was only half-finished, and she was completing the puzzle to recreate the tower on the right side.

I gestured her along. "Come on, Sanders. She's free."

The scientist in her wouldn't leave it alone. "If I'm going to do it, I'm doing it right."

I strolled forward while Sinope introduced each of us. The young girl curtsied at each name and inclined her head demurely, a common gesture in Kingdom. She was as cute as a button—blonde hair; expressive, hazel eyes; heart-shaped lips —but a little heavier than typical depictions of the fairytale princess. Tower completed, Sanders flew up beside me and alighted on my shoulder. Sinope introduced her last.

While Rapunzel bowed her head, Sanders said, "Hiya, Rapunzel."

Her mouth dropped open. "How do you know my birth name? The name I've gone by all my life is Raquel."

Sinope eyed us also. "I found that curious, too."

Rapunzel's eyes widened at me and Sanders. "Are you my parents?"

While such wasn't out of the question, Sanders and I were a bit young to be Rapunzel's parents. Yet, her eyes were wide with hope.

I shook my head. "I'm sorry, no."

Rapunzel stepped forward. "But you knew my parents. You must have, to know my name."

Ugh. How to explain this one. She seemed so eager for news of her parents that I hated to let her down. Sanders flew off my shoulder and landed on the ground, growing to her human size. She took Rapunzel's hands. "Unfortunately, no. We must have heard it from somewhere."

"But no one knows my name." She cast her eyes down, and I could tell she was trying to hold back tears. "I thought for sure…"

Sanders put her arm around the girl. "I think you're in for some exciting times, but first we have a quest we must complete. You may find a family at the end of it."

Certainly, she meant the queens, but Rapunzel looked puzzled. The girl wrinkled her nose. With a few questions, I found out Rapunzel was twelve-years old. She looked around the field and ran her hand through the grass and then touched a tree. "I haven't been able to touch outside things without Sinope bringing them to me." She grinned. "Branches don't snap off easily. I wasn't expecting that!"

Sinope took Rapunzel's hands and smiled; the first time I had seen the sprite turn the corners of her mouth upward. "I will take you to Graddock, and then Rapunzel and I will find a place to live far from Town."

I felt disappointed to leave the fairytale princess so soon. Rapunzel shook her head. "But, Sinope, this is your chance. You can return to your birth family. Now that your brother has found you and I'm free, you can reunite with them."

Sinope sprinkled sparkles from her wings. "Rapunzel, I was planning to take you with me."

"Your brother said your sprite family hates humans. They'd never accept me."

Sinope narrowed her eyes. "I'll make them."

"We've had this argument before." Rapunzel squared her shoulders. "And you know that won't happen. You must go there alone. They'll never accept you if I'm with you."

"But you're my little sister!" Sinope wiped her eyes. "I can't abandon you."

Rapunzel looked at me and Sanders. "I think I should go with them."

She still thought we were her parents. I wasn't about to lead her on, but I was certain one of the queens would adopt her. "I agree."

Everyone turned toward me in surprise except Sanders. My wife took my arm in solidarity. "So do I."

Wysdel motioned us away from the others. We followed her to a spot in the clearing and kept our voices down. The peasant revolutionary frowned at us. "We are on a perilous quest. She cannot join us. Her life will be in danger."

"The queens, even when they were fairytale princesses, weren't defenseless," I countered. "Rapunzel may have Cinderella's ability to charm, or Snow White's resistance to weapons. And if Piper finds out she's a fairytale princess, her life will also be in danger since all fairytale princesses become queens here. If we leave her behind, we won't be there to protect her."

"How would he find out she's a fairytale princess?" Wysdel nervously fidgeted with the lace at the base of her neck. "In Kingdom, we do not know the stories. Only people from other worlds do."

Sanders' wings slumped. "Any Traveler could tell him."

Wysdel protested, but I stuck to my guns, and she eventually relented, shaking her head. Sinope also wasn't sure, but Rapunzel defended her decision. The last part was in whispers, and I was certain she thought we knew where her parents were located. In the end, Sinope agreed to take us to Graddock and then decide what was best for her and Rapunzel.

Our growing party made its way through the smelly forest and the plains of Kingdom. Rapunzel turned out to be delightful and nothing like Sinope. We had to pause our march several times for her to stop and smell a patch of bluebells, or listen to a woodpecker knock on a tree, or wander into a stream and watch the water flow over her toes. She plucked wild strawberries off a bush and ate them greedily, savoring their taste. Certain experiences we had every day were all new to her, delighting her senses.

Rapunzel didn't walk but hopped around, much like a child with a gift card rushing up and down the aisles of a toy store. For no reason, she would hold her arms out their entire length and twirl around, telling us she didn't have to fear hitting a wall. Rapunzel had a pleasant, low voice that sounded like the hum of lazy bees waking up to meet the day. She spoke mostly to Sinope, and they held whispered conversations, but occasionally she would point out something and ask what it was.

At one point, Sinope and Rapunzel strolled beside me and Sanders, the sprite like a barrier between us and the girl. Rapunzel cleared her throat nervously. "My sister says you go on quests. Are you typical of knights?"

I snorted. "I'm not a knight."

"And he's not typical," Sanders rolled her eyes. "Very atypical, in fact."

The girl blinked. "What are you, then? Don't knights go on quests?"

I spoke in an exaggerated, masculine voice. "A soldier of fortune, mostly. A guardian of the oppressed."

Ruffling my hair, Sanders said, "He's a normal guy. You, on the other hand, are special."

"Because my mother locked me in a tower?" Rapunzel's eyes fell from ours. "I am afraid that I missed out on so much. I never want to be locked away again."

"We'll explain it later, but my husband and I believe you have a destiny to fulfill, an important one." Sanders reached around Sinope and put her hand on Rapunzel's shoulder. "You'll help us, right?"

Rapunzel cocked her head, and with the motion, she reminded me of a bird. "Me? I have a destiny? My only hope is destiny grants me a normal life, away from alchemists and locked towers. I want to be with people like me and experience everything I missed out on my entire life."

"First, you're about to have an adventure." Sanders changed into her pixie form, sparkles dropping to the ground. "After that, we'll see where life takes you."

When our troupe arrived back in Town, Sanders restored her Charlie disguise so that we wouldn't attract attention. Wysdel and Lenore walked behind, while Sinope led us to a section that bordered the river where the soldiers quartered. Night had descended, allowing us to crawl closer to a field where the army trained. Tents were arranged in straight rows, but at the edge stood a wooden construction of seven-foot posts with boards nailed between them. A pen.

Sinope pointed to the wooden quarters, keeping her voice low. "Graddock used to frequent the *Thirsty Wench* until a couple of days ago. On that day, soldiers entered and grabbed him, saying they were pressing him into service to train the king's patrols. I learned later they had quartered him here as a prisoner of war."

"He spars with the soldiers?" asked Wysdel.

"They won't give him a weapon." Sinope floated to the ground. "The king's forces use only blunt instruments, but still the results are brutal."

Rapunzel gasped, and Wysdel's mouth was a thin line.

"They use him as a live training dummy, then," I said. "Come on, we have to get him out of there."

"How?" asked Lenore. "I don't see a door on the pen."

Sanders gritted her teeth. "They must use magic to take him in and out of there. I'll have to teleport them."

Sinope held out her arm. "Wait. We have come at the changing of the guards when the wooden jail is briefly unmonitored."

"Quick! Let us not tarry," said Wysdel.

Crouching down, we moved across the field in a line until we all reached the wall of the pen. The boards were close enough to prevent escape, but far enough apart that we could see through them. As I peered through the cracks, I spotted a half-dozen or so men lying on the wooden floor. I tossed a rock inside to make a pinging sound, which woke one sleeping nearby. "Hey, you."

The man opened one eye and grumbled. "Not dawn yet."

Wysdel whispered, "We are looking for a man named Graddock. Is he here?"

The sleepy man kicked his partner and growled, "Guards want you."

The man who was kicked sat up and shook his head. He looked at the wall separating us. "What do you want now?"

Sanders put a finger through a crack and a thin beam of light, like a penlight, shined on a patch of floor near the seated man. She lifted it up to his face. Though he was thinner and sadly drawn, the light hair and round chin of Graddock stared back at us. A purple bruise spread across his jaw. "Yup, that's him."

"Indeed, 'tis," confirmed Wysdel.

Graddock put a hand up to block the light. "Remove that! What is going on?"

Wysdel turned to Sanders. "Can you teleport him out of there?"

"I can try."

Before she could start gesturing, the sound of a flute drifted out from a dark tent in the distance. The entire field was filled with light as if it were a stadium and someone had switched on the lights. After my eyes adjusted, I spotted Piper strolling from the tent with five golem soldiers, weapons drawn. Piper squared his shoulders, causing his royal robe to ripple as he observed us. He smiled at us like a cat who had caught the canary. And in our case, a raven, too.

17 - VIVACE

When Radiance awoke the next morning, she peered out her window and spied Pennilane and Sylvia's tent. The selkie was performing battle movements with her spear, and the human woman was exercising and practicing defensive moves. The bed had been so warm and cozy, and they'd had to sleep on the ground. Radiance swore she wouldn't forget them and resolved to visit them later.

Radiance dressed and went downstairs to find no trace of Roger anywhere except on the kitchen table. On a plate sat a small fig tart with a short note. "For you."

She sat and ate the sweet breakfast, picturing him across from her. "How did you sleep?" he would ask. "Oh, wonderful. The bed was fit for a queen." They would then both laugh. Truth was, she had awakened multiple times the prior night and once reached for his reassuring arms before she realized he wasn't there. Still groggy, she felt terribly alone.

What was wrong with her? Radiance had to remind herself that she didn't like him. Didn't like him? No, despised him. Yet "despise" required a lot of energy, and Radiance didn't have that in her. In all honesty, she really didn't hate anyone— especially Roger. When she had been reunited with him a few days before, she had said she hated him but had lied. Angry with him? Totally! Frustrated that he had reappeared after all these years? Naturally. But despised him? No. She could never really hate Roger Jolly.

Radiance ascended the stairs to the second floor with a desire to view the well in the daylight. The vantage point inside, safe from pesky insects, suited her tastes as if...as if it were built for her. Wondering where Roger had gone, she advanced to her glass-enclosed alcove and spotted him standing a short distance from the well.

Shirt off, Roger adjusted a grip on an ax, eyeing a few logs placed on stones. His bulging muscles strained as he lifted and swung the tool, cutting a large log into kindling. Radiance's eyes widened at his effort, and she stood mesmerized by his body's movement. Unaware of her presence, he swung the ax again while Radiance's heart drummed inside her chest.

Roger stretched his back, pulling his muscles taut. Radiance drank in his broad shoulders and strong arms. Staring? Sure. She knew she was staring, but so what? Why not take a nice, long look. After all—

After all, what? Radiance blinked then closed her eyes. Once she did, she breathed in deep and stepped backward, out of the alcove.

She put a hand on a wall to steady herself. "What is happening? I must not look at him undressed. I'm not his wife."

But why did her declaration make her feel bad? Nonsense. Radiance would steal another peek, ignoring the fluttering inside. She took a step forward and craned her head for one last look at Roger. She pictured his bare arms around her, and a smile spread across her face, while she started to lose herself in a daydream.

Again, she stepped back. "Stop this!"

She decided to go outside, confront him, and tell him to put his shirt on and keep it on. Radiance found the back door to the chalet and closed her eyes. She exited and put her hands out in front to keep from bumping into items in the yard. Moving forward on a crushed-stone path, she stumbled when someone's rough hands caught hers. "What are you doing?"

Turning to the sound of his voice, she replied, "Please put on your shirt."

"I have."

She partially opened her eyes to test whether Roger was lying, but he wasn't. Radiance cleared her throat. "I think it best if we are discreet and maintain our proprietary." He flashed a grin and she snapped, "That means keep your shirt on!"

"Not a problem." Roger released her hands. "However, if I am your husband, I am sure you have seen me without—"

Radiance lifted her chin. "Do not finish that sentence."

Gesturing to the round construction beside him, Roger asked, "Have you noticed the well?"

"I spotted it last night."

"It is the exact replica of the one where we met."

Annoyed, Radiance looked away. "I am aware."

"Perhaps I built it for you as a reminder of the beginning of our relationship."

"Relationship? I can sum up our relationship in eight words. You made a mistake, and I gave up."

Shoulders slumping, Roger put his hand on the edge of the well. "Are you ever going to forgive me?" His words dripped with regret.

"Oh, Roger. I suppose I could one day." Radiance stepped up to the side of the well. "But my forgiveness doesn't mean we can go back and have the same feelings we had before. So much time has passed."

Roger picked up a pebble and tossed it down the shaft. "I am not asking you to go back and become the young girl I knew. The person before me is more interesting to me than she was."

Radiance ran her finger along the well's ledge. "How will I be sure you won't abandon me again? How do I know you will not treat me as a servant one day? When we are married, will you ask me to clean up after you? Radiance, run to the market. Radiance, cook me dinner! I do not want that kind of life. I deserve better."

"You do deserve better, but you have to trust me that I will only treat you as sweetmate, an equal."

"But how can I trust you?" asked Radiance.

"I made a mistake, Radiance." Roger toed the weeds along the well's foundation. "I did not purposely do anything wrong. I spent all my fortune seeking you. I was starving to death. Life wasn't worth living without you."

Putting a hand on her hip, Radiance frowned. "Without the mysterious maiden, you mean."

Roger reached out and took her hand. Her first instinct was to pull it away, but she found his touch oddly comforting.

"Without you."

She swallowed. His sincerity was like a beacon of light in a dark tunnel.

Squeezing her hand lightly, Roger continued, "The mysterious maiden and the woman before me are one and the same. I cannot tell you how joyful Hero made me when he revealed you were my maiden. The beautiful, mysterious lady of my dreams is also my best friend. I was the most fortunate man in the world."

Stomping her foot, Radiance pulled away from his grasp. "Why is it that when I want to hate you the most, you say something like that?"

"I will not apologize. 'Tis the truth."

Radiance took a deep breath. "You spent all of your money?"

"Yes. I was a disgraced, one-legged soldier." Roger hung his head. "I would have given it all for the one person who made me feel alive again. This is why every time you insult or spurn me, I do not turn away. You are the only person who saw someone who was worthwhile. I could not see it in myself."

"Of course you were worthwhile!" Radiance relaxed her shoulders. "Do you know I prayed every day when you were in the army? Do you know how frightened I was that I would hear the news you had died? And then the day they announced you had come home, and you had lost your limb, everyone else thought you a coward since all your companions had died. They would not say it to your face because you had lost your leg, but rumors spread that you had injured yourself after you ran away."

Roger's scowl deepened.

"I did not believe any of it." Radiance swatted the air as if batting away the gossip. "I did not care if you were a hero or a coward. All I cared about was that you were home, and you were alive. I went to church and prayed for hours in gratitude. I was never so relieved in my life.

"And then I heard about your despair. I heard you were coming to the festival, and I went to my mother's grave and cried, hoping someone would bring you a little joy that night. The ghost of my mother, Wyndolyn, answered my prayer and dressed me like a noblewoman. She styled my hair, produced a mask, and gave me the golden slippers. But she did not give me one thing—my determination. By God, I was going to pull you out of the pit of despair or die trying. I did not care if you recognized me or not. I only cared for you."

Radiance stopped her confession and stared at him with wide eyes. Roger walked over and held his arms out to her. Slowly, she stepped into his embrace and put her head on his chest.

"You did not pity me?" Roger asked.

"I would never," she responded.

Taking a deep breath, Radiance broke away from him. "I

do not pity you. I do not hate you although I said I did. But I am not the girl I once was. When I look at you, I see my life in Julia's camp gone. I favor my home in the Forest of Death. I was safe there."

"You restored your heart there, and you are afraid of it shattering again."

She raised her chin. "Yes. Nothing is wrong with that. You almost starved to death, but the girl you knew did starve to death. Her love for you withered away years ago. The rest of me has lived on, and I enjoy my life now."

Turning around, Radiance walked away, despite the sourness in her stomach. She owed him the truth, and she had given it to him. In some way, they'd had it all out now. They did not have to hide behind looks and jibes. He knew what he had to overcome to win her, and he would fail if all he had was the rest of this one day.

Radiance's muddled thoughts needed straightening out, and she thought back to her resolution to see her selkie companion. Pennilane was outside. A mid-morning walk with her best friend might be the best way to clear her mind.

She went outside and grabbed Pennilane's arm, asking Sylvia to remain behind. The two longtime friends headed away from the chalet to a field. Pennilane spent the entire time questioning her on what was going on in the chalet. Radiance redirected the conversation to what Pennilane and Sylvia were doing. The selkie explained she had spent her time foraging and hunting, and Sylvia was watching and drawing birds.

"Roger brought Sylvia a quill and parchment this morning." Pennilane rolled her shoulders. "Birdwatching was a hobby someone named Snow White had introduced Sylvia to."

Hmm...Snow White again? "Someone defaced trees with that woman's name. I wonder who she is."

"Stop avoiding the subject, Radiance. What has been going on inside the chalet?" Pennilane's whiskers twitched, awaiting an answer.

Radiance quickly recounted the time she had spent with

Roger.

Pennilane scowled. "We should leave. We can start off now and find a boat to take us home."

"I gave my word," replied Radiance. "I am an honorable woman and will not go back on it."

Pennilane eyed the sun. "Perhaps you could stay outside here with me the rest of the day. At night, you could sneak back into the chalet and avoid him."

Without thinking, Radiance said, "I am not going to remain outside. Avoiding him is not an option, Pennilane."

Pennilane halted in her tracks. "You are not required to interact with him. You never promised anything of the sort."

"I know, Whiskers, but the entire point was to spend time with him. Why did I choose to come if only to avoid him? Besides, the chalet is very comfortable."

Pennilane sensed the lie immediately. "'Tis not the chalet."

Radiance wouldn't give her friend the satisfaction of a reaction. She had tired of this conversation and wanted, more than anything, to return to the castle named after her. Return...and talk to Roger.

Radiance performed an about-face and marched to the chalet, leaving behind a disappointed Pennilane and an inquisitive Sylvia. When she entered the romantic cottage, she decided to keep the conversation light for the rest of the morning. She wouldn't be seduced by his charms. She would treat him pleasantly—he had earned that much.

At tea, Radiance asked him about the people in the area where they had lived, and he deftly avoided the subject, apparently knowing she didn't favor anyone in her home village. Roger asked her about Pennilane, and she admitted the selkie hated men. He pointed out that Pennilane would hate him the most of all.

Roger asked her to stay at the table while he slipped into the kitchen. He returned with a plate of various fruits and cheeses and had arranged it in a smiley face. When she saw it, she grinned and reached for a wedge of cheddar. They discussed his garden and how much he loved growing herbs. He had learned how to cook in the last six months, and he was surprised how much he enjoyed it. The conversation, centered on food preparation and the meals he described, made Radiance eager to try them. Only if, of course, she stayed with him.

"You didn't spend a long time with Pennilane this morning," Roger observed.

Radiance squinted out the window. "Long enough. About as long as we have been talking."

Roger shaded his eyes. "By the position of the sun, I would wager we have been talking for two hours."

Two hours! Radiance sat back. "You must be mistaken."

But she knew he wasn't.

They spent the rest of the afternoon exploring the house together. While they had run through it the night before, they now decided to play a game of pretending Hero's story was true. They were married, and Roger had built the chalet. They entered each room, trying to guess what he was thinking when he designed it, and what she would've thought of it. When they came to the pink room, Radiance tried to pass it by, but Roger slipped around her and opened the door. He looked about the room in amazement. "I know what I was thinking when I designed this."

"And I know, whatever you were thinking, is not going to happen," she snapped.

Roger smirked at her, and she grabbed his arm to lead him out of the room. As they walked down the hallway, with her hands around his forearm, he stopped and looked her in the eyes.

Her thoughts flew to the pink room. Absolutely not! But the draw to return to her chamber was palpable.

Biting her top lip, Radiance stepped away. "I am done pretending for the day."

Roger nodded. "I will make dinner."

Radiance retired to the pink room and examined a chest filled with beautiful dresses. They all matched her taste perfectly. Curse this cottage!

Radiance selected a gown that she thought Roger would favor, then threw it on the bed. Did she want to make an impression on him? Her traitorous heart desired it.

Dinner exceeded her expectations. Afterward, Roger poured wine into goblets for them. As he handed her a goblet, she stared at her reflection in the shiny golden surface. What was she doing? Was this the right thing? Was she not her own woman? She did not need him! Yet she wanted him. Desire was different, was it not? Desiring him did not mean requiring his presence.

Roger suggested they go into the front room with the massive fireplace. They sat on different couches, staring across the expanse of the room at each other and sipping their wine. Radiance smacked her lips. "Elderberry and something I can't identify, but it too is sweet."

Staring at the fire, Roger said, "As sweet as you."

Radiance blushed, and silence descended on the room like new-fallen snow.

Barely above a whisper, Roger asked, "Do you believe you are a queen?"

Radiance laughed. "Honestly, that part of the story I have not considered. Imagine, me—a queen! I do not care if I am royalty. What interests me about Hero's story is the part that concerns you."

She broke off, wary of continuing that line of thought. Instead, she held her hands out to the fire.

Roger leaned forward. "And do you believe that part?"

She wanted to. More than anything. But she didn't want her heart to break. Curious, though. Her heart was the part of her most convinced the story was true.

Perhaps a test?

Radiance rose to her feet. "Move your arm."

Roger looked at her curiously until she walked over

and sat next to him. She cuddled up and put her head on his shoulder. Roger put his arm around her shoulders and pulled her in. He smelled of burnt rosewood and mulled wine, a delectable combination, and she could feel the tips of her fingers tingling. In his arms, everything felt right as if her favorite shoe in the market fit her foot perfectly.

He turned his head, his mouth even with hers.

The kiss was inevitable. His eyes glistened in the firelight; she moistened her lips. He moved closer, his lips the width of a feather from her.

Roger said, "You are so beautiful, Cinderella."

And with those five words, the dream vanished. She pulled away and leaped to her feet, spilling both of their drinks. Her nostrils flared. "What did you say?"

"I said you were beautiful."

She pointed at him. "You called me Cinderella."

"Did I? I hardly noticed."

Radiance's eyes bulged in indignation. "How could you? How could you call me that name?" Her lisp became pronounced. "Cinderella is the name my evil stepsisters called me when they wanted to shame me. How could you forget my name, the name my beloved mother gave me, in favor of that insult?"

Roger stood. "Honestly, Radiance, I do not know why I said it. I have not heard that name in years."

She stepped back. "Deep inside, you want me to be that slave, don't you? I'm not going to give in to your charms. To think how close I came."

She marched toward the stairs and slipped off her slippers at the bottom. Gripping them in her hand, Radiance declared, "I will not give you that excuse a second time."

She stormed upstairs, grasping her slippers like an animal she had choked to death, and once inside, slammed the door of the pink room. Radiance threw herself on the bed and cried—her body making a line through the heart shape. Weeping for several minutes, she hated herself for every tear that fell.

When she wiped her eyes, she spied a smaller version of her and Roger's portrait on the nightstand. She picked it up and studied it. He was dashing, and his eyes were filled with tenderness. If this rendition of him was as a husband, he adored her.

Shifting to her own depiction, Radiance imagined her portrait talking to her. "Don't fool yourself. You are Cinderella."

"I am Radiance," she whispered. "Never Cinderella."

"Cinderella or Radiance. Your name doesn't matter. You are still the true-hearted maiden of the Hartstones. If you lose Cinderella, you lose yourself."

Radiance knew she had overreacted when Roger had called her the wrong name. Clearly, he didn't mean it. She sat on the edge of her bed for a couple of hours, trying to decide whether to return to him.

In the end, she stood and snuck down the stairs. To her disgust, Roger was sprawled out over the edge of the couch, snoring. At first, she was upset that he had fallen asleep, but then she spotted the two empty bottles on the table next to him and the smashed glass in the fireplace. No, he had decided to drown his sorrows.

Radiance approached him, observing his chest rise and fall.

What if she kissed him now? If he didn't know, she could determine whether Hero's story was true without Roger knowing. She could also find out how kissing him would be. She leaned over, and her lips hovered over his. She pouted and remained there, just above him, for a minute, deciding.

Eventually, she straightened up, found a blanket, and covered him. Turning on her heel, Radiance returned to bed.

18 - ROCK, PAPER, DAGGERS

Sondra

Piper stood before our little group, grinning like a hamster on a wheel. Well, not a hamster on a wheel. That's not the simile I was going for. And you don't see hamsters grin often, do you? You know what I mean. He had the element of surprise, had us in his sights, and had us pinned against a literal wall. Wysdel and Lenore, Sinope and Rapunzel, and Hero and I stared back.

Piper surveyed us all in a regal manner, staring down his perfectly formed nose and square chin, and then waved away each but three of his guards. As he waved, I noticed his hands were nice too. Nice, but villainous.

The false king spoke in a loud voice. "And this is the

result of your many efforts. You failed at the Inn of Five, you failed at Halifax Manor, and you have united two at the Retreat, but they refuse to do what you proposed."

Hero flinched at Piper's surprisingly accurate summary of our adventure. But I wasn't going to let him get away with dismissing all our hard work. "They will kiss. They just need time."

Piper flashed a boyish-yet-manly grin that would melt the hearts of all his fans if he were a famous Hollywood actor. "Time is something, I'm afraid, you do not have. Even if you manage to lure the man you seek here to the toy shop in Tusk, they will not fall in love. Valencia and her husband were a mismatched pair from the beginning."

Did he just tell us where Valencia was? I think he did. How dumb was he?

Piper's eyes narrowed. "But you will not take him there, because I have decided, Hero, to let you think about your failure in a royal cell."

Oh, not that dumb.

Hero said, "We'll win. You'll see."

"This isn't a prophetic quest, Hero. You do not have the requisite skills or the pre-ordained hand of destiny guiding you on this occasion. Think about that as well as my previous offer, while you and your wife rot in prison."

Our adversary gestured for his golems to advance. The eyeless, human-shaped soldiers marched forward. I decided to pull the same trick as at the Inn of Five and dropped my disguise. "You wouldn't arrest your queen, would you?"

But the guards didn't halt, and Piper smirked. "I have warned them that a magician might take the guise of their queen. 'Wouldn't,' Sanders? Your contraction gave you away."

Cat's piss. Stupid contractions.

Piper snapped his fingers, and something descended from the sky. Hovering above us was a creature made of stone and shaped like a demon with bat wings. The thing was at least nine feet tall with a wingspan of fifteen. It squealed a piercing cry.

"This is Barnaby, my gargoyle commander. Wait for my command, my servant."

Before the gargoyle or the guards could reach us, Lenore turned into a bird and Wysdel drew her short sword. Hero reached down for rocks on the ground as I prepared a spell. Sinope grabbed Rapunzel's hand and ran for the shadows, but a guard flanked them before they could get away. We were surrounded.

The guards stepped forward as electricity crackled from my fingertips. Wysdel advanced on them, a gutsy move. She called, "I have the guards. Sanders, the gargoyle."

Hero shouted, "I know about you, Piper. I know how you used your musical abilities to rid the town of Hamelin of rats. And then when the mayor didn't pay you, you had all the children follow you into the side of a mountain."

Piper threw his arms out. "Halt. Hero, rumors imply you have a preternatural knowledge about our affairs. Knowledge of events you should know nothing about." The handsome villain strode forward, drawing the dagger that used to belong to my husband. "Leave the loudmouth to me. I have decided he shall go to the dungeons bleeding. Take them!"

The guards rushed us, and Sinope cast an incantation to sever one of the golem's hands. This gave our side an advantage. Wysdel parried another golem's slashing motion and kicked the creature in the kneecaps. Crack! It wouldn't be getting up anytime soon.

One guard grabbed Rapunzel. I detached my left fist and sent it flying toward the guard, punching him in the throat. The disembodied hand took him by surprise.

The gargoyle descended, so I took to the air, dodging his blows. His skin was made of stone. A fizz spell, electricity, and fire weren't going to be effective. What worked best on stone?

I flew over Piper and Hero. Piper had cornered my hubby and sliced his arm. Hero dodged the imposter's second blow, but I knew my husband wouldn't last long.

After I retrieved my hand, I flew in a loop to circle behind the gargoyle. The winged fiend swung his head, but I saw that Sinope had cast a quick spell to separate his fingers from his palm. The pebbles rained down on our enemies, bounced off the guard's helmets, but crowned the false king. So to speak.

"Nice one, Sinope!" I called.

Rocks! Yes, I know what works with rocks. Rock-paper-scissors. Paper wraps rock!

I cast a giant nylon canvas and sprang it at my pursuer. It wrapped around the gargoyle's eyes and wings, forcing it to the ground. When the monster hit the soil, I created multiple tent spikes to pin it to the ground. Success!

But my defeat of the creature was not enough. Initially, we had countered Piper's welcoming party, and they were off-guard at the resistance. But when a golem stabbed Wysdel in the gut despite Lenore clawing at its head, my stomach dropped. The golems were too relentless to be brought down by a bunch of amateurs. The only one still holding her own was Sinope who cast sparkling lights in front of Piper's eyes.

The so-called king pointed at Rapunzel's companion. "Kill the sprite! Worthless little buggers."

A golem grabbed Sinope and pulled back his sword to pierce her stomach. But as he tried to bring the weapon forward, he found he couldn't because Rapunzel's hair fully encircled his wrist. She leaned back, holding him from completing the thrust.

Yes, I know. We just said Rapunzel's hair was short, not long. But her tresses elongated before my eyes, pooling around her feet. Apparently, she could lengthen and shorten her hair at will. And control it, too.

Go, Rapunzel! I knew she belonged with us!

"Kill the little girl if you must." Piper pointed at Rapunzel. "She is not important."

I swung my attention to where he and Hero tussled. Piper had Hero pinned against the wall with one hand, and the other was thrusting forward with Hero's knife. I had to think of something quickly or he was going to die. In my anxiety, my mind went blank.

Then the knife seemed to take on a mind of its own and swung away from Hero. I couldn't explain it, and my husband looked shocked too. I thought Sinope had thrown a spell, but she was busy with another golem. What had just happened?

I flew to Hero to protect him, but Piper tried to stab Hero again. This time, the big bad's arm stopped in mid-air, and instead of completing its trajectory, reversed it. Piper dropped the weapon and its point sliced open his leg on the way down.

I arrived at Hero's side as his opponent cried out in pain. Point down, the knife stuck into the ground next to Piper.

"How did you do that?" I asked my husband.

"I didn't. But you need to get us out of here. Now!"

Teleport. I needed to do it correctly this time and get us far away from here. I swallowed down my fear. "Here goes nothing."

Hero clenched his jaw as I completed the spell. I had envisioned the people I wanted to transfer and the clearing of Rapunzel's tower as the destination, but instead, we found ourselves standing in a dark enclosure. I waited for my eyes to adjust.

"They are in here!" shouted a rough voice.

When I could finally discern my surroundings, I realized where we had ended up. We stood in the pen with the prisoners. A dwarf was pointing at us. "Here!" he shouted again.

"Grundymail, shut up!" yelled Wysdel, holding her hands over her abdomen. She knew him.

I hadn't teleported us far, but a quick count of noses told me I had left no one behind. Graddock stood next to Hero. I put my hands together and pulled them apart as if I were executing a move in the cat's cradle game. "I'll get us out of here."

The sound of pipe music floated through the cracks in the walls, and my head exploded in agony as if a rose vine with thorns had encircled my brain. I couldn't think and clutched my skull.

Hero grabbed my arm and said something, but I couldn't focus through the searing pain. I screamed as I pictured the vines, digging like worms into the tissues that made up my brain matter. If this continued, I was going to faint.

Hero put his hands over my ears, and the pain subsided. He mouthed a question to me which I thought was "better?" and I nodded. While the pain lessened, the faint music from outside shifted to a different tune. Then voices whispered inside my cranial cavity about how nice it would be to be queen, and I saw myself wrapped in Kris Heaven's arms in a bed larger than my bedroom. I felt wonderful, smelled even better. Something told me this was what living in paradise felt like.

The music stopped, and I shook my head. The musician called from outside. "How about it, Sanders?"

I gritted my teeth. A dreamboat he might be, but I was going to sink that ship right now. By God, I'd teleport us as far away as possible from here with Graddock.

Hero's hands were still over my ears, but I removed them. "I think it's over."

"Wysdel, do you need to be healed?"

Our companion stepped into the darkness. "The man's blade barely touched me."

That was not what I saw.

"Sanders, get us out of here," said Hero. "Teleport us anywhere."

"Gladly."

I pictured all of us standing inside of the pen and pictured another section of Kingdom in the Forest of Death. Carefully, I formed the spell, but the pipes started up again outside, distracting me. We disappeared and then reappeared behind the golems and Piper.

For the moment, everyone was stunned. My mind was like the crawl of stock market prices you see on the bottom of financial shows on TV, but instead of numbers, four-letter words marched across. The music continued, louder now, and Hero grabbed my arm in alarm.

I looked around in a panic. Piper and golems hadn't noticed us yet, but that was just a matter of time. Wysdel held her stomach, Lenore flapped her wings around, Sinope and Rapunzel were fear-shocked by the sudden teleportation and seemed frozen solid. I tried to quiet my brain and cast the spell. I'm a top-notch scientist, but I'm still learning the ways of magic.

Sinope made a flicking motion with her fingers and conjured a pebble out of the air. The small stone rushed forward and knocked Piper in the back of the neck. While it probably didn't hurt as much as a bee sting, it stopped Piper from continuing with his disorienting music.

The false king turned, his face contorting in rage. "They are behind us!"

I pushed as much out of my mind as I could and pictured the Forest of Blood. We wanted to go to Tusk, which bordered that forest. I said the incantation, and then we disappeared. Success. Well, almost. Admittedly, we ended up in the Forest of Blood, but "ended up" may not be the best description of how we landed there.

The Forest of Blood

19 - TEARFUL SEPARATIONS

Harold

We landed in the Forest of Blood, but Sanders had teleported us sideways. We all appeared as if we were levitating on our sides three feet above the ground. Then as the spell ended, gravity took over and forced us to the ground. The air left my lungs when I smacked the forest floor, preventing me from cursing. Everyone else either cried out or grunted when they landed.

I stood, using a hand to steady myself against a tree and brushed dirt off the side of my pants. I glared at Sanders. Seated on her rump, she lowered her head. "I'll get better."

My wife shook her head as if restoring her equilibrium and then flew to Rapunzel's side. "How are you? Okay?"

"I'm adapting." Rapunzel opened her mouth and winked with one eye.

Graddock examined our surroundings. "We're in the Forest of Blood. Eft-end."

Eft meant "east" in Kingdomese. I'll give my wife this—she'd teleported us over half of this world. Her distance was improving, but her technique still left something to be desired.

Wings extended, Sanders lifted into the air and darted over to Wysdel. The freedom fighter had an arm around her stomach but no expression of pain on her face. My wife started conjuring. "You're hurt. Let me see if I can help."

"I am fine." Wysdel shook her head. "Do not worry."

After Sanders' teleportation misfire, Wysdel clearly didn't trust my wife to heal her. I can't say I blame her either. I hadn't seen what had happened, but the wound must have been superficial.

Rapunzel slid her hand up and down the bark of a tree resembling an elm, nearly hugging it. "These trees are different from any I've seen before. And so many exist, in all directions."

Graddock rose to his feet and observed us. "Who are you people, and why did you bring me here?"

Sanders turned away from Wysdel. "Hero, will you do the honors?"

While Graddock leaned against a tree, I explained Piper's curse and the real events of Kingdom. I focused on Queen Valencia and how he had fallen in love with her. His scowl deepened through the discourse. I had talked without him interrupting until I mentioned his marriage.

Graddock held up his hand. "Are you telling me I wed a queen, and I am royalty?"

"You're not royalty, but you married a queen, yes. You declined taking the title of prince, thinking yourself unworthy of the honor."

Stone-faced, Graddock stood back while I finished my story. At the end, he crossed his arms. "I do not believe you and do not know what you are scheming. Thank you for saving me, but good day."

"I know this is hard to believe, but we need you," I said. "If you kiss the queen, you break the spell and both of you will remember who you really are."

Graddock turned to leave. "Yes, a queen of Kingdom will want to kiss someone like me, a loyal soldier to the odious former king. I practically live at the Thirsty Wench."

He was leaving, and I couldn't stop him. Not with the truth, so I had to switch to another tactic. "You owe us."

Graddock halted, only one side of him facing me. His left eye glanced my way. "I owe you nothing."

"We freed you. Your enemy is Piper, and so is ours. He wants us dead, and after seing us with you, he'll want you dead too. You're better off with us than on your own. I'll say it again. You owe us for releasing you from that prison."

Though a bit of rogue, Graddock had some sense of honor. I was poking his pride hard.

"What do you want?" Graddock heaved a sigh. "And I will not entertain joining you and completing this fool's quest."

Crap. His idea was exactly my proposition. What could I do to keep him with us?

"Escort us to the queen," said Sanders. "We just learned her location because Piper is an idiot and gave it to us. We need to find a toy shop in Tusk. I teleported us as close to Tusk as I dared."

Graddock considered Sander's suggestion, rubbing his chin.

Sanders flew over and hovered in front of him. "Meet her. You can do that much, right? And then make up your mind about her."

Graddock held out his hand. "Alright, we have an accord."

Sanders cast a spell to separate her hand from her wrist, enlarged it to human-size, and held out her hand. Graddock didn't seem fazed by the gesture, and he clasped my wife's palm. Though her hand was disconnected from her wrist, my wife winced.

Wysdel urged us to leave, worried the surrounding area was a common habitat of hobgoblins and giant bats. We journeyed east toward the city of Tusk and made camp for the night about two miles within the forest's edge. Everyone except Graddock agreed to take turns watching in pairs for the night. He created a makeshift hammock eight feet in the air away from the rest of us. Apparently, he didn't trust any of us while he was sleeping, preferring to be far off the ground.

Sanders and I took the last watch near dawn. I nudged my pretty wife to wake her up, but she only mumbled something about Kingdom needing to discover coffee. I let her sleep and kicked dirt over the campsite to ensure the fire was out, though I was certain it had extinguished hours earlier. Stirring the ashes with a stick, I reflected on our progress... or lack of it. Penta at the Inn of Five—strike one. Beauty at Halifax Manor—strike two. Cinderella at Radiance's Retreat— three strikes, I'm out. And now Valencia at Tusk, and Helga in a convent in the Marsh of Wishes. How was I going to convince —?

"Hey, handsome, how about I shrink you and we make out in the tulip heads?"

I turned around to see Sanders, pixie-sized, grinning from ear to ear. She raised her left brow playfully.

"That's what you're thinking right now?"

She put her hands on her hips. "I'm joking, Droopy Dan. Why the long face?"

I toed the remains of the fire with my shoe. "I don't know, Sanders. Perhaps we should head home."

"What? Why?"

"Maybe the situation is under control around here," I replied. "And I've only made it worse. Now it's going to be twice as hard to convince Penta since she thinks she's already in love. I didn't bowl over Beauty with my words. And I haven't heard any news from Roger and Cinderella."

JIM DORAN

Sanders waved a hand at me. "Maybe you haven't heard from Roger and Cinderella because they're together in the tulips?" She smirked.

"I doubt it. I wish I had a way to communicate with Sylvia."

Sanders grew to her normal height. "What's the first thing Cinderella and Roger are going to do when they kiss, Hero?"

"Find us."

"No, they're going to find their children and make sure they're safe. Then maybe, they'll find us. Perhaps that's why we haven't heard from them yet."

She was right. "When we started, everyone thought I was the guy to convince the queens to kiss their princes. I'm not so sure anymore. Maybe we shouldn't interfere. Maybe a queen dies because of my overconfidence."

"Or maybe you get over yourself and do your job." Sanders took my hand. "I believe in you, and so do they. They just don't know it yet."

She released my hand and swung her arm around me. I rested my head on her shoulder. "I'm not the man I used to be."

"And that's a good thing," she replied. "Because you're wiser. Now hush, a sunrise is coming, and we shouldn't miss it."

After a breathtaking sunrise, we started to wake everyone up but found Lenore missing. I was sure she had been sleeping when I woke up, and we started to call for her. As we did, Lenore, in her raven form, swooped into our campsite and landed, transforming into a human woman. She beamed with excitement and approached Wysdel. "I have wonderful news."

Lenore took a breath. "I was scouting Tusk when I ran into a blue jay who had been at Halifax Manor. She informed me that Beauty kissed Grr."

Wysdel hugged Lenore. "We have one! Finally."

Sanders jumped up and joined in the celebration by embracing Lenore. When they released each other, she hooked

188

her arm around mine. "See? There you go. Success!"

"I wasn't there. Maybe I had nothing to do with it."

"Oh, Hero." My wife turned back to Lenore. "When are they joining us?"

Lenore and Wysdel parted, and the were-raven addressed my wife. "They won't be. Beauty wants to gather reinforcements in Faerie Forest first. She and Grr are headed there."

"Did she thank us for stopping by and putting the idea in her head?" asked Sanders.

Lenore faltered. "No. I'm not sure our visit had a hand in their pairing."

I kicked dirt into the circle of charred wood, but this time, not to put out a fire.

Sanders nudged me. "You gave them the idea, Hero."

Wysdel caught on to my frustration. "I'm sure you did. Likely, she would have ignored Grr if you hadn't made an impression and said...whatever it was you said."

Nice try, Wysdel, but I wasn't buying what she was selling. You'd think with one of the queens restored I'd feel better about being here, but I felt worse.

Turning, Wysdel put a hand on Lenore's shoulder. "Lenore, I want you to fly to Faerie Forest and meet Beauty and Grr at Sparkles Pond."

"Sparkles Pond?" asked Rapunzel.

Rapunzel, Sinope, and Graddock were all listening to the news with varying levels of interest, but at the mention of Sparkles Pond, Rapunzel perked up.

Wysdel nodded. "Yes, my friends there need reinforcements, and Lenore will arrive well before any of the rest of us could."

"Not Sinope," declared Rapunzel. "She's fast."

Sinope turned her head sharply toward her sister. "Why would I go to Faerie Forest?"

Rapunzel took her hand. "Isn't that where your brother said your birth parents lived? They have a nice sídh near the border of the forest. You'll be escorted to Sparkles Pond with someone who knows the way. You must go with Lenore."

Sinope grew as large as Rapunzel. "I told you that I'm not leaving you!"

Rapunzel threw her arms around Sinope. "But you must. I'll feel sad if you don't. You must be reunited with your family, as I will be with mine."

Sinope pointed at me and Sanders. "But they don't know your parents."

Rapunzel smiled. "They know something. I must go with them, but I'll see you again. I promise, Sinope."

The argument dragged on another ten minutes but eventually Rapunzel convinced the sprite. Grudgingly, Sinope agreed to go to the pond, but on one condition. Sinope flew up to Sanders. "You will protect her? The rest of them are human, but you are a pixie. We small creatures must stick together, and the pixies have always been friendly with sprites."

Rapunzel stepped forward. "No one can take your place, Sinope."

Before Sinope could answer, Sanders broke in. "I won't take Sinope's place. But you can rely on me, Rapunzel."

I was surprised and unsure why Sanders sounded so confident. She looked over at me. "Him too."

"Yes, I am sort of a princess protector."

Sanders rolled her eyes. "Hardly, but together, we're quite a team."

Tearfully, Rapunzel turned to Sinope and hugged her as tightly as a human girl can logistically hug a sprite. We walked a distance away to allow the two of them a private conversation. They weren't the only ones speaking in low tones, however. Lenore and Wysdel huddled together, whispering.

They broke off, and Lenore approached us. "After Sinope and I leave, Wysdel would like to speak with you two alone."

I leaned back. "Why didn't she ask us herself?"

"Do you trust her?" Lenore asked.

The jury was out as far as Wysdel was concerned. A freedom fighter suddenly appears to Sanders and has all the information we need? Both Sanders and I had witnessed a golem stab her, yet she didn't die. Was her "wound" all for show to gain our trust?

I returned my attention to Lenore. "Do you know if spies exist in the resistance movement?"

Lenore grimaced. "That is one of the reasons she wants to talk to you alone. But the main reason, you'll want to hear."

"I trust you," I said. "So we'll meet with her."

When Sinope and Rapunzel returned, a tearful Sinope followed our were-raven friend into the air. She waved at Rapunzel and then gave us a significant glance. I interpreted it as "if she comes to harm, I'll hunt you down." With a flourish, Sinope flew off to the north, racing after Lenore.

Graddock stretched his back. "If the sentimental partings are over, shall we be on our way to Tusk?"

Nervously, Wysdel cleared her throat. "I need one more conversation with Hero and Sanders."

Graddock sighed then pulled out a sword Lenore had left behind. "Very well. I suppose I am not in a hurry. I shall guard the lass Rapunzel but make it quick."

Sanders and I walked with Wysdel further into the forest. Her eyes darted back and forth. "I must make sure no one else can hear us."

Wysdel strolled forward with purpose while my wife and I followed cautiously. After a few minutes, Wysdel stopped, glanced around, and folded her hands.

"Please don't hate me," she said.

I stepped back. "Why are you using contractions? Kingdomers don't use contractions."

Wysdel held up her hand. "We're beyond that now. The resistance movement has spies, mostly Travelers who were stuck here. Piper has promised to send them home if they infiltrate us. He's recruited other Kingdom residents, too. Enemies of the queens. I can't be sure of anyone, especially

Sinope, and meeting her prevented me from telling you the truth. But now that she's gone..."

She must be a Traveler to speak in contractions, I guessed, but who? She wasn't Alice, and I didn't know many other people in Alice's guild.

Wysdel reached up into the lace she wore around her neck and pulled it away from her throat. A small twig was stitched into its lining. With the tiny stick away from her throat, Wysdel announced in a birdsong voice. "I'm so glad to see you two."

That voice could only belong to one person. If I removed her overbite, dyed her hair black, and reshaped her face into a perfect oval, I knew exactly who it was.

"Snow White!" yelled Sanders.

20 - INTERMEZZO 2

Fifteen Years Earlier

The priest at Old Saint Mary's hadn't given Penta shelter as she had expected. He had instead sent her to this place called a station. A station to her was a guarding place for sentries, not this busy room, and it didn't seem like a better place than the cathedral. The uniformed people here had asked her many questions, the same ones, over and over. Clearly, they hadn't believed her story. And magic? They claimed magic didn't exist. Absurd! Magic was everywhere here. Yet, these *officers* absolutely refused to acknowledge its existence.

This place, this police station, was no refuge. She sat on a chair by a table in a room with a glass wall, listening to the sound of woodpeckers again. Not truly woodpeckers at all, but people tapping little squares on flat objects. Someone had called them "laptops," a word she had never heard before today.

People in this region used a lot of unfamiliar words—gun, narcotics, trafficking. She prayed to calm herself. *Oh, dear Creator! Would you intervene and cancel your adversary's spell so as to return me to my father's smithy?* Closing her eyes, she pictured her father dropping his tools, smelling of iron ore, and turning toward her. He would open his arms and flash his mostly toothless smile. His hearty voice would call out "Come here, Penta."

Penta slumped in her chair. Her adversary wouldn't make it so easy. Her plan was to find a magician, despite everyone claiming magic didn't exist. It must. She'd prove magic existed here, find a mage, and ask her to cast a spell that would transfer her home. Despite what these people said, this world had more magic than Kingdom as evidenced by their laptops and squad cars. Locating a spell-wielder would be easy once they acknowledged magic existed.

She looked up and ice ran through her veins.

The demon—the one who had sent her here—stood outside her glass room, staring in at her. The infernal creature smiled as their eyes locked. He was here! She was trapped unless she married him.

She prayed, her lips pouring forth words she had memorized since she was a small girl. Creator Father. Ruler of All. Your name alone reigns above all else. Your Kingdom come. Your—

Her adversary shook his head, cutting short her prayer.

No one in the station noticed him. This seven-foot tall, horned creature in Kingdom clothes, stood outside her small room. The people in the station all walked around him. One woman in blue headed straight for him, reading something in her hands. Instead of running into him, she went out of her way to circumvent a collision. They must accept him here!

Pointing, the demon's fingernail touched the glass. Penta followed his eyes to her hands. Her palm and fingers were restored. The demon had given back her hands. Holding them up, she examined them, but they dissolved into her stumps once more. She knew the price to restore her hands. No, she wouldn't do it! She rubbed the ends of her wrists against each other. She would never succumb to his demands.

"You're trembling, dear."

She had been so transfixed by her hands, she hadn't noticed the woman in the doorway. Older than Penta by at least two of her lifespans, the woman tugged on her blue-gray jacket as she entered. The woman had silver glasses and a small nose. Penta's eyes zeroed in on her lapel where a small silver cross caught the light. That same symbol was in the cathedral, a holy shape in this weird world.

The woman removed her coat, revealing a white blouse with purple flowers, nothing like the uniforms the police officers wore. Placing her coat around Penta's shoulders, the woman asked, "Is that better?"

Penta nodded. Her eyes returned to the devil, but he was gone.

"Can you speak?"

Penta whispered, "Yes."

"What is your name, child?"

She licked her lips. "Penta Emily Corden."

"What a pretty name," said the woman. "I am Sister Joan. I'm glad to meet you."

Penta didn't say anything, her eyes wandering around looking for her nemesis. Sister Joan took a seat next to her, but not too close. "Father Francis sent me. He's worried about you."

The priest at Old St. Mary's! Maybe he would be useful after all.

The woman placed a sheet of paper on the table next to her. "You told Officer Palmer that you were from another world and that you needed to return home. This happened because the devil asked for your hand in marriage, and your father..." Here the nun swallowed but continued. "...removed your hands and gave them to him."

Should she trust this woman? The sisters in Kingdom

were holy, but some nuns worshiped demons.

Penta nodded.

Sister Joan folded her hands on her lap. "Tell me, Penta, did you take anything recently? A pill...or something else? I won't tell the police, I promise."

Penta shook her head.

"Did someone offer you a drink? They poured it and gave it to you?"

What an odd question. "No."

"You said your father lives in your home world? And since you outsmarted the devil, the devil was furious and sent you here from a place called..." Sister Joan consulted the page. "Kingdom? Is that right?"

"Yes."

Sister Joan said, "Penta, do you like to read? Have you ever read fairy tales?"

"I do not know what a fairy tale is."

Sister Joan ignored her answer. "Perhaps where you live now isn't like what you've read in stories. Perhaps you wish you could live in a story? Or maybe, you never had a home, and someone has been introducing you to adults for a night. Those people...are they your devil?"

Tired of these questions, Penta asked, "All I want is a spellcaster who can take me home. Do you know one?"

A voice growled to her left, out of her view. "No magic exists here, girl!"

Penta started at the interruption and turned to the voice. The devil stood there, an arm's reach away. She tumbled out of her chair and the woman caught her before she hit the floor. The nun asked, "What is it, dear? What's frightened you?"

The devil folded his arms. "They won't believe you. They're going to lock you in a dungeon for the rest of your life."

No! Losing her father and trapped in this odious place? This couldn't be happening. She had been pure-hearted and followed the path of the righteous.

The tears welled in Penta's eyes. "Help me! Help me!"

Sister Joan started to rise. "I'll call a doctor."

"Yes." The devil's eyes glinted. "Bring a doctor. They are the ones who judge and send people like you away."

Penta stood but stepped away from her adversary. "No doctor. Nothing is ailing me."

Lines appeared in the woman's forehead. "Perhaps I should anyway."

How could this nun not see that horrible creature in the room with them? How could she not hear him? "You do not see him, do you?"

The devil curled its lip into a grin.

The nun turned to look to the corner of the room where Penta was staring. "No one's there, dear."

The devil grew in height until his head touched the ceiling. "That's right. Even those who should sense me cannot in this world. They do not know how much I have conditioned them to overlook me. The people in this world have made bad choices, all in the name of good, to a point where they don't know right from wrong. This is *my* world, Penta, and you are trapped here for the rest of your life. The only way out is to marry me."

The devil only wanted to marry her to prevent Penta becoming a queen. Such a creature could never love anyone else. She turned to Sister Joan. "Please, I beg of you to look again. Please."

Sister Joan nodded. "If you return to your seat, I will look."

With all her nerve, Penta stepped toward the eldritch being, righted her chair, and sat.

At first, Sister Joan gave a passing glance, but something caught her eye and the devil frowned. Suddenly, the nun's eyes widened, and she stepped back, gasping.

Maybe...just maybe. "Do you see him?"

Sister Joan's lips looked bloodless. "Something's here."

The devil shrank back into himself, trying to obscure

his presence, but the nun had the scent and the more she focused, the more she trembled. Sister Joan leaned away from the foul creature, and at the same time swung her arm around Penta. "Go away. I don't know what you are, but in the name of Jesus Christ, I command you to go away."

The devil snarled at Penta. "I will have your hand in marriage."

But Sister Joan replied, raising her voice. "I compel you to leave at once!"

The demon disappeared, and Sister Joan's shoulders lowered. She turned and embraced Penta. Penta buried her face in the woman's chest and cried. The nun rubbed her back. "You're coming with me. I'll pull every string I have, but I'm not leaving you alone with whatever that was."

The Forest of Blood

21 - THE WATERFALL
OF RENEWAL

Harold

Stunned, I observed the youngest sister queen with my mouth hanging down. The revelation, however, didn't keep Sanders from speaking her mind. "Of course! You called me Sondra when we first met. You weren't here when my name changed to Sanders. I should've known."

Snow White untwined her fingers from the lace around her collar and reached for us. Both my wife and I stepped forward into an embrace she was known for. And if I'd had any doubts before about Wysdel's identity, I had none now. The loving gesture was everything I remembered of the fairest in the land. We were in the presence of a Kingdom queen and legend.

She spoke with both of us pressed against her. "I'm so sorry I couldn't tell you before, but I never had a chance without people listening in. Sanders, I wanted to tell you but thought it better to wait when we reunited with Hero."

Because Sanders would've blurted it out when we came together in Town. Snow White was being nice, but she knew my wife well.

When she released us, I swayed unsteadily on my feet. "But why the voice-changing twig and the disguise? No one remembers you from before."

Snow White touched her face. "'Tis not a disguise at all. This is my face now. In fact, the false Planet has copied my technique to alter her appearance as well."

Sanders blinked. "This is why the queen resembles Planet even when viewed through tears?"

"Same as me," assured Snow White. "She and I have had a spell cast on us to remold our faces into a different shape. The perfect disguise is not a disguise at all."

"But why?" I leaned to the side as if examining a work of art. "I have so many questions."

"Allow me to put the twig back in place." Snow White adjusted the lace. "Let's rejoin the others and I will explain further on the way to Tusk when the others are out of earshot."

We returned to the camp and found Graddock and Rapunzel ready to travel. The rogue knew the most direct way and led our group through the forest. He estimated we would make Tusk before nightfall.

The trees in the Forest of Blood were not as densely packed as in its center, allowing for a slightly easier journey. We found a well-trodden path of branches and multi-colored leaves.

Snow White, Sanders, and I allowed ourselves to fall behind to continue our conversation. Snow White eyed Rapunzel skipping alongside Graddock ahead. "I believe we're far enough behind where they can't hear us now."

"Yes, spill it. What's going on?" I asked.

"I should start with how I survived the aging curse when I sailed away from Kingdom." Snow White caressed a white tree trunk as she passed it. "If you recall, Valencia spoke of a waterfall that could lift any curse, and she used her good-fortune ability to point me in the right direction. I found that waterfall."

I ducked under a branch. "How about Dear?" Dear was Snow White's true love who contracted the curse to accompany her in her journeys.

Snow White gulped. "No, he died before I made it there." Tears formed in her eyes and she wiped them away.

Taking a deep breath, she continued. "The waterfall is called the Waterfall of Renewal, and it cured me, but at a cost. I lost my memory when I emerged from the water."

"Jeez." Sanders shrunk and took to the air in her pixie form. "Is losing your memory the new thing in Kingdom?"

Snow White avoided an exposed root in the road. "This was different. I couldn't remember who I was. A month passed before my sister queens found me but kept my return a secret. How my memory was restored and who did it is another story, but it ended with me secretly marrying my second true love, after Dear."

Sanders' eyes bugged out. "Another prince in Kingdom?"

"No. Another long tale, but my husband cannot be a prince of Kingdom." Snow White giggled. "The queens and I agree on that point. For love, I abdicated the throne, leaving all the residents of Kingdom—with only a few exceptions—with the impression I was dead. This was years ago, and we've settled down on a farm with my two daughters–"

"Two?" asked Sanders.

Snow White raised two fingers.

"Do they resemble the before-you, or the after-you?" Sanders floated backward in front of our friend. "I'd be curious whether the magic works at an epigenetic level."

I gave Sanders a sidelong glance. "Save your disturbing

scientific questions for later. Go on, Snow."

Snow White patted the twig on her lace. "Piper's spell affected me in the same way it affected the queens. I was at home when he cast the spell on my sisters. I forgot all about them, thinking I was a commoner. Since Piper didn't know I existed, however, he couldn't prepare a new history for me. Memories of my husband, our wedding, our children, all remained, just without my sisters. After a day of chores, I kissed my husband goodnight and he and I remembered everything."

"True love's kiss." I waggled my eyebrows.

"Indeed. This is how Lenore and I knew it would work." Snow White caught a cottonwood seed in the air between her fingers. "After that, as Wysdel the resistance fighter, I started recruiting people who weren't born in Kingdom. We began hanging the signs about Snow White to attract more people who know the truth. I've sent people all over Kingdom looking for my sisters. And I had a feeling you'd show up one day, Hero. I kept Lenore on lookout."

"Fat lot of good my showing up has done you so far," I said.

Pouting, Snow White blew the cottonwood at me. "My little skyward sweeties, the birds, have told us Beauty and Grr are reunited. Sanders has connected with Celeste."

"But we haven't even approached Helga or Valencia yet. And Cinderella and Roger—"

"Are together," interrupted Snow White. "'Tis only a matter of time before those lovebirds kiss."

Floating backward in front of us, Sanders crossed her arms. "You didn't see them."

"I know my sister." Snow White made her eyes widen like Cinderella's, and then she rolled them. "I've seen her upset with Roger, but she loves him with all her heart."

"But then there's Penta," I said. "Lenore told us not to worry, but all the queens must kiss their true loves to break the curse on everyone else. Penta has no true love."

Snow White peered to the south. "I've come up with a plan. More than one way exists to break the curse, Hero, even as strong as the one Piper cast."

I scratched my head. "Do you have some magic artifact in the queens' vaults?"

"Many, but none that would break this curse, or I would've tried to obtain it. No, with Penta, our path leads to the water. We must restore Valencia's and Helga's memories, and then convince Penta to go to the Waterfall of Renewal. The same waterfall that removed my curse."

Sanders floated back through a cobweb and then dusted herself off. "Do you think it will work?"

Snow White paled slightly. "It must. Otherwise, Penta is lost. But we need Valencia because her luck will navigate us there, and Helga is the best ship captain in Kingdom."

"That's why Lenore spoke about three queens restoring Penta." From her hair, Sanders pulled a strand of webbing that stuck like taffy.

"But we've been working on the wrong ones." I kicked dirt off the trail. "We have you, Beauty, and possibly Cinderella."

Snow White chirped, "Cheer up, Hero. Beauty has already come up with a plan to raise an army. Her ingenuity is only matched by her courage. And Cinderella? She's our matchmaker sister. With her on our side, Helga and Valencia don't stand a chance."

Sanders brightened. "You're going to tell Sylvia too, I assume?"

"Though she's a dear friend, I'd like to keep this from Sylvia. Doing so pains me, but the fewer people who know my former identity, the less likely someone will reveal it. So far, only the queens, their husbands, and my friends Rose Red and her husband Lol know. Because of the situation, I've revealed it to you two, but I'm stopping there for the sake of my family's privacy."

Sanders returned to her human form. "She's going to be

pissed at you, Snow White."

"This is what I mean." Snow White thrust out her jaw. "Don't call me Snow White. For the rest of the time together, I am Wysdel." She broke off and looked around. "Now, we should hurry to Tusk. No one else must know about this. When we succeed, I want to return to my farm as Wysdel, matriarch of the Spring family. Will you keep my secret?"

We both immediately agreed.

Snow White—em, Wysdel—placed a hand on my shoulder. "And will you keep this out of your next novel?"

"On that," I replied, "I make no promises."

We continued our journey through the forest, and when the sun was directly overhead, I found myself once again alone with Wysdel. When we passed another "Snow White Lives" placard hung from a branch on a tree, I bumped Wysdel with my hip at one of the signs, and she flashed a quick grin but whispered, "The signs bother me."

"In what way?" I asked.

Wysdel picked a burr off her skirt. "I abdicated, Hero. Everyone who is not a queen kisses their true love every day and does not remember. But I did. The magic in Kingdom still believes I'm a monarch." Her face drooped. "And I don't want to be. I thought I had given up that life for my comfortable family and farm."

I avoided a muddy patch along the way. "The fact you remembered has helped us, though. If you hadn't regained your memory, we wouldn't know how to break the curse."

Wysdel's shoulders slumped. "I suppose you're right. And I do want to have my sisters remember their lives as well. These adventures, though. Hero, the last one nearly killed me. I worry about this one."

Her words struck a chord in my heart. Would Wysdel be better off without us? Were we leading her to her doom?

Wysdel glanced over at my wife and Rapunzel who were chatting. "Another princess of Kingdom! What a delightful addition!"

"And with the perfect hair to match."

Wysdel giggled, then snorted. I had forgotten about her ugly snorting when she laughed. The abrasive sound was completely incongruous with her former beauty. Yes, she was Snow White for certain.

Wysdel brushed a lock out of her face. "This spell Piper has cast against my sisters and my niece Beauty is unforgivable, but he has also sinned against Kingdom and her people. His curse makes me furious. We must right this, but I've been struggling until you came. I feel better with you here."

"Nothing's certain, and I have a bad habit of someone dying on my adventures," I replied. "I'd like to have one where no one dies."

"Yes, I would like that too."

After we crossed the border of the Forest of Blood into the muddy plains leading to Tusk, Wysdel accompanied Graddock, attempting to persuade him to stay with us after we found his wife. I walked along with Rapunzel and Sanders. Sanders, in human form, reached for Rapunzel's hair. "May I touch it?"

Rapunzel's cheeks colored, but she nodded.

My wife pinched a strand through her thumb and forefinger. "I'd love to see if your hair grows when detached from your body."

"Always the scientist." I nudged my wife then turned toward the young girl. "With everything that has happened, I forgot to ask you about how you're able to control your hair growth."

She grabbed the ends of her hair and twisted it nervously. "Yes. Mother always told me not to do it unless I was attacked."

Sanders put her arm around the child. "You were

marvelous and brave. Unlike my husband who nearly had himself killed thinking he's a knight."

Rapunzel put a hand to her mouth to suppress a laugh.

"Oh, yeah?" I said. "You nearly killed us when you teleported us between Piper and his army."

Sanders lifted her chin. "An honest mistake. And I flew us out of there."

"But not on the ground!"

Rapunzel put her hands between us. "The two of you must start treating each other better. How do you get along with all this bickering?"

"Like this." I leaned down and planted a kiss on Sanders' mouth. "What do you think of that?"

Sanders fluttered her eyelashes. "I think that Kris Heavens is a better kisser."

"What?"

Before I could finish, she leaned forward and gave me a friendly but too-brief smooch.

Rapunzel brightened at our display of affection "When I first met you, I wasn't sure you were in love."

"Love is a funny thing." I swung my arm around Sanders. "Sometimes we tease each other to show our love for one another."

Sanders scratched her ear. "And sometimes, we're completely normal. Almost boring. We have jobs, a home, and a son."

"The two of you have a son?"

Sanders said, "Hard to believe, I know, but true. I miss Fitzie's little face."

"Boring sounds wonderful." Rapunzel's hair lengthened down to her waist. "I wish my life was boring sometimes. Parents, a home, maybe a family."

Sanders lowered her head. "I'm sure they miss you, Rapunzel."

"Then why have they not sought me out? When Mother Gothel died, they could have returned and rescued me!"

Sanders cradled Rapunzel's head in her shoulder, and I was amazed at how familiar my wife was with our youngest member, but they'd had a long talk alone earlier that day.

Sanders stroked the girl's hair. "They may have a reason. Rapunzel, don't worry about it. I've known you less than a couple of days and I think you're an amazing young lady. Anyone would be proud to call you their daughter. You have a very bright future ahead of you."

Rapunzel lifted her head and looked at Sanders. "Can you help me find them?"

"Your parents?"

"Yes. If we found them, then I would feel truly home. I would have a family and Sinope could come and visit with us. My life would be perfect."

We had no more time for side quests or after-the-epic-quest quests. "I don't know—"

Sanders interrupted me—an annoying habit of hers. "Of course we will."

Rapunzel brightened. I admit seeing her happy made me feel good, but I flashed a "what the hell" look at Sanders, who wrinkled her nose at me.

We approached Tusk at mid-afternoon.

22 - TENERAMENTE

With Beauty in the lead, a contingent of resistance fighters entered the grove near Sparkles Pond. The wood elves had revealed their destination the prior year for Valencia's birthday, but the queen had never visited the site. Now, when they pushed their way through a barrier of pine trees, the scene in the clearing confirmed they had arrived. Beauty uttered its name for Sinope's sake. "The Grove of Kor. Kor the Mystic was adept at infusing powerful magic into ordinary items. Two of his greatest accomplishments, his mystical sword and shield, are here."

Sinope raised a trembling finger. "Not there, I hope."

She pointed at a permeable wall of fire and ice pellets. The ice formed the outer ring—the fire, the inner. The flames reached up twenty feet where the ice pellets formed and dropped like missiles to the ground. Neither element consumed the floor of the grove, and neither fire nor water changed the condition of the other despite their proximity.

Lenore transformed back into her human form. "I never understood this legend. Why fire *and* water?"

Beauty found a strand of hair wrapped around her finger—one of her nervous habits. "This ice could freeze anyone with a touch, and the fire is all-consuming. Those who can withstand fire are often more susceptible to cold, and the reverse is true as well. I know of no species resistant to both."

Sinope gazed skyward. "I s'pose you can't fly over it."

"You'd be met with ice pellets and fire missiles," said Beauty.

Grr pounded his chest, indicating the word "I." "See the sword and shield in the center."

"Yes, every so often, you may catch a glimpse of it. Kor was a righteous magician, hoping his artifacts wouldn't fall into the hands of fiends. Legend says he constructed them to loan to those who won't abuse their power. We're fortunate the wood elves gave the location to the queens for Valencia's birthday—otherwise, we would never have found it."

Peering through the ice, Lenore asked, "What is so special about the sword and shield?"

Beauty's eyes glistened. "They raise armies. Now, I shall summon the guardian."

Striding forward, Beauty knelt before the barrier and kept her head bowed. "Great spirit guardians, I, Beauty Shaina Corden, lady of Halifax and queen of Kingdom, have come to borrow the treasure you protect. The land needs their magic."

Two giant-sized faces bulged from the ice and fire. As one, they spoke. "The price is steep, young quest-seeker. For only those who love may take what we possess, and even then, at great cost."

Beauty raised her head. "I understand Kor did not wish these gifts to be handed over to the undeserving. I assure you that I will use them only to defeat an evil magician who falsely calls himself a king."

The faces performed a quarter-turn to regard each

other. They appeared to be communicating silently. They nodded and turned back to Beauty. "We have judged you to be worthy. However, you must make an exchange."

Beauty stood. "I will pay anything for Kingdom."

The fire face said, "In place of the sword and the shield..."

"...you must ransom that which you love the most," finished the ice guardian.

Beauty curled her lip. "What do I possess that you desire? I will gladly give it to you."

Behind her, she heard someone...someone she knew all too well...thump his chest.

Jaw dropping, she turned around. Grr lifted his fist. "They mean—" and he struck his breast once more.

Beauty pointed back at the wall of ice and fire. "They require an item. A trade."

Grr shook his head. "They said 'ransom.'"

Twirling around and sucking in a breath, Beauty held her hands out, begging. "You do not refer to a person, do you?"

The heads said in unison, "He is sufficient."

"No! Not him!" Beauty pleaded, holding up her hands in supplication.

Grr came and gripped her hand. "They make sure you not delay returning weapons."

Beauty grabbed his other hand. "But I have no idea how soon we will overthrow Piper. You may starve."

Grr nudged a bag slung over his shoulder. "Have rations for three days. Long time without food."

"But Grr—!"

Grr leaned forward and kissed her, interrupting her in mid-sentence. "You rule Kingdom. Queen first. Friends second."

Knowing he was right, she pulled him in for a crushing embrace. "But true love, always."

The tears slipped out of her eyes. Could she forego the sword and shield of Kor? Not likely. They needed to quickly raise an army, and these weapons were the best means to do it.

Beauty pulled away then leaned in for a long, desperate kiss. She never wanted to let him go, but then forced herself to break away. Wiping her eyes, she stepped back.

Her ability, to surface the beauty within a living creature, flowed out of her and enveloped Grr. In seconds, her lover became a handsome Black man. His eyes were filled with emotion.

She laid her hand on his heart. "I love you."

"As do I you," he said.

Her breath hitched. This was the first time he had ever used the pronoun "I." Beauty had always suspected that for Grr using "I" was a step toward admitting his feelings, making himself vulnerable.

Grr sucked in a deep breath and turned toward the ice and fire. The guardians spoke at the same time. "Step forward both of you. Quest-seeker, take the artifact but leave your heart."

The wall of ice and fire parted like a curtain, and Beauty grabbed Grr's hand. They rushed through the opening and approached the gleaming silver sword and shield. The only crest on the shield was a large scripted "K."

Beauty turned to Grr and kissed him as if their separation were a final good-bye. The ice wall cleared its throat. She had a mind to tell it off! Instead, she grabbed the sword and shield and departed from the interior before she could change her mind.

As she stepped away, the ice and fire wall closed behind her and the steadfast suitor, Grr, raised his hand in a salute. "You are doing the right thing."

Taking the sword and shield didn't feel like the right thing. When the wall closed, however, Beauty realized she was on the hourglass, so to speak. She turned to Sinope. "Do you know the way to your home?"

Sinope, her complexion a paler purple and her jaw hanging open, only nodded.

"Very well. Thank you, friend sprite. I hope to meet you again."

Sinope bowed her head in reverence. "I'm staying. If what you did wasn't the act of a queen, then I don't know what it was. I'm at your command!"

Beauty made a gesture of appreciation. Her eyes then shifted to Lenore. "Do you still have the birdseed?"

"I do."

"We shall return to the Inn of Five. There, I will attempt to convince my mother she is a queen."

Lenore crossed her arms. "That didn't go so well for Hero."

"I shall be craftier."

When Radiance walked down the stairs in the morning, she paused at the bottom and peered into the massive fireplace room where she had stormed out on Roger the night before. He wasn't near the fireplace but across the room, facing the back garden. Roger stood with his back to her in front of a window with a spectacular view of Grok's Teeth. He was as still as a sentry, his hands folded behind his back. She considered slipping out of the chalet without saying good-bye, but she couldn't leave without saying something. Honor dictated she be the better person.

Radiance entered the room. With that pose, Roger could be a prince. The straightness of his shoulders and the rigidity of his body screamed regality. For a split-second, she imagined she was a queen, approaching her prince. What a lovely life that would be.

Too bad it wasn't reality.

She walked up next to him and stood by his side while Roger stared out of the window. He cleared his throat. "It is beautiful."

"We agree on that, at least."

Roger's placid face showed weariness. "I apologize from the depths of my soul. I did not call you that odious name because I think you are beneath me. I could never demean you in any way."

"I know."

The words escaped her lips before she could take them back. Clearly, he hadn't meant anything by the insult, and she had overreacted. She could take his hand now and continue where they left off. Why not? History, of course. If only Roger had found her soon after she left for the forest.

Roger turned his head and looked into her eyes. "You accept my apology?"

She met his gaze. "Yes."

They didn't speak for a half-minute. Radiance licked her lips. "I must go. I cannot return to that point in the past after I lost my slipper. What we almost did last night...I think I would have regretted it. I'm sorry. I wish I were the maiden you love, but I'm no longer her."

Roger's eyes darted to her hands. If he took them, if she felt his touch again, she wouldn't leave. She wanted him to gently hold her hand, but she knew he wouldn't. She read Roger's feelings in his eyes. He was letting her go though the sacrifice was breaking his heart.

"Separating again makes me sad, but I understand," Roger said. "We are no longer the friends at the well, or the couple at the festival. Too much time has gone by. But I want you to know one thing."

Radiance gulped, afraid of what he might say next. Roger's eyes softened and focused on hers. "I will always be grateful to you. You gave me meaning in my darkest hour. I have no better way to say 'I love you' than by saying that."

Radiance's head felt lighter than air, and she flushed. Deep inside of her, she wanted to kiss him, but her memories prevented it. She had to leave. Now! "Good-bye."

She turned and raced across the entry room and left the castle. While sprinting away, she recalled the nights of the festivals and leaving him behind while she rushed off. All because of a silly dress! If she had stayed and reverted into the slave girl he knew, he would've accepted her. True, he didn't try the slipper on her, but she didn't make it easy on him either.

Radiance proceeded across the bridge to the other side where Sylvia stood at the end. The birdwatcher spread out her hands. "Did you kiss him?"

Radiance shook her head. "I must be on my way."

Sylvia walked alongside her. Soon, Radiance spotted Pennilane in the distance. If she could reach Pennilane, the selkie would intercept Sylvia. Sylvia wasn't going to leave her alone. Radiance's mind screamed to hurry away; her heart whispered to return.

Sylvia wrung her hands. "Don't leave now. Give it more time."

Radiance didn't acknowledge Sylvia. Her companion hadn't said anything she didn't know. Yet Radiance's silence didn't deter Sylvia from trying again. "When someone loves you the way Roger does, you shouldn't run away. True love is a rare thing."

Radiance and Sylvia had reached Pennilane, and Radiance addressed Sylvia without looking at her. "Tell everyone good-bye."

Turning, she and Pennilane hurried off, leaving Sylvia behind. Pennilane stepped beside her, carrying her spear by her side. "You are making the right decision. He was not true to you in the past. Why would he be in the future?"

Eyes forward, Radiance marched along. "He would be true."

"He should have known the maiden at the festival was you. Overlooking you is unforgivable. As if your stepsisters were worthy! The shame of it."

"Please, Pennilane. Let's not discuss this any longer."

They advanced down the hill, but Radiance had an itch she had to scratch. She had to take one last look at the chalet. She halted and turned around, and the idea he had built this beautiful retreat in the mountains for her calmed her. The chalet, the painting and the signature, Roger's earnestness. She belonged here with him at Radiance's Retreat. *Radiance's Retreat*, not Cinderella's Retreat.

Something there...

The selkie took her arm. "Come, Slippers. He is not worth this. He is not a good man."

Radiance kicked a rock out of their path. "That is just it. He *is* a good man. He is a *wonderful* man."

"Perhaps for a different woman, but you deserve better. You will see. He will move on and marry another and forget about you."

Roger with another woman? Like a jarring note in a swirling symphony, the thought made her clench her fists. "He had better not court another woman!"

"But, Radiance, let him dally with another. They would both be beneath you. He—"

Radiance shook her head. "I cannot have it both ways. I must let him go, yet I cannot let him go. What am I to do?"

Pennilane put her hands on Radiance's arms and made the human woman face her. Her own whiskered face showed her compassion. "Let him go and return to the forest with me. You are safe there. The time has come, Radiance, for you to be yourself again."

Radiance reflected on this advice, and the truth in the simple statement resonated. She should be herself. Up to this point, she hadn't been, thinking of every reason to hate the one person in the world who loved her more than life itself. And she realized in that moment, too, that she had never stopped loving him. She was furious with him, wanted to spit when someone mentioned his name, but deeper down, in a central part of her, her love for him overflowed as the waterfalls behind her spilled over the mountainside.

Pennilane was right. She must be true to herself. She loved him, but more importantly, she forgave him for the lost time. She *was* the girl at the well. She *was* the maiden at the dance. And now, she would be the wife of her true love.

Radiance hugged the selkie. "You are right, Whiskers. I must be true. Not just to him, but to me."

Turning she ran toward the castle. Pennilane started after her, but Radiance had a good head-start. The selkie, carrying the spear, struggled to catch up. "But...let us discuss this."

Radiance threw her arms into the air. "No need. I love him!"

Sylvia watched her approach, grinning broadly after hearing Radiance's confession. Pennilane was on Radiance's heels, but Sylvia stepped in front of her, allowing the maiden to approach the bridge into the castle. As Radiance stepped onto the bridge, it widened and formed sides. Golden metal poles sprung from the sides, curved inward, and made arches overhead, covering the walkway. Plant vines entwined themselves around the poles and sprouted tulips, daffodils, and all varieties of colorful plants.

Radiance paused for a moment, and the realization hit her. *She* was doing this. Her longing for him, her desire to be in his arms, expressed itself in the beauty on the bridge. Smiling to the point where it hurt, Radiance again raced across the bridge and through the front door.

She found Roger remaining in the same position, standing by the window. He turned and emitted a cry of surprise as she crossed the room and threw herself into his arms, hitting him with such force that he stumbled backward against a wall. In less than a heartbeat, her lips met his and she kissed him hard.

Bliss and sweetness followed. She didn't care about Kingdom customs, or the past or future. The moment was right. Pure. She'd never before felt so confident in a decision.

Roger wrapped her in his arms, and she shut her eyes, enjoying the moment. The absorption of the kiss lasted briefly, and a moment later, *Cinderella* remembered everything.

Images flashed through her mind: Roger finding her in

the forest years ago, her coronation, her marriage, Piper and his flute. The memories marched along all at once, almost too much to bear, and her eyes flew open. She was tempted to break the kiss, and Roger pulled back, but Cinderella kept her lips on his. This was a kiss for the books, and she wasn't going to let it end prematurely. She reached up behind his head and kissed him the way she knew he liked, remembering exactly the way to do it. Cinderella saw her best friend, her prince, her husband, the father of her children, and her lover and adored every single role he played.

When Cinderella finally moved back, she and Roger stared at each other. Recognition shone in their eyes; they didn't need to ask each other whether they remembered. Cinderella put her fingers to her mouth. "The children!"

Roger clenched his jaw. "If something happened to them, I am going to kill Piper."

Cinderella set her hand on his chest. "No. Lenore told me their names and said they were being cared for in the royal city. I had no idea what she was talking about at the time, but she knew I'd think of them first after we kissed. We must go to them immediately."

"Indeed. And then I run a sword through Piper," growled Roger.

"Not yet. First, we join Hero and Sanders. We must make Valencia and Helga remember too. And Penta." Cinderella bit her lip. "Without a true love, Penta will need a different solution."

Roger's hands tightened on her shoulders. "And we must find Valencia's prince, Graddock, and Helga's prince, Danforth. That false king has separated them as well."

"Piper!" Cinderella's cheeks burned. "Oh! What I'm going to do to that man is unspeakable. You better talk sense to me for I'm considering torture."

"He'll be dead by my hand before you get a chance."

Cinderella released a long, shuddering breath then put a hand on his cheek. "When this is all over, promise me one thing."

"Anything."

"A night in the pink room." Cinderella smirked.

23 - TUSK

Sondra

Before entering Tusk, Wysdel reminded me of my disguise and requested Hero and me to appear as Rapunzel's parents. Her reason? "This might be best in the city." Wysdel believed ne'er-do-wells—I always wanted to use that word—wouldn't target her as much if they thought she was our daughter. I transformed into my Charlie disguise and hid any sign of pixieness from view. Holding Rapunzel's hand, I marched forward as we entered the city.

Truth to say, I worried about the young lady beside me. Rapunzel had grown up in isolation and had spent the last several years in a tower. A town can be overwhelming for someone unaccustomed to crowds. However, she was resilient beyond my expectations. She took in everything and savored the scene the way someone thirsty enjoys a drink from a clean spring. Rapunzel continued to mention how much Sinope would love the place, and she smiled at everyone and everything. The buildings, the streets, the crowds were all new to her, and she experienced everything tactilely. So much so that we had to apologize to a few people.

Truthfully, Tusk was new to me too, and I found it a bustling metropolis. Like a picket fence themselves, a ring of homes surrounded the inner city. The houses were stone-based with flat roofs, most of them of only one or two stories. They were ornate and colorful, with lush-though-contained grassy yards. Graddock, having been stationed here when he was in the king's employ, provided a history of Tusk and explained that the people who worked in the city lived here. He noted we had entered through the more prosperous part of the town.

After passing the suburb, as it were, we entered the downtown proper. This section was circular in layout, and all concentric roads led to a central point—a temple. The shops and other buildings were three or four stories, again made of sandstone or limestone, and decorated with corbels designed with fleurs-de-lis and curlicues. Ropes up, down, and between the buildings had buckets attached to them. The ropes moved on their own and delivered product to vendors. The constant activity made me imagine the city as a giant clock with gears and sprockets always in motion.

We followed a road toward the temple. Graddock said that Tuskians always used that structure as the starting point to one's destination when describing directions. Wysdel educated us about the Temple of Shaole as we made our way down a busy market street.

"The Temple of Shaole is the oldest structure in Tusk. Residents speak of different legends as to how it came to be, but they all agree that the two mammoth tusks at the temple's doors were made from a mysterious, giant boar. Many people worship in the temple. Some worship the Redeemer god, some, the One-Truism god, and still others Animus and other exotic gods. Above ground are several beautiful chapels. However, in its subterranean vaults, evil ministers practice dark magic and abominable creatures lurk."

I hugged Rapunzel closer. "Sounds like fun."

Wysdel eyed me. "The temple, and the town for that matter, attracts certain types of persons. Some honorable, some not." She sighed. "I am sorry to say many are poor."

As if on cue, several beggars approached us with dishes. The most heartbreaking sight, though, was when a biped creature with an orange-and-white cat's head and paws approached us and showed us an illustration, asking if we had seen the subject. Graddock responded negatively, and the cat-person slouched away, despondently.

"Poor felinorians." Graddock scratched his chin. "The Basilisk Battle last summer was the hardest on them."

Wysdel gritted her teeth. "The queens could have prevented that from ever happening if they had been in power at the time."

We rounded a corner and spied the top of the temple above the stores. The structure's shadow loomed over the other buildings the way a puppeteer hovers over a marionette. In only moments, we stood in the center of the village, and I was left speechless.

The temple reminded me of the Parthenon in Greece, but was larger and granite gray. The building's columns hid shadowed hallways, and I noticed one door that nearly blended into its wall. A half-dozen turrets sprouted from its roof, and all the windows were triangular and shaded a dark red. The window above the front door bulged from its edifice like a cyclops' eye. In the courtyard, a group of dwarf and troll children pelted each other with skulls, of which plenty were piled against the walls.

I whispered to Wysdel. "You've been underneath this place?"

Shuddering, Wysdel answered, "I've been down there only once. On that topic, I will say no more."

221

As we viewed the temple, Graddock stopped a two-headed giant fetching water. The massive creature gave directions to the only children's store in Tusk—Mangiafuoca's Toy Shoppe.

We turned north. The buildings in this section of the city looked more desolate and deserted. Ivy grew over many of the structures, and the stone forming statues and fountains was cracked or worn smooth. We passed people who wore their hats so low we couldn't see their eyes.

At one intersection, a pair of Black women in light mail and shields marched across our path. Their bucklers had a broken sword insignia painted on it. Eyeing us warily, they stopped and stepped aside. Wysdel nodded as we passed on. "Daughters of the Oracle. They are the self-appointed law in Tusk."

Their eyes never blinked as we crossed the street. "Can we trust them?"

Graddock cleared his throat. "The Daughters and Sons of the Oracle are great warriors and live by their own code. As long as we do not break the law, they shall leave us be."

"The queens and the Daughters and Sons had an agreement as well," added Wysdel. "They had great respect for each other."

Rapunzel walked between Hero and me. I noticed a door with a severed pig's head nailed to it.

"Gross." I wrinkled my nose at the smell. "Graddock, are we close to our destination? Do you know anything about it?"

"Rumors." Graddock scratched his ear. "I have heard this section in town traffics dark magic. I wouldn't be surprised if the proprietor sells cursed items retrieved from the temple in addition to childrens' toys. The wicked merchandise is not sold to the young, of course, but to their so-called parents."

Hero bumped Wysdel with his shoulder. "Another thing the queens will set right once they regain their thrones."

Wysdel's lips pressed together in a straight line before speaking, "Unfortunately, the black market thrived here during the queens' reign."

Hero knitted his brow. "Do you mean the queens let shopkeepers sell evil magic?"

"They did not condone it." Wysdel lifted her chin. "Hero, the queens see their role to inspire and instill righteousness in their citizens. This makes for a strong Kingdom—not its rulers running around squashing every instance of disobedience. The queens act on conflicts that require a united Kingdom, but local issues are left to the people they love and trust."

We turned off the avenue to a smaller road. Hero said, "I thought they were more involved."

Wysdel touched Hero's shoulder. "I understand, but their best weapon is not power but love. They agreed at the beginning that at the root of their laws had to be trust in their people. Their philosophy is not to correct minor offenses but believe the local law will handle it."

Graddock snorted. "Love? Give me a halberd any day instead. I am not sure these queens would be better than King Piper."

Wysdel frowned and eyed us warily. The months had not been kind to Graddock, and he seemed far more hardened than I remembered.

Around a corner, a woman troll strolled with a fuzzy creature on a chain. The animal rushed along excitedly like a dog. Rapunzel pulled on my arm, but I reassured her. "Tardalong, Rapunzel. I can face at least five at a time."

Graddock grinned. "Little beasties. The shop is ahead on the right."

In the light of the setting sun, we arrived at the toy shop. The narrow building was made of slate, with glass, round windows at the front for a display of its wares. Hanging by twine, a puppet held a placard announcing the name of "Mangiafuoca Toy Shoppe." We entered, and our eyes adjusted to the dim lamplight inside.

A toy shop should be a place of joy, but this one

reminded me more of a museum. Even with a family of gnomes browsing, a sepulchral mood hung over the store. Wooden dolls without movable joints, blocks with pictures on their sides, jump ropes, miniature weapons, and other items I couldn't identify littered the store in piles. I noticed magical toys as well: a wizard's hat where obscure sigils rotated around on their own, a fuzzy doll unicorn that moved its head at any sound, and a life-sized female doll wearing a purple polka-dot dress seated on its bottom with a "Pinch Me" sign around its neck. The last toy remained motionless as the child gnomes pinched it.

The counter to purchase wares stood in the back of the store. Behind it, a broad-shouldered, heavyset lady lorded over the shop. She had white hair shaped like a judge's wig and a flowing red robe. Her eyes narrowed at us as we entered.

No sign of Valencia anywhere. I noticed a door in the back leading to another room. Perhaps the proprietor had her trapped back there.

Our group allowed Hero to take the lead, and he nodded to the proprietor. Passing the gnome children who giggled while knocking on the life-sized doll's knee, we approached the counter. Hero cleared his throat. "Greetings. My name is Hero."

The woman answered, "I am Mangiafuoca. What toy are you interested in, Mr. Hero?"

Her voice was soft and silky, catching me off-guard. Hero continued in an even voice. "I was hoping you could give me information about a missing person. I have it on good authority that she is here."

The gnome children laughed behind me, continuing in their game to abuse the masochistic toy. The woman shrugged. "I do not deal in missing people. I only sell toys."

Hero reached into his pocket and jingled a bag of coins Wysdel had given him. "Perhaps I could buy a toy and while we talked, you might remember this woman? She is human, short, with long blonde hair and freckles?"

"I do not know such a person. I cannot help you."

He glanced my way for my opinion. I could almost read his thoughts. Trust her? Nope, not a smidgen. I put on the expression I use whenever Fitzie tells us a fib, and he nodded at me.

Hero eyed the door in the back. "Does anyone else live here with you? Or someone who works here?"

The woman crossed her arms over her chest. "I do not live here, and the room is a storage room where I keep my most private toys for trusted customers. If you are not going to buy, I suggest you leave."

Without warning, Hero darted toward the door. Mangiafuoca rushed after Hero, but with a flick of my fingers, a pile of toys fell off the counter and blocked her. She had to dodge the falling playthings, giving my husband enough time to enter the back room. He grabbed a lamp on the wall near the doorway and lit the room. I spied piles of items—weapons, lamps, jewelry, but no sign of anyone.

Mangiafuoca grabbed Hero's tunic and yanked him out of the room. "What are you doing? This is my private collection. You cannot come back here without my permission!"

Hero lifted the lamp as a barrier between himself and the proprietor. "Where is she? I know you're lying."

Snatching the lamp from his hand, Mangiafuoca pointed at the door with her other hand. "I demand you leave my store, or I will shout for a Child of the Oracle."

Graddock shifted uneasily, and Wysdel stepped backward. The gnome parents grabbed their children's hands and led them to the front of the shop. We didn't want to attract this type of attention.

Hero swallowed. "Fine. We will just...shop. Everyone, look around."

He was stalling, and we all knew it. I noticed Mangiafuoca nod at the gnome father who nodded back, then left with his family. Not a good sign, but we needed time.

Hero and I wandered around the store as the rest looked

on. Rapunzel had been fascinated with a small collection of blocks that built themselves into different structures on command. I grabbed a doll of Planet and held it up. "How much for this?"

The woman ignored me and approached Hero. "I want you to leave immediately."

"I'm a paying customer. Aren't you open for business?"

As he went to step around her, the store owner blocked him. "I do not need your money."

Hero tried to pass her again, and she sidestepped again, intercepting him. What was he doing? But I could tell my husband had a plan. He pointed over her shoulder. "Perhaps I will buy the large doll behind you?"

Her tone was deep and threatening. "It is not for sale."

All eyes were now on the toy with the sign around its neck. Upon closer inspection, the porcelain face could be a mask. The toy wore an oversized dress, gloves, stockings, and slippers. Not a stitch of skin was exposed.

Hero glared at the store owner. "Perhaps I will name her Valencia."

At the sound of her name, the head of the doll moved slightly. Wysdel stepped forward. "'Tis her."

The owner's face turned red. "No. She is a magically enhanced doll and nothing more. Many of my toys move."

At that moment, two Daughters of the Oracle entered, swords drawn. One, her hair styled in ringlets, spoke. "A customer has reported a disturbance here. Trouble, Mangiafuoca?"

The proprietor squared her shoulders. "Escort out these intruders. They are threatening me."

The Daughter of the Oracle who had remained silent stepped forward, touching the hilt of a scimitar. "One of your *exchanges* gone bad?"

Flaring her nostrils, Mangiafuoca said, "I do not know what you are talking about."

The scimitar woman stepped toward my husband, but

he held up his hand. "Hear me out first. This storekeeper has kidnapped a woman and disguised her as this doll."

The Daughter drew and pointed the scimitar at Hero. "Exit. Now."

"I will leave after you take the mask off the doll."

The Daughters looked at each other. Wysdel out held her arms. "We mean no one any harm, but our dear friend recently lost her memory. We believe she is here. If the doll is our friend, finding her will be a great relief to us. Please, will you help us?"

Wysdel was playing to their sense of justice. The Daughters regarded us with less aggression. They examined the doll and then Mangiafuoca. The one with braids nodded. "'Tis not an unreasonable request."

Mangiafuoca eyes narrowed. "This is my store. How dare you Daughters listen to them?"

"How dare you question us," responded the one with ringlets.

"They are strangers!" shrieked Mangiafuoca. "I demand you escort them out right now."

Apparently, commanding the Daughters was a bad idea. The second Daughter shifted her sword from Hero to the toy store owner. The other woman pointed at Wysdel. "Unmask the doll."

Mangiafuoca held up her hands and stepped aside, and Wysdel stepped forward and reached for the mask. The head pulled back as Wysdel removed the porcelain cover. Behind it, the frightened countenance of Valencia stared back at us, blinking rapidly.

Wysdel shook with excitement, Hero grinned, and Rapunzel's jaw dropped. I caught a glimpse of Graddock who examined Valencia with a faint trace of a smile. I returned my attention to the freckled queen. "Greetings, Valencia."

Her muumuu-like dress allowed Valencia to move fluidly. She jumped to her feet and stepped behind Mangiafuoca. I admit, I didn't expect her to side with the proprietor. Mangiafuoca glared at us. "You found out my little secret. I have committed no crime for employing a homeless, uneducated woman. Now, Daughters, I request you leave with these people."

Eyes alight, Wysdel said, "She is our friend. She does not remember us, but I am certain." Her attention turned to the proprietor. "And unlike this charlatan, we love her very much. We would not allow others to hurt her for profit."

The Daughters looked back and forth between Mangiafuoca and the rest of us. The ringlet one nodded at Valencia. "Can you speak? Is your name Valencia?"

Valencia gripped Mangiafuoca's arm. "Yes."

"Do you recognize any of these people?"

Valencia examined us, one by one. She lingered on Graddock slightly longer than everyone else. "No."

Mangiafuoca threw her arm around Valencia and my stomach turned. She cooed to Valencia. "This group will tell you lies. They want to hurt you and abandon you, my dear." Mangiafuoca tucked a strand of hair behind Valencia's ear. "You do not want to go with them, do you?"

Valencia looked panicked, and she shook her head vehemently. "No, I want to stay here."

Mangiafuoca turned to the Daughters. "You heard her decision."

"Will you give me a moment," Hero said. "I would like to speak to her in everyone's presence. Agreed?"

The Daughters nodded toward him. Hero stepped forward, and Valencia shrunk further behind Mangiafuoca, who smiled at him triumphantly. Hero cleared his throat.

"Valencia, Mangiafuoca is wrong. We do not wish to hurt you. I know you do not remember us, but we know you. We know that you lived in Exile. You were penniless, yet you still helped the poor. You...have a lot of money. I can explain how later, but you have used it to help others and have done wonderful things with your riches. You defend the helpless, those without a voice, the ones who need you the most."

As he described her personality, her eyes enlarged, and her mouth twisted. The spell had taken away her memories but not who she was. "You say I was impoverished but then wealthy? And philanthropic?"

"And intelligent," answered Hero. "Tell me, what uneducated person uses the words 'impoverished' or 'philanthropic'? You have been studying since you acquired your money."

Valencia tried to step out from behind Mangiafuoca, but the owner blocked her. Valencia leaned around the bulky woman. "I do have a head for numbers. I can multiply and divide, but I do not recall how I learned how to do so."

"You sold matches in Exile," said Hero. "You remember that, I am sure. I don't know how you ended up here, but you almost died in a snowstorm."

Valencia said, "King Piper found me while on patrol and brought me inside. He saved my life."

Hero scratched his chin. "Why would the king have been on patrol in a prison city? Did he ever explain it?"

"He...I do not remember."

"Meeting the king seems fairly important to not remember details. Maybe Mangiafuoca here told you this story over and over until you thought it must be true."

The Daughters glanced at each other, puzzled. Hero had found a false memory and exposed it. He continued, "Sequences of time in your past do not add up, do they? Join us, and we can help you remember."

Mangiafuoca broke in and turned Valencia to face her. "They are liars and cheats and like the others who would not feed you on your journey from Exile to here. I was the only one who opened my house to you, remember? You were dying of hunger when I saved you. You had nothing, and I—"

Hero cut in. "Another false memory. Dressing her up as a doll to sell your wares is not being a loving guardian."

Valencia looked at Mangiafuoca as if seeing her for the first time. She stepped away. "I do not know which of you is lying. I—"

She never finished her sentence. Mangiafuoca reached into a pocket and produced a short wand. Wysdel stepped back in alarm. "Where did you get that?"

She brandished the wand. "Stand back! She stays with me!"

The Daughters advanced and Graddock drew his sword, but Wysdel threw out her arms. "That wand can summon a vengeful spirit. We will all be haunted the rest of our lives."

"But Wysdel, we—"

"We must leave, Hero!"

Mangiafuoca grinned. "Be so good as to see yourselves —"

Before Mangiafuoca could continue, Rapunzel flicked her head. In a heartbeat, her much-longer hair snapped across the room and stung Mangiafuoca's fingers, forcing her to drop the magic object. The proprietor snatched back her hand and buried it against her body as the wand clattered to the ground. Graddock stepped forward and scooped up the item.

Valencia looked with horror at the owner. "You would have used it?"

Wysdel glared at the proprietor. "*He* gave that to you, did he not?" Clearly, she meant Piper but wouldn't say his name in front of the Daughters. "You are working for him."

"I do not know who you are talking about." Mangiafuoca raised her chin.

The Daughters stepped forward and grabbed the store owner's arms. "We will take you to the Council. We have suspected you were hiding evil weapons, Mangiafuoca. 'Tis time for you to face the courts."

They dragged her from her shop, straining to remove her from the building. Face contorting in anger, Mangiafuoca protested. "I shall appeal to the king. He will not let me languish in prison. And when I escape, I shall have justice."

The Daughter with the scimitar pushed her out of the store. "We shall deliver justice, woman, rest assured."

After they left, I embraced Rapunzel. "Wonderful! You go, girl!"

When Hero and Wysdel approached her, Valencia hugged her arms and stepped back. "I was safe here."

Wysdel reached for her, holding out her hands. "No, now you are safe. Come with us, we have much to tell you."

24 - A ROUND

Harold

I n the toy shop next to a display of dolls that looked like miniature golems, Valencia moved her hands up and down her arms and huddled away from us. We made a semicircle around her and took turns introducing ourselves. I spied a tear in the corner of Wysdel's eye that she wiped away. Valencia graciously curtsied to everyone except Sanders. Sanders revealed her fairy wings but kept in place her Charlie disguise, not wanting Valencia to think she was the queen. Valencia's gesture of respect to my wife was brief—a grimace etched on her face. The Match Girl had been cheated by a pixie early in her life and distrusted them as a result.

When Valencia curtsied to Graddock, her eyes lingered on him, and she didn't lower her head. Good! For his part, Graddock made a flourishing bow to Valencia. Maybe this wouldn't be so hard?

Valencia chewed on her lower lip after I asked her to join us. "My home is Tusk," she said. "I know little of the rest of Kingdom."

So untrue. Piper's spell had not only removed her memories but most of the confidence she had gained over the years.

Now that we had found Valencia, I was worried Graddock would depart. A little ego-stroking might be in order for him and reassurance for her. I patted Graddock's shoulder. "With this man at our side, we can offer you protection. This gentleman here is one of the most skilled soldiers in Kingdom. Certainly, he could accompany us to the Marsh of Wishes."

Graddock snorted, seeing right through my attempt. "Lucky for you, I am traveling to the Forest of Death, so the marsh is on my way."

Success! Graddock had never said where he was headed. I wondered if a certain Match Girl had made him decide to set a new course. No matter, as long as he remained with us.

We left the toy shop and headed north to leave behind the city of Tusk. With me on one side of our newfound member and Graddock on the other, I informed Valencia I knew all about her early life as a merchant girl in Exile. I asked her what she had done since that time. Valencia recounted her departure from Exile to Tusk, nearly starving before Mangiafuoca took her in. She turned to me. "But you say someone has altered my memories? Yet I vividly recall my past."

I countered by listing Valencia's adventures and her charitable works, being careful not to yet broach the subject of her reign over Kingdom. The Match Girl was surprised to hear she had siblings and curious about them. I glanced at Wysdel, wordlessly prompting her to reveal she was Snow White. She only shook her head, preferring to keep her identity a secret for now. Too much too soon.

An hour later, we found ourselves on the outskirts of

Tusk with its rolling hills and pockets of trees. We stopped near a small lake populated by a flock of swans and a log full of toads. The amphibians' collective baritone, a southern breeze, and the setting sun created an ideal place to rest.

Once we were seated in a circle, Valencia's attention focused on me. "Do you have a plan for removing the spell?"

Across the clearing, Graddock's eyes shifted from her to me. He raised his eyebrows and smirked. I hunched my shoulders. "We know of a way, yes."

I didn't know how to proceed, so she tilted her head toward me and wordlessly egged me on.

I rubbed my chin. "You have to kiss your true love."

She leaned back and fiddled with the folds of her oversized dress. "So, there is no way then?"

"Actually, there is."

Intuitive to a fault, Valencia picked up on my meaning immediately. "You know who is my true love? And you are taking me to him?"

No time like the present, I guess. "Actually, I brought him here." I nodded at Graddock.

Graddock, seated on the ground across from her, grinned sheepishly and lifted his hand.

Valencia tapped her chin with three fingers. "Are you certain? When I met him just now, I felt no *coup de foudre*."

Valencia was known for speaking in French from time to time. *This*, she remembered, but not Graddock. "I met you both years ago. You'd grown quite close."

Wysdel reached out to put her hand on Valencia's, but the Match Girl pulled her hand away. Undeterred, Wysdel spoke in her dulcet tone. "You are married to him."

Valencia's head swiveled from Wysdel to Graddock. "I think not!"

"Yes, you are." Wysdel's tone was firm.

"I believe I would remember marrying someone, spell or not." Valencia placed her hand on her breast. "I look at him and my heart feels nothing."

Graddock leaned back on his forearms. "And while you are an entirely fetching maiden, I share your sentiment."

At his compliment, Valencia blushed but addressed Graddock. "You do not remember any of this either?"

"These people have told me I have lost all of my memories too."

Valencia asked, "Do you believe them?"

"Mangiafuoca acted strange about keeping you around." Graddock crossed his boots near the fire. "She could have replaced you with any street urchin but seemed determined to keep you. I sense something about you, milady, that is more than meets the eye. Even as charming to the eye as you are."

A second compliment. Clearly, Graddock was taken with her.

Valencia ignored the compliment this time. "But do you believe them?"

"The entire incident in the toy shop has supported their story. One does not use an artifact of great power to keep a slave from departing. My presence here is to repay a debt I owed them. I was to escort them to you, and then take my leave. Now, I find myself intrigued by their tale. Do I believe them? Not entirely, but something is not as it seems."

Sanders brushed back a lock of blonde hair. "We risked our lives to break you out, Graddock. And almost went to jail for you, Valencia."

Valencia stood and clasped her hands. "This is quite a lot to take in."

I rose to my feet. "I understand. You don't need to believe us immediately. All we ask is that you come with us and give each other a chance. If it weren't for Kingdom's customs, I would tell you to kiss each other now, but I know you won't do that."

Both spoke at the same time. Valencia's voice was high and distraught. "Kiss him? I do not know him!"

Graddock's was low and more like a scoff. "If I am going to kiss a maiden, I am going to make up my own mind!"

235

Valencia and Graddock turned their attention to each other. A moment of protest and solidarity. "See? You have your resistance in common," I said.

Valencia twisted the fabric of her polka-dot dress in her fist. "You said you were escorting me somewhere. Why?"

"One of your sisters lives in the Marsh of Wishes. My wife will teleport us there."

Graddock peered at Sanders. "Will you land us on the ground this time?"

Sanders put her hand on her right hip. "That only happened one time. Get over it. Is everyone ready?"

The queen looked at my wife in disgust. "I do not know about—" Valencia paused then spat. "Pixie magic."

Sanders ran her hand along the edge of her wings. "Listen, I was born human and then became a pixie. It's a long story, but you can trust me."

Valencia pressed together her lips.

Sanders ran a hand along the side of her cheek. "I'm in disguise, but I'll show you what I really look like. But don't freak out...uh, become distressed...when I do."

Valencia crossed her arms as Sanders removed her Charlie façade. She lowered her arms when Valencia recognized her. "You look like Queen Planet."

"I'm not Queen Planet. This is how I normally look. No wings, no tricks. Truce?"

"For now."

Sanders nodded and started her spell. Everyone stiffened as the crackle of the teleportation drowned out the toads' chorus. On the final word, we blinked away...

...into a bog, ankles deep in muck, and sinking fast.

"I am stuck!" said Graddock.

"I am too."

"Me also."

"Sanders!"

Now up to her knees, Sanders exclaimed, "It's a marsh! It's huge! What did you expect?"

She gestured again and we found ourselves back in the middle of Tusk, mud-covered up to our waists. Graddock stomped the muck off his boots. "We are an hour's journey in the wrong direction from the place where we were just resting. Probably for the best. Let us get a room at a Tuskian inn and spend the night here."

I brushed mud off my pants. "A sound idea."

Graddock led us to an inn called The Lock. With windows shaped like keyholes and drinks stirred with a lockpick, the building had to be Kingdom's watering hole for thieves.

After a brief night of rest, we gathered for breakfast in the morning in the common room and discussed how we would spend the day. In particular, the route we would take to the Marsh of Wishes.

"I suppose teleporting is off the table," I said.

In her Charlie disguise, Sanders sighed. "I need Celeste. I should try to recruit her again."

"What about me? Are you leaving me behind?" asked Rapunzel, wrapping her arms around her body.

Sanders swung her arm around the girl. "You can trust Hero as you trust me. We're like the same person except I'm the cuter one, and the smarter one, and the more creative one—"

"And the more conceited one," I finished. "I will protect you until Sanders returns, Rapunzel. I won't leave your side."

Rapunzel softened and smiled, her expression rivaling a sunrise.

Sanders eyed a map of Kingdom on the wall. "I'll pick up Celeste and then check on Cinderella." She regarded Valencia. "She's one of your sisters."

Sanders and I stood. She nodded to Graddock, Valencia, and Wysdel, and she hugged Rapunzel. She patted the twelve-year-old girl's arm before stepping away. "I'll return. Trust me."

Sanders and I walked out of the inn together and stopped on the street. I gazed into her eyes. "Be careful."

"Never."

Taking her hand, I led her to a nearby alley to say good-bye. Though she resembled Charlie, I recognized Sanders' nervous expression of biting her lower lip. "Then be careful with Rapunzel, at least," I said.

Her goofy grin turned solemn. "She's a lost soul, Hero. No family. An unfamiliar world. She's two years younger than Snow White was when you met her, and Snow White was *young*."

I entered the alley and turned to face her. "Assuming we restore the queens' memories, how are we going to stay here and find her family? What about Fitzie?"

"Yes, I know." Sanders placed her hand on her heart. "I miss him terribly. But helping her is wrapped up in the principles of Kingdom. Here, good repays good, and she has already helped us twice."

I looked at her piercingly.

She tapped her forehead. "Call it pixie intuition."

"I'm worried you have another reason."

Her face softened and a faraway look stole into her eyes. "Perhaps, but don't you remember our conversation last month about our family? Maybe she's the answer."

The statement took me off-guard, and I didn't know how to answer. Sanders jerked her thumb toward the inn. "Valencia has been giving me the stink-eye since I met her. Work on her, will you? And think about what I just said."

She kissed me and squeezed my hand, and then started the spell to teleport.

I stepped back. "I'll convince Valencia while you're gone. She should be easy compared to Helga."

Sanders' eyes went wide, then she vanished. Why the look of alarm? I'd have to ask her when she returned.

I went back to my traveling companions, and we started our trek north. I was stunned by Sanders' statement concerning our family, but I knew exactly what she was referring to. Three months before, Sanders and I had discussed fostering a child, but we weren't sure we could handle it. Now, Sanders was acting like a foster mom to Rapunzel until we found her parents—an interesting way to see if we measured up.

As we set out, I decided to walk with Rapunzel. Her hair was shorter today and she stared at her feet. I ducked to get into her line of sight. "What's wrong?"

She shrugged. "I liked your wife."

"I like her too as it turns out. She'll be back. What did you do to cheer yourself up in the tower?"

"I sang."

I nudged her shoulder with mine. "Why don't you sing a little?"

I was sorry I encouraged her. Rapunzel sang, and her scratchy voice startled a flock of birds, which took to the sky. Off-key, Rapunzel trilled a song that made no sense. The verses rhymed but the words sounded as if put together using a word search puzzle.

Graddock winced, and Wysdel rubbed her temple as if she had a headache. To spare my companions, I suggested, "Why don't I teach you a song from my world?"

Rapunzel brightened. "That sounds nice."

"Have you ever sung a round with Sinope? A round is when two people sing the same lyrics but at different times."

Rapunzel furrowed her brow. "Sinope wouldn't let me sing."

Now I knew why.

I used "Row, Row, Row Your Boat" as an example of a round and taught Rapunzel the lyrics. Though her voice was the equivalent of fingernails on a chalkboard, she was a fast learner, and enjoyed the songs I chose. After she learned the round, I swung my arm around her, and she leaned into me.

We traveled north along the edge of the Plains of Safe Passage with the Hills of Despair on our right. Rapunzel asked if I had traveled this way in Kingdom before. I told her I had traveled south through the hills with the giants on my first adventure. Valencia joined us as I described the places I'd been in Kingdom. When I had finished, she observed, "I am envious. You have traveled extensively."

"And so have you," I said. "With Graddock and your sisters."

Valencia bit her lip. "Tell me about this sister I have. Cinderella. What is she like?"

I described Cinderella in broad strokes. As I did, Wysdel and Graddock were also listening in. I finished by saying, "She is accompanied by a selkie named Pennilane."

Wysdel gave me a sharp look. "Poor Pennilane! She must have returned and was trapped by the spell."

"Returned?"

Wysdel explained. "Pennilane lives off-world with her husband half of the year. When Piper cast his spell, it was her time to be away from Kingdom. She must have come back early."

"Off-world?" Valencia shook her head. "This is madness. How am I to believe any of this?"

Graddock nodded in agreement, and I didn't dare bring up that Valencia had Traveled extensively outside of Kingdom.

Valencia sniffed and quickened her pace, pulling ahead of us. Graddock did the same, walking in line with her. When they were out of earshot, I kicked a stone in our path. "I don't know what we need to do to convince her."

Wysdel tucked a strand of hair behind her ear. "Patience, Hero. She'll come around."

We camped for the night in a small grove of trees. While I was watching Rapunzel scale a tree to examine a purple squirrel, I realized Valencia and Graddock had wandered away. Alarmed, I consulted Wysdel who pointed at the birds in the trees. She raised her eyebrows. "My little spies say they're not far, talking to each other."

I had forgotten Wysdel could understand birds. With

Rapunzel in the tree watching the wildlife, I saw an opportunity. "Maybe we could sneak up on them and listen in?"

"Oh, Hero. That would be completely improper." Wysdel lightly tapped me on the arm, then grinned playfully. "But my winged darlings do not know any better."

A blue jay landed on her shoulder and chirped. Wysdel interpreted, eyes alight. "Graddock has complimented her beauty once again. They are discussing the possibility of your story, particularly of their being married."

Wysdel shrugged and the jay flew off. Moments later an oriole landed on the palm of her hand. "Valencia has said she doesn't remember consenting to a marriage. She doesn't fall in love because someone tells her to. Graddock has replied that many would settle for the security and routine of a marriage even if love was not present."

A goldfinch swooped down and hovered in front of her. After it sang its song, Wysdel nodded knowingly. "Valencia wants to love and be loved. Graddock shares her point of view." Wysdel sucked in her breath after the finch interrupted her. "And has admitted his attraction to her."

I leaned forward. "What about Valencia?"

A robin appeared and settled on Wysdel's other hand. "Valencia blushed but didn't respond. Graddock offered his sword to protect her in return for her company. Valencia has agreed and conceded she has a connection with him because they are the only two who don't fully believe our tale."

A hawk landed on the grass in front of us, and the other birds scattered. Wysdel breathed in quickly. "They return."

The hawk preened itself while Wysdel rubbed her hands together. "Valencia and Graddock took forever to admit they were attracted to each other. I hope it will not take that long again for them to kiss."

241

25 - CALANDO

Sondra

C at's piss, Hero! He should've known better than to speak to a spellcaster when she's in the middle of a spell. 'I'll convince Valencia while you're gone,' he said. 'She should be easy compared to Helga.' He totally threw me off from focusing on my destination. And now I was standing in an exquisitely groomed yard wondering where the hell I had appeared. I could be anywhere in Kingdom.

The immediate area resembled the grounds of an historic house. Ahead, a gray-brick, three-story building with shuttered windows indicated people lived here. Large hedges surrounded me, and I had materialized on a pathway between them. The smell of violets and honeysuckle drifted through the air.

Believe you me, was I going to tell off my husband! I

shook my hands, readying another teleportation spell. I had already used up a decent portion of the magical essence I had. You only have so much each day, you know. Before I started my incantation, however, I heard someone muffle a sob around the corner of a hedge.

None of my business, I know, but my maternal instinct wondered if a child was in danger. The mourner hitched their breath. No, this was someone older, likely female. I rocked on my heels. I didn't have time for a distraction, and I was trespassing. Yet, someone was grieving—something with which I was all-too familiar—and I couldn't ignore them.

Unfurling my wings in case I had to fly away quickly, I crept up to the hedge's corner and peered around it. There knelt a lady in an alcove next to a stone bench. In the center of the area was a four-foot column splitting out to a Y-shape with wings. I recognized the statue as one of the sacred symbols of Kingdom.

The woman wore a long gray robe with a white sash and sandals, her back to me. Her body trembled in her sorrow.

In a flash, she turned around and rose, spotting me before I was able to duck behind the hedge. Helga Helvys—another queen who had lost her memory—stood in front of me. And what I had mistaken for a robe was a nun's habit.

Helga's eyes narrowed, and her face, the only part of her head I could view in her wimple, pinched. I gulped. Spying on Kingdom's legendary warrior queen was never a good idea.

"Helga?"

Helga clenched her jaw. "Who are you? Why are you here?"

I nearly said "mistake" before I realized I could turn this lemon into—one of my favorite beverages—a lemon drop. I had found Helga. Could I convince her of her true past myself? If not, perhaps I could gather some intel for the others. A tall order, yes, but I had to try.

I spread my arms. "I was drawn here...because of you."

Because Hero had mentioned her, I had teleported to

her so I was telling the truth. Mostly. Anyway, I hoped Helga would sense my sincerity. Helga was a popular figure before Hero's first adventure. Everyone in Kingdom knew of her. She wouldn't question my excuse for suddenly appearing.

Shoulders still tensed, she stepped forward. "The sorcery that surrounds this convent is powerful. No one simply magicks their way in."

Unless their magic is unconventional, and they can't throw a proper teleportation spell. But I couldn't tell her that. I had to flip the conversation away from me. "I didn't mean to interrupt you, but maybe I could help?"

Her face softened at the offer. "I do not know who you are or why you are here, but you cannot help me. Return from where you came, and I will not report this."

"Perhaps talking about what's troubling you would ease the ache," I said.

Helga moved forward, now three paces away. Though a warrior, Helga was a woman of peace and wouldn't attack unprovoked. If I made a sudden move, she'd take me down faster than a hummingbird flutters its wings, but I had no plans of startling her.

"Perhaps, you were sent to me." She bit her lip. "An answer to my prayer?"

Well, why the hell not? Mute, I waited for her to continue.

Helga took another step toward me. "I do not know why I weep. I am often sorrowful in the morning with the rising of the sun."

I scanned the horizon around the gray building. Half of the sun peeked above the line of earth and sky. "Maybe the sun reminds you of something?"

Helga never took her eyes off me. "I do not believe it has anything to do with the sun itself."

Sunrise. Waking up. Daybreak. Dawn. Why would they —? Dawn! Wasn't that Helga's daughter's name? The one with Down's Syndrome?

Helga read the expression of revelation on my face. "What? Do you know something?"

How could I tell her she was missing a daughter she couldn't remember? We had already determined the spell removed the subject's memories but not the resonance of those memories on a person's emotions. Helga was worried about her missing daughter, but she didn't know why. If I told her, she would think me crazy and hand me over to Piper. I had to focus on Helga, not her plight. What could I say...?

Aha.

"I cry sometimes for reasons I don't fully understand," I said. "My body grieves for something, and my mind doesn't understand what. But letting the tears flow helps."

Helga rubbed her hands together. "But I have everything I want. I am at peace with my Creator, and the Eternal has provided for me here. Is my faith not strong enough?"

Now I stepped forward. "You are one of the most faithful women I know. But sometimes you must believe in something you don't understand yet to find peace."

My words plucked a heartstring in Helga like a harpist plucks a harp. She breached the gap between us and embraced me, breath hitching. She cried on my shoulder, and I tenderly wrapped my arms around her.

After several sobs, she parted and looked at me through tear-filled eyes. "Thank you, my angel."

Oh! She meant my sudden appearance and Charlie's features. She does look like a traditional angel. And the fact I had wings. Though my wings didn't look anything like an angel's wings, but who knew what an angel looked like in Kingdom? "I'm not an angel."

Helga's face fell. "I thought for sure. You speak in contractions—the old way. You appear, though strong magic should keep you away, and you speak with wisdom."

I reached out and held her hands. "I'm a friend, Helga. Look into your heart not your memories, and you'll know it's true."

Helga squeezed my hands. "I do know 'tis true."

If I said any more, I might ruin the moment, and I had to find my way to Celeste. "I must go now, but I'll be back."

Helga released me. "I will eagerly await it."

Sitting beneath her house in Faerie Forest next to a beautiful birch tree, Celeste was arrayed in a plain yellow dress and black slippers. Her golden hair caught the sunlight just right as she tilted her head.

"Let me see if I understand," she said. "You are not my sister, but you look exactly like her. You are not only human but from another world, and some adventure in Kingdom transformed you into a pixie."

"I can transform back and forth like a pixie, but my birth form was human."

Celeste held up her hand. "I am afraid to say it, but this is the easiest part to believe. According to your claim, I have been a court magician serving under five queens and three princes for over a decade. In that time, you and I have become close, as close as sisters."

"Yes." Tears formed in my eyes.

"And I bear the title of Celeste the Extraordinary?"

"You've earned that title."

"And I have been in your world because…and I do not know how to react to this…I am the godmother of your son? But you were not here when the king cast a spell that not only took away my memories but replaced them with false ones of his ascension to the throne. And you are here because you need my help on your current adventure to restore the memories of the queens, defeat the king, and turn Kingdom over to its rightful rulers."

"Yes, that's about it."

Celeste leaned forward. "If you are not Planet, where is

she?"

She had asked the question that I feared. With her mother dying in the house above us, I didn't have the heart to tell her that her sister was dead. "I cannot answer that."

Celeste said, "If we are friends, why not?"

I squirmed. "I would rather you remembered."

Celeste looked off in the distance for a while. "But I cannot leave. My mother is dying!"

I pulled up a tuft of grass. As I tossed it, sparkles emerged and showered to the ground. "I know."

"There you two are!"

We turned our attention to the person who had interrupted us. Da Constellation floated down. "Ma is asking for you, Planet."

I had appeared a couple of hours before to hugs from Da and a hardened stare from Celeste. I had asked Celeste to join me for a conversation to tell her everything. At the time, Celeste's mother had been resting, which allowed me to unburden everything on my chest to my best friend across two worlds.

Celeste threw me a cautious glance. I grimaced. "Does she really want to see her wayward daughter?"

Da nodded energetically, his bowler hat bouncing up and down. "But why would she not? Your departure before was abrupt, but you promised to return. And here you are."

Celeste sighed. "We do not have much time left before..." She faltered.

The guilt washed over me with that statement. How could I refuse? I rose and floated behind Da into the house.

The one lit candle hardly illuminated Ma's room. As before, the bed and the small accompanying table were the only furniture in the small space. The gaunt form of Mrs. Constellation, or Ma, lay in the bed. Her arms were stick thin. Her wings, devoid of their brilliant green and pink colors and now a pale gray, splayed beneath her on the pallet.

Planet's mother turned her head toward me, her

rheumy eyes taking me in, tired but curious.

I pulled up next to the bed, floating in the air but positioned as if I were seated. "I am here."

She examined me closely, squinting at times. "Amazing."

"What is amazing, Ma?"

The skeletal pixie tilted her head. "Who are you?"

I pulled back. "Huh?"

"You are not Planet."

"But—"

"When you carry your child for six months before childbirth, you form a bond. Who are you?"

I wanted to reassure her that I was, indeed, her prodigal daughter. She didn't have to die without knowing what had happened to Planet. I should provide comfort, not distress, on her deathbed. Yet, could I? Wasn't giving her a false memory to placate her exactly what Piper was doing to the queens?

"You are correct, Mrs. Constellation. But I'm not here to hurt you or anyone here."

"Why do you look so much like her?"

I hesitated. How could I tell her? And like Celeste, she would want to know about Planet. I could lie to Celeste, knowing she would eventually remember her sister died, but her mother? That was too heavy a burden to bear. Yet I saw no way of avoiding telling the truth. I would have to explain.

Steadying myself, I told her about Earth, who I was, and how Planet was my parallel. I described how I had come to Kingdom in the past, and through a spell, could become a pixie. "And that is the truth. I'm sorry for deceiving you last time I was here."

Her eyes softened. "I enjoyed our talk before, but I knew you were not Planet. I am not in a position to defend myself, thus I went along with your fabrication. Yet, at the end of the conversation, I sensed your heart was pure."

I scratched my temple. "Why didn't you confront me?"

"I wondered why you had come, and I sensed Celeste

knew, so I assumed you had told her. You came for her, not me." Her trembling hand reached out and touched a wayward strand of my hair, tucking it back in place. "You are so much like her, but you are not her."

I hung my head. "I could never be as heroic as Planet."

Cat's piss! How did that slip out? I meant it to be a compliment to Planet, but all it did was make her mother want to know more.

Ma Constellation's raspy voice cut across the silence. "You know where she is."

"Please don't ask me."

The elderly pixie shut her eyes. "She is dead."

The lump formed in my throat. "I can't…"

Trembling and unsteady, she reached for me. When I took her hand and stared into her eyes, all I could see was a concerned mother. I lost it. I mean I had a lot packed away in the overstuffed suitcase I called my heart, and the lock sprung open. Everything came out—all over this poor woman on her deathbed. I could only nod to confirm her daughter's fate, and Ma Constellation's tears dripped down her cheeks. Without knowing what I was doing, I hugged her, crying on her shoulder. Wasn't I supposed to be the comforting one? But the moment didn't work out that way. Her arms embraced me, her heart beat against mine, a rare moment of closeness between two people suffering in their own ways.

When I pulled back and wiped my tears, she pointed at my heart. "You are in pain."

"That doesn't matter. What can I do for you?"

"Tell me why you are hurting."

I swallowed down more tears. "It isn't important."

"On the contrary, 'tis important to me."

"Planet saved Kingdom." I wiped my eyes with my index finger. "Because of her, my husband was able to return to Earth and marry me. I owe her everything."

Ma Constellation's steady gaze peered deep inside of me. "That is not why you are hurting. I have known for a while the woman on the throne is not my daughter, but who would believe me? I have suspected the king killed my daughter after she helped him overthrow the former despot. And then you come in, and I thought at first you were her. But as we talked, I was sure you were not. Still, you knew her fate, and your avoidance of the truth confirmed she was dead."

"I'm sorry" was all I could manage.

"Do not be distressed." Ma Constellation's rustling voice calmed me. "You do not realize this is exactly what I needed to hear. She awaits me. My baby is alone and needs her Ma, which shall make my passing easier."

Fresh tears littered my face. "She'll be angry at me."

"Not Planet! Not with you. If she loved your husband, and if you do so now, how could she hate you? Planet was not that type of person."

I wiped my eyes, and she reached out her hand again. I took it and held it gently. She said, "Tell me what is wrong with you, child."

"I...I lost someone whom I was close to. I have not had a heart-to-heart with anyone since..."

"Your mother," said Mrs. Constellation. "You lost your mother. Do not forget that Celeste is a prognosticator. She inherited it from me."

I nodded, unable to speak.

"I am missing a daughter, and you are missing a mother. Are you surprised you are here? Now, grant me a final wish. Let me be a surrogate for you. Do not pretend I am your birth mother, and I will not pretend you are Planet. Unburden your heart to me about your birth mother."

And then I told her everything. The pain flowed out of me like Niagara Falls flows over its watershed. Ma Constellation calmly listened, speaking only now and then, and yet every word she spoke was exactly what I needed to hear. In that short hour, she adopted me, even calling me Sondra, one of the few in Kingdom to do so. For the first time, I felt like a true Constellation.

The conversation lapsed, and I knew we had come to the end. The storm within me had become more serene. Choppy waters, yes, but currents I could navigate. For Ma Constellation's part, I sensed she had given me everything she had. My newfound pixie parent was tired, and I wouldn't take any more of her time. I said, "This is my last conversation I will have daughter to parent."

"My sense says it is not the end, but as with all things in life, it will change. Be open to the change, Sondra. We have an old saying in Kingdom: 'Nothing ends, it renews.' My dear, thank you for staying with me and helping fill my final hour with life."

She put her hand to my cheek, and I put my hand on hers. She closed her eyes. "Please send in Celeste and her father. I will say good-bye to them now."

I left and did as I was told. Da seemed surprised I wasn't invited but he agreed to go in with Celeste. I waited in the front room where Hero had once knelt in front of a lifeless Planet, and Ma Constellation had said, "See how much he loved her." This house would always be a sad memory for Hero and me.

Fifteen minutes later, Celeste entered the room, gushing tears. The pixie, weeping into her hands, sat on the couch. When she looked up, tracts like rivulets streamed down her face. I couldn't help it, but I hugged her, holding her close. She didn't resist. In fact, she welcomed it. She didn't remember me, but Piper's spell couldn't erase her heart's memories. Somewhere in her subconscious, she recognized me, and she desired her best friend's comfort. We cried and hugged each other.

Da entered the room a short time later, as downcast as I've ever seen a person. He fell into a chair and stared at the floor like a man hit with a hammer who was struggling to remain conscious. "Ma has traded up her wings and is now at peace."

My mother's death hurt so much, and this felt the same. I had lost my mother, had her back briefly, and lost her once again. Celeste wailed, openly weeping, and I joined her.

Da managed to compose himself for a moment. "She wants to delay her funeral. I am to put her in stasis."

Celeste regained her composure. "She sensed something from you...Planet." Calling me her dead sister was only for the benefit of her father. "She knew you needed me right now for a period. Ma wanted me to go with you and help you before the funeral."

I put my hand over my mouth. "You cannot. You must be here for your family."

Celeste held up her head, her eyes glistening. "This was her dying wish." My best friend took a shuddering breath. "I am yours to command. Whatever you need of me, whatever you ask me to believe, I am at your disposal."

I gave Celeste some time to grieve for her mother. At moments, the pixie wanted me by her side, and other times, she wanted to be alone. I did as I was told until nightfall when she appeared before me and said she was ready. I asked her to use a location spell on Cinderella.

"The one you call Cinderella is outside of Town near Grok's Teeth. Three others accompany her."

"Is one of them a man named Roger Jolly?"

Celeste closed her eyes. "Yes. And two others in their party."

"Can you telepor...magic us to them?"

Celeste took my hand and the next thing I knew I was freezing. The chill winds of the mountains of Grok's Teeth swept over us. We had appeared behind the queen and her companions.

I called out to them. "Greetings! We have returned."

Roger drew his sword, Cinderella had her hand outstretched, Pennilane pointed her spear, and Sylvia assumed a martial arts defensive position. After their initial shock, they relaxed, and Cinderella ran to us. The queen hugged me fondly, very un-queen-like, but much like her. Roger approached and kissed my hand, and Sylvia and I embraced. Naturally, Pennilane remained aloof.

My eyes went back and forth between the queen and the prince. "So...you kissed?"

"Kissed?" Cinderella arched her eyebrows. "Let's say we had a difficult time not entering the Pink Room."

Roger blushed.

Cinderella noticed his face flush. "And that is why we call it the Pink Room."

Celeste had remained a few steps behind me, but Cinderella spotted her. "Celeste?"

Celeste hugged herself from both the cold and the awkwardness. I stepped back and placed my hand on her arm. "She doesn't remember."

Celeste examined the three women. "Are you the queens?"

"I am the only queen here," said Cinderella. "Has Sanders told you who you are?"

Skepticism lined her face. "Yes."

Cinderella approached her and slowly put her hands on the pixie's arms. "Greetings, Celeste. I am your friend."

Celeste's eyes widened at the queen's familiarity. I whispered, "Ma Constellation died today."

Cinderella put her hand to her lips. "No! Oh, my dear, I am so sorry. You do not remember, but I knew her as well."

Celeste looked away and swallowed down her grief. Cinderella turned to me. "This curse of Piper's is the pits. What he stole from all of us, what he continues to take, I will make him pay for it." Cinderella held her hands out to Celeste. "You have my deepest sympathies."

Celeste nodded, and a tear formed in her eye.

I said, "We have located Graddock and Valencia. They are heading for the Marsh of Wishes. With Wysdel and Hero."

Cinderella brightened at her sisters' names. "And we

will join them. We have snuck into the orphanage and have seen our children. Dreadful that they didn't recognize us and asked us to adopt them. They shall be safe if we keep away from them."

Shaking from the brisk air at the foot of the mountain, I asked, "What are you doing here?"

"Looking for wyverns to ride. But now that we have Celeste the Extraordinary, travel shouldn't be a problem."

Celeste's head jerked at her title, but she didn't respond.

Roger asked, "How are Graddock and Valencia getting along?"

"Umm, fine, I guess? When I was with them, they weren't rushing into each other's arms."

The queen and prince flashed each other knowing glances. Cinderella smirked. "'Tis high time for some sisterly interference, I think."

Kingdom

26 - THE PIPES OF PERRINGON

Harold

As we traveled north toward the Marsh of Wishes, we crossed broad meadows, stretching out to the western horizon. Lazily flapping grass greeted us and waved farewell after we passed through. The plains gave way to hills on our left, capturing the breaking sun in the morning with a red tint on their summits, reminding me of piles of ice cream with a cherry topping. The sweet scent of untainted grass, the enveloping wind cooling us at midday, and the virgin air with its slightly salty taste, all combined to deliver a pleasant journey. And the fact that giants only threatened us twice, and that Graddock chased them away both times to Valencia's admiration, added to the charm of our sojourn.

Rapunzel and I traded jokes as we walked. After a knock-knock joke of...

"Unicorn."

"Unicorn who?"

"Unicorny guy, Hero."

...Graddock flinched and suggested another singing round. Apparently, Rapunzel's scratchy voice was less offensive than our humor. Rapunzel squeaked at the idea, and we sang "three blind mice." She was a little put out by the lyrics but sang it energetically. Even Valencia smiled at her enthusiasm.

At the doorstep of the hills north of the Gnome Lands, the air wavered and we stopped our march. Graddock stepped in front of Valencia, and I did the same for Rapunzel. Wysdel grabbed my arm. Something was about to happen.

With the sound of a whip cracking, Sanders, Celeste, Cinderella, Roger, Pennilane and Sylvia materialized thirty yards ahead of us. When Rapunzel spotted my wife, she ran to Sanders before I had the chance. The young girl nearly tackled her with a bear hug of an embrace, and Sanders enfolded the child in her arms.

Cinderella strolled toward Valencia after winking at Wysdel, her sister, clearly knowing her true identity. Roger remained behind her at a respectful distance, and Pennilane remained where she appeared, observing the proceedings.

As Cinderella approached her, Valencia huddled away. Her focus was on Celeste, not her sister, and she glared at not one, but two pixies. In contrast, I was excited to see Celeste. A true friend and accomplished sorceress, Celeste being here made our quest seem achievable.

Cinderella stopped short before Valencia. "You don't remember me, do you?"

Examining her curiously, Valencia replied, "From what I have heard, you are the one they call Cinderella?"

Cinderella beamed. "I am. Two days ago, I couldn't remember you or anyone else, but what everyone's telling you is true. You are my older sister...and my friend."

Valencia put a hand on her heart. "This is too much to believe."

Cinderella's eyes shifted to Graddock. "How do you fare, Graddock?"

"In good spirits. I apologize for not being on familiar terms with you, beautiful matron."

Cinderella reached over and moved Graddock's chin so he faced Valencia. "You keep your eyes on her."

Valencia blushed.

Cinderella said, "I was your matron of honor, Valencia. You confessed your love for this man in front of me and my husband."

Roger stepped forward and bowed. "Queen Valencia."

Valencia lifted her shoulders, like a turtle withdrawing into its shell. "If this is true, I do not know if I will ever become used to it."

"Even as queen, you were never partial to royal titles." Cinderella flung her arms wide. "May I?"

Valencia offered her hands instead, and Cinderella squeezed them, tears in her eyes.

Roger turned to Graddock. "You old dog. I owe you money for our card game six months ago. I demand a second chance."

Graddock eyed the full pouch on Roger's belt. "If only we had a deck."

Roger reached into his tunic to an inside pocket and produced cards wrapped with twine. "Picked some up in town."

Valencia glanced over Cinderella's shoulder. "And now we have two pixies?"

Cinderella said, "Yes, both are true friends, and Celeste is the best spellcaster in Kingdom. The cavalry is here." Her eyes sought me out. "Calvary is the correct Earth term, Hero?"

"Affirmative."

Cinderella turned my way and hugged me. "Always good to see you."

"We've met earlier on this adventure."

"But I did not greet you properly then. 'Tis freaky to see you."

I grimaced. "That's not quite the right word."

Cinderella patted my cheek and moved on. "And Wysdel? How do you fare this fine day?"

Wysdel had told us that her sisters knew her real identity. I could tell Cinderella and Wysdel were struggling to keep the reunion formal. For her part, Wysdel blinked back tears. "My...queen."

Cinderella wrapped her arms around her. "My sweet. I'm so happy to find you here."

When Cinderella parted from Wysdel and words unsaid crossed the distance between their eyes, she turned to the young girl beside me. "Sanders told me you found this young girl. Rapunzel."

Rapunzel let her hair grow long, and she placed it around her mouth like a mustache and beard. "See? I can disguise myself. I'm a barbarian of Nor!"

"I don't think you'll fool them." Cinderella stroked the girl's shoulder. "You are exceedingly pretty. I hope my daughter Snowy Vallee grows up to be as fair as you."

Listening in, Valencia said, "Snowy Vallee is a pretty name."

Cinderella turned to her. "Not surprising. Vallee is short for Valencia."

Valencia blinked rapidly. "You named her after me?"

"Naturally, I love you very much. Roger and I wanted to honor you."

Valencia put a hand to her heart. Even though she could not remember her sister, she clearly favored her among the rest of us. After more introductions, I took this break in our journey to recommend we use a little magic to set up camp.

Around the campfire later that night, Rapunzel told a series of knock-knock jokes to which Cinderella responded with enthusiasm. The princes were engaged in a card game.

Once everyone formed a circle around the fire, Cinderella cleared her throat to call our attention.

"We must be careful. Piper has the Pipes of Perringon."

Gasps erupted around the campfire from the Kingdom residents. Sanders asked, "What are the Pipes of Perringon?"

Cinderella rubbed her hands together. "A powerful magic item capable of changing a person's behavior in all ways except to love or hate. With that artifact in Piper's hands, he played a tune to put a spell on Kingdom. This is what caused everyone to forget our reign as queens."

"'Tis a legendary item, to be sure." Graddock drew on a pipe between his teeth. "But I do not know if the pipe's power could ensorcel an entire world."

Celeste floated in the air above a log. "It could."

"Look around you." Cinderella gestured to the darkness surrounding the campsite. "And I was there when he played it and erased my memories."

I leaned forward, setting my elbows on my knees. "Piper told us that he was wronged, and the queens didn't serve justice to his enemies."

"A half-truth." Cinderella grimaced. "He drove the rats out of Haylon, and the mayor didn't pay him. He came to us with an appeal but had to wait. Hero, the queens cannot be in the middle of every slight done to our citizens. We appointed judges to rule fairly. Unfortunately, he didn't receive satisfaction or money to live. He decided to play a concert for the children near the mountains, hoping to make some coin."

I grabbed a stick near the fire. "He didn't kidnap them like in the Earth fairy tale?"

"No, far worse." Cinderella averted her gaze to her hands. "The people of Haylon, feeling guilty, encouraged each other to attend the show, and so all the children were there. When he was playing his music, a landslide occurred, burying the children and many of the parents."

I poked the fire, still riveted on her every word. "But Piper survived?"

Cinderella breathed in deep. "He did. Witnesses there said the landslide pushed him back into the mountain into a newly uncovered passage. He told us later he found the Pipes of Perringon within seconds before he played them and cast the forgetting spell."

"How do you know this happened?" Wysdel leaned forward, eyes glued on her sister. I realized she hadn't been there when Piper mesmerized her sisters and was hearing this for the first time too.

"The mayor and aldermen of Haylon brought him before us. They claimed he magicked the landslide in retribution. Piper said he would never hurt children."

Roger placed down a card. "I believe him on that point. Despite everything he has done to us, he has not harmed our children. They live in relative happiness in the orphanage without their memories."

"We queens didn't know if what he said was true," Cinderella continued. "But the mob in the court was turning ugly, and we needed to separate them from him. We asked for a recess and quietly told the guards to take Piper to a different room for questioning. While we adjourned, we discussed the matter and were favoring his side of the events. But Piper, thinking the guards were a sign we were going to jail him, had the pipes out when we returned to the room where he was waiting."

Valencia's jaw hung down. "So, you recognized the pipes when he played them?"

"No, my dear." Cinderella pointed at Valencia. "You did. You said their name, and that was the last moment of free will any of us had before he erased our memories. You, my brilliant, scholarly sister, know the legends of Kingdom better than any of us."

Valencia put a hand to her mouth. Cinderella stared at her. "Now, do you believe me?"

Valencia dropped her gaze to the fire. "Everyone in Kingdom knows the Pipes of Perringon legend. They know the story that the citizens of Perringon destroyed their own town when the governor played them. The pipes are hardly a secret."

"But not known by sight," countered Cinderella. "You saw a picture of them in your books, I'm sure."

Valencia stood. "I want to go for a walk and clear my head."

Graddock rose to his feet. "I will accompany you in case giants lurk nearby."

Cinderella watched them walk away, firelight dancing in her eyes. When they were out of earshot, she giggled. "Ha! They'll be smooching before you know it."

Wysdel brushed a stray curl away from her face. "Queen Helga will not be so easy."

"Indeed. We will have both Valencia and Helga on our hands." Rubbing her temples, Cinderella raised her eyebrows. "But perhaps we could delay meeting Helga and give me time to convince Valencia."

Sanders rubbed her fingertips to produce tiny, blue sparks. "You don't want to teleport into the convent where Helga is staying? I've been there." She proceeded to tell us of her mistake—which she blamed on me—and how she had met Helga.

Cinderella said, "I have no idea what to do when I meet Helga without Danforth. 'Tis not as though we can teleport in there the way you did, Sanders."

"Why not?" asked my wife.

Cinderella held up two fingers. "Two reasons. The first is it's warded against teleportation, and Helga was right. Your unconventional approach to magic allowed you to slip through." She glanced at Celeste. "Celeste could likely overcome it, but the second reason is too important."

"And that is?" I tossed my stick into the fire.

Tilting her head, Cinderella regarded me like a professor whose straight-A student missed an easy question. "You don't know? The church isn't subject to the queens' rule. All land owned by the religious is independent of Kingdom. I must enter as a guest. Otherwise, I break the sacred covenant between Crown and Worship."

"But Cinderella, we are in dire times," Sanders interjected. "A time of war even. I don't think anyone will hold it against you."

Cinderella straightened her shoulders. "Sanders, I am a queen of Kingdom. I must act like one, even in these times. I will not break such a foundational rule of Kingdom."

"She's right." Sylvia sighed. "Many times I was tempted as mayor to break the law for the greater good, but I'm glad I didn't do it."

"So, we're not going to teleport into the convent but outside of it?"

Roger stroked his beard. "How about going to Ghael's Inn? The new building Helga dedicated two years ago?"

Cinderella patted his hand. "A sound idea. The inn is about a half-day's journey from the Saint Bonadventure's Convent."

"Great!" I nodded to Celeste. "We'll teleport to this inn in the morning."

Cinderella pursed her lips. "Could you give us the morning to journey? I would like time to try to convince Valencia she is a queen. If her memory is restored before we meet Helga, I think together we can convince our stalwart sister."

We agreed to the plan. But Sanders and I exchanged a worried glance. Another day without Fitzie. How many more?

We all agreed to take turns on watch during the night. Minutes before dawn, Celeste woke up Sanders, who nudged me. I cleared the sleep from my eyes while Celeste pulled Sanders to her feet. "We must leave. Giants approach."

I shook my head as the others awoke, though Cinderella and Roger were already on their feet. Graddock reached for his sword, but Roger placed a hand on his shoulder. He nodded at his wife. "Let her take care of it."

Valencia swayed on her feet, looking ready to bolt.

"Cinderella? What can she possibly do against three giants?"

Roger straightened up. "Prove to you she is a queen."

Kingdom

27 - BERCEUSE

Harold

Three two-headed giants emerged from the predawn darkness with long pikes in their hands. Their black hair matted with sweat, their faces red, they resembled rhinos ready to charge. Over ten feet tall each, the giants sent six sneering expressions glaring at our party. The last time I had encountered giants, I was with Helga. Those odds were far better.

Undeterred, Cinderella marched toward them, lifted her hand, and spread her fingers wide. Huzzah! She was going to use her ability to appeal to their conscience, hopefully drawing out their sense of justice and mercy.

Cinderella cleared her throat. "Stop! In your hearts, you know you do not want to take our lives."

She stood upright, though two times smaller in height

than any of them. Roger was a skilled swordsman; usually he accompanied his wife. Yet now, he crossed his arms and gazed at the scene as if watching a movie.

The giant in front had scraggly black hair with a blond streak. "We will kill you!" growled one head. The second followed with "Indeed."

Graddock drew his sword and stepped in front of Valencia. Sanders put Rapunzel's head against her breast and grabbed Celeste's arm.

The giants advanced on Cinderella and loomed over her like three, long-stemmed thistle plants crowding out a sprouting daisy.

"Is this what the giants have descended to?" Cinderella's eyes flared. "You would take the lives of human travelers who wish you no harm? We are scarcely an army, only desiring safe passage to the Marsh of Wishes."

The giant with blond-streaked hair pointed his pike to the west. "Then go around giant territory." The other five heads nodded.

"This land belongs to no one and everyone." Cinderella tapped her foot on the ground. "You would constrain yourself to this patch of Kingdom? Do you not wish your own children might walk freely anywhere in our nation? The time is coming when they can, when you may take your family to Grok's Teeth and view the sunset, or buy trinkets in the markets of Town, or sit at table in any inn barred to you now. These days will only come to pass if you allow our simple caravan to move across these lands to the swamp."

The lead giant's head swiveled to its twin. Another one of the brutes' heads, this one bald, nodded at Valencia's guard. Roger whispered, "Put away the sword, Graddock."

Graddock complied, and Cinderella swung her pointing hand around at them. "What is your answer? Freedom or brutality?"

The main giant lowered his weapon. "We will let you pass because your party is few, and your ideas are amusing.

You speak pretty words, but you are a dreamer. T'would be a shame to kill a dreamer who does not know how the real world works."

Cinderella curtsied. "We shall not tarry."

We picked up our belongings and rushed past the giants. They murmured they would send word to ensure we would not be detained again, and Cinderella thanked them. When she returned to us and the two-headed beings couldn't hear her, she whispered. "How sad to be stuck in the present, unable to envision a better future."

Valencia's eyes were riveted on her sister. "Where did you find the confidence to stand up to giants?"

"Oh, Valencia. This would be child's play for you too, if only you would remember."

After an hour of traveling, we paused at a small lake behind a line of trees. Cinderella took Roger and Graddock aside and asked them to bathe. She whispered something to her husband that the rest of us didn't hear. I considered joining them, but she asked me to stay back. After the men left, she asked Valencia to take a walk with her. A *cri de couer* rang out moments later, and the two queens came stumbling out of the woods, Valencia blushing and Cinderella with a smug expression. Later she told us the two had "accidentally" come across the princes, and Roger had dropped down into the water to hide. Valencia had taken a long look at Graddock. Cinderella lowered her eyes, surreptitiously. "Valencia could not keep her eyes off of him."

We started the journey to the north. As we walked, Cinderella took Sanders' and my arms and escorted us, again proclaiming how happy she was to see us. "I never get to spend enough time with the two of you."

"Where is Valencia?"

Cinderella looked ahead and we followed her gaze to spy the Match Girl and Graddock walking together out of earshot of everyone else. They were walking side by side, close together but not touching. The queen winked at us. "Sanders, will you cast a spell to listen in on them?"

I protested. "We really shouldn't—"

Sanders had cast it before I finished my sentence. Valencia's voice sounded as though she were standing next to me. "...father died, I journeyed across the tundra from Exile to Tusk. I was starving when I entered the town because no one would give me anything to eat."

"They were cruel to you." A trill of menace undercut Graddock's sympathy.

"Mangiafuoca found me soon after I entered Tusk. She brought me to her store, fed me, and said I could work there as a doll if I did not mind children."

"I found it deplorable how those children treated you."

"They are rich, and I am poor." Valencia's voice was full of despair.

"If you were rich or poor does not matter to me, no person should be treated in such a manner."

They fell quiet for a few moments until Valencia spoke again. "What if this entire thing is a ruse? What would you think of me then?"

"I would be glad we met. Say it is a ruse, what will you do now?"

"I do not know," answered Valencia. "Return to Tusk, perhaps? I know no other option."

Graddock cleared his throat. "Why not go with me? I would like to build a little cottage at the edge of the forest and live a sedentary life. The house may be humble with only a couple of rooms, but it would suit me fine. You may wonder what I would do to pass the time. I am fond of rocks, and I would love to sit by a roaring fire at night after a day of collecting them."

"Sounds peaceful."

"Lonely, too. My only fear is that I will grow bored. I may not like the seclusion. Perhaps, if you are so inclined, you could accompany me until you know what it is you would like to do?"

Valencia laughed. "I... I am flattered. Your offer is

generous. I will consider it."

Cinderella put a hand on Sanders' shoulder and my wife stopped the spell. Cinderella said, "Valencia will not believe that she is a queen or that we are related, obstinate sister of mine, but she does favor Graddock. I am doing everything in my power to get them to kiss."

Cinderella diverted her attention to Sylvia and Rapunzel who were walking ahead and chatting. "And now we have another fairytale princess in Kingdom? She will play a part in all of this. Her hair-growing ability is unique."

"I don't think that is her ability." I squinted against the sun. "Her mother was an alchemist, and she gave Rapunzel several elixirs to keep her safe. Her hair growth is a result of her mother's protection."

"We do not know her ability yet?"

Sanders eyed the girl. "I think she can do a lot of things. She either hasn't told us yet or doesn't know. She confessed her mother wouldn't tell her what all the potions she made her drink did."

We continued our trek until Valencia asked for a bathroom break. After she went into the bushes, Sanders said, "I think I will join her. Nature isn't only calling but screaming into a megaphone."

"Bonding over blipsie-doodling?" I asked.

Sanders eyed me warily. "Such a guy!" she huffed and flew off.

And then a shout from my wife. "Oh, my God!"

We were on our feet in a heartbeat. Graddock had his sword out and rushed toward the brambles. Roger also stood, but Cinderella held his arm to give Graddock a head start. Sanders flew out and held up her hands. "No one comes back here."

Graddock growled, "Why not? What is wrong?"

Valencia's voice called out over the bushes. "*Ta Gueule!* Do not tell them!"

Sparkles rained down as my wife shrugged. "But,

Valencia, you have nothing to be ashamed of."

Valencia emerged from the bushes adjusting her purple dress. "I should have figured it would be a *pixie* who found out. You had to sneak your way into my privacy. Stay away from me!"

Cinderella reached out and put a hand on Valencia's arm. "Please do not insult Sanders. She's a dear friend."

Valencia pulled away from Cinderella, and Graddock stepped closer. She edged toward him. "She is not my friend, and you are not my sister! I do not trust any of you!" She turned to Graddock and gave him a look that indicated he was excluded.

"Valencia!" Wysdel tossed her head back. "Truly? After how we have treated you?"

Twisting her loose-fitting dress with her hands, Valencia raised her voice. "You are giving me false hope about queens and families and wealth. I am not the person you think I am, and I want you all to stay away from me!"

We all stepped back at her venomous outburst. All of Cinderella's hard work to entice Valencia to trust us had evaporated from Sanders interrupting her peeing? That made no sense.

I winced as my wife spoke, her voice calm and low. "Show them, Valencia."

Valencia bared her teeth at Sanders, who remained placid. My wife floated in the air, arms at her side, never more serious. "They don't understand. You'll find out just what kind of people they are if you show them."

Valencia shifted her gaze to the rest of us, then glanced at Graddock, blushing. Certainly, she didn't want to show us her secret. Him, least of all. However, my wife's judgment, always sound in a crisis, forced her hand. She sighed and slowly took her dress and pressed it against her stomach. A bump, the size of a child's bowling ball, formed near her belly.

Cinderella's hands went to her mouth and Wysdel paled. Rapunzel looked at Sanders and me. Graddock's arms dropped to his sides. Celeste, the least astonished of all of us, stated it plainly. "You are with child."

Valencia slumped her shoulders. "Yes. I do not know how. I cannot remember it happening."

Cinderella and Wysdel both hugged her at the same time. Valencia stiffened, but she didn't resist. Cinderella's eyes were filled with tears. "But do you not understand? This proves our version of what happened!"

"How?"

Cinderella gazed down at her stomach. "Valencia, I have birthed two children. You do not forget what happened unless forced to."

Valencia took a deep breath. "Perhaps I have removed it from my mind. Perhaps what happened was so horrible that I do not want to remember."

Cinderella eyed Wysdel. "Pish-posh. Before Piper came, you and Graddock decided to have a baby. Piper did not create a memory of it because he didn't know."

Graddock dropped his sword, and Valencia looked at him as if regarding him for the first time, her mouth agape, and then she displayed a slight smile. Had she never considered Graddock the father? Perhaps, Valencia had never combined our story with becoming pregnant, keeping the two events separate.

Graddock stepped back. "I am not the father. As you said, you do not forget something like that."

Wysdel said, "The spell was cast about seven months ago, and Valencia appears between her seventh and eighth month."

Cinderella smirked. "And now I remember you offered to take Snowy Vallee for a few nights. I thought you were being a good aunt, but you wanted to be close to a baby."

Graddock clenched his fists. "I tell you I am not the father!"

Valencia recoiled from that remark, but Cinderella approached him and stabbed her finger into his chest. "Of course you are. What do you think of my sister? She is honorable and faithful, traits she has taught you. You can say what you want, but I know Valencia, and she has only one man for her. I have no doubt she carries your child. This is your happiest moment."

Valencia stepped forward. "How can it be his happiest moment when he does not know it is his? Do not badger my—"

Cinderella swung toward her. "Your what?"

Valencia stepped back. "My…friend." Valencia continued, "If your story was true, Cinderella, why did you not know I was with child when we first met? You are supposedly my sister. Would not I have told you?"

"You don't share enough with your sisters, Valencia." Cinderella stiffened. "You keep your secrets and have always been a little guarded. When you regain your memories, we're going to have a long talk."

"While I want to believe…I still have doubts." Valencia's eyes looked down. "I so desperately wanted to tell someone."

Cinderella again embraced Valencia. Though the Match Girl tried to slip out of her sister's arms, Cinderella wouldn't let her go. "I am by your side through this. You stood by mine during my first childbirth, and you have my solemn promise that I will not leave you during yours. You will be cared for when the time comes. Roger will help you, too. And the other queens, when they remember, will be there for you."

I glanced at Wysdel, and she nodded, slightly.

Valencia started to cry. "Really? I will not be alone?"

"Never." Cinderella held her hand above Valencia's baby bump. "May I?"

Valencia nodded, and Cinderella gently laid her hand on Valencia's stomach. She smiled and looked at her sister. "Now I cannot wait until you regain your memory. Kingdom will have much to celebrate! We will have a three-day festival!"

Roger cleared his throat. "Perhaps we should not make a woman with child march across Kingdom."

Cinderella threw an arm around Roger and pulled him

close to her. "An astute observation, dear husband. Celeste? Will you magic us to the inn outside the Marsh of Wishes?"

28 - GHAEL INN

Sondra

C ompared to most buildings in Kingdom, which were ancient, Ghael Inn shone with new bricks and a bright green-tiled roof. The structure stood guard on the edge of the marsh as a lonely soldier would at the border of a new country. Tall pine trees surrounded the inn on both sides, arranged in a crescent formation as if hands cupped around a treasure. A three-story lodge served as the entrance to two smaller hallways behind, spreading out in a Y-shape.

Cinderella looked around, nodding with pleasure. "Valencia, we were here at the dedication of this inn two years ago. We named it after Dame Hildegrant Ghael, a true hero of Kingdom."

Sylvia gasped. "You dedicated a building to my friend, Hildy?"

Cinderella laid a hand on Sylvia's arm. "I forgot you were there when she gave her life for Kingdom."

As we approached the thick, eight-foot-tall wooden doors, I changed my appearance so that I looked like another friend of ours, Paisley Nepta, who had short, mousey hair. Hero nudged me. "Give up on Charlie?"

"Yeah, I thought a change would do." I examined my nails. "My hands aren't the same coloring as Paisley's. I suppose I should change these too."

Cinderella grabbed Valencia's wrist. "Oh, I nearly forgot!"

Valencia examined Cinderella's sudden action but remained silent. For her part, Cinderella guided Valencia to a shrub near the door and circled around it. We followed them.

"Where are we going, my dear?" Roger asked, peering over his wife's shoulder.

"Before we dedicated this building, Penta told us about a tradition on Earth where people put their hands in soft stone," Cinderella answered. "I didn't understand it then, but she had Celeste cast a spell on a stone behind this shrub and demonstrated what she meant."

Cinderella pointed at a flat white rock the size of a headstone. Imprinted in the rock were five handprints. Under each was a single letter—P, H, V, C, and B.

Cinderella set her hand on the letter C. "This is my handprint. Valencia. Why don't you place your hand in the impression near the V?"

Valencia bit her lip. "Impossible. I have never been here."

"Won't hurt to try." Cinderella gestured to the slab.

Timidly, Valencia held out her hand to the handprint above the V. When she set her hand in the impression, it matched.

Cinderella waggled her eyebrows. "What did I tell you?"

Valencia withdrew her hand and eyed the stone. "'Tis interesting, but my hand is a bit larger."

"Oh, Valencia! Your hands may be swollen. Admit that it fits."

Valencia remained unconvinced, and we turned and approached the inn. The lodge fronted the two hallways in the back where the rooms were located. The three floors of the main building were shaped as rectangles, but each level's dimensions were smaller than the one beneath it, giving it a pyramid shape. This mammoth construction was at least three times the size of the cozier Inn of Five.

The bottom floor was constructed like a music hall for dancing. The middle floor was a typical tavern with tables and the top floor was a private club for intelligent swamp inhabitants displaced by the new inn. Cinderella told us the ceiling of the first floor and floor of the second were magical and became transparent based on events at the inn. Today, no one was performing, yet the floor was see-through. We walked in to view tables apparently floating in mid-air with waiters and waitresses running up and down invisible stairs.

Graddock leaned to the side and looked up. "I see why the waitresses wear pants. I can only imagine what the Thirsty Wench would do with a ceiling such as this."

Valencia wrinkled her nose, obviously displeased with Graddock's observation. Roger noticed it too. "I've missed your responses to your husband's ill-timed comments, Valencia," he said.

The tiny woman nodded at Roger.

We climbed the spiral stairs, passing a sign announcing Gilbert Grossenroid as tonight's storyteller. Barmen and barmaids rushed back and forth, and we had to wait for a table. A person with cornrows-styled hair and a forked tongue approached us. "We are full at the moment."

Valencia murmured to Cinderella, but loud enough for us to hear. "Surely, queens are not turned away at the inns they've established."

All at once, a band of dryads stood, and moved toward the exit. They dropped coins in the waiter's hands as they passed us. "Cornrows" did a quick count of the dryads. "The exact number of people in your party. Your table awaits," they said.

Cinderella nudged Valencia. "How fortunate. As if luck followed someone everywhere she went."

Valencia beamed at the observation of her queenly ability. Now that her secret was out, she held herself more confidently.

After we sat at the circular, oaken table, Cinderella ordered a roasted lamb and bread bowls with salad in them. Roger ordered mead and something called Druid's Root, an earthy-smelling ale. Graddock and Roger had a contest over which of them could finish their tankard first. Hero and I didn't order anything. You can drink Kingdom water if you are used to it, but I almost contracted dysentery just by looking at the pieces floating in the liquids.

Cinderella asked about our mutual friends, including Alice. At the mention of Alice's name, Hero perked up. "Cinderella, have you ever heard of Joseph Macquin? Alice would like us to find him while we're here."

Cinderella touched her chin. "I can't say that I have."

"Give up looking for this dude, Hero," I said. "We have more important things to do."

Hero frowned, then retrieved the *Swan Princess*'s spyglass and placed it on a nubbed end, twirling it around on the table thoughtfully. He had taken a powerful magic item and transformed it into a fidget spinner. "Cinderella, Roger? How well do you know this marsh? Could you lead us safely through it?"

I nodded to Celeste. "Her Extraordinariness will transport us close enough."

Hero gave the spyglass a nudge. "If Valencia doesn't mind walking, I'd rather reserve Celeste's magic."

"Why, hubby?"

"I suspect Piper is keeping tabs on us. He might have people in this inn. And now that we have two queens..."

Roger set down his tankard. "He will make a move. We need a guide."

We ate and drank, discussing the benefits and dangers of teleporting. We agreed to journey now on foot. After a couple of rounds and succulent forkfuls of dinner, we asked our host if anyone in the inn could be hired as a guide.

As they thought about it, a man with a tricorn hat, a black leather jacket, and green leggings tucked into small boots stood up at the table next to us. He wore a bandana over his mouth and nose with ties around his ears extending over his dundrearies. His piercing green eyes took us all in.

His muffled voice addressed us. "I could not help but overhear. You seek a guide to the convent?"

Everyone looked at Hero. My husband was like our human litmus test of whether to trust someone or not. He was uncomfortable, so I put my hand on his knee under the table. Hero pushed the spyglass in a circle but stared at the man. "You've been there?"

The spyglass distracted the masked man for a moment before he answered. "Many times."

"How far is it from here?"

The man scratched his sideburns. "Most of a day's journey. We can leave in the morning. Three gold."

We didn't have that much gold, but his eyes locked on Celeste. I didn't like his lingering stare, so I spoke to turn his attention to me. "Deal."

"An accord!" corrected Roger. "Sanders, recall we only deal when we play cards."

The stranger seemed unperturbed by my slip of the tongue. "My name is Cillian Puttè. I go by Cilly."

Hero extended his hand. "Of course you do."

The man stared at Hero as if about to say something but then only shook his hand. He surveyed us again, and I noticed he lingered a little longer on Pennilane. Just what we need, a perverted guide. When his eyes met mine, he spoke. "I will meet you at the front of the inn tomorrow just after dawn."

The guide turned on his heel and slipped between the inn's patrons, heavy pipe smoke obscuring his exit. Pennilane grabbed her butter knife like a weapon. "He is a seal hunter. I know his type. We should find someone else."

"Are you certain, dear?" asked Cinderella.

Pennilane nodded and squinted.

"We have an accord." Roger lifted his tankard to the waiter, indicating he wanted more. "Unlike in Hero's faithless world, my word is my honor. Pennilane, you do not remember, but I am a friend. I will protect you with my life if needed. He may be troll droppings, but he is our guide."

Picking at my salad, I spiked a leafy piece of radish. "I don't like the mask."

"Some adventurers wear masks to hide scars or deformities." Wysdel pointed at her face with her fork. "He would consider us rude to ask him to remove it."

We reserved rooms at the inn for the night, inviting Rapunzel to sleep with us. The room was elegant for this world, with two beds and a small oval table. A window in the ceiling admitted light.

As we were settling into the room, the chambermaid said, "Your daughter will like the smaller bed in this room."

When she left, Hero scratched his head. "Daughter? Why not sister?"

I smiled. "For that comment, you are my hero! But clearly Rapunzel looks more like our daughter. I've crossed thirty even if you haven't."

Rapunzel giggled. "*Mom*, will you tuck me in?"

I laughed. "Right after I ask *Dad* how he thinks he's going to get three gold coins?"

Hero grimaced. "Stop that. We'll ask Celeste to transform some of Wysdel's iron trinkets to gold."

"Celeste's not going to like that. She's an honorable pixie, not one of the tricky ones, the kind Valencia hates."

"We don't have a choice. Now, let's go to sleep. I'm exhausted."

As I was falling asleep, someone banged on our door. Hero grumbled and asked the person to identify himself, and the inn owner replied. He said he had an urgent message.

Cursing, Hero crossed the room and opened the door while I transformed into my Paisley guise. The innkeeper stood there with a gun pointed at my husband. A gun! An object unknown in Kingdom.

Hero stepped back and held up his hands. "Where did you get *that*?"

The innkeeper trembled. "I do not want to hurt you, but the king himself entrusted me with this and told me to make you come downstairs. Only you and your wife."

I raised my hands, and Rapunzel stared at the scene with a bedsheet up to her nose. "I will not leave our daughter."

"She may lock the door and barricade herself with the table." The innkeeper gestured to the room key hanging on a hook. "We must not tarry. The king awaits."

The innkeeper marched us down the hallway into the main building on the first level where all the chairs were stacked on the tables except one in the middle. At a square table sat Piper and a woman who resembled me with slight differences. So this was "Queen" Planet.

Piper swung a hand toward two empty seats on the other side of the table. We took our places warily, and the innkeeper gave the revolver to Piper who set it on the surface in front of him. "Curious item my predecessors collected from your home world, Hero. I found it in their vault."

"The queens didn't bring it here," said Hero through gritted teeth. "Their adversary did."

Piper waved away Hero's explanation. "I have discharged it once as practice, so I suggest you listen carefully to what your king and queen have to say."

The false king dismissed the innkeeper, and the only light in the room was a lantern on the table. I transformed back into my normal features.

Piper cleared his throat. "Both Planet and I are—"

"She is *not* Planet," I hissed.

The woman frowned but said nothing.

"—ensorcelled to prevent any magic spell from affecting us. So even with your legendary skills, Sanders, I would think twice before casting a spell."

I rubbed my hands together under the table, calculating my next move. I couldn't cast anything on them but could still cast something on me. Should I grow large like a giant? Wall up the room? Or change my appearance to startle him? I pondered my options.

Hero's eyes blazed. "What do you want?"

"Direct, are you not?" Piper cracked his knuckles, one by one. "I told you I was not the villain of your adventure, but you ignored me. I tried to capture you at the soldiers' quarters."

"You tried to stab me! Here." Hero touched his ribs.

Piper snorted. "A wound to detain, not to kill. I would have healed you. I told you I admire what you have done for Kingdom in the past."

"Well then, give back the throne to the people who deserve it." My fingers clenched, aching to throw a spell.

Piper scowled at me. Clearly, "as if," or however you say it in Kingdom, reflected on his face. He set his hands on the table. "You have refused my gracious offer. After some reflection, I now understand asking Sanders to be my queen and to part from her son is unjust. Please forgive my presumption. I meant no offense."

He hung his head and looked so much like Kris Heavens that I wanted to forgive him. He was distracting me from the problem of the gun, though.

"Whatever," said Hero. "I'm sure you didn't drag us out of bed to tell us you're sorry."

"Planet and I—"

I pounded my fist on the table. "She is *not* Planet! Call her by her real name or I'm not going to listen to you."

He tapped the revolver. "I have the gun."

I cast a spell and removed my ears then pointed at the

sides of my head. "I can't hear you." I could hear him but he didn't know that.

Piper gestured to restore my ears, and I complied. "Fine. Her original name is Janus. Janus and I discussed this in detail. Turns out, she wants to go to Earth and experience your world."

The near-replica of me took the opportunity to speak. "A Traveler told us about television and airplanes. I want to see them." Her eyes sparkled.

Hero grimaced. "I still don't understand."

Piper made a motion between Hero and himself. "We swap. Maybe for part of the year. I get Sanders for half, and you get her for the other half."

So…why didn't I lose my shit at this idea? Truth was, his suggestion was so absurd, I couldn't speak. For once.

"This is worse than your first proposal!" Hero pointed at Janus. "I'm not going back to Earth with her. She's not my wife or Fitzie's mother, and I certainly am not going to leave my love here with you!"

Janus winked at Hero. "I could be your wife. Think about it. Diversity in the bedroom might be to your liking."

I stood. I couldn't take another word coming out of this evil twin's mouth. "I may not be able to throw a spell, but I can still knock your block off, sister!"

Piper put his hand on Janus's arm. "Calm yourself, my pet. Remember what we said."

I breathed heavily through my nose like a bull about to charge. Hero's next words, though, slowed my rush of anger. "Sanders is the love of my life and the only one for me. Tempting me with other women is a lost cause." He glared at Janus. "And everything is fine in the bedroom."

Janus shrugged. "'Tis not like your marriage is over. You would have two where you had one. And I will even let little Fitzie suckle on me if he wants."

Hero grabbed me, and a good thing he did. I shouted, "Fitzie is six years old, you bimbo. There'll be no suckling while

I'm alive."

Perplexed, Janus said, "Oh, I thought he was a babe."

Leaning forward, Piper said, "Sit down, Sanders." His tone was no longer cordial but threatening.

I sat and glared at Janus. What a floozy! Hero's next question stunned me when he addressed her.

"Why are you putting up with him, Janus? He's willing to trade you away. What's the attraction?"

Attraction...that word. Something there.

Janus moved her finger back and forth. "Oh, no. You will not turn me against him. He made me a queen the day after I was in the stocks. And you know who put me there?"

I felt a headache coming on. "The queens."

Nostrils flaring, she sneered, "Pickpocketing! All I did was take a few money purses. For this, I end up in the stocks?"

But my mind went back to the word "attraction," and I quickly thought of an idea. I hid my hands under the table and whispered an incantation, hoping it would work.

Piper's frown deepened at Hero's question. "Enough of this. You two are coming with me. I cannot allow you to continue with the queens. You have done enough damage restoring Beauty's and Cinderella's memory which I shall have to remove from them again. I cannot have Valencia recalling her past as well."

He reached for the gun, but I had finished the spell. I raised my hands, transformed them into two huge magnets, and pointed them at the weapon. The gun's barrel slid across the table away from the false king. I quickly restored my hands and scooped up the revolver.

Piper blanched, and Janus stiffened. I cocked the gun. "You're leaving now. My father taught me to shoot muskrats when I was three, foxes when I was five, and bears when I was ten." I squinted my right eye and raised the gun, aiming at the royal faker. "Shooting you will be my pleasure."

"You will regret—"

I interrupted Piper. "—this. Yeah, I know. I could've been

a queen. I could've had riches beyond my imagination. Blah. Blah. Get lost."

The fake king and queen stood, and Piper took Janus's hand, then hummed a trio of notes. As the music ended, their bodies became translucent and vanished. Not invisibility, teleportation. I knew that much. He had to exit with an advanced teleportation spell! Show off.

Hero stood up and hugged me after I lowered the revolver. "You never shot a bear when you were ten. You never even shot a real gun. You're the only person I know who shot herself playing paintball."

"Oh, shut up. Let's go tell the others. Piper is becoming desperate."

We were dressed and ready at sunrise. Rapunzel was having a time of it calling Hero "Dad." I could tell the nickname made him uncomfortable, but he'd get over it, the big baby.

Cillian, I couldn't honestly call him Cilly, came around. Again, he fixed his gaze on the women, particularly Pennilane. Roger glared at him with his hand on the hilt of his sword. Cillian understood the non-verbal warning and looked away.

At the break of dawn, we set off directly into the marsh. Celeste was upset about tricking Cillian, but she agreed to transform three worthless hunks of metal to gold. She and our guide went at a distance to make the transaction. When Cillian was satisfied, he returned and told us to follow him.

Unlike Hero, with his fifty-cent words like "verdant" and "willowwacks," I can't properly describe the marsh. He would say, "The plashing morass stretched before us with narrow tracks of firm ground made of paludal soil and tree roots. The rising marsh gas was a silvery-purple color instead of green, creating bubbles as we passed. Humid yet frigid, the air felt oppressive because of low-hanging cumulus clouds. Though rotting barks shot up through murky waters, the marsh didn't smell of decay but had a light, honeysuckle scent to it." I, on the other hand, would describe it as "The swamp was wet and dirty, and we trudged through."

I'm a scientist, not some fancy writer.

We moved slowly across the marsh with Cillian in the lead. A wide pathway of solid ground cut across the bubbling bog much to my relief. I had pictured us hopping from one point to another last night, but fortunately we didn't have to play hopscotch today. I wondered why we had hired Cillian until we crossed intersecting byways. The trails here were a maze.

Most of the morning, I flew next to Celeste and used my power to float Rapunzel along when I could. She hovered next to Hero, saying, "Watch your step, Dad." He grinned a few times, warming up to her teasing.

Rapunzel's "Dad" and "Mom" horsing around made me think of my own mother and the scene with the Constellations Ma. Hero and I fell back from the others. With a lump in my throat, I explained what Ma Constellation had said to me. Recalling the conversation brought it all back—a grief like a hole that I could never fill with my tears. I finished, sniffed, and grabbed Hero's hand. "My visit with her helped. You know I'm not much of a believer in an afterlife, but somehow, I know my mother was there, Harold." Our real names seemed appropriate to this conversation.

Hero squeezed my hand. "I'm sorry, Sondra."

My eyes dotted with wetness. "It's so silly. She wasn't my mother, but...for a moment...I felt..."

Hero slung his arm around me, and I put my head on his shoulder as we walked. My throat loosened as I talked. "You wonder why I'm so protective of Rapunzel. It's because I understand her need for a family. Since my mother died, I've felt lost. My mom was my anchor, Harold. For months, my life has been like a ship in a whirlpool, descending into nothingness."

Clenching his jaw, he started to speak but I cut him

off. "But now, I feel I've moved on from the vortex. Ma Constellation and Rapunzel have helped.

Hero didn't respond. We walked in the sunshine, the chirps of marsh creatures the only sound. I cleared my throat. "You've been wonderful. I'm glad you're in my life. But that talk with Mrs. Constellation, I'll never forget it. It's reminded me of what I've lost, but it's also given me hope."

Ahead of us, Wysdel, Sylvia, and Cinderella all laughed at one of Rapunzel's silly knock-knock jokes. Wysdel surreptitiously put her arm on Rapunzel's back, and Cinderella was holding Rapunzel's hand. I thought about the succession of queens for the first time. Beauty had taken Snow White's place before Snow White turned thirty. I tensed my shoulders picturing Rapunzel as a queen. What if we only convinced some of the sisters that they were queens and not all of them? Would they reclaim the throne without breaking the spell over everyone? Penta was going to be a challenge. Would the others expect Rapunzel to take the throne from Penta after she came of age?

Hero interrupted my thoughts. "Let's join them."

We caught up to the rest. The conversation had changed from humor to geography. Wind whipping her longer hair, Rapunzel asked, "Why is this called the Marsh of Wishes?"

Cillian brushed his fingers along the tops of fronds growing in the wet patch next to us. "Bards sing of legends of how it received its name. One popular song says if you find a will-o-the-wisp in the marsh, make a wish. If you are pure-hearted, the creature will grant it."

Rapunzel gazed across the marsh. "I hope I see one!"

An hour later, Cillian called for a rest, Roger and Graddock sparred off to the side. Graddock continued to disarm Roger again and again. Cinderella stood by the side of the battle, eyes on Valencia. Now Roger was a top-notch swordsman, and I could see Cinderella's hand in his "defeat."

When Graddock beat Roger three times in a row, Cinderella hugged Roger and gave Graddock a kiss on the cheek.

Graddock stiffened at her gesture. "Should you not be kissing your own husband?"

"You forget." She patted his cheek. "I am your sister-in-law, and victors should be rewarded." She turned to Valencia. "You should reward him too."

Wysdel lowered her head. "Cin—" She caught herself before calling her sister by her name informally and revealing her own real identity. She cleared her throat. "Queen Cinderella. Perhaps—"

Cinderella ignored her and grabbed Valencia's hand, pulling her so that she stood in front of Graddock. Panicked, the two of them looked at each other, and I groaned mentally. What a ploy to get them to kiss. Only Cinderella.

Valencia mechanically lifted her arms and put them straight against Graddock's sides in the stiffest and most awkward hug I have ever seen. Cinderella bumped her with her behind and Valencia fell against Graddock. He caught her gracefully. The act had succeeded in getting them into an embrace.

Valencia lifted her head, blinked, and flushed. For his part, Graddock stared at her wide-eyed. For a moment, I thought he was going to kiss her. The moment hung in the air preserved like a fly in amber, and everyone held their breath. Valencia stood on her tiptoes and lightly gave him a kiss on his right cheek. They parted and stepped back. Then, Cillian suggested we continue.

The convent was four hours away, and we marched along, hour after hour, in an increasingly less jovial mood. After a while, Hero called for another rest. The Kingdomers frowned, used to walking long distances, but Hero and I weren't. My wings were sore.

We found a nice cul-de-sac off to the side of the trail and Valencia chose a seat furthest from Cinderella. Sylvia sat down next to her and shared a stick of lamb we had procured from the inn. After Valencia thanked her, Sylvia said, "I was close to your sister who died, Valencia. Snow White. She and I would write to each other."

"What was she like?"

Seated within earshot, Wysdel toed the dirt. Sylvia, who had no idea Snow White was among them, continued to describe her to Valencia.

"Friendly. Possibly the most thoughtful woman I'd ever met. When I first came here, I had to pretend I was her to confuse the queens' enemies."

Valencia lowered her half-eaten meat and examined Sylvia. "You resemble her?"

"A spell disguised me, but I have her general features. If she were here, you would love her. I know she would be so happy about your baby."

Wysdel smiled.

Valencia lowered her head. "I would have liked to have met her."

Sylvia placed a hand on Valencia's shoulder. "She inspired me like no other person ever has. Kind, yet wise. She'd willingly give her life for her sisters. We could all learn from her. I wish I could be like Snow White."

And then we spotted a tiny ball of light, an ignis fatuus, rise out of marsh. From it, a high-pitched voice said "granted" then winked out.

We all jumped to our feet, and Wysdel put her hands over her mouth. In seconds, Sylvia's face and body stretched and bubbled, reforming itself. When it was done, Sylvia was the spitting image of Snow White.

Sylvia gazed at herself in a puddle at her feet. Wysdel rushed forward, shaking her head. "Oh no. No. No."

Cinderella ran to Sylvia's side, tears pooling at the corners of her eyes. "Amazing! I couldn't tell the difference."

Sylvia removed her glasses and blinked. She handed them to Wysdel. "I don't need these. I can see without them."

"If Piper finds out, he is going to kill you." Wysdel handed Sylvia's glasses back to her. "Reverse the wish. Say it."

Sylvia went to speak and then stopped. "Why should I?"

Wysdel grabbed her arms. "Because your life is in danger, that is why. Sylvia, reverse the wish."

"She has to mean it," Hero said. "I don't think she will."

Sylvia straightened her shoulders. "Let him come for me. Like those signs say. 'Snow White lives.' It's time to give people hope."

Wysdel spent the next half hour on the walk trying to convince Sylvia to take the wish back, but Sylvia was adamant about maintaining Snow White's form. We continued marching on with Wysdel, the old Snow White, pleading with Sylvia, the new Snow White, to change back. Her attempts to involve Cinderella only resulted in a question. "I wonder if you have Snow White's gifts as well. Speaking to birds? And her ability to withstand pain and death from violence?"

Sylvia whacked her hand against a tree near the side of the path. "It doesn't hurt."

Wysdel said, "Sylvia, I think—"

"I think, my *wise* resistance fighter—" Cinderella winked at Wysdel. "—we have a powerful ally. And right now, we need all the help we can get. We can sort out this situation after we retake the throne. With her abilities, Sylvia is safer than she was before."

Wysdel glared at her sister, but her features softened with reason. She nodded, and we continued.

The Marsh of Wishes

29 - BELIEVING
NUN OF IT

Harold

We decided to stop for a rest along the path through the Marsh of Wishes. Cillian had asked us to watch our step at this point as we were in the most dangerous part of the bog. "The quicksand here will hungrily devour you, it being deeper than Ghael's Inn. And the moving moss may trip you into it."

The party huddled together until my wife moved to the edge of the trail. Just like her, after the warning, she heads toward danger! "Where are you going?"

She reached in her tunic and produced the gun she had retrieved from Piper. Cinderella gasped. "We need to lock away that odious artifact, Sanders."

"No!" proclaimed my wife. "I won't have this stupid thing pointed at my husband again. First, his knife is used against him, and then this gun. Your vault isn't safe."

Roger eyed the revolver. "What do you mean to do with it?"

Sanders extended her arm over the muck and dirt. "This!"

Her hand detached from her body and floated out over the bog, holding the weapon. When it reached about twenty yards away, her fingers released the gun into the mucky water. The item hit the sludge with a slurping sound, which gurgled as it swallowed the firearm, producing one bubble.

The hand returned to my wife's wrist. "There! I hope to never see that horrible thing again."

While this was going on, everyone but two people were watching us. Nonetheless, I noticed Cillian slipping something into Valencia's hand. Valencia gave him the smallest of nods. I filed it away under something I would have to ask her about later, away from our guide.

While pondering Cillian's actions, I was tapped on the shoulder by Cinderella. "Sanders mentioned your knife. Was it used on you?"

I described the scene where we freed Graddock from his cell and how Piper had attacked me.

Cinderella lifted her eyebrows. "And how did that work out for our beloved *king*? Did he strike you?"

She was being callous about a potential life-or-death situation. "No. He tried to hit me, but the knife turned the other way."

Cinderella clapped her hands. "It worked. Penta had Celeste cast a spell on that dagger so that you could control its actions."

Celeste's jaw dropped. "This is advanced magic. I am not sure I am capable of such a spell."

Cinderella waved at her. "Of course you are." She turned to me. "After so many others have used that knife against you,

Penta swore no one would ever do so again. That blade is yours to command, Hero. If he went to strike you, and you hoped he would miss, the knife would read your thoughts and purposely deflect."

I grinned. "Exactly what happened."

Roger stroked his beard. "He still possesses the knife. We could use this to our advantage, Hero. If he attacks you again and you direct it, you could have him stab himself in the leg."

I liked that idea.

Sondra

After twenty minutes, we started on our way again with Cinderella prattling on to Valencia about her baby. "When you remember, you will be so happy. You and Graddock will make wonderful parents. Snowy will be delighted to have a friend close to her age. I know you will be a great mom."

Valencia stopped, and since we were in a mostly straight line, everyone halted. She turned around to Cinderella. "You have so much confidence, but you have no way to know for certain."

"Oh yes, I do." Cinderella eyed her then shifted her attention to Graddock. "Kiss your husband."

Valencia stiffened. "I am not willing to do that yet."

Cinderella inclined her head toward the two of them. "Your love for each other is obvious to everyone here. Once you kiss him, you'll have your life back, and I'll have my sister back. And you will help me to convince Helga if you have your memories."

Valencia bit her lower lip. "What if...what if I kiss him and it does not work? What if we do not recover our memories?"

Cinderella put her hand on Valencia's arm, "It worked for me and Roger."

"But maybe the kiss will not work for us. Maybe I

291

married him, but he is not my true love."

Cinderella's eyes lowered to Valencia's belly. "Graddock is your true love. You are carrying the proof."

"But perhaps this is all a ruse, another way to humiliate me. I cannot help but think, after the kiss, the rest of you will laugh at me, and I will be alone with my child."

"This will not happen, Valencia." Cinderella's shoulders sagged. "What more can I say to convince you?"

"How about 'Valencia, I trust you'll make the right decision.'" Hero rubbed his chin. "When the two of them are ready—and only then—will they kiss. Having us hover around them isn't helping."

Valencia straightened her shoulders at Hero's admonition to everyone else. "Quite right!" she declared. "Onward."

Another hour of walking and we spied the spires of the convent in the distance. Cillian pointed at it. "Our destination. Unfortunately, they will not let you in."

"Why not?" Hero asked.

Cillian said, "Single men, in a convent? Selkie warriors? A married woman, Wysdel, without her husband, but with other single men? What are they going to think? Do you have a holy request?"

Wysdel touched her chin. "We were going to ask to see Bonadventure's famous grotto."

"Many ask, few are admitted."

I changed my appearance to my Charlie disguise, the one I was using when I unexpectedly landed in the convent walls. "I met Helga Helvys a few days ago and promised to return. I teleported inside."

Cillian scratched his sideburns. "I suppose that is all right if she knows you. But you will have to get past the sister who answers the door. What was your plan?"

"Without a clue" would most accurately describe our expressions. Cillian snorted. "You may be able to convince the doorkeeper as long as you are not asking after Helga Helvys, the most popular nun in Kingdom. Recall she was known for her legendary battle skills before entering this convent."

We answered him with silence.

He shook his head. "Do you know how many people seek out Helga? She is famous. She sees no one."

Pennilane shook her head and turned away. Valencia eyed Cinderella. "You have dragged us all out here, and we cannot even see her."

Cillian folded his hands behind his back. "I can get you an audience with her if you trust me."

I didn't. "How?"

He ignored my question and headed for the convent. Reluctantly, we followed as he led us to the front door and knocked. An elderly nun appeared in a window above the entrance and glared down at us. "What is it you want? We are about to have our supper."

Cillian bowed his head. "We have come for repentance. We are pilgrims who are seeking benediction for our trespasses against Nor. The elders there said we must confess our sins to Sister Hildegard, or we shall receive no penance."

The nun tilted her head so we could see only one eye. It rolled around in its socket taking us all in. "This is highly unusual."

Cillian's voice cracked as he pleaded. "Please, do not leave us in a state of disgrace."

"She will not leave the convent. You must go to her."

"A private room, then," he said.

The nun shook her head. "The back garden. You will have privacy there."

"Very well."

The nun shut the window, and Cillian turned and gathered us around. He whispered as footsteps approached the door. "You must trust me. Hero, let me speak to her first. Squinkle?"

The *word*. Squinkle. Both Hero and I looked at each other and at Cillian. Squinkle was a code word the queens used.

If no one remembered the queens, how did Cillian know about it?

I wanted to ask Cillian questions, but he had timed his little speech perfectly with the opening of the door. The elderly religious woman gestured for us to follow her and placed a finger to her lips. A vow of silence—my worst nightmare. We walked down a long hallway of the convent, adorned with pictures of Kingdom's Redeemer, and then out a back door into a walled-in garden about the size of half a football field. The walls were ten feet high and topped with spikes. No easy egress would be found out of here, except for Celeste and me, who could fly.

We were in the back of the convent and the high structure stared down at us as if frowning. Two dozen windows faced us, and from each one, a nun stared at us. In all of them, the holy sisters watched us, their arms at their sides. Despite the setting sunlight shining on us, I shivered. "I'm officially weirded out."

Ten minutes passed before the back door opened again and a nun, head bowed, entered the garden. When she looked up, I couldn't help but smile. There she was, the second eldest queen, the warrior of her age, the holiest woman I knew. She was Helga the Bone-Crusher, Helga the Valiant, Helga the...nun.

Cinderella swayed back and forth at seeing her sister, and Wysdel's eyes moistened. Helga ignored them but spotted me and quickly approached. She spoke in a raspy voice, one that was hardly used. "My confidante! You have returned."

"I have brought friends. We have something to tell you. Our tale may sound ridiculous, but hear us out."

Helga made a gesture at me that I think was a blessing. I eyed Cillian. He knew the word squinkle, and he wanted to speak to her. "Our guide, Cillian Puttè, has something to say."

Hands shaking, Cillian stepped forward. Why was he so jittery? Just in case, I started a fizz spell to use against him if I needed it.

Cillian cleared his throat. "Sister Hildegard. The holy elders of Nor told us to come to you to complete our absolution after our confession."

Helga regarded him suspiciously. "Why me?"

"Because what I am about to say chiefly involves you. You see you have been wronged. A great injustice has been done to you, and you do not even know it."

"I think you are mistaken." Helga stepped back.

"Please, I beg of you, hear me out. At the end, I will make my request, and then you may make up your own mind."

Helga glanced around him at me, and I shrugged one shoulder. I wasn't sure where he was going with this ruse, but I was ready one way or the other. I was worried about the nuns in the windows behind us, the setting sunlight reflecting off the glass.

Cillian squared his shoulders. "Sister Hildy, or rather, Helga, a spell has been cast on you, one you do not remember. The current king placed it on you seven months ago. He has stolen your memory."

Our attention swung toward Cillian. He knew the truth!

"You are not a nun, but a queen! Not the queen of Nor, but the queen of all of Kingdom. Helga, years ago, you ascended to the throne, and you and four sisters united this land where people have lived in peace and prosperity, a peace far better and far more lasting than Piper's. His is a false peace, but you and your sisters have ushered in a golden era."

Helga opened her mouth to speak, but Cillian held up his hand. "Please, let me continue. The people with me all know this is the truth, and two of your sisters are behind me. One is even here in spirit."

Not surprising he would mention Valencia and Cinderella, but to know about Snow White? Who was this?

Without lowering his eyes from Helga, he gestured behind him to the rest of us. "Your sisters love you and have risked their lives to come here to tell you the truth. None of them know the danger they are in right now." He looked over at Celeste and she nodded. "But even if they knew, they would still be here."

Above us, window shutters opened.

Celeste started gesturing and cast a quick spell that I couldn't identify on Cillian and Helga. Damnit, Cillian had convinced the pixie to do something behind our backs! A popping noise, and multiple lights winked around them, then faded. Whatever she threw didn't seem to work.

Helga ignored Celeste, leaning away from Cillian. "Why should I believe you?"

Celeste turned and cast the same spell on the queens. Rapunzel happened to be standing near them and the same lights blinked above her. Now I trust Celeste to use magic responsibly, but what was she doing?

Cillian lowered his voice. "Because, Helga, you have had many adventures, and in one of them, you met a man. You fell in love. He is in disguise, standing before you now."

Danforth!

Cinderella sucked in her breath. "Is it you?"

Lowering his bandana, Danforth, Helga's husband, ignored his sister-in-law's question. He stared at Helga. "You do not understand how important you are to everyone here, especially me. I have been miserable without your presence. Just to hear your voice is like Eid al-Fitr. I know you do not believe me—I did not expect you to. But Helga, I have proof. If you accompany me, I will prove you are a queen of Kingdom!"

Her eyes went wide at his declaration. Danforth continued without allowing her to interrupt.

"By Saint Peter's beard, my love, please, please believe me enough to come with me. I want nothing but you, no matter if you are Helga the Virtuous, Queen Helga, or Sister Hildegard. I know that you've forgotten me, but you would believe God would want this wrong righted. That is why I am here."

"Danforth!" shouted Hero. "Why didn't you tell us who you are?"

Danforth didn't answer. We stood in that courtyard in the dying sunlight with those austere women scowling down at us. Cinderella was biting a nail, and Valencia was squeezing something in her hand. I held my breath.

Placidly, Helga said, "May I speak?"

"Your words are a symphony to my ears."

Helga's face hardened. Uh oh. "You are a liar. I do not understand why you wanted to see me and tell me this human short story, this bedtime fable. I will not stand here and be complicit with someone who lies about confession and absolution. I have a mind to—"

But then Helga moved and grabbed Danforth and shoved him to the side. Where he stood a moment before, an arrow pierced the ground. I looked up, my jaw dropping at the sight. In the windows stood nuns with longbows aimed at all of us.

When the door swung open to the back room of the Inn of Five, Beauty observed Penta, her mother, startle at seeing someone else in the kitchen. Penta gracefully recovered before nearly dropping her tray. "Lady Halifax. What are you doing here? And dressed as a soldier?"

Beauty took a deep breath. This was it. Her speech would require her full effort. "Penta, you and I are friends. And friends do not lie to one another, do they?"

Penta slid the platter on a table near the sink. "You are a lady. I am a commoner. Friendship—"

"You are anything except common," interrupted Beauty. "Others have told you before me, but you are a queen of Kingdom whose memory has been stolen."

Penta turned around and leaned against the table. "Not you, too."

"Would a lady fib about such an important matter?" Beauty pointed in the direction of the royal castle, miles away from the inn. "The imposter king occupies your castle. He has locked the throne room because of the thrones placed inside—yours and your sisters. Your court magician bespelled anyone from removing them."

Color rose in Penta's cheeks. "'Tis absurd to think multiple monarchs rule this land. Who would conceive of such a thing?"

"You did. Years ago. You could have ruled alone being the oldest, but you shared your power with your siblings. 'Tis time, my queen, to take back what is rightfully yours."

"Time? Actually, 'tis closing time, Lady Halifax. And I will gladly serve you a free pint if you remove yourself from my kitchen and return to the main room."

Beauty stepped forward and held out her hand. She longed to hold her mother's hand once again. "Before, you and I were very close. You have counseled me wisely since I was a girl. Please, try to remember."

Penta stepped back. "That odious freedom fighter, Wysdel, tried to convince me of the same nonsense. Have you joined her cause?"

Beauty bit the inside of her mouth. Penta had forced her to expose one of the gaps in the innkeeper's life. She might hurt her mother, but all would be forgiven when Penta came to her senses. "Where is your father, Penta?"

Penta snapped, "He is lost to me. Somewhere in Kingdom."

"No, he is not." Now for the other hole in her memories. Perhaps her mother would make the connection with her father. "What happened to you when you were sixteen? Do you recall that stage in your life?"

Penta stiffened. "No different than any other year."

"Your father made a powerful enemy, and that enemy sent you to another world called Earth. Your father went looking for you, and—clever man that he is— he ended up off-world too. He is not in Kingdom, Penta. I can take you to him, and he will tell you the truth."

Penta slammed her fist against the table. Gulping, Beauty realized she had gone too far.

"You will not speak any more of my father. Though I am a commoner, I have rights that protect me even from a noble's privilege. You do not belong here. Though I cannot bar you from the main room of my tavern, I demand you exit the rooms off-limits to the public."

Though rebuffed, Beauty felt a small pocket of hope stirring. This imposing woman, speaking above her station, was the true Penta. Her mother had disciplined her before with the same authoritative tone. She had hated it then, but now Beauty welcomed it.

"I have failed you, and I sincerely apologize."

Penta shrunk against the sink. "I have always admired you, Lady Halifax. I will not inform the king of your beliefs, but you must never again speak of this ill-founded rumor to me. The next time, I will tell the king he has an insurrectionist in his nobility."

Couldn't have that. But Penta, being a good citizen of Kingdom, should've reported her. Why Penta resisted telling Piper spoke to her affection for her. Again, hope! But Beauty decided leaving this to Hero, Sanders, and her aunts might be best.

Beauty slid past Penta to the door to the tavern room. Penta sniffed. "How did you get back here? I did not see you while I was serving."

Beauty nodded backward. "Back door. I have a key, Penta. You gave it to me. You'll notice a silver key on your own keyring." Beauty gestured to a keyring on the wall. "That key unlocks Halifax Manor."

Penta rushed over and touched the key, her brow furrowing.

Grinning, Beauty put her hand on the door to the main room. "Think about it."

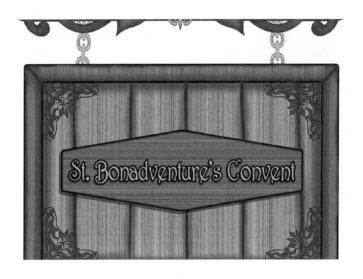

St. Bonadventure's Convent

30 - DISCORDANCE

Harold

Holy shit. In this case, a half-truth. The holy nuns were aiming arrows at us, and I'd rather be pelted with poop than what they had loaded. Kingdom manages to surprise me over and over, but this trap had to be one of the strangest of all.

With a twang of their bows, the first arrows rained down on us. Celeste and my wife sprang into action. Celeste had formed an enormous wooden bird above her, sheltering us from most of the ammo. My wife pointed at a volley of arrows, transforming each one's molecules into water—her scientific brain intersecting with her magic abilities. Nonetheless, being hit by the remains of a watery arrow felt like being beaned with a water balloon. Fortunately, this combination of defensive moves saved us from the first onslaught, but the renegade nuns wasted no time reloading.

The spellcasters weren't the only ones spurred into motion. Wysdel and Sylvia stepped in front of Rapunzel, forming a barricade around her. Roger stepped in front of Cinderella and raised a round shield to protect his head and upper torso. For her part, Cinderella started pointing at the nuns, using her ability of charm to convince them to stop. Graddock stood in front of Valencia and retrieved a handful of throwing darts from a pouch on his belt. Helga still had a grip on Danforth. From under his cloak, Danforth handed Helga a short sword. "They are not nuns! They're spies."

Helga shouted upward. "Stop, sisters! What are you doing? Please—"

Helga's plea died in her throat as she chopped an arrow in half with her sword, deflecting it right before it hit her. She grabbed a branch and tossed it, intercepting another arrow aimed at Graddock.

An arrow whizzed at Celeste, but she had turned herself intangible and it passed through her and embedded in the ground. My wife, though busy with transforming arrows into water, asked, "How do you do that?"

The nuns Cinderella pointed at had stopped firing on us, and I hoped this would be the end of the battle. Yet, they were shoved aside by more assassin women in habits. With a sinking heart, I realized Piper had assigned an all-woman warrior group to replace the normally non-violent sisters. With the sheer number of adversaries and their chance of hitting her with an arrow, Cinderella had to take cover. Who knew how many Piper had placed here? We might have to face hundreds!

An arrow sliced the top of Wysdel's shoulder, and she shrieked. Blood poured from the wound and many of us gasped. Snow White's ability was known to prevent her from being hurt by weapons. How had our adversaries overcome this? Celeste instantly started a healing spell.

An arrow whistled through the air directly at Helga who

used her sword to bat it away. "By Saint Peter's beard, this is madness!"

As Wysdel crumpled, Sylvia spread her arms wide in front of herself as a shield. An arrow sliced through the air, piercing her chest. While the missile knocked Sylvia back a step, the arrow did no further harm, Sylvia now having Snow White's abilities. Rapunzel crouched in Sylvia's shadow.

"Syl, be careful!" screamed Wysdel. The twig she used to change her voice had been knocked loose, and Snow White's high-pitched tone rang across the garden.

Sylvia turned around, eyes wide. "Snow?"

An arrow sliced through Sylvia's throat, again with no apparent damage. Wysdel put her hands on Sylvia's hips and swung her so Sylvia could face the battle. "You must still be careful. Your body has limits."

Sylvia deflected a bolt with a jiu-jitsu move. "It *is* you, isn't it?"

Wysdel clutched her friend's shoulder. "I'm sorry that I didn't tell you sooner."

More arrows started to whiz across from the doorway to the garden. This time, instead of coming down at us, they fired horizontally, and one missed Cinderella by only centimeters. Roger couldn't use his shield to defend from above and forward at the same time, and Sanders and Celeste were in the middle of their spells. I had to make it to that door and shut it.

Danforth shouted, "We must escape! Piper has been tracking our movements through his spy. No more!"

He had said "spy," not spies. Danforth couldn't be referring to the nuns for he had used the singular form of the word. But I couldn't focus on that right now, as another volley of missiles flew toward us.

Valencia hadn't been cowering all this time but digging something out of her pouch. "Now?" she shouted at Danforth.

"Almost. Hero, the spyglass."

I had been crawling on the ground to avoid being a target. The spyglass? What would I do with that?

Moving along on the ground next to me were long, golden-colored strands of hair like snakes but far cuddlier. They slithered rapidly to the door, although arrows pinned a few tresses to the garden's soil. They reached their destination, the door, and wrapped around the handle, slamming it shut. The crossbeam barrier fell into place.

Rapunzel, of course. She had single-handedly sealed off the killer nuns' means of entry.

I crawled over to Danforth and stood. He threw a rock against the ground, and it exploded into a cloud, temporarily obscuring the nuns' line of sight at the two of us. He ripped off his bandana. "We need to hide from Piper, and from each other, if we are to succeed. Use the spyglass, Hero on those remaining here after we escape."

"Remaining? What do you mean?"

Danforth never answered me because Helga grabbed him. "Stop this immediately! This is holy ground!"

"Not until I reveal the spy." He called over to Cinderella. "Has no one told you that Kingdom is cut off from Travel? Don't you see? Pennilane was off-world when Piper threw his spell!"

I had forgotten that Pennilane married a man who lived in another world, and they spent only half of the year in Kingdom. If she was off-world, *how did she return when the rest of us couldn't?* But if the selkie next to Cinderella wasn't Pennilane, who was she?

Cinderella turned to her selkie neighbor. "What does he mean by cut off?"

Pennilane shook her head. "No! He is lying."

But the nuns targeted the selkie. Perhaps for her failure? I'll never know. Roger pulled Cinderella out of the line of fire. The false Pennilane tried to dodge the arrows racing at her, but one embedded in her heart and pushed her to the ground.

Whether she was Pennilane or not didn't matter to Cinderella. Under Roger's shield, she dropped to her knees beside the fallen woman. Graddock's throwing darts provided covering fire.

While convulsing on the ground in the garden, Pennilane's face sharpened and altered slightly. This water creature wasn't Pennilane, and Cinderella kneeling next to her looked on her faux friend in horror. She exclaimed, "Pennilane's cousin, Pollytheenpam!"

Celeste had finished healing Wysdel who continued to hold her shoulder though no wound was evident. Sylvia had multiple arrows sticking out of her like pins in a pincushion, but the blood immediately congealed around her wounds. Meanwhile, my wife had separated her body into multiple parts—arms, legs, torso, head—making her less of a target.

As if things couldn't get weirder, a rainbow rushed from the sky, originating outside of the convent's grounds and ending next to Helga. Exiting its interior, a female, dark-skinned leprechaun stepped out of the prismatic display next to Danforth.

The newcomer surveyed the garden. "Wot have I got meself into?"

"As we discussed!" Danforth put his hand on Helga's shoulder. "The two of us."

"Right-o," replied the leprechaun.

Now, Valencia!" shouted Danforth.

Valencia closed her eyes and started whispering.

Cinderella knelt by the dying selkie, holding her hand. "Why? Were you that jealous of your cousin?"

Without answering, Pollytheenpam pulled the arrow from her body and thrust it with all her remaining strength into Cinderella's waist. The serrated edge cut deep into the queen's midsection. Cinderella gasped, eyes bulging!

Roger screamed. At the same moment, Danforth, Helga, and the leprechaun were sucked into the rainbow and flew away inside of it. No one could teleport inside the convent, so riding a rainbow must have been a different matter entirely.

Roger started toward his wife, but a fresh barrier of projectiles prevented him from reaching her. At the same time, Valencia opened her eyes, finishing whatever she was mumbling. Now I understood what Cillian-as-Danforth had given to her. A wishing stone! In a blink of an eye, Valencia disappeared along with Cinderella, Wysdel, and Rapunzel.

In a far corner of the garden, I had removed the spyglass and was centering it on our group. Trying to get them all in view was tough with my wife spread out all over the place, but I managed. As a camera centers on a QR code, an image froze into place when I had them captured, and we were the last group to be whisked away from the garden.

Sanders, Roger, Graddock, Sylvia, Celeste, and I stood on board the *Swan Princess* once again. Not expecting the heavy rocking of the ship, we couldn't maintain our bearings and fell over onto the deck. A rainstorm's torrent poured down on us in faster succession than the arrows.

Roger found his sea legs first. He helped Celeste up but didn't let her go after she rose to her feet. "Take me to her!"

Graddock reclaimed his bearings next. "Me, as well."

"Snow is helpless without me." Sylvia huddled to keep the rain from washing over her. "I stole her abilities with my wish."

Hair plastered to her head, Sanders shouted, "All of us will go!"

"No!" I shouted, still seated on the deck.

Roger turned to me. "Not your decision, Hero. I am a prince of Kingdom, and my love is dying!"

Shakily, I stood. "Are you able to heal her, Roger?"

Roger ignored me. "Celeste, this is a direct order. Take me to her."

Celeste didn't start a spell. "Cillian told me to cast an incantation to confuse locator spells."

Aha. This was the spell that seemed to have done nothing before the nuns started shooting at us.

"I do not know much about magic," said Graddock. "But I know a caster can dispel their own spell. Take me to Valencia. I love her."

"Great time to figure that out." I reached for the main mast to steady myself. "And even more of a reason not to teleport."

Roger ran his hand through his wet hair, brushing away a handful of rain. "God's heavens, Hero, stand down! You are not in charge! You hold no position in Kingdom."

Celeste lifted her chin. "Cillian consulted with me and Valencia privately the night we stayed at Ghael Inn. He had me throw a truth detection spell on him as he told us who he was and why he wanted to go to the convent."

The truth detection spell was a great idea to convince people to trust you. Wish I had thought of it.

Celeste continued, "He said we had a spy among us and outlined the plan he executed in the convent. Since Piper was tracking Hero and Sanders through his spy, Cillian guessed we might be attacked. He believed we had to split up to keep Piper's attention off the queens. The false king will be looking for traces of transference magic if I bring you to Cinderella."

I huddled against the rain. "Cillian—Danforth is his true name—was right to separate us. How long has Pollytheenpam been with us, and we didn't know she was a spy? Roger, if you go to them, you risk all their lives, especially Queen Valencia's. You are a prince of Kingdom, sworn to protect all the queens. Going there will expose them to Piper!"

Roger glared at me through tear-filled eyes. He shook his head and sent water splashing in all directions.

My voice hitched as I spoke. "You can't save your wife. You can only endanger her family."

Roger turned from me and stomped to the bow. Graddock looked pale as he watched him leave. He turned back to me. "Do you think she is…?"

"I don't know. Your wives have lived through many deadly encounters, but I don't know how Cinderella could have survived that one."

Sylvia pulled an arrow from her waist. "Do we have a plan?"

Sanders interrupted her question and put her hand on my shoulder. "Rapunzel shouldn't be there. *We* promised to protect her. Danforth was wrong to tell Valencia to include her with the queens."

I raised an eyebrow. "She'll be safe with them."

Sanders wiped the rain from her face. "No, you don't understand, Harold!"

I tensed at her mention of my real name.

"We can't leave her there with them." Sanders tightened her grip on my shoulder. "Just tell me where they are, and I will teleport there and get her and bring her back. I can keep her safe."

"I understand perfectly."

"No, you don't!"

I took her hands. "If Celeste had teleported Fitzie with Valencia, I'd still be doing the same thing. Danforth understands Rapunzel's importance in all of this. She's a fairytale princess."

Sanders clenched her jaw. "She's not a pawn in a game, Harold."

"I know, but if we go to her, we'll risk her life. Celeste didn't throw the spell on us."

Quirking an eyebrow, Sanders stated, "We're the distraction to attract Piper's notice."

"Correct. But I'm not sure where we should go."

Celeste gestured to the sails. "Danforth told me, and I will set a course. We are all going to meet tomorrow morning. We converge on a place called the Inn of Five."

I nodded. "And this time, we must convince Penta."

31 - INTERMEZZO 3

Sixteen Years Earlier

"Hey, Penta. Want to see a kitten video?"

Edwina Alderston held out her phone. Penta's instincts were to turn away immediately. Edwina had never been anything but dismissive or downright mean. But Sister Joan had just taught a lesson on love in theology class. She had ended with a challenge to the girls of St. Theresa's Boarding School to treat each other better than those in any other school of the nation. Maybe this was Edwina's way of showing love?

Hesitantly, Penta leaned forward and looked at the viewing screen. No kittens. Just a man and a woman. Penta wasn't surprised by what they were doing. She was well aware of what the girls at St. Theresa's called "the act." However, she had never seen it being done. Her father had only described it to her.

Before she could stop her stupid tongue from speaking, she blurted out, "That's not kittens."

Naturally, Edwina and her friends broke into laughter. They had played Penta for a fool many times before, and she knew they'd post a picture of Penta next with the meme: "That's not kittens." Stupid! Why hadn't she walked away when Edwina called her over?

When Edwina stopped chortling, she stepped closer to Penta and put a hand on her shoulder. "No, Penta. They aren't kittens at all."

A fresh round of laughter. Beatrix Chandler said, "She doesn't even know what she saw."

"I know what it is," snapped Pena. "It isn't very loving."

"But it's accurate." Edwina again. "True love doesn't exist, Penta. I know you believe it does, but you're wrong. Certainly not for someone like you!"

Penta turned to leave. Edwina called after her. "Don't worry, Penta. No one will ever do the act with you. Most men prefer women with more than one finger."

The girls started giggling again while Penta walked away. A voice from behind all of them stopped her in her tracks. "If Penta had a finger, I know which one she'd be raising."

Penta swung around. Behind the girls was a guy in her class. His name was Jacob, or John. Something starting with a J. Most Earth names were weird compared to the names used in Kingdom.

Edwina's lip curled at the boy. "You stay out of this. Or are you in love with her?"

The boy rolled his eyes but didn't answer.

"Maybe you want to make kittens with her?" Edwina grinned. "Make her Mrs. McStumpy?"

That was enough! It was one thing to tease her, but she wouldn't stand for Edwina picking on anyone who defended her. Oh, would she give it to that little snot!

309

Penta marched forward, grinding her teeth. She grabbed Edwina's arm while her attention was on the boy across the way. She'd teleport her just a little—a few centimeters. Just enough to be disorienting.

When Penta touched her, Edwina shifted locations a tiny amount. No one would notice as they were looking at the J guy. But to Edwina who wasn't expecting it, her eyes widened and her face went white. She put her hand over her mouth and darted to the bathroom.

Just the effect Penta was going for. A little stomach flop.

Edwina's abrupt departure attracted the attention of the rest of her gaggle. Beatrix glared at Penta. "What's wrong with Edwina? What'd you do?"

Penta mocked surprise. "Me? I didn't do anything."

The Forest of Blood

32 - POLYPHONY

Wysdel estimated that Cinderella had about two minutes to live.

She, Valencia, Rapunzel, and Cinderella had appeared at the southwest edge of the Forest of Blood. As they had moved west, sunlight brighter than at the convent shone down on them. Stately beech trees surrounded the four teleporters on both sides, leaving an inlet of plains, like a peninsula or a firth of land extending into a forest rather than a body of water. This natural alcove provided them with privacy.

Upon spotting Cinderella, Valencia dropped her wishing stone. Retracting her hair short, Rapunzel put a hand to her mouth. Wysdel knelt by Cinderella's side and went to work, ripping off a piece of her shift to make a bandage. She folded the cloth, rolled up her sister's shirt, and applied pressure to the wound. Wysdel's voice trembled. "I will save you!"

The words, meant to be a statement of truth, came out pleading. Wysdel whispered a prayer while stemming the flow of blood, hoping the Redeemer-God would grant her request.

Valencia lowered to a crouch on the other side of Cinderella. "Cillian said the rock had only one wish. Otherwise..."

Cinderella reached for Valencia's hand, her face contorted in pain and her fingers stained with blood. "Valencia, Wysdel is your sister, too. You ought to know before I die."

The material in Wysdel's hands had soaked through with blood. She ripped a sleeve for another bandage.

Cinderella's voice was a whisper. "Snow, Valencia. I love you both dearly. Please help Roger to raise Cuthbert and Snowy, and..."

Valencia, eyes swimming with tears, moved a stray piece of hair from her face.

Tears also welled up in Wysdel's eyes, and she blinked them away. The bleeding wouldn't stop no matter her effort. If only she were a doctor or a magician or a cleric...

Wysdel's eyes locked on Cinderella's. Though she didn't speak, Wysdel recalled happy and sad scenes with her closest sister. Birthing their children, being kidnapped together, Cinderella's public marriage and her own secret one. Anguish and bitterness fought for control. How could Cinderella's life end this way?

Cinderella set her hand on Wysdel's. "The roles have reversed. You showed me how to face death with courage when you left on the boat and—"

"Excuse me."

Rapunzel muscled her way past Wysdel, nearly knocking her over. The impertinence! Did she have no sense of how important this final speech was to Cinderella? And she studied Cinderella less like a dying woman than as a doctor ready to do an operation. Stone-faced, the young girl appeared completely unmoved by Cinderella's plight.

Biting her lip, Rapunzel asked, "What can I think of that's really sad?"

Wysdel stumbled on her response. She'd teach this upstart of a fairytale princess a lesson later. For now, she turned to her sister. But Valencia voiced the words going through her mind. "Rapunzel, you are being quite rude."

Rapunzel sucked in a breath, a gasp in reverse. "A bird once flew into my chambers and hit the wall. The poor thing died in my hands."

Wysdel glared at the girl, then grabbed Cinderella's hands. "Dear—"

Next to her, Rapunzel's eyes welled up with tears, and they dripped from her eyes onto Cinderella's wound. Wysdel reared back as she heard a hissing sound when the water mixed with blood. Cinderella breathed in sharply—a sound of relief, not suffering. Rapunzel's tears spread over the wound and stemmed the flow of blood.

Rapunzel continued to cry. "That poor little birdie flipped and flopped in my hands."

The tears flowed from her eyes, and Cinderella's skin started growing from the edge of the wounds, knitting itself back together. While magic was common in Kingdom, miracles were not. In Wysdel's book, this was a miracle. "Whatever you are doing, keep doing it."

Valencia laid a hand on her own cheek. "How are you able to do that, Rapunzel?"

Rapunzel sniffed twice. "A potion administered by my mother. Wyvern tears were a key ingredient."

The girl stopped crying, but the healing continued. Cinderella's hand tightened on Wysdel's slightly, and that was all the sign she needed. Cinderella was recovering!

Unable to stop herself, Wysdel grabbed Rapunzel and hugged her tightly. "You saved my sister's life. Oh, dear one, you are truly a treasure."

Rapunzel blushed. Valencia leaned across and hugged

the girl. "You are full of surprises."

Still weak from the loss of blood, Cinderella whispered, "You're so young that you don't even understand how incredible you are, do you?"

Rapunzel took a tuft of hair and wrapped it around her finger. "So incredible that my parents abandoned me."

Wysdel tapped herself on her breastbone. "My stepmother sent a huntsman to kill me and eat my liver."

Valencia looked shocked. "I was beaten by my stepfather when I did not make enough money."

Cinderella raised a trembling hand. "My stepmother tried to prevent my marriage. Then, she banished me and my sisters from Kingdom to take the throne and steal my husband."

Wysdel giggled and then snorted, putting a hand over her face. "The point is, I think we all wish our parents had abandoned us."

Cinderella closed her eyes, "You are a sunflower, dear."

With the crisis averted, Wysdel locked eyes with Valencia. Now, Valencia knew her identity. "You are my sister, too?"

Wysdel leaned over and embraced her. "I am so glad you are with child. What a terrible time to be carrying a baby, but we will defeat Piper, and set all things right."

"But you look nothing like me!"

Wysdel leaned back. "I didn't look like this originally, and Helga and I resemble our father's family more. You and Cinderella inherited your features from our mother's side."

Rapunzel sat back. "Where are we?"

Wysdel shaded her eyes, peering south. "Near a friend's house where we can spend the night. Danforth knew where to send each of us. I have a plan to get us all to safety."

"Danforth mentioned we were in danger and asked me to wish us here." Valencia examined the natural enclosure. "He told us to meet him at a place called the Inn of Five at the zenith of the sun tomorrow."

"He hopes we'll convince Penta," Cinderella said.

"Exactly." Wysdel stood. "Rapunzel, will you accompany me to my friend's house? She's married to a were-bear. We shall be back before the sun is completely down. Valencia, please watch over our sister. If danger comes, Cinderella should be able to use her ability."

Valencia squared her shoulders. "I will."

Wysdel again leaned down and embraced her injured sister lightly. "And my dearest, we need to have a talk about your trusting nature. How could you mistake Pollytheenpam for Pennilane? Didn't you see her true self through your tears?"

"She always walked away when I cried, claiming tears made her uncomfortable." Cinderella folded her hands on her stomach. "I never suspected her. Pollytheenpam was always jealous of Pennilane, arguing my friend shouldn't have been admitted to the colony."

Wysdel broke away and grimaced. "But Pollytheenpam?"

Cinderella waved at her. "Yeah, yeah, yeah."

Wysdel turned to Rapunzel and held out her hand to the long-haired teen. "Rapunzel and I shall request shelter from true allies now. Friends who knew me before I became a queen and know me still."

Wysdel and Rapunzel hurried away.

Three figures appeared on a mountain pass. A stiff breeze blew around them, ruffling their clothes and hair. The rocky trail only had fragments of vegetation.

Adorned in her traditional robe and habit, Helga spun around and pointed the short sword at the man with her. The black-clothed leprechaun jumped back in alarm and screeched. The man held his hands up and stepped back. "Helga, I have to pay the leprechaun."

Helga's eyes shifted to the fairy. "She goes nowhere until

I return home."

The leprechaun, realizing she was in no danger, growled at the man. "You tricked me. 'A simple grab and go,' you said. I just kidnapped Helga Helvys in the middle of a battle zone."

"My purse is on my belt. Take it if you must," said the man.

The leprechaun snatched the purse. The ring the man had used to summon the fairy flew from his finger and into the leprechaun's palm. "This too."

"The ring was not part of the deal."

But he was too late. The leprechaun had disappeared. Helga anticipated it, but she had her eye on the larger prize. She would force answers from this man, even if she had to resort to violence. The nuns would disapprove, but they had taken up archery behind her back! Her entire world was off-kilter right now, and she was going to force this man to set it back on its axis.

Helga recognized the path where they had appeared, slightly alarmed that the man had chosen this place. They were in the mountains south of Nor, a place she knew intimately. A cold wind blew past her, a refreshing breeze that felt like her hometown enveloping her in a welcome-back hug. Though pleased by the location, she was not supposed to be here. She needed to be back in the convent. "Take me back."

The man clenched his jaw. "They will kill you."

"They would not do that. They have taken vows to uphold the Creator's law. Murder is a profane act."

"Helga, you saw what they did," he said. "They are not religious. Piper put them there to keep an eye on you and ensure you did not escape. That usurper is crafty, imprisoning you in a place that appeals to you."

The king was behind this treachery? Unbelievable. "Who are you?"

"My name is Danforth Tyreeph. I know you, Helga. You have a deep faith, and someone like that seeks the truth. Please allow me to tell you the truth before you speak."

With an economy of words, her prisoner started with the story Helga knew too well. She was cursed to be evil during the day and virtuous during the night, but nighttime came with a cost. She turned into an enormous, ugly frog. His story deviated from her memories when he said a man in the garden with them, a person named Hero, had saved her. He had revealed that she was a prophesied queen. Not of Nor, but all of Kingdom.

When he paused, she lowered her sword. He was delusional. She had four sisters and had overthrown the king before King Piper? She had ruled justly and brought about the golden age? The very words were treason.

Danforth cleared his throat. "You are queen, wife, sister, aunt, warrior, but the one thing you are not is a nun."

Helga eyed Danforth suspiciously. "And if our king cast this spell to make everyone forget, why have you retained your memory?"

"I wondered that myself, but I discovered how from my companions. Piper's spell had a flaw. It only affected those born in Kingdom. I was not born here."

"You say you love me." Helga switched the sword to her other hand. "But even romantic love has limits. Why would you do this, risking your life to take me from the convent?"

Danforth swallowed. He looked uncomfortable, and he glanced at a ring on his finger. She had sized him up as she approached him in the convent and had known he was married. What had being married have to do with his quest—?

No! He couldn't think...couldn't conceive of...

Helga stepped back near the edge of the path. "You are daft! You believe we are married."

"I know how it sounds," he said.

A rush of wind swept over them, and Helga waited for the roaring sound to quiet down. "How could I possibly forget the man I love?"

"Piper has the Pipes of Perringon. And he used it to remove your memories."

The Pipes. A powerful and evil artifact capable of influencing one's actions. If anything at all could create that kind of an outrageous scenario, the pipes were capable of such magic.

Against her inclinations, Helga decided to continue to prompt her so-called husband. "And you think you know how to break the curse?"

"I had a plan, but the others knew a different way. One of your sisters still did not have her memories and they were urging her to kiss her husband. True love's kiss, Helga, will break the curse."

Helga guffawed. "I must kiss you?"

"That is the long and short of it. I know this sounds impossible, but I have proof of everything I said. We are close to it. Your hidden cave is near."

Helga glanced up the trail. The winding rock-strewn path led higher between three boulders, a makeshift trellis to her hiding spot. "No one knows about that cave. I spent years as a child constructing a secret entrance to it."

"No one knows except your husband." Danforth rocked back and forth.

Helga gestured with her sword. "You walk ahead. I will stay behind you."

Danforth moved forward but lowered his arms. "I know you, Helga. You will not kill me. You detest the taking of another's life. I know I could snatch that sword away if I really wanted to, but I will not. I love you too much."

"I know plenty of moves I can make with a sword that would not kill you."

Danforth looked over his shoulder with a pained expression. "Fair. Please allow me to get to the cave."

As they kicked rubble while striding along the path, Helga asked, "How long do you think we have been married?"

"A little over five years."

"And no heir?"

Danforth stopped and turned around. Helga raised the

sword again, but Danforth ignored it. His voice sounded strained. "Why do you ask?"

Danforth's face expressed several emotions of which pain seemed the most dominant. Helga was taken aback, and she lowered her sword. "What is it you are not telling me?"

"I would rather restore your memory than have to tell you."

This man was holding something back. He wasn't lying to her. Deceptions were born of speaking words, not withholding them. If his story was true, he knew something about her, something important, that she didn't know herself.

Helga raised her chin. "I refuse to follow you unless you tell me. I want to know all of it."

"This, you do not want to know."

Helga stepped forward and faced him, peering deep into his eyes. "Tell me."

Danforth said, "Something inside of you knows about our children. You have been troubled over it."

Now Helga's turn came to flinch. "If this is all true, and if we have a child, then it would explain how I feel in the dead of night, yes. I have an ache I cannot explain."

"It's not what you think. Please don't make me tell you."

"Tell me, or we go no further. I will bind you and carry you back to the convent."

Danforth closed his eyes and sighed deeply. "I have one request then. Let me take your hand."

Helga eyed him suspiciously and then offered her hand. Danforth took it gently. "You mentioned one child and not children, proving a part of you knows. You and I had a child. She was a beautiful little thing, but she came early. She died the same night you gave birth to her. Melda Akira Penta."

A lump lodged in Helga's throat. No precise image of a baby formed in her mind, but love swelled in her heart. Though loving someone you didn't know was impossible, Helga believed strongly in a baby named Melda Akira Penta.

Danforth managed to speak the child's name but then

stopped. Tears ran down his face as he continued. "You were holding...her the morning she... The sun rose and cast a glow...around the two of you. You were...holding her...and she breathed her..."

Helga pictured herself holding her daughter—heart shattered. The image came easily. Perhaps not an accurate picture of what had happened, but a true one.

Danforth wiped his face. "We were devastated, but then we had another girl. Her name was Dawn. You named her because she was a difficult birth but survived the night, a fighter, though she was a—"

"Gliff," Helga uttered. Again, no memory, but the word emerged from her heart.

"Dawn Radiance Wyndolyn Tyreeph-Helvys,"

The name was a symphony in Helga's ears. This man gave her a reason as to why she cried so hard in the mornings. Mourning a dead child, missing a live one. His words felt like the words to a song she had long forgotten.

"Dawn is in the cave, safely guarded. She doesn't remember us. Though she trusts me, she feels abandoned. Her longing for her parents is the cruelest fate suffered by a child because of this spell. She cries herself to sleep at night and—"

Overcome with emotion, Danforth couldn't proceed. Tears slipped out of Helga's eyes also, not recalling the memory, but in empathy. Love, sorrow, and despair mixed into a word that didn't exist, and it hurt her far worse than any wound she'd ever received in battle.

This story Danforth told her couldn't be true. It couldn't! The scandalous king, the loving sister queens, the lost prophecy that put her on the throne. She was a member of the Order of the Beatific Vision, not a warrior queen, or a traveler of worlds, or a...a caring mother and wife.

But one thing Helga learned in the convent was that the more absurd the premise, the more the Creator liked it. Trusting her faith and her emotions, Helga leaned forward and kissed Danforth before he knew what she was going to do.

The kiss wasn't sensual or long, but sweet and to the point. The loving gesture restored her memories immediately. A rush of tenderness and vulnerability flooded through her —emotions Helga hadn't experienced since her last intimate moment with Danforth.

When she pulled away, she breathed deeply to take it all in, but she wasn't surprised it worked. She had expected it to.

Her heart ached with the memory of the night Melda had died. She recalled that long night. Helga held the tiny body, too tired to cry. She was a spent match, but she flared her love just a little longer for her dying child. She gave her infant the last little bit of peace she could as the newborn took her last breath. Helga had never been defeated in battle, but that day conquered her soundly. It took everything from her and left her nothing in return. She treasured even this memory, full of pain and sorrow.

Danforth eyed her. "You kissed me. I didn't think you would."

So many emotions roiled within her, Helga had to respond lightly. "Danforth? How did you ever come up with the name Cillian Puttè?"

He hugged her and kissed her again, this time harder and longer. When they parted, he said, "I had Cusp in the cave to restore your memory. Dawn is there with it."

"You left her alone? And how did you come by my holy sword? Cusp chooses to come to its wielder. How did it come into your possession?"

Danforth squeezed her. "I was at my lowest, wandering around Nor, trying to think of a way to save you. In the middle of the night, I sat by the statue of you in the town square and whispered to you, hoping you'd somehow help me. You didn't hear me, but Cusp did. Your statue withdrew Cusp from its granite scabbard and handed it to me, then returned to its original pose."

Helga's eyes widened. "That is quite an honor."

"Cusp has communicated with me and has kept me out

of trouble. And it talks to Dawn as well. Cusp, the legendary and holy artifact, makes a good babysitter too."

Helga smiled. "I wouldn't have expected it, but that blade is full of surprises. Quickly, I want to see my daughter."

Together, they proceeded up the trail toward the cave. Passing by gray granite boulders, Danforth cleared his throat. "We should get our last conversation out of the way."

"You mean when you left me?" asked Helga. "I wanted to revoke the title of princess from Dawn to give her a normal life, and you wanted to keep it."

They ascended the uneven path with Danforth in the lead. "I flew away on a wyvern to think it through, Helga. After I learned what had happened with Piper's spell, I realized our differing opinions didn't matter. Whether Dawn is a princess or not, I need both of you in my life. I went after Dawn on my wyvern mount. Our daughter was hiding in the castle in one of her places, the red wardrobe. We moved into a house in Nor. I assumed a new identity, wearing the mask and going by the name of Cillian."

Helga gritted her teeth. "I can still hear those pipes. My mind was blank after he played them, the false memories replacing the true ones. I only knew I must hurry to the convent, and when I arrived, I thought I had lived there for years."

They entered the secret passage into the cavern—a one-room, stony interior fit to hold about four people around a fire. Helga and Danforth stopped in their tracks. At the other side of the chamber, their daughter, Dawn, waved the holy sword Cusp around, a weapon twice her size, as if it were a toy. When she saw her parents, she dropped Cusp and ran to Helga with her arms wide. "Mommy."

Helga embraced her and lifted her off the ground, kissing her cheek. She eyed Danforth. "I thought she didn't remember."

Danforth merely shook his head. Cusp's voice rang through the cavern. "Once you were restored, Helga the

Valiant, I returned her memories to her. An innocent such as she should not be denied the truth."

Helga lowered Dawn to the ground. "'Tis good to hear your voice again, Cusp."

"Now pick me up, Helga, and restore Kingdom to its glory!"

An hour passed after Wysdel and Rapunzel left Valencia. Cinderella napped to restore her strength while Valencia stood guard. The Match Girl examined her companion, holding her hand. Could she be her sister? They looked alike, certainly. But Wysdel looked nothing like either of them.

Cinderella's eyes fluttered open. "Oh, how long have I slept?"

"Not long."

Valencia rubbed Cinderella's arm. The weakened queen was cold and started shivering. Valencia wished she had a cloak to give her. "Perhaps I could build a fire."

Eyes closed, Cinderella said, "No. Talk to me. A conversation with my sister will help to take my mind off my pain."

"What should we talk about?"

"How about Graddock?"

Pouting, Valencia toed the dirt. "I understand what you are scheming, and while I cannot say I have discounted your story, I also have not ruled out other possibilities. Perhaps, I have a past hidden from me, but how do I know King Piper is bad and you are true? What if kissing Graddock triggers a spell that implants new, false memories into my mind? Have you thought of that?"

Cinderella rolled her eyes. "Oh, Valencia, your wonderful intelligence is playing against you this time. You are thinking too much about this and not listening to your heart.

The truth is you are afraid to kiss him, and you are thinking of any scenario, no matter how absurd, to prevent it."

Ouch! The truth stung. Valencia tossed her hair over her shoulder. "Why are you so interested in our pairing?"

"Because you and I weren't just sisters, we loved each other. And you were joyful when you were with Graddock." Cinderella teared up. "Since we've reunited, I haven't seen you happy like you were when you were married. Now, you're avoiding the subject. You love him."

"But how do you know?"

"Because our story is true." Cinderella held up a hand to cut off Valencia's next question. "You may ask why you should trust us? Examine how we have treated each other. Do evil people look out for each other and share in each other's sorrow and joy? Would wicked people support you when they found out you were with child? Examine us with your heart, Valencia."

"'Tis a fair point." Valencia crossed her arms. "But Graddock has hinted that he has kissed another woman. Has your Roger kissed another? You do not understand. You have a perfect husband."

Cinderella smacked her lips. "Not perfect, but you are correct, he has kissed no other. Tell me, are you attracted to my husband?"

Valencia pulled back. "Of course not. He is a fine gentleman, but I do not feel that way about him."

"And yet I know you are attracted to Graddock. If my husband is so perfect, why is it you are not attracted to him? The reason is he is *my* true love, and he fulfills *my* desire of what I seek in a husband, as does Graddock for you. You and I are different, sister. You aren't the most obedient among us. You give Penta gray hairs with your secret adventures. Your rebellious ways do not align with someone like Roger. You would rather have a man who secretly courted you without your sisters' permission. Graddock is honorable, just, and scrupulous. He is also secretive, roguish, and daring. He's your perfect match."

Her words did strike at what Valencia most liked about Graddock, but she turned her head so that Cinderella couldn't read her expression. Nonetheless, the wounded queen continued.

"Don't you see? Hero and Sanders tease each other all the time. Their love thrives on it, but I find it exhausting. Most men fear Helga, but Danforth adores her too much to be intimidated. Her walls are down completely around him. Are you and your love the picture of domestic tranquility? Hardly. You and Graddock are the example of adventurous liaisons. Valencia, true love exists, but couples demonstrate their true love in different ways."

Valencia listened in rapt attention. "But how do I know?"

"Stop listening to your mind and forget the past and the future. Graddock is not here. Do you miss him? If he were here, would you kiss him?"

The answer sang through her mind like a choir. Before Valencia could answer, a giant bear lumbered out of the forest at them. Valencia jumped up, but Cinderella reassured her. "No worries, Valencia."

The bear turned into a man as he approached. "Our friend Snow White told us you were hurt. Are you the maidens Cinderella and Valencia?"

Cinderella grinned. "Yes. Greetings, Lolander."

33 - TUTTI

Harold

The *Swan Princess* had docked on the river named River in the middle of the night. If we'd had to walk to the inn, the trek would've taken us days, so Celeste teleported us closer to the tavern. At this point, if Piper was tracking us, he'd figure out we were headed for Penta. Hopefully, we had distracted him long enough to allow the queens to converge on the scene to gain their older sister as an ally.

We were a scruffy band. Roger was morose and surly, preferring to keep to himself. Graddock was focused on leading us to the inn but said little. Sylvia was impatient to have words with Wysdel about hiding her identity, and Sanders and I were anxious about Rapunzel.

In the distance, I saw a group of people standing

together on a ridge. Because the dawning sun was in my eyes, I squinted and counted four people in front of us. One tall and angular like Wysdel, another short like a twelve-year-old child. But if this was Wysdel, Valencia, and Rapunzel, could the last one be Cinderella?

Roger shaded his eyes with his hand and cried out his wife's name as a soldier called for his sweetheart across a crowded train station. He bolted toward the group and was in front of Cinderella in seconds, lifting her into the air. He swung her around and whooped with joy. She, in turn, screamed with delight. Before they said a word, they kissed, not breaking contact even after the rest of us arrived.

Graddock and Valencia approached each other. Eyes locked on him, Valencia offered her hand and Graddock took it. Tears flowed from both of them as Valencia pulled him into an embrace.

Sanders and I ran up to Rapunzel with our hands clasped. When we came to her, we swung around and hugged her from both sides. She shook with delight, proclaimed that she had saved Cinderella, and proceeded to relate the entire tale.

Sylvia ran up to Wysdel and threw her arms around her. When they parted, Sylvia stuck out her chin. "How dare you keep this from me!"

"I'm sorry for the deception, dear Sylvia." Wysdel lowered her head. "I should've told you."

Sylvia hugged her again, eyes sparkling. "Piper will have his hands full with two Snow Whites."

I was standing near Valencia and Graddock and overheard their conversation. Graddock held Valencia's hands and stared into her eyes. "I was worried about you. It took our parting to realize I have loved every minute I have been with you. I believe their story."

Valencia blinked back tears. "Their story does not matter to me."

Graddock leaned closer. "I want to kiss you, but I fear

that I will lose this feeling of newfound love. If we break the curse, what will we think of each other?"

Valencia turned up her chin. "Who cares? I want to kiss you too. Whether we have known each other for many years or the past two days, I love you, Graddock. I want to be with you in a castle, or in our small cabin in the woods. Our future does not matter to me if I am with you."

Valencia closed her eyes. Their light kiss transformed when Graddock pulled her closer and Valencia put her hands on the back of his head. What appeared at first to be a five-second peck between first-time lovers transformed into a lengthier gesture of affection between husband and wife.

Valencia wiped away tears. "We fell in love with each other again!"

Graddock kissed her knuckles. "You doubted it?"

"Do you regret it now? Losing the newfound feeling?"

"I have not lost it. I feel the same way, except with all my memories back."

"I feel the same." Valencia glowed with happiness. "And we will build that cabin just like we dreamed, but it may have to be a little larger."

Graddock squeezed her hands. "We are going to be parents! By all that's holy! The baby, just as we had planned."

"You'll make such a great father."

She kissed him again, and then they turned and looked at everyone. Rushing to each of us, Valencia embraced us as old friends. The Match Girl blushed when she came to the end of the line and stood before my wife. "Oh, Sanders. I am so sorry."

My wife shrugged. "We're all good, Valencia. Friends again?"

"*Absolutement.*" A tight embrace between queen and pixie.

After everyone greeted each other, a whooshing noise sounded from above like a giant bird rocketing through the sky. The creature was coming from the north, and I peered up at the drifting clouds. My jaw dropped. Helga and Danforth flew through the air with Helga's outstretched hand clutching a sword. They soared as fast as an airplane and landed on the ground outside of the inn, taking only a few steps to stop themselves.

Valencia stepped next to Cinderella. "She can fly?"

"With her recounting her prior exploits all the time," Cinderella said, "there will be no living with her now."

Helga sheathed Cusp and addressed us. "I am Helga the Cusp-Bearer, Helga the Restored, Helga the Queen." Her eyes sparkled and she ran forward and embraced her sisters. "I am grateful for you."

"You have broken the curse?" asked Cinderella. "You allowed Danforth to kiss you?"

She leaned back, smirking at Cinderella. "He is my true love. Why would I resist?"

Valencia hugged her. "'Tis so wonderful to have you here."

Cinderella put a hand on her hip. "How long did it take? Did it take you a day?"

"I will discuss it later." Helga patted the hilt of her blade. "Cusp, the legendary sword came to Danforth, and he hid it in a cave outside of Nor with Dawn. I've left her with my parents."

The queens all expressed their relief at the news of Dawn.

"Only a true queen can bear Cusp." A smile tugged at the corners of Helga's mouth. "Also, it has granted me the power of flight."

Cinderella asked, "The sword convinced you to kiss Danforth?"

Helga looked at her sister strangely. "No. I kissed him after we parted at the convent."

Cinderella looked as though she was going to have a headache. She caught Roger's eye, and he shook his head. No more questions.

Helga gave me a rib-crushing hug. I'm not sure how Danforth stands it. She lingered at Wysdel and whispered something in her ear then turned to Sylvia. "Sylvia, is it you?"

"Yes. Danforth told you, I assume."

"You are Snow White's spitting image. Wishes can be dangerous things, dear friend."

"I believe in myself."

Helga slapped her arms. "Good. Kingdom needs a Snow White for our upcoming battle."

Then she moved to Rapunzel. "Our newest member."

We were interrupted when two unicorns raced toward us from the southeast. On one of them, in full battle armor, sat Beauty. Riding the other unicorn, to my astonishment, was Sinope, looking as small as a cricket riding a dog. A large raven who could only be Lenore flew above them.

The queens hailed Beauty who directed her steed to them. She dismounted, and the reunited queens all kissed her cheek. For her part, Sinope flew to Rapunzel and grew large enough so that the two could embrace.

Beauty explained she had been keeping watch on the inn, and sharp-eyed Lenore had spotted us and directed Beauty and Sinope here. While Beauty was enveloping Cinderella in a hug, Valencia asked the question we were all wondering. "Where's Grr?"

Beauty's face fell, and my blood froze.

The youngest queen retrieved the shield from its position on her back and lifted her sword. "This is the shield and sword of Kor."

Valencia examined them as a scholar would, and Helga touched them as a soldier would. Only Cinderella didn't seem interested. "But where is Grr?"

"I obtained these weapons to build an army to oppose Piper's golems, but I'm only borrowing them. I had to leave Grr behind..."

"As collateral," finished Valencia. "These are incredible, Beauty. If what the legends say are true, we shall be a force to be reckoned with."

Helga eyed the Inn of Five. "We won't need an army if

Penta remembers her past. Breaking the spell on the last queen will restore everyone's memories. But without a true love..."

Valencia said, "If she did have a true love and kissed him, she'd be furious at Piper. Our sister's temper..." She shook her head.

Wysdel stepped forward. "We should sail to the Waterfall of Renewal with Penta. The waterfall will be strong enough to break the spell."

Helga turned around. "Best idea I've heard yet. Cinderella, Valencia, Beauty, Wysdel, and I will go in and convince her to join us on this quest. Hero, please come with us as you're gifted at this sort of thing."

I didn't feel gifted. All the queens had kissed their husbands at the promptings of their own passions. I hadn't convinced them to do a thing. And my presence would put Penta on the alert. "Maybe this is a family affair."

Helga put her hand on my shoulder. "And you are our brother. If not in flesh, then in spirit." Her features softened. "If Penta had her memories, she'd want you there even if you say nothing. She loves you, Harold."

Using my real name, Helga's counsel touched a chord deep inside. She was right. Penta would want me with them.

The queens and I started for the inn. While we marched to the front door, I had an idea. "Helga, can't you use Cusp to restore everyone's memories?"

Helga lifted her chin. "Divine intervention into human affairs is rare and usually reserved to oppose demonic forces. Piper is human, brought to life by the Creator. Our Redeemer loves him just as much as he loves me. Directly interfering in our human disputes would be an abuse of power from our Creator's point of view."

"But Cusp broke the spell on your daughter."

"As a personal favor to me," replied Helga. "Cusp knows Dawn will not influence the outcome of our conflict with Piper. Cusp is not a weapon or wand to be used against humans. If I used it as such, it would likely depart from me.

No, it is a symbol to remind people of a higher world than Kingdom, a world where the consequences of our actions here come due."

"Hero, you'd be surprised how little that sword does," murmured Cinderella.

Helga snorted. "Cusp heard that, sister."

Cinderella blanched.

When we reached the door, I halted the other five. "Wait a minute. Penta teleported all of us away the first time I visited her. Sanders was the last one she sent away, but before she did, my wife told Penta about the true love's kiss solution. Uh..."

"Spill it, Hero," said Cinderella.

"Penta kissed a guy in the bar, another bartender."

The sisters looked on in disbelief. Penta's daughter Beauty voiced their concerns. "She kissed a man? You mean...on the lips?"

Valencia touched her chin. "I wonder. Maybe she put her bottom lip on his top lip. You know it's a common way of getting around the kissing custom."

"She kissed him, as in pecked, smooched, osculated, canoodled. She got it on with him, gave him sugar, played—"

Helga held up her hand. "If you continue, I am going to have to put you in the stocks for vulgarity and insolence. She is my sister and the high queen, after all."

"Sorry."

Helga stiffened with resolve. "This does complicate things, but I suggest the five of us approach her with you behind us so that she cannot see you at first. We will gain her trust by telling her about the times she was a great sister and mother." She looked at her other companions. "Do each of you have an example?"

Heads nodded except Beauty's. "Perhaps I should stay back as well. I didn't impress her when I visited her before."

Wysdel tapped Helga's shoulder. "I think best would be if you, Valencia, and Cinderella blocked the rest of us from view."

I raised my cowl and followed the others into the barroom. The inn was busy as always, and Penta was behind the bar, washing glasses, her back to us. I looked around and whispered, "I don't see the other bartender. Lenore said he worked in the castle. He was a garbage guy or something."

"She kissed Quin?" Cinderella frowned. "He has always been fascinated with Penta."

The women approached the bar, and I hunched down behind the queens next to Beauty. Helga spoke in a loud voice. "Penta Emily Corden!"

Penta turned around and wiped her hands on a towel. "What can I get for you girls?"

Helga squared her shoulders. "Do you recognize me?"

Penta narrowed her eyes. "Should I?"

"I am Helga Helvys. Have you heard of me?"

Penta backed up a step. "Helga of Nor. The warrior turned nun?" She raised her eyebrows. "Did you retire your wimple?"

"I assure you I am Helga Helvys, no mere common maiden of Kingdom. Others have told you, and I shall repeat it. You are a queen, Penta."

Penta huffed. "You must be an imposter. Why do people keep saying I am royalty?"

Helga said, "Why would I, in all respects a queen myself, come here to tell you that you are a queen unless I speak the truth?"

Throwing down the rag on the counter, Penta's nostrils flared. "'Tis impossible. I am only a barmaid. I do not know why people persist in this deception."

"I will stake my honor on this story because it is the truth." Helga twirled her finger to indicate herself, Cinderella, and Valencia. "We are your sisters who love you, and you are a queen of Kingdom."

"As if! How do four sisters share power in Kingdom?"

"Listen, and I will tell you how." Helga's voice lost its royal tone and softened. "I had a child, and you were her godmother. She...died."

Helga paused, and Valencia and Cinderella instantly took her hands and squeezed them. Helga cleared her throat. "You gave the eulogy, Penta. You provided comfort to me and my husband. Your words...not hollow...but sincere, and from a grieving heart." Helga's voice trembled and became quieter. "You led all of Kingdom in mourning, and showed everyone what it means to love, even something as tiny as a babe."

Helga lowered her head and choked up. Penta's lip quivered, and she held out her hand. "I am sorry for your loss."

Valencia put her arm around Helga but kept her eyes on Penta. "I, too, am your sister. My name is Valencia. At the start of our reign, my friend was falsely accused of treason, but we didn't know if he was a traitor or not. As queens, we voted on whether to send him to the dungeon. The vote was split with two for and two against. You had to cast the deciding vote. By all rights, you should have convicted him, but you showed mercy and pardoned him. Because you did this, I was able to continue to see him, and fall in love with him, and now we are going to have a baby! Your mercy demonstrated to Kingdom that we cannot settle for easy answers. You're a woman who seeks truth, not expediency."

Penta put her hand to her mouth while she looked at Valencia's belly. Cinderella reached out and took her other hand and gripped it. "I know you can send me away now that I've touched you. I trust you won't. I have faith in you as you had in me once. When Helga was with child, we decided she could no longer lead the army until after the birth. We needed to appoint a new queen to command the soldiers. You found me crying in my room. I had overheard a soldier say that he hoped it would not be the party-planner queen. Me.

"The soldiers dismissed me out of hand. You were the army's choice to replace Helga, but you asked me if I would do it. You told me you believed in me. I accepted and led Kingdom's infantry in a battle against the pirate skeletons of Andwar. We won, Penta, and I have you to thank for it. And now, I return the favor. I believe in you."

Penta stared at Cinderella's hand clutching hers.

Beauty stepped forward next to Cinderella. "You adopted me, but I've always thought of you as my birth mother. I love a man who most look on with horror. He has no dowry, no title, no power. To this world, he is less than nothing. The nobility has courted me, and a well-placed marriage would have solidified your rule. But you've always stood against it. You've championed my lover in your speeches and your actions. And you've always encouraged me to make him my prince, no matter the cost to your throne."

Flustered, Penta squeaked, "How could... I don't remember any of this!"

Valencia held out her hand. "We are your family. We're going to take on Piper, the false king, but are incomplete. We need you to stand with us."

Penta looked at each woman in turn. "But...the entire thing. 'Tis a fairy tale."

I lowered my cowl and stepped around the others. "Where did you hear that saying? Fairy tale?"

Alarmed, Penta recognized me but answered my question. "I do not know. Somewhere."

"The phrase 'fairy tale' is unknown in Kingdom. It's your subconscious that Piper couldn't erase. Deep down, you know this is all true."

A voice interjected from behind Penta. "There is only one problem."

Quin, or "Big Mac," entered the bar area from a back room. He took in all of us, eyes narrowed. "She kissed her true love, but her memories have not returned. How do you explain that?"

"You aren't—" I stopped myself from finishing my sentence. The kiss had worked five times now. Clearly, he was not her true love, but calling him out was not the way to win Penta over.

He raised his eyebrows. "I am not her true love? Show

them, Penta."

She reached in and pulled out a necklace from which hung a charm of a circular disc with a hole in its center. The object was a flat piece of metal without a gem anywhere to be seen. Penta fingered the item as if it were jewelry. "I cannot put this ring over my gloves. Big Mac and I are engaged."

I leaned forward and examined the disc. "Wait a minute. That isn't—"

Sanders burst into the bar. "Piper is here with a golem army! Everyone outside."

The queens turned around and without hesitation ran for the door. I didn't follow them, opting to stare at Big Mac. "This isn't a ring. It's a metal tab from a soda can."

And then it hit me. I had dismissed his name as another silly moniker of Kingdom, but I was blind. The man across from me was from Earth, and I knew exactly who he was. Mac and Quin. The journal Alice found!

Big Mac crossed his arms. "Nice to meet you, Hero. Name's Joseph Macquin."

34 - INTERMEZZO 4

Sixteen Years Earlier

"**D**ear diary. I am Princess Penta Emily Corden," Penta said aloud. Her tutor had encouraged her to speak the words she wrote to become better at writing. She had to go slow, using her plastic prosthetic hands, the only ones freely available to an orphan.

Penta reviewed her first sentence and ground her teeth. Not quite right. She lined out her first effort and started again. This time, she didn't talk aloud.

Dear diary. Hi. I'm Penta. Sister Joan gave me this book early for Christmas to capture my memories. I live with Sister Joan and the Little Sisters of the Assumption at a boarding school. Sister Joan is my 'aunt.' Not really, but she bribed a few people to make it look that way. Sister Joan said in a world where millions of children are lost in human trafficking, faking my identity in the system was easy to accomplish.

Thunder rumbled outside. Ick. Penta wanted snow.

I've lived here for about eight months with several foster kids. Sister Joan says the school's existence hangs by a thread every day. Some of our computers don't work, the few smartboards we have glitch all the time, and we always have a bathroom problem, or a heating problem, or an electrical problem. But to me, St. Theresa's is my temporary home, and I love it.

The rain tapped against the window. Sister Joan said it should snow this time of year. Snow was rare in Kingdom, and Penta longed to see some. But today's weather brought only rain. Penta sighed and returned to her writing.

Sister Joan didn't believe my story until I teleported her across the room. After that, she drank something from a tin canister and sent me away, but an hour later, she came to me and hugged me tighter than ever. She told me she'd do anything to help me go home. She showed me a book and read it to me. It was a fairytale, like Kingdom's bedtime stories, one that was about me! *Sister Joan and I think this isn't a coincidence and maybe I can find a way home.*

Penta observed the bed across from her that belonged to Edwina Alderston. Ugh. Why did she have to bunk with that girl! *The girls here have a clique called the Queen Bs. Not 'bee' but 'B' as in the first letter of a word I refuse to write down! They make fun of me because I don't have hands. They spread rumors that my parents had cut my hands off to trade for drugs.*

Most everyone here ignores or teases me, except one boy. Joseph Macquin. The first time I noticed him he was staring at me in math class, and he blushed when I caught him. I thought he'd be like the others, but he doesn't stare at my stumps. Mostly he looks at my hair. Says he likes the color. They call it 'russet' here.

She stopped writing and thought of Joseph. When she and Joseph were talking at lunch yesterday, Edwina had interrupted them, asking if he'd give her a hand because "you know, Penta doesn't have one." She and the Queen Bs laughed and walked away. They only teased Joseph because he talked to her. And to think, Joseph had given up a field trip to be with her.

She set the pen down and stared out her window. Rain fell over the pane in streaks. The weather forecasters had promised a white Christmas this year. What she wouldn't give for a little elf magic now. Oh, to see an elf just one more time would be glorious.

Christmas was different on Earth than in Kingdom. In Kingdom, Christmas was known by another name and was far less glitzy. A minor holiday in the year. The lights, the songs, and the efforts by Earth people to be charitable...Penta admired it all. Kingdom could celebrate in the same way. If only she could return, she'd introduce her home world to Christmas trees, sparkling lights, and lip-smacking cookies.

Another raindrop fell on the window and dripped down. Earth felt like a new shoe to her now. Though stiff and unfamiliar, she had adapted to it and appreciated some of its customs. They spoke in the old way, using contractions, but it was fun. And the way they spoke about reproduction. All the time and in various, graphic ways. Videos on the internet were full of it.

One drop landed on the pane of glass outside and began a zigzag pattern downward. Penta placed her finger on it and followed it. But...Earth had its charms. Flushing a toilet beat an outhouse any day of the week, electric light allowed her to read at night, and they valued education here. She was receiving an education with a private tutor. And the Penta story! How Earth knew about Kingdom, she wasn't sure, but these fairy tales gave her hope that a way home existed.

A flash of white. Was that snow? Sister Joan had told her about large snowfalls in Detroit, and she couldn't wait to see one. She leaned forward to take a closer look when someone knocked on her door.

"Come in!"

The door opened, and Joseph stood there. Oh, Joseph. He had told her last night that he had given up going to his foster family for the holidays to spend it with her. What a good friend. Earth people continued to surprise her. The world told them to acquire everything they could from their neighbor, go with the majority, or not to believe in old traditions because that makes you small-minded. Yet, the people rose above what others said. The devil was wrong—he didn't control this world.

"Hey," greeted Joseph.

Penta stood as he entered. "You're not allowed in the girls' rooms."

"I think we can bend the rules today." Joseph grinned. "Are you excited? You said yesterday your parents didn't celebrate Christmas."

"I said that my father never celebrated it in this way. But yes, I'm a little excited."

Joseph stepped across the room. "Well, I'm going to make it one to remember. I've got something I want to tell you."

"Should we go somewhere?"

"Here's as good as anywhere."

Joseph sat on the bed, and Penta sat next to him. She had no idea what he was going to tell her, but his leg was bouncing up and down, making the bed move.

"Penta...you and I are good friends."

She chuckled. "You're my only friend. But yes, you're a good friend."

"Sometimes friends don't stay friends. Sometimes they drift apart, but sometimes it goes the other way. You know?"

What did he mean? Just as she thought she understood the people in this world, something came along and surprised her. Was there a friendship ritual on Earth he was going to do? Penta gave him a questioning glance and a small smile.

Joseph leaned forward. "I'm going to go for it."

Now what did *that* mean?

"Penta, I love you."

He...what? Did he use the word 'love'? Who could love a girl without hands, who constantly made mistakes and made a fool of herself? Her only goal was to return home.

Penta's eyes widened. She stood. "I...I'm honored."

"Honored?"

How could she explain it? He was her only friend, but she had to be honest, no matter what. "I'm sorry, but Joseph, I don't feel the same way."

Joseph looked down. "I think...I think if you gave me a chance you might feel different. You might like me and don't know that you do."

Penta almost laughed, but Joseph was so earnest. How could she let this poor boy down? Of course! She had an out —her past. He'd think she was crazy if she told him about Kingdom. Sister Joan had warned her not to tell anyone when she first entered the boarding school, but Joseph was a friend. If she told him, he wouldn't believe her, and their relationship would be over. But with his confession of love...didn't she end their friendship by rejecting him anyway?

Wouldn't discussing her true past with someone on this holiday be nice? It would push him away, but why not? Her father had figured she was one of the prophesied queens, and her mission was to return home. Sister Joan had suggested perhaps God's hand was in her exile here. Possibly she had to learn something before she returned to Kingdom. Certainly, her destiny wasn't tied to Joseph even if he was a true friend.

She sat down next to him again. "Let me tell you something, and you'll see why I can't return your feelings."

She told him everything about her past. At first, Joseph asked if she was kidding him, but her expression told him she believed it completely. "I would never ridicule you, Joseph."

With that, he quieted down as she told him about the demon and how he had sent her here. She finished with her arrival at the boarding school.

He eyed her. "You can't prove any of this."

"Actually, I can, but I don't want to."

"You're afraid of love. It's okay to be afraid. I was too when I walked in, but now that I've told you, I feel better."

This wasn't going as she had hoped. "It's not that, Joseph."

He put his hands on her wrists as if he were holding her hands. "I love you. I really do. Just…keep your mind open. That's all I ask for now."

"Will you keep yours open?"

"How?"

She teleported him across the room to the door. Joseph sat on the ground there for a moment, collecting himself. He pointed to where he had landed, and his mouth dropped open. "How…?"

"I used my ability. The prophesied queens all have some power. I teleport other people to different locations. If you tell anyone, I'll deny it. Sister Joan told me never to show anyone else."

Penta thought this would push him away, but it didn't. Surely, he'd think her bizarre. Instead, he ran across the room, his mouth agape. The word he said Penta knew from the B girls, but he said it in a completely different way. In awe, not in cruelty.

And then she realized he believed. She had proved it, all right. But it hadn't repulsed him at all.

Penta cleared her throat. "Listen, I'm a freak, right? You shouldn't have anything to do with me."

His eyes sparkled, reflecting the rain running down the window. "You're telling me the truth. I want to hear more."

And they talked about Kingdom for hours, dropping the subject of his love for her. Their conversation filled the afternoon, and she enjoyed every minute of it.

Christmas morning was a new, delightful experience for her on Earth. The Little Sisters of the Assumption, Joseph, and Penta enjoyed a cozy morning in the teacher's lounge. The nuns prepared syrup-drenched waffles, Eggs Benedict, and a minty tea for breakfast. After the hearty meal, they gathered around a fully decorated tree and a smattering of presents. Penta received six gifts from the nuns and one from Joseph. She unwrapped them with her prosthetic hands. Excited like a small child, she found believing they were all for her difficult.

Joseph's present was a book, *Around the World in Eighty Days* by Jules Verne. He had told her the book was his favorite and possibly the best book ever written. In her room that night, Penta lay in her bed, reading Joseph's present. She had removed her stiff prosthetics and was using a hands-free page turner clipped to her wrists. The device was a stiff rod with a rubber end that caught the pages and flipped them.

Joseph knocked on her open door. "Hey, Penta. Just wanted to say goodnight."

Penta shook off the page turner. "Come here."

She squirmed to a sitting position as he stepped up to the bed. He put a soda can on her nightstand.

Penta hugged the book. "Thank you for everything today. You made me happy."

"Of course. I told you I loved you."

Penta tilted her head. "Really? Still? Joseph, you can't love me. I'm going to return to Kingdom one day."

Joseph hooked his thumbs in his belt loops. "And I'll come with you. Why not?"

"Because you belong here with someone who will really love you back. The other man pursuing me is a demon. You don't want him to know how you feel about me."

"He doesn't scare me."

Penta held up her rounded-off wrists. "He should. This is what happens to people he wants to marry. Imagine what happens to a rival." She touched his arm with her forearm. "I am going to go back and I'm going to unite my sisters. I'm not waiting for some stranger to do it. Then we're going to take the throne away from King Shade and I'm going to rule Kingdom. I don't think I'll ever have a husband. I'll be far too busy."

"After you do all of that, send for me. I'll come. I

promise."

Her eyes sparkled. "You're sweet. Truthfully, a small part of me would like to stay here."

"Make me a promise." Joseph bit his lip. "If you turn eighteen and you haven't gone back to Kingdom, you'll consider staying here with me. We'll go around the world, just like in the book. I'll save money for it. I'll reserve us first class tickets by plane, train, and boat and we'll go everywhere."

"Oh, Joseph. You're funny."

"Promise me."

Penta fluttered her eyelashes teasingly. "Sure. It'll be fun. But I don't love you, my friend. Kinda wished I did, but I'm sorry. And you've been so kind, I'll give you what I can. You remember what I said about kissing in Kingdom?"

"You said it was like a marriage proposal."

"Indeed. Some Kingdom maidens, not always of the best reputation, know a way around it. I shouldn't, but I'm here, and I feel a little reckless. Hold still."

She leaned forward, and her top lip connected with his bottom lip, kissing half of his lips and his chin. She pulled back. "There! A princess's kiss is supposed to grant favor. I hope your life is favorable, Joseph."

"You gave me a pseudo-kiss."

"It's the pseudo-best I can give."

"I told you I wanted to give you jewelry earlier, but I didn't have any money." He reached for his pop can and snapped the ring off. He presented it to her. "Here's a ring! I'll make you a necklace for it!"

Penta put her wrist on her chest in staged admiration. "Oh, it's lovely! Look how it sparkles without any gems or diamonds. I'll treasure it."

Joseph's smile faltered, knowing she was kidding him. Penta rubbed her forearm over his hands. "I will treasure it, but because it's from you. Any other ring wouldn't do."

Joseph said, "Will you think about going on that trip? I'm serious."

Penta sighed. "Sister Joan finds out a little more every week about this thing called Traveling. I don't think I'll be here for another year. But—" she held up her wrist as he was about to protest. "Yes, if I'm here and if I'm not on the verge of going back, we'll go around the world."

Joseph stepped away. "You'll fall in love with me. I'll warn you. That's my evil scheme."

"Oh, is it?" Penta quirked an eyebrow. "Well then, I'll be on my guard."

Joseph walked backward toward the door. "Guard all you want, I won't give up. You don't love me now, but one day I'll be worthy."

"You keep trying, Sir Joseph, and we'll see. Maybe one day, when I'm old and cranky, you'll wear me down. And I'll be proud to wear your discarded trash on my plastic fingers."

Joseph was at the door. "It'll be the jewels of nature. Try to resist in Paris, or New Zealand, or Hawaii. You'll see!"

She threw a pillow at him as he shut the door. She laughed when he departed.

But he was serious.

35 - A ROUND
AT THE INN

Harold

Penta's head swiveled from Joseph—or using his Kingdom name, Quin—to me. "Do you two know each other?"

My nostrils flared. "I never met him, but I followed his instructions to Travel here."

"Is that how you made it?" Quin rubbed his jaw. "I wondered."

I leaned on the bar counter. "How did you ever find the back door?"

"They call it a back door? Let's just say, I appropriated notes from Sister Joan. Her writings gave me insights into Traveling, and some research led me to a bookstore in

Cambridge. The shop has all sorts of so-called back doors."

Penta placed a gloved hand on his arm. "Quin, what are you saying? I thought you'd lived in Kingdom all your life."

Joseph took Penta's hand and folded it in his own. "No, I came here from the same place as Hero. The difference was I followed my heart to you. I came here only for that purpose."

I pointed at him. "You're a spy for Piper."

"No. I was here long before King Piper." Joseph thrust out his chin. "When I arrived, you had already come and set events in motion. I was older and balder, and no one recognized me." At this, his eyes shifted to Penta, the only one who would know him. "I started at the bottom and worked my way up, hoping and praying for an audience one day. And then King Piper came."

I addressed Penta. "Do you hear him? He's validated my story."

Penta furrowed her brow. "All he said was you and he share the same birthplace, and that he came here a long time ago and worked his way up to be my assistant. And when King Piper's rule came, he told me he loved me. He did not say I was a queen or that I had sisters."

Yelling erupted from outside the inn. I put my hand on Penta's. "I know you can send me away, but I'm begging you to listen to me. You *are* a queen. A legend. You and your sisters banished the demon who caused you to lose your hands."

Penta raised an eyebrow.

I continued. "Please, let's go outside, just you and me. Witnessing what will happen will prove to you Piper is your enemy and we aren't."

Penta ground her teeth, debating my proposal.

"Please, don't send me way up in the air to fall to the ground," I begged.

She removed my hand, pinching it as if she held a mouse by the tail. "Again, you do not know me. I have honor. I would never do such a thing." Penta reached for Quin. "The three of us shall go, and I will publicly declare my loyalty to the king."

We exited the inn. Surrounding the building some hundred yards in all directions was a row of golem soldiers. The eyeless figures in armor stood in rows like headstones in a graveyard. I let out a shaky breath, wondering how we were going to survive the coming battle.

A slight distance to my left, Helga stood with the other queens. She waved me over. As I approached her, Valencia lifted a flag with a green banner.

I eyed the pennant. "What does that mean?"

Helga took my arm. "We're going to discuss terms with the enemy. None of us want this conflict, and perhaps Piper will surrender."

"Unlikely," I responded. "Where is he?"

Helga directed me around the corner, and I spied two figures in the distance—a human-sized Janus-the-pixie and the queens' doorman, Lyken. Under the queens' rule, Lyken judged who would have an audience with the monarchs. I hadn't seen him this entire adventure, and although he was on the opposite side, his presence gave me hope. He was the type who could be persuaded.

"I don't know where Piper is." Helga's eyes roamed across the makeshift infantry. "But I sense he's close, directing the golems. For now, you and I will negotiate with the false queen and my former trainer."

"I forgot Lyken was your mentor. But why me and not one of your sisters?"

Helga gave me a sidelong glance. "You have the gift of persuasion, Hero. We all agreed you should be present."

Maybe in the past I could sway others. I couldn't admit to Helga that I had lost my mojo.

We strolled toward the rendezvous point on the field. Helga spoke out of the side of her mouth, keeping her voice low. "What say you, Hero? I could take her hostage and force her to admit her deception."

"People will say you coerced her. But could anything

cause her to make a mistake? Is there something only a queen can do that she can't?"

Helga slapped me on the arm. Ow. "You're a genius, Hero! Let's proceed."

Genius? I wanted to know what she had planned, but we were rapidly approaching the false queen.

When we reached a point where we could hold a conversation, Janus held up her hand. "Proceed no further!"

Before us stood a woman who could be a twin of my own wife. So much so that only I could see the differences. To call the experience "disorienting" would be an understatement.

Janus pointed down. "Kneel before your queen."

"Who should kneel before whom?" snarled Helga. "Where is Piper?"

Lyken touched the hilt of his blade. "Helga Helvys, your insubordination will leave you lying in your own pool of blood."

Janus touched Lyken's arm. "Remember, my faithful guard, that Helga is again under the curse. Beautiful but wicked in daylight, and ugly but remorseful at night. Her evil side presents its face to us now."

Helga cocked an eyebrow. "So, this is what you've told the people who know me? I assure you I am under no curse. Lyken, I am the true queen of Kingdom, and this woman is nothing but a cutpurse. She is not Planet."

Janus grinned. "We cannot believe a word she says."

Helga thrust out her jaw, frustrated. I leaned over to my royal companion and whispered in her ear. "However I inspired you, I say go for it."

"I'll give her one more chance," Helga murmured to me.

Wind rustling her hair, Helga used a tone of authority. "Janus, you know you are up against queens with the Creator on our side."

"Now to the terms of surrender." Janus continued, ignoring Helga's threat. "King Piper the Great will allow this little act of rebellion to be overlooked if you submit yourself to him in the throne room."

"To remove our memories again, no doubt." Helga's hand clenched the hilt of Cusp.

Janus ignored her interruption. "You will return to your present lives safely under the jurisprudence of King Piper's rule. The rebels Hero and Sanders will leave here and not return to Kingdom under threat of death. No blood spilled, and everyone winds up with what they want."

Helga lifted her chin. "I asked before. Where is Piper? I will only deal directly with him!"

Eyes flashing, Janus screeched, "I am the queen. You are fortunate to have an audience with me!"

I stiffened. How much more taunting could Helga take before she attacked Janus? Lyken was no match for the warrior queen Helga had become, and I knew she could take them both if she wanted. But Helga abhorred violence and nudged me instead. "Thank you for the inspiration."

Helga squared her shoulders. "If you are the queen, then a holy artifact would recognize you as such. Is that not so?"

The blood drained from Janus's face. "Naturally."

Helga unsheathed Cusp as Lyken drew his sword at the same time. Upon recognizing Cusp, however, Lyken lowered his weapon. "It cannot be," he whispered.

"'Tis," answered Helga. "The holy sword Cusp, forged by the divine, and borne only by royalty of pure hearts." Helga held it up in front of her face. "Cusp and I are in communion, proving I am the true queen."

Lyken fell to his knees. "Truly, no evil or cursed person could wield Cusp." Indecision flashed across his face, and he eyed Janus.

Splotches of red sprinkled over Janus's cheeks. She held out her hand. "Cusp has come to you so that you could reward me with it. Give it to me."

Composed and statuesque through this entire conversation, Helga tensed. "Janus, do not try to take Cusp.

You must know the fate of the unworthy thief Jazlar and what happened to him when he attempted to steal it."

"I am worthy! I am the *queen!*" Janus' eyes widened. "Now present me with Cusp."

Helga clenched her teeth, kneeled, and held out the sword to Janus with both hands. Greedily, the faux-queen's eyes lit with fire as she reached out and snatched the handle of Cusp. I had heard the sword was heavy in anyone but Helga's hands, but Janus lifted it up and pointed it at the sky. Her face displayed plainly her ambition and hunger for power... and betrayal. With her fierce expression, I wouldn't want to be Piper.

But then her smile faltered. Her fingers unclasped the hilt, but the sword stuck to her palm. Her complexion turned a darker color, a hue of green. She began to tremble, and Lyken and I stepped back. Within seconds, her wings contracted, her legs came together into one stump, and her arms shrunk into her torso. She shrieked but the sound died out quickly, ending in a hiss. When she no longer had hands, the sword floated in the air before her. Scales emerged from her skin in rapid fashion, and when she opened her mouth, a forked tongue came out.

Rapidly, she shrunk down into a small creature. A simple garter snake slithered in the grass. Helga reclaimed Cusp and stuck its pointed end into the tail of the reptile, lifting it into the air. "I warned you, Janus. Now, I will have to put you in a pen next to the so-called spider monarch."

She opened a pouch, slipped Janus into it, and closed it. "So much for Kingdom's queen."

Lyken kneeled. "Helga. You are royalty."

Helga smiled. "Faithful Lyken, everything I have told you is true. Now, where is Piper?"

Rising to his feet, Lyken nodded to the eyeless army. "Disguised as a golem."

Helga surveyed the creatures. "As I thought. You have a squadron of human soldiers far yonder. Could you keep them from attacking?"

"That goes against royal orders," Lyken said.

"He is not your king." Helga straightened her posture, striking a queenly pose. "Here is my royal edict. No soldier under your command may engage in battle. Can you do it, Lyken?"

Lyken stood. "I can."

Helga said, "Be off, then." Lyken marched away.

Helga turned to the golems. "Piper! Throw yourself on our mercy. You were wronged. We queens were about to proclaim justice for your situation the day you played the pipes, but you mesmerized us before we had the chance. Though treason is punishable by death, if you come to me now and kneel, we will spare your life."

No one answered her, and Helga sighed. She turned and directed me back to our small band of adventurers. I said, "We need to break this curse on everyone, but Quin will never admit Penta's a queen. He loves her too much."

"Penta will see reason soon, Hero. Have no worry. Right now, we have a golem army to fight."

When we arrived at our small gaggle of heroes, the creature army started marching across the plain in unison. They moved slowly but with purpose. I turned to see scores of golems advancing toward us. Helga quickly outlined a plan using the inn to protect our backs, though her strategy also cut off any retreat. She sheathed her holy sword, saying, "Cusp cannot turn hearts of stone. I must use another weapon."

The odds appeared impossible to me, but I had to grin when Helga unsheathed her old flail with the ball and chain in her free hand, and Celeste and Sanders lit up with glowing auras. When the golems were about thirty yards in front of us, the queens and their allies sprinted forward and attacked.

Sondra

Weapons flashing, Helga had defeated three golems

before I cast my first spell. I created a trench of quicksand inspired by my time in the Marsh of Wishes. Though I took out four golems with my bit of magic, my sister-in-spirit Celeste downed twenty with a whirling blade that chopped off their heads.

Everyone was engaged except my husband, Penta, and the bartender dude. Cinderella's ability was useless on creatures without a conscience, so she was back-to-back with Roger using his shield as a weapon. Valencia sliced her opponent's knees with a short sword. But Beauty's tactics surprised me the most. She wasn't fighting, just holding the sword and shield of Kor out as if ready to engage. Instead, she would jump back a few inches. A replica of her sword and shield would appear out of thin air and attack the nearest golem. She had created at least five of these copies of her weapons, and they were effectively keeping our enemies at bay.

Out of the corner of my eye, I spied Rapunzel snapping her hair at a soldier. I screamed, "Someone get that child out of this battle."

An eyeless monster rushed at her and reared back to strike her. Rapunzel tensed, awaiting the blow. I cast a quick spell and turned Rapunzel's body into fog. The thing's hand passed through without harming the girl. Graddock grabbed the golem after that and swiftly dispatched it.

Faintly, the sound of pipes drifted from behind the advancing army. "No!" yelled Celeste, clutching her head.

I was about to help Celeste, when at the same time, Rapunzel's misty body returned to flesh. But she wasn't out of danger yet. Fortunately, Hero was ahead of me and convinced Penta to teleport him next to the youngest princess. My husband was hugging Rapunzel as I arrived.

Hero asked, "Rapunzel, have you ever tested just how much hair you can grow?"

"No."

Clutching her arm, Hero urged, "Rapunzel, let down your hair. Grow as much hair as fast as you can. Can you do it?"

"Watch me!"

A great mass of hair flew out of her head, and Hero grabbed an end and ran around in a circle. Her locks were heavy and sturdy when bundled together. The princess directed her tresses to follow the circular pattern Hero had started, the locks swirling like spun sugar in a cotton candy machine. In a short time, a wall of hair encircled Rapunzel, Hero, and Penta.

While the makeshift barrier wasn't the thickest of strongholds, it deterred the eyeless golems. When they touched it or brushed against it, they recoiled, clearly confused. As long as our enemies left those inside alone, I was satisfied.

I flew over to Celeste who stood focused on a spot on the ground. Sinope was a few feet away, conjuring a transparent shield to protect Celeste.

I grabbed her shoulder. "Celeste. What's wrong?"

Eyes filled with tears, she asked, "Que et el majours en pleh!"

"What does that mean?" I asked.

Celeste huffed. She pointed at her head then at her lips then made a slashing motion. Oh no! "Piper has messed with your ability to speak?"

Celeste closed her eyes. "Language." She hesitated. "Broken."

"She won't be able to cast anything until she slowly speaks the counter spell," remarked Sinope. "She'll need to concentrate on each word. This level of magic is above me. How about you, Sanders?"

"I don't know it, either." I was going to learn it, though, if I ever got out of here. Cat piss! Stupid Piper messing with people's minds again.

I continued using my scientific magic to confuse the golems. I cut them in two then turned their upper halves around in a semicircle so that they couldn't see where they were going. I also created miniature bicycle horns with the big bulbs at one end. They floated around honking, startling the golems just as they were about to strike.

The others were also fighting furiously. Helga and Valencia were back-to-back, twirling around while they moved through the creatures, knocking them down with their weapons. Beauty's twenty-and-growing animated swords and shields defended our flanks.

A guard advanced behind Sinope and raised its sword. I conjured a giant catcher's mitt behind her, blocking the attack. I yelled at Sinope. "Guard Celeste."

Sinope threw out her jaw. "You're not leaving me out of this."

"Don't worry, Sinope." I gritted my teeth. "Leave the handsome villain to me!"

Nearby, Hero overheard me. "Really, Sanders?"

Sometimes my kidding goes too far. "Don't worry, Love-of-my-life. I have a Planet-sized score to settle with him!"

The bartender outside of our wall of hair, held up his arms, indicating he wanted no part in the conflict. I had zero idea who he was, nor did I expect him to help. Even without any assistance, we were slowly evening out the odds. I surveyed a cluster of the golems moving slower than the others, as if protecting someone. In the middle of them stood a man with a flute in one hand and a knife in the other. Like the golems, his helmet only covered the top of his head. I pointed at him. "I see Piper."

Hero shaded his eyes. "He has my knife again!"

I materialized a red cardinal and a slingshot. I pulled back the sling and propelled the bird at Piper. "Here's a little thing I call pissed-off birds."

The bird bounced off Piper's helmet, knocking it off. The "king" curled his upper lip and lifted the flute like a weapon. "Enough!"

I readied to charge him, but he pressed the instrument to his lips. Music drifted from it like bees floating on a summer breeze. A voice in my head commanded me to stop any activity and enjoy the melody. Everyone else's faces went slack as well. The golems stood down.

Piper paused to speak at certain intervals. "Futility, futility, futility! Hurting my army will achieve nothing."

When he stopped playing, my mind began to clear—the haunting melody drifting out of consciousness. Our party struggled to fight the golems, and I had difficulty remembering the incantation for my quicksand spell.

Piper played again, sapping our energy, causing everyone to slow down or stop. Yet, he was so arrogant that he would pause and speak in between using the pipes.

"Hero and Sanders, you have failed. You did not know that I allowed you to travel through Kingdom, did not care who you found, or what you did. I needed time to perfect my spell, the same one I cast before, but more potent. This time, it will impact those who were not born here!"

A chill ran down my back. He was going to erase all our memories this time. The Resistance would be wiped out.

More music, then words. "No more Hero and Sanders. You will become Harold Tray and Sondra Saturn, simple merchants who like each other but don't dare to express it. I will implant a suggestion that the other rejected you cruelly. You want your knife back, Hero? Unrequited love is the sharpest blade of all."

"We have a child!" I cried out.

"You should have thought of that before you opposed me."

Piper played more notes, disrupting a spell I had started. Cat piss!

Then he spoke again. "Everyone else resets to six months ago, except the visitors to Kingdom and this new Snow White. Our immigrants will receive a new history, and Snow White will end up deep in my dungeon with no idea why she is there."

Tears rolled down Beauty's face. "If I forget, Grr will die of hunger! Don't do this!"

Hero turned to Penta. "Do you hear this? Do you believe us now? Help us!"

Penta frowned in indecision. But her *hombre*—Quin, I think I heard Hero call him—looked worried. Over the sounds of the continuing melee, he shouted. "Spare Penta and me! Do not reset us. I am loyal and will remain so."

Shrugging, Piper said, "You were never worthy of her."

Quin was not a spy, apparently. I had no idea why Quin did what he did next. He must've known the consequences. My romantic heart said he chose her against all odds.

Quin spoke to Penta over the barrier of hair. "They're not lying, Penta. You are a queen of Kingdom. The best one."

Penta gasped. I could see in her eyes that she believed him immediately. If he convinced Penta, we could end this. If she teleported behind Piper and ripped the flute from his fingers, the battle would be over.

Breathing in deep, Piper nodded at one of his soldiers fighting one of Beauty's animated swords and shields. The golem broke off, unsheathed a knife, and threw it. The knife soared end-over-end directly at Penta's head, but out of her field of vision. But not Quin's.

Quin stepped in front of the blade's trajectory. It sliced deeply into his chest and knocked him to the ground.

"Quin!"

Penta teleported next to him, cradled his head, and cried his name in anguish.

Hero pointed at Piper. "You call yourself a just king? Killing people who tell the truth?"

Piper raised his flute in victory. "His death is of no consequence. His life had no more value than that of a common sprite."

Again, he set the flute against his lips and broke out in a calming melody. I tried to concentrate and launch another bird at him to distract him, but the song was hard to ignore. The music occupied my mind like a fat spider spinning its web in a high-ceilinged corner. The spell captivated all of us. After everything we had faced, I couldn't believe *music* would defeat us.

No, I wouldn't succumb. I was Sanders Saturn, pixie, wife, and alchemist. Wait, that wasn't right. I was something like an alchemist, though.

Everyone lowered their weapons as the golems stopped attacking. Penta ceased consoling the dying Quin. Lenore and Sinope landed on the ground, unable to focus on flying.

Piper's song was beautiful and terrible, haunting and hypnotic. I tried to block it by thinking of essential facts about my identity. I was Sanders Saturn. I lived on Earth. I was married to...someone. I had a child. Or did I? Oh God, I didn't know.

Piper's words of new beginnings floated in my mind like a rocking boat on a rolling river. "The world is darkness and light. Creation and destruction are the same and everything returns to whence it came."

And then a high, stark voice cut across the music. The voice sang something different...enchanting...wonderful.

"Row, row, row your boat."

36 - LACRIMOSO

Harold

Her voice was the sound of audible honey, church bells at Midnight Mass, and the giggles of a delighted child. The singing was clear, confident, on-key. She trilled "Row, Row, Row Your Boat" as if a professional singer performed it. The tune cut across the field and snapped me out of my hazy funk.

"Gently down the stream."

I glanced sharply at Rapunzel, the originator of the round. Gone was the scratchy voice and lack of confidence, replaced with poise and determination. Also gone were the false memories Piper had planted in my mind. I was not Hero Tray, a destitute seller of hair tonic. My name was Harold Saturn, husband of Sondra, and father of Fitzie, and I was one determined-to-win adventurer.

"Merrily, merrily, merrily, merrily."

Rapunzel had made herself a target of our evil and powerful adversary while surrounded by his army. What had pushed her over the edge? Possibly the sprite comparison to Quin's life. His disregard for the value of sprites signaled he might not just wipe Sinope's mind, but kill her. Sinope, her stepsister, whom Rapunzel loved dearly.

"Life is but a dream."

Sanders' eyes focused, Helga gritted her teeth, and Sylvia's nostrils flared. My shoulders relaxed as the memories of my life on Earth returned. We had escaped Piper's spell.

Piper's brow furrowed when he zeroed in on Rapunzel. I stepped in front of her, ready to take whatever he decided to throw her way. Instead of attacking her, however, he raised the flute to his lips while everyone else returned to the battle. The royals continued to fight, Sanders floated into the air, and Penta resumed weeping. The queens lacked their usual vigor, and Sinope struggled to form spells. Again, Piper's music made us pause, and his words lulled us into a false security.

"Depression is happiness if only you embrace it. In the struggle is the joy, not in the achievement. Work is pleasure. Love is pain. Life, a burden."

Sinope landed on Rapunzel's shoulder. "Sing! I scolded you to avoid using your ability near magic but ignore me now. Keep singing with your real voice!"

And then. "Row, row, row your boat. Gently down the stream."

Again, Piper seemed stymied in his efforts to mesmerize us, and he glared between the seams in the twelve-year-old's hair with murder in his eyes.

Rapunzel's shaking hand reached for mine and clasped my fingers. She was not as steady as she appeared, and I worried she wouldn't be able to keep countering Piper's flute. I breathed in deep and belted out the beginning of the round. "Row, row, row your boat, gently down the stream" while Rapunzel continued with "Merrily, merrily, merrily, merrily, life is but a dream."

Sanders landed in our circle of hair and grabbed Rapunzel's other hand, also shielding her with her body. She thrust out her chin and cleared her throat. Another ally.

From behind us, Penta sobbed. "Quin, please do not die. We were meant to be together until our elder years. Always in love."

Music, then Piper again. "The moon is an illusion. The stars are tiny. The night sky is not a place of wonder but a void ready to swallow us all."

And Rapunzel's response. "Row, row, row your boat, gently down the— The..."

Then Sanders' discordant voice. "Stream! The stream, Rapunzel!"

My mind whipped back and forth like a carnival ride. I was Hero Tray—no, Harold Saturn—no, Hero Saturn. I imagined my memories as a flag on a rope in a tug-of-war between Piper and Rapunzel. On the one hand, you had a master magician and on the other, an inexperienced twelve-year-old girl. My entire future depended on that girl. Despite the peril, my heart swelled with pride at Rapunzel's effort.

But this song, from my earliest childhood, I could remember as Harold and learn quickly as Hero. As I sang it, I taught it to the identity Piper was creating for me. I swallowed. "Row, row, row your boat, gently down the stream."

And then, Piper's voice. "Words are meaningless. Love is dangerous. Hope is out of reach. Will you stop that singing!"

"Merrily, merrily, merrily, merrily, life is but a dream," sang Rapunzel and Sanders together.

Piper blew a note that was clearly wrong on the flute, and his eyes narrowed.

As I started the "merrily" verse, Sylvia and Danforth, my Earth-born friends, joined in. Sylvia's high-pitch and Danforth's steady baritone aided our efforts. When Sanders and Rapunzel sang the "Row, row, row your boat" line, they were joined by all the queens, Sinope, and Lenore. Soon, we'd have everyone singing for their lives except for one person. Penta.

Focused on Rapunzel, Piper had forgotten about the Penta who emitted a loud wail. Penta shouted one word. "Dead!"

My attention turned to her and Quin. His head lay to the side, eyes glassy. While not a fan of the bartender, I still swallowed down a lump in my throat. He meant something to Penta, and because of my affection for my friend, I felt her loss.

Gracefully, Penta leaned down. "I love you, Quin."

With those words, she kissed him gently on the lips. I should've turned back to Piper and Rapunzel, but when Penta parted from the kiss, our eyes locked. In them, I spied something unexpected. Recognition. She was no longer Penta, humble barmaid of the Inn of Five. She was now Queen Penta Emily Corden, a royal force to be reckoned with.

True love's kiss breached the void of the living and the dead.

Penta stood. Watching her, my skin broke out in hackles. I had seen that look before. She had resolve, determination, and murder in her eyes.

I raised my arms higher than Rapunzel's hair barrier as if to flag Penta down "No!"

Was I nuts for attempting to save Piper's life? No. I knew Penta. She was going to do something terrible, something she would regret later. She wouldn't be able to live with herself. Certainly, she'd step down from being a queen, and perhaps go further into depression.

"Sanders, stop her."

Sanders teleported herself outside of Rapunzel's wall of hair, but unfortunately, she landed ten feet behind Penta. She tried a second time and this time she was fifteen yards to her right. She shook her hands as if trying to ignite a spell.

Piper had noticed Penta advancing on him and stepped back, turning as white as marble. He nodded at the golems nearest Penta. She ignored them, her fists clenched, arms at her sides. When the creatures approached and swung their swords, I thought for sure they were going to cleave her in two. But the instant the sword touched her flesh, the instant before it could pierce any of her skin, she teleported each of them fifty feet into the air. They fell to the ground with a stone-splattering sound, crumbling into pieces. After she dispatched six golems this way, she had a clear path to Piper.

Everyone had stopped fighting—all eyes on Penta. No one moved but the other queens. Helga, Beauty, Valencia, Wysdel, and Cinderella hurried to her. They all surrounded and embraced her, halting her ten feet away from her target. The faux king looked relieved as her sisters held Penta back. Directly in front of her, Helga tightened her embrace. "We have him. We've won."

Penta didn't look at any of them. Instead, her eyes bored into Piper's as he shrank back. Penta didn't say anything either, not acknowledging any of the women surrounding her. I thought it was over—Penta respected her sisters and daughter above all else in Kingdom. But I underestimated her, and the next thing I knew they were teleported fifty yards behind her, all embracing each other.

Face set, Penta strode forward. Piper had lost his composure and withdrew my knife. He started slashing the air in front of him and to either side. If Penta teleported next to him, she'd likely be cut by the blade. My pulse quickened. He was going to kill her with my knife. I had to do something. But what? I was encircled by hair.

Hold on. I was the master of my knife.

But the revelation came too late. Penta appeared directly behind him. By the time he realized it, she had already reached out to the back of his neck. With her index finger, she tapped his skin and they both disappeared.

Where had they gone?

Above their current position, Penta and Piper were falling like stones to the spot where they had stood a moment before. Piper had let go of the knife and it tumbled through the air with them. Penta fell through the air beside him, arms wide, accepting her fate. I thought she was going to murder him, but she had a different idea—a sacrifice play. If she was going to take his life, she was going to pay for it with hers.

They approached the ground rapidly. Penta was going to die. My best friend from Kingdom was going to die!

But I was not powerless. I used three words, talking in shorthand. Fortunately, my love understood immediately.

"Sanders, teleport Rapunzel!"

For the moment, I forgot Sanders was, shall we say, teleportation challenged. But this time, when it counted the most, she nailed the spell. In an instant, Sanders had teleported Rapunzel to the location not directly under but near the plummeting Penta and Piper. In particular, she had teleported Rapunzel's hair and had transformed it in one act. The hair, which had been in the shape of a ring around her, Sanders had mashed together into a large cushion about five feet high. Her thick tresses appeared just below the two falling figures. They dropped into Rapunzel's tangles, and it slowed their progress to the soil below. The trick hadn't stopped them from hitting the ground but acted like a buffer and cushioned their fall. Bones still snapped as they connected with the packed dirt.

Along with them, my knife flew point down into the cushion of hair. I concentrated as the dagger fell below my line of sight into Rapunzel's makeshift netting, and I heard a wet, gurgling sound.

Sanders and I raced to Rapunzel's side. The queens were still behind us, trying to make their way to the scene, and the golems had frozen in place. Everyone else stood as still as their adversaries, eyes glued to the brambles of hair.

Mortified, Rapunzel rapidly retracted her hair, and I noticed blood spatters on her golden sheen. She placed a hand over her mouth, looking sick. Lying on the ground was Penta, not moving. Next to her was Piper, also still, but for a different reason. The knife protruded from his throat.

Rapunzel stared in horror, and she buried her face in Sanders' chest. Celeste teleported immediately to Penta's side and voiced a spell. With the golems transfixed in place and Celeste's language restored, I assumed Piper's death had dispelled his magic. But what of the mesmerized people across Kingdom?

I heard Lyken's squadron at a distance start to raise a cheer for the queens, shouting out all of their names.

Celeste finished her spell, one that I recognized from having received it before. She had put Penta in a stasis to prevent any damage from spreading.

The queens surrounded Penta's body, but left a space for the kneeling spellcaster, knowing she was Penta's best chance of survival. Celeste leaned down and placed her ear on the prone woman's chest. My heart froze for a moment. After everything Sanders and I had done on this adventure, would it end this way? Was Piper right about his prediction that one of the queens would die?

Celeste lifted her head and released an unsteady breath. "She lives."

The Queens' Palace

37 - POSTLUDE

Sondra

Everything happened fast after the battle. Celeste whisked us to the royal palace where all the soldiers, servants, and townspeople had gathered to await their beloved queens. Helga gently carried Penta to the royal physician.

A crowd gathered outside of Penta's recovery room. Valencia retrieved a wishing stone from her collection and wished all the royal children back to the castle. While the families joyfully reunited, a pall hung over the scene, waiting on news of Penta's condition.

Valencia wished a few of our old friends to the castle. Hero, of course, wasn't pleased to see Turducken. Turducken and I immediately apologized to each other for my deception and his squaring off against Hero, and I hugged him tightly.

Stiffly, my husband accepted the elf's apologies.

Penta regained consciousness an hour later. Once we learned Penta had suffered no serious injuries, the remaining queens addressed the massive gathering outside. Hero and I visited Penta during this time, the doctor allowing us a few minutes. Penta wasn't exactly cold—remarking how pleased she was to see us—but I felt a distance between us. She may have been alive, but clearly something inside of her died in that fall.

After leaving Penta, Hero and I met with Rapunzel privately. We described her fairy tale and her destiny in Kingdom. Now that it was all out in the open, we discussed her future. When we had finished, Turducken appeared with Sinope and offered to take Rapunzel and Sinope on a tour of the castle. Hero and I decided to go off on our own.

We proceeded outside to a spot where Hero declared his love for me, one of our favorite places to visit. On our way, a steed appeared from midair a slight distance ahead of us. Bree, my stallion! I called his name, and he neighed and excitedly shook his head. I sprouted wings and flew to him, wrapped my arms around his neck, and buried my face in his mane. Bree was far more than a ride home to me. After wiping a tear from my eye, I wagged a finger at him. "Never do that to me again."

He tossed his head back, and I patted him.

While we led Bree to the stables, we came across Lyken talking to Celeste and joined them. He handed her the Pipes of Perringon. "I have buried Piper in an unmarked grave. Here are the pipes for the queens' vault."

Celeste raised her chin. "I bespelled the vault so that only the queens may enter in. They are enjoying a little private, family time now. But I will remove some of the magic from this odious artifact with some ancient spells I know."

Lyken frowned. "Careful, Court Magician. This is a powerful item."

"And I am Celeste the Extraordinary." Her eyes sparkled and shifted to me. "As someone has reminded me, though I am not worthy of the title."

I grabbed her hand and squeezed it. "You earned it, again."

"We shall have a long talk." Celeste's eyes moistened. "But first, I must retire to my magic study to disenchant this instrument. Why not visit with the queens properly? They are in the center of the castle's hedge maze."

I hugged her, and we parted from her and Lyken. Hero and I strolled into the maze and along its well-trimmed pathways, discussing the future. Soon, we entered the large garden-like center inhabited by the queens and their princes. Benches were arranged facing each other, and the queens and their husbands sat mostly on one side. Valencia sat between Graddock's legs, facing outward, his arms around her belly. Helga lay on another bench, her head resting in Danforth's lap. Beauty's arm was around Grr's waist, and her other hand was around his front, hands clasped together. Cinderella was sitting sideways, and Roger was massaging her back. I found it hilarious that we had come upon the queens and princes relaxing, but Hero blushed and excused us.

"Stay!" commanded Helga, waving for us to remain. I thought the queens and princes would move apart because of our intrusion, but they did not. Nor did they stop what they were doing.

Hero and I sat on an open bench. He was clearly ill at ease, but he didn't realize that the elegant, noble, gracious queens were comfortable sharing a moment when they could be themselves. We were family, though we hardly spend any time together unless someone threatens Kingdom.

Cinderella's eyes softened. "Throughout this entire adventure, I forgot to talk to you like a normal person. How fares Fitzie?" she asked me.

We talked for a few minutes, answering Cinderella's questions about our son. Cinderella inquired about mutual friends until Helga interrupted.

"Cinderella, give us all a chance to talk to Hero and

Sanders. You had the most time with them on this adventure."

Cinderella side-eyed her. "I always get ripped off spending time with them." She looked at Hero when she used the words "ripped off" and winked. "I was the last queen Hero found the first time he was here."

Beauty sidled up to Grr. "My time with them was limited as well. I had to trade my items back to restore Grr."

Cinderella rolled her head back on Roger's shoulder. "True, favored niece, but I still would've preferred more time with Hero and Sanders."

Roger tilted his head toward her. "If you had kissed me sooner, we could have had more time."

Cinderella looked at him askance. "If you had asked for me all of those years ago when you had the slipper, I wouldn't have been so bitter."

Swinging her feet, Valencia gestured to Roger. "Are you still going to hold that over him? Has not this adventure taught you anything, Cinderella? Piper was able to manipulate you with your resentment of that event. Roger is right. The way you two are, you should have kissed him at first sight."

Cinderella snorted. "Are you honestly lecturing me, Valencia? How long exactly did it take to get you to kiss Graddock? Two lunkheads pining for each other but...oh no...'I just do not know.'" Cinderella mimicked her sister's voice.

Valencia lifted her nose. "Unlike you, *dear sister*, Graddock and I fell in love a second time. You knew you loved Roger from before, but you wouldn't act on it. Graddock and I were complete strangers to each other with entirely different histories, and yet we fell for each other again. No matter how you separate us, across worlds, or remove our past, we always fall in love."

"Nice try. You still took too long. You two are the most stubborn love birds I have ever met."

Valencia said, "You were not as fast as Helga. It took her...what...a day? A day and a half?"

"An hour," answered Helga.

All the queens looked at her, astonished. Cinderella leaned forward, pulling away from Roger. "Is this the same woman who once said, 'Do you think I am won so easily' when you first met Danforth? Whatever happened to Helga the Bone-Crusher?"

Helga squeezed Danforth's hand. Danforth didn't regard the rest of his family when he responded. "Shared pain unites people quickly."

He was referring to their infant daughter who had died, Melda. A hush fell over the scene until Helga broke it with a steady voice. "We are better now, sisters. Danforth and I need time together, but to put it in Hero's language, we are going to be okay."

Danforth leaned over. "That we shall."

Helga lifted her head and kissed him with a short peck. "My dear, Silly Putty."

Rearing back, Danforth blushed. "That was my code name to Hero and Sanders to let them know I was from Earth. I had hoped they would see through my disguise and trust me."

"Well, you earned yourself a new lover's name," Helga said.

"Oh? Well, you'll always be my Frisky Froggy," responded Danforth.

Giggles and clapping met this response. Helga pulled away. "Must you? And in public? Call me what you will but remember which one of us can fly."

Valencia rolled her eyes. "Oh, here we go again."

Cinderella's shoulders went up, and Beauty looked at her warrior aunt with embarrassment. Helga continued, "Like an eagle, soaring across the landscape. I flew straight as an arrow, whistling through the air."

"Able to leap tall buildings in a single bound," murmured Danforth.

Helga looked quizzically at him. "I don't understand the reference."

Danforth smiled and cupped her chin and the two

kissed lightly. Cinderella nodded her approval. "Yes, I think you two will be okay."

Beauty said, "I tell you who will not be okay is my mother. She damaged a bone in her leg. She refused any spell to heal it and made the doctor treat it without anything to relieve the pain."

This was news to me, but the decision seemed consistent with Penta's resignation.

"She wants the pain," said Danforth. "Sometimes pain helps."

Beauty frowned. "It worries me. I don't want—"

Penta suddenly appeared in the middle of all of us, leaning on a cane. The queens didn't move when Hero and I entered, but for Penta it was a different story. Helga scooted away from Danforth, and Graddock dropped his arms to his sides. Cinderella stood up and reached out for Penta who ignored her.

Hunched over, Pena didn't make eye contact with anyone. "I am convening a council. We will meet in thirty minutes. The princes should attend, including Grr though not officially a prince yet. We shall also include Hero, Sanders, Rapunzel, Wysdel, Sylvia, and Celeste as well."

That was quite a list. Helga lifted her chin. "Penta—"

"Helga." The tone of her voice was an audible stop sign.

Helga's jaw tightened and Penta vanished.

"I don't like it." Helga shook her head. "She's going to say something she will regret before we have a chance to react to it."

"She may refrain in front of Beauty," remarked Cinderella.

Helga put a hand on her niece's shoulder. "Beauty is no longer a child. We have been reminding Penta of this for years, but I am afraid she is going to choose this day to take our advice. Beauty, whatever she says, I know I speak for your aunts when I say that we stand together. Remember, she is not entirely herself."

Beauty hugged Helga, and Cinderella and Valencia joined in the embrace. We left the alcove and found Rapunzel and Celeste and relayed Penta's message.

We all gathered in the queens' throne room, a mammoth, pillared chamber in the center of the palace. Arranged in a semicircle were the queens' thrones with their crowns arranged on the seat of each. Snow White's throne resembled a tree with a carved inset where she could sit. Valencia's was a plain four-legged chair you'd find in anyone's home, while Helga's was wooden with a stave architecture. In the center, Penta's marble throne was a massive seat studded with diamonds, and next to it stood Cinderella's silver swinging chair, aligned with her playful style.

At the extreme left stood a new throne made of burnt-umber redstone. Carved around its back were faces with snouts and tusks, which puzzled me at first. But as I moved to view it dead-on, the faces transformed into human features. Awesome!

"'Tis not magic," whispered Celeste who appeared behind me. "Beauty wanted something carved into her throne from your planet. You call it an optical illusion, I believe? The faces are different depending on where you stand."

The queens approached their thrones with Penta leaning on her cane. As one, each sat in her respective chair of authority except Wysdel, leaving Snow White's seat empty. The rest of us stood in front of them while I held Rapunzel's hand wondering what her throne would look like.

Pale, Penta set her cane next to her throne. "Though my sisters summarized what has happened, one day I shall learn all the details of Piper's treachery. But that day will have to wait. Today, we have business to attend to. With the remarkable way my daughter has conducted herself on this mission and with her steadfast and sacrificial suitor, I'm very pleased. As we promised you before, Grr, the courtship to Queen Beauty is over. Let the wedding preparations begin."

Grr bowed his head, and when Beauty looked at him,

she used her ability to change his form into that of a handsome prince.

Penta turned her attention to Wysdel and Sylvia. "And now, we must address the problem of too many Snow Whites."

Wysdel stepped forward. "I have no voice here after abdicating, but the spell affected me too. Though I was done ruling, Kingdom itself wasn't done with Snow White as a monarch. The spell treated me like a queen, not a commoner. But as you know, my husband and I don't desire a royal life. I am afraid for my marriage if I become a queen."

"But the rumors are rampant now, Snow White," said Beauty. "You put up signs stating you lived, and people witnessed you fighting at the inn."

Wysdel turned to Sylvia. "They witnessed Sylvia, not me. The wish in the marsh has taken away my abilities and given them to my Earthen friend. She is the true Snow White now."

I'd wondered if this would come up. All eyes locked on Sylvia. Penta cleared her throat. "Dear Sylvia, what is your true heart's longing? Many speak wishes in the Marsh of Wishes but are turned away empty. Yet the will-o'-the-wisps granted your wish. Do you want to become Snow White and live here permanently?"

Sylvia clasped her hands together. "My parents passed away a few years ago, and I have no siblings. I'll miss my friends, but...I have friends here, too. Becoming a fairytale queen? I would be crazy to say no. However..." With trepidation, she glanced at Helga.

Helga knitted her brows. "You think I would disapprove?"

Sylvia squared her shoulders. "I'm not Christian, Helga. I'm Jewish."

Confusion stole over Helga's face, and she looked to her husband. Danforth held up his hand. "Sylvia, if I may. I'm Muslim yet married to a Christian. Religious beliefs aren't as contentious here as they are on Earth. In fact, in Kingdom, the

Jewish people are known as One-Truists."

Helga returned her attention to Sylvia. "You're a One-Truist? And you think only a Redeemerist may sit on the throne?" She shook her head. "Sylvia, Kingdom would be honored to have a One-Truist sit on her throne. And I would take no personal offense."

Wysdel rolled her eyes. "And with that extremely minor detail settled." She leaned across and hugged Sylvia. "I renounce my former name to Sylvia who, from this point on, will be known as Snow White. And what a Snow White! Unlike the rest of us when we started, she brings leadership experience to Kingdom."

"Here, here!" yelled Hero.

Cinderella stood and rushed over to Sylvia, now Snow White, and took her hands. "I move that our new Snow White joins us as a queen."

This motion was unanimously passed. Cinderella eyed her sister. "Wysdel, would you do the honors?"

And with little ceremony, Wysdel took the crown made by the seven dwarfs of wood and jewels and set it on the new Snow White's head. Taking her by the hand, Wysdel led Snow White to the long-abandoned tree throne. With tear-filled eyes, the newest queen sat down. Wysdel backed away and kneeled, along with everyone else in the room.

After the ceremonial trappings were dropped and everyone had a chance to congratulate Snow White, Penta allowed her attention to land on Rapunzel. "It seems Hero and Sanders have found a new princess of Kingdom. Rapunzel, you are far too young to be a queen, but the perfect age to be a princess. And for the wonderful things you have done for us, we cannot fully express our gratitude."

Valencia grinned. "She whipped Mangiafuoca's hand, freeing me."

Delightfully, Cinderella waved her hand. "She saved my life as I bled."

Helga nodded at her. "She locked the door at the

convent, likely saving mine."

"Mine as well," said Penta. She sounded less concerned for herself and prouder of the twelve-year-old girl. "You are talented in many ways, and I suspect we have only begun to understand your spell-dispelling singing ability."

Penta straightened her shoulders, ready to make another royal proclamation. "And so, as queen of Kingdom, I move that we officially confer the title of Princess onto Rapunzel."

I stepped forward. "Excuse me? May I say something before you vote?"

Penta blinked. "Assuredly."

I reached over and grabbed Rapunzel's hand. "This extraordinary young woman has saved Kingdom. She certainly deserves the title of princess." I turned to her. "Hero and I have spent our time in Kingdom guarding her, and in that time, the three of us have grown close."

Rapunzel gulped. Her eyes shifted from mine to the queens and back again.

"We'd like to adopt her into the family she desires."

Rapunzel squeezed my hand, trembling, but I was calm. The queens would see it our way.

Gently, Helga said, "I think it's wonderful you're planning to adopt her, but take a moment to consider the situation. Rapunzel is clearly a princess of Kingdom. She has abilities similar to ours. And the best evidence I can present exists in your own home world. Did they tell you, Rapunzel, that, in their world, people tell stories about you as a fairytale princess? She belongs here."

Rapunzel clenched my hand so hard it was starting to hurt, yet she defended herself. "I want a family. I would love to be a princess, but not if I don't have a Mom and Dad."

"We will be your family." Valencia held out her hand. "Sylvia will become a sister to us all and an aunt to Beauty. We shall treat you the same way."

Rapunzel pulled in her hair to a short bob, a sign I knew

of her nervousness. "Who will be my mother? Or my father? I wanted to meet the people who gave me to Mother Gothel, and I'm still curious about them. But they're not my parents. These two are my true parents!"

Wysdel asked, "What about Sinope?"

Rapunzel observed her feet. "She's found her birth family, and they won't take me in. Her family was mistreated by humans."

Helga sighed. "As painful as it is for me to ask this of you —"

Penta interrupted, "Maybe you should not ask it then."

Helga raised her eyebrows at the interruption but deferred to her elder sister. Penta touched her chin. "On Earth, I learned many lessons that prepared me for being a queen, some of which I've brought to Kingdom. Rapunzel, if you go to Earth, when you come of age—and on Earth that is eighteen—will you consider coming back and becoming a princess?"

She faltered. I put my arm around her. "Rapunzel, it's okay. It will be up to you. The important thing is you'll always be my daughter. No matter where you live or what you choose to do."

Rapunzel leaned against me. She nodded.

Penta picked up her cane and set it before her. She pounded the end of it like a gavel "Then I dismiss my current request to make Rapunzel a princess. And I offer my congratulations."

We hugged Rapunzel along with everyone else, each person in the room taking their turn. When the queens returned to their thrones, Penta called everyone to attention to continue the meeting.

Helga cleared her throat. "As glad as I am for the Saturn family, we may have a problem. There are now six queens, an even number. Many times having an odd number has been to our advantage."

Penta glanced thoughtfully at the floor. "An astute observation, one I had hoped to avoid with Rapunzel as tiebreaker as Beauty was before her."

Valencia said, "I wonder…"

Everyone knew this phrase was Valencia's way of thinking through a problem, and they let her "wonder" for a few seconds. Her eyes brightened. "I move the eldest queen gets two votes if we are ever an even number. This will always ensure an odd number of votes."

The queens nodded enthusiastically, all except Penta. "While I favor the idea, I would rather confer the two votes on Helga."

Helga leaned back. "On me?"

"Look how you defended our traditions to Hero and Sanders. You stand up for what you think is right for Kingdom even when at odds with good friends. You had the courage to do so. You deserve the double vote."

Cinderella snapped, "I second it."

When the rest consented, Helga touched her crown reverently. "I accept but will not abuse this power."

Penta closed her eyes and sighed. "And now for the final business. I will relate what I know of Quin that it may help you understand."

She told us about her history with Quin on Earth while staring mostly at her hands. When she finished, she said, "So it must have come as a great shock to many of you that the dustman of the castle was my lover at the Inn of Five. But he told me a month ago that if I were not a barmaid, if I were more than that, he would have been too embarrassed to tell me how he felt. He said he would have strived to become noble, worthy of me. When Piper threw his spell, Quin saw an opportunity.

"He helped at the inn and paid me compliments, and for my part, I thought he was handsome. Piper sought to implant a memory where I would feel trapped as a lonely barmaid all my life. He did not foresee Quin. Quin gave me hope of a new life, a married one to a man devoted to me, but a man, as you know, I didn't truly love. Not at first."

Cinderella spoke, and I thought that was brave of her.

"I'm sorry, Penta. I speak for all when I say our hearts ache with yours."

Penta nodded slightly to her sister, tears in her eyes. "Life is sometimes cruel. Life was cruel to save true love's kiss for my last one with Quin. Sometimes, in saying good-bye to someone, you discover how deeply you love them. No matter what came before, I was truly in love with Quin, and I seek your approval of him posthumously. Joseph McQuinn—" Her voice cracked on his name. "—should have been a prince."

All the queens spoke as one. "Granted."

Penta blinked away the tears. "While we were not married, this still makes me a widow of sorts."

Beauty, tears running down her face, could contain herself no longer. She rushed to her mother and hugged her, though Penta was still seated on her throne. When they parted, Penta laid her hand on her daughter's shoulder and then addressed the room. "We have established that I am mourning a lost love, and so I'm going to take a furlough. I have something I need to do, and I'd prefer to do it alone."

Trust my husband to say either the wrong thing at the wrong time, or the right thing at the right time. This time it was the right thing. "Do you think that's wise, Penta?"

He purposely didn't say "queen," addressing her as an equal. She recognized it and took no offense. "Perhaps not. Perhaps, if they want, I can stay with friends."

Her eyes darted between Hero and me. I blinked. "Of course."

Valencia inquired, "You're going to Earth?"

Penta nodded. "I thought I would travel around that world."

"But for how long?" asked Cinderella.

Penta flashed her sisters a wistful smile. "I thought about eighty days."

The queens looked down. Penta stood and limped to Valencia's throne, laying her hand on her sister's. "I know I will miss a great many things. Valencia giving birth to her first child, Beauty's early wedding preparations, my special nephews and nieces who've grown so much in seven months. Yet, this journey is something I must do. I will stay with Hero and Sanders, but plan to travel extensively and only inconvenience them briefly. Please, sisters, please let me do this."

Beauty's voice cracked when she spoke. "Granted."

Valencia followed up. "Seconded."

The rest of the queens assented. Tears formed in Penta's eyes. "Thank you."

The Saturns

38 - CODA

Harold

As we prepared to leave on Bree, I couldn't help but feel I needed to do one more thing. Sanders and I discussed it, and she encouraged me to look in on Penta. She hadn't joined us for breakfast and had spent the night in her room away from her sisters and daughter.

I knocked on Penta's door, but no one answered. When I entered, I found Penta in her elaborate annex to her bedroom. She sat with her back to me at her desk, her cane leaning within reach. Out of the corner of my eye, I noticed that the full-length Mirror of Reflection—a magic item that reflected her innermost thoughts—was smashed. Pieces of glass littered the floor. I stepped up carefully behind her.

Penta held an open, ceramic box in her hands and spotted me in a mirror on the lid. "What are you doing here,

Harold?"

She had set the mood of this conversation by addressing me with my Earth moniker. I gulped loud enough to hear. "I thought you might want to talk about it."

"I don't."

"You were there for me when I needed you. When Planet died."

She retrieved several items from the box, examining each one. She held up a Detroit Lions football ticket, a photograph of a tall Christmas tree near a skating rink, and a book: *Around the World in Eighty Days*. "Piper brought some women into the castle, and they took some of our personal things. Quin retrieved this box for me after the spell was cast. I thought it was his when we worked at the inn. He promised me he would show me the contents one day. Funny, him showing me my own things."

I didn't know what to say so I let her continue. "I've kept these reminders of my time on Earth and take it out from time to time. Now I want to burn it all."

"Don't do that."

"Wise counsel from the *Hero* of Kingdom." She spat my name. In all my years of knowing her, I never received such a cutting remark. I went to say something else, but she held up her hand. "Not now, Harold. I may say something I regret more than that last statement. Tell me, did you direct the knife into Piper's throat?"

I grimaced. "He's dead, and that's all that matters."

Her eyes regarded me from the box's mirror. "I'm not fond of murder."

"I'm not fond of it, either." I thrust out my chin. "I saw my best friend in trouble, and I made a call."

"You'll have to live with that choice."

"I'll sleep easy, I assure you."

Penta snorted. "Take that knife with you to Earth. I don't want it in Kingdom any longer."

I nodded, and Penta's attention returned to the items

on her dresser. She picked up a necklace with a soda can ring attached to it from the dresser. Allowing it to slip from her hand into the box, the tinkling sound of metal hitting the other treasures in the container filled the silence.

I folded my hands behind my back. "Are you sure I can't help you?"

Heaving a sigh, Penta stood up and turned around. "Harold, does the grief ever stop?"

"No, but it does change." I paused, choosing my words carefully. "At first, the sorrow intrudes into your life, and you want it to leave you alone. It's not an enemy, though. It leaves unexpected gifts behind, but you only realize they're gifts later."

Penta stared at a point over my shoulder. I could see her struggling to maintain her composure and wanted to comfort her. But I also sensed she'd reject it.

Penta bit her lip. "Did you ever stop loving Planet?"

"No."

"Better not tell Sondra."

"She knows."

"Then that's true love."

"'Tis," I replied.

Penta's hands touched mine. "Farewell, Hero. I'll see you in a couple days, but please leave me for now."

When we arrived home, we had to create an identity for Rapunzel and adopt her. While I won't say everything we did was legal, it was all done with her in mind. Sometimes you must bend the rules to do the right thing. I'm not sure Helga would agree, but she holds a high standard.

Penta arrived at our house two days later as she had promised but set off immediately. She didn't traverse the world as much as pop in here and there. She'd teleport to a location and return to her room. Sometimes she'd spend a day at a location, sometimes a week, but we rarely saw or heard her. She'd leave us postcards on the small side table where we set our mail. I sensed a theme from many of the locations she had visited.

On the eightieth day of Penta's journey around the world, the queen agreed to join us for dinner. Sondra's older sister, Karen, had wanted to meet her, so we invited her over. Karen had been a little put out about Sondra choosing Celeste as Fitzie's godmother until she learned about Kingdom. Now she was at peace with our decision.

Sondra and I prepared an Italian dinner with angel hair pasta and wine. Karen made a sauce to compliment it, a delicious Saturn concoction that her mother had passed on, and Karen had promised to share with Sondra one day.

Penta came down mid-afternoon, informing us of her last trip to Rosario, Argentina. She presented hand-wrapped gifts to Fitzie and Rapunzel. I observed her carefully, and while gracious as always, she was still distant. Even the "welcome back" embrace from her was stiff.

Penta excused herself to dress for dinner, and Karen went into the other room to talk to Fitzie and Rapunzel, leaving Sondra and me with a moment alone. We were in the kitchen, preparing last minute details and getting in each other's way.

I lifted the lid on the saucepan and stirred it with a wooden spoon. "Penta's still not back to her old self."

Sondra retrieved plates from an overhead cabinet. "You can't seriously think she'd be all better. She's grieving the loss of a husband."

Taking the spoon, I dipped it in the sauce to taste it. Just like Sondra's mother's version, it would give the pasta a tangy lift. "It's been eighty days. In her travels, she's been to Wot Rong Khun, the Vatican, Nasir al-Mulk Mosque, Angkor Wat. I expected at least a smile."

"You don't smile at the Wailing Wall, Harold. My favorite was the picture she took outside of the bookstore in

Cambridge, the same one Quin used to Travel to Kingdom." Sondra opened a silverware drawer with one hand. "The plaque dedicated to Quin was a nice touch."

"Maybe there's something I can say to her—"

Sondra held up her hand. "No. She has to go through this. You couldn't make stubborn people who were obviously in love kiss each other, *Chosen One*. Similarly, you can't make this go away. You weren't in Kingdom to get her to kiss her true love but to save her life. Now's the time to be her friend."

I squeezed her hand. "Seeing her like this is hard. Same as it is with you."

Sondra drew me closer. "A little at a time, life becomes more bearable. Not the same, mind you. Karen and I cried when she arrived. But you've lived up to your Kingdom name with me while I mourned my mom. Our mom." She put her hand on my cheek. "And I love you more each day for it."

Rapunzel's laughter cut through our moment, and we stepped away from each other. I eyed the other room. "Rapunzel wants so much to impress Penta, but Penta's not in the mood."

Sondra handed me the dishes and patted me on the shoulder. "Everything will be fine as long as you stop tasting that sauce!"

When we started to set the table in the dining room, Karen, Fitzie, and Rapunzel arrived from the living room. I nearly dropped the dishes when I saw my daughter. "What the hell!"

Rapunzel was sporting a mohawk that trailed down to a long braid that came to her mid-back. Sondra put a hand on her hip. "No way, young lady."

Rapunzel straightened her shoulders. "Aunt Karen likes it."

Karen said, "She's beautiful no matter how she has her hair."

Sondra was about to explode, so I cut her off. "You won't impress Penta with that updo."

Blossoms of color appeared on Rapunzel's cheeks. "Fine!"

My daughter grew out the sides of her hair and the braid came free. Fitzie guffawed. "Told you."

"Shut up, squirt."

Rapunzel and Fitzie fight all the time. She refuses to babysit him. 'Princesses don't babysit bratty little children' she had told us. I thought she might turn into a spoiled princess in Kingdom. Little did I know she was turning into a spoiled princess right here in the United States.

Penta came down the stairs and entered the dining room, remarking on how good everything smelled. I offered her the seat at the end of the table, but she declined. Noticing Karen's attention, she said, "I'm just a guest tonight. Not a queen or anything else."

We started eating. I twirled the pasta on my fork and asked about Rosario, which was met with brief answers. The conversation around the table was polite yet constrained. Before I could think of another topic, Rapunzel joined in. Leave it to her to broach a sensitive subject. "Will you please let me keep Clive Prince's phone number in my cell's address book. It's so annoying to have to ask you to dial his number for me."

"I don't like Clive," I said.

"He helps me with homework." Rapunzel took a drink.

Karen leaned forward. "Is he cute?"

Rapunzel brightened. "He has dreamy eyes." She pointed to her chin. "And a dimple right here. You know what? If I married him, I'd be Princess Rapunzel Prince."

I paused, my fork halfway to my mouth. "Married him!"

Karen waved at me. "Don't worry, Harold. We're just talking."

"No one is marrying anyone until she is twenty-five!" exclaimed Sondra. Glad she adjusted up, last week it was only twenty-three.

Penta raised an eyebrow.

Rapunzel appealed to Karen and Penta, sitting opposite

her. "Do you see what I have to put up with? I wanted to dye an orange stripe down the center of my forehead last week, but these two went berserk."

Sondra set down her wine glass. "Not this again. Orange is a horrible color on you."

"I can grow it out in a minute!" protested Rapunzel.

"And what would people say?" I interjected. "'Raquel, how did your hair grow out so quickly?' No daughter of mine is putting a no-passing line down the center of her head!"

"I should've never left the tower," grumbled Rapunzel.

Fitzie laughed and then shifted. "Mom, she kicked me."

Sondra shut her eyes. "Can we please enjoy our meal? We have guests."

Fitzie furrowed his brow. "It's only Aunt Karen and Aunt Penta. They're not guests. They're family."

Penta's face softened a bit at Fitzie's remark.

Rapunzel swallowed a forkful of pasta. "No mohawk. No hair dyeing. Everyone at school thinks I'm Amish with how I dress and style my hair! If you'd let me get a little tattoo—"

"No." Sondra and I, in unison.

"Even if it wasn't visible, it would mean a lot to me."

"Absolutely not!" I said. "We've discussed this. You have beautiful skin, please don't cover it up with something you'll regret later."

Karen cleared her throat. "Maybe a little tattoo wouldn't hurt."

Grimacing, Sondra glared across the table. "Is this my sister or a parallel from some other world? I thought you were a conservative mother."

Karen clenched her jaw. "I am a conservative mother. I also happen to be a liberal aunt."

"Karen!"

"Oh, Sondra. When did you get so stodgy?"

Rapunzel broke out laughing, throwing her head back. "I like that word."

We returned to our meal. I was about to discuss Alice's

latest trip to Kingdom and the news of Valencia's son when Fitzie interrupted me.

"Oh, gross! There's a hair in my food!"

Fitzie pinched the offending strand and held it up to Rapunzel. "It's one of yours."

Rapunzel rolled her eyes.

Fitzie appealed to me. "Ever since she came here, it's like we've had a new dog. Hair everywhere."

Sondra plucked the strand from Fitzie's fingers. "It's no big deal. Eat your food."

Fitzie growled, "You always take her side."

Rapunzel nudged him. "You're such a whiner. Don't embarrass me in front of our aunts."

Fitzie pointed at Penta. "My godmother would agree with me if she lived here all the time, wouldn't you, Aunt Penta?" He turned to his sister. "You grow hair like a yak."

Penta froze, her fork hanging in midair.

"And my godmother would agree with me." She glanced at Karen and received an encouraging nod. "My hair has saved people's lives, I'll have you know. You little booger."

I exhaled loudly through my nose. "We talked about the name calling, Rapunzie. Please apologize to Fitzie."

Shocked, Rapunzel replied, "He called me a yak. And call me Raquel like everyone else. Rapunzie sounds like a baby. Like Fitzie."

Fitzie frowned. "Better than bedhead. I heard that's your nickname at school."

Rapunzel threw down her fork. "Where did you hear that?"

Fitzie grinned. "I'm not telling."

"You little tardalong butt! I'll show you!"

Rapunzel stood and leaned over Fitzie's plate. In moments, her hair grew down and mixed in with the angel hair pasta and sauce, covering it.

Sondra had retreated to the kitchen to throw away the strand of hair, returning to the assault on Fitzie's dinner. She gripped the doorjamb. "Rapunzel!"

But our children ignored her. Fitzie parted his sister's hair, picked up the remains of his dinner and shoved it into her face. "Take that, *princess*."

Rapunzel shrieked and wiped the sauce and noodles from her face. She snorted like a bull, and screamed, "Oh, yeah?"

Her hair lifted out of Fitzie's food and into the air. Rapunzel suspended the ends of her hair, covered with tomato sauce like several spears dripping blood. Fitzie jumped up and pointed at them. "Mom, she's doing the Medusa thing again."

Fitzie bolted out of the room with Rapunzel racing after him. "Come back here. I'm going to whip the sprite outta you."

How did this happen? I leaped to my feet, but Sondra put her hand on my shoulder. "Sit down, Harold. I have this."

After speaking, my wife marched out of the dining room like a pixie on a mission. "You two better come back here right now, or so help me I'll get Piper's flute and I'll..." The words trailed off.

I turned to Karen and Penta. Karen had her napkin over her mouth, clearly suppressing her mirth. I turned to apologize to Penta but stopped. For the first time in eighty days, Penta had a broad smile planted on her face.

AFTERWORD

Thank you for reading this novel. I hope you enjoyed it. If you are so inclined, please leave a review on Amazon or Goodreads. Reviews help author's books get noticed.

If you are interested in reading more about Kingdom, three novels and two collections are listed in the books section. Also, check out my website at jimdorantales.com. I've posted free short stories there, including many set in Kingdom. One called "The Green-Haired Abductor" is the story of Sinope and "Raquel" before the events in this book. There, you'll see more wonderful art created by multiple artists, many of which are from the paintbrush of this novel's artist, Daniel Johnson. Over fifty illustrations and twelve free stories await. Why not check it out?

Jim Doran
jimdorantales.com

Daniel Johnson
artisticknack.com

ACKNOWLEDGEMENT

Valencia: Penta, why have you gathered us together, and what's in that cardboard box?

Penta (opening box): Alice dropped off copies of Hero's latest book, *Will Be Done*.

Cinderella: I'll bet this is his best novel ever.

Helga (rolls eyes): You would say that. You're in a lot of it.

Penta (hands out books): How much you're in it doesn't matter, Helga.

Valencia: Before I read the story, I enjoy reading the back matter first. I like reading Hero's acknowledgements. Though I don't know who all of the people are.

Penta: When I was living with Hero, he admitted it takes a lot of people other than the writer to bring a novel to life. For instance, Natalie Gaspar. She read the novel before it was published and helped specifically with the first chapters, so critical to a book.

Beauty (reading): And from what it says here, author Felicia

Change also read it and made many contributions to the final manuscript.

Snow White: And I know Hero has talked about Michelle Tang to me back when I lived on Earth. She's a dear writer friend who he consults with for most of his novels.

Cinderella: Just look at this cover! I'd like to meet Hero's artist, Daniel Johnson, one day and compliment him! He captured me beautifully.

Valencia: I don't think that's you on the cover, Cinderella. I think that's our newfound friend.

Cinderella (flipping through the pages): Well, inside is a depiction of Radiance's Retreat. It's stunning.

Beauty (skimming): I'm amazed at how he gets all these details right and keeps the action flowing.

Snow White: He has an editor, G. Miki Harden, who helps him. He once told me his books are elevated quite a bit by her work.

Helga: I see he's credited another author friend, Kristiana Sfirlea, as an inspiration. She's a gem.

Valencia: He also lists a lot of names. Ed Hosmer, Phillip Doran, Paxton Doran, Tom Doran, John Doran, Judy Malecke, Tricia & Bill Wittenberg, Ken and Carla Graham, Scott McCarthy. I wonder who they are?

Penta: I've met a few. Friends and family who encourage writers are super important to them.

Snow White: And there's Hope Doran. Someone who's always been super sweet and loving.

Beauty: I liked how he phrased this. "Since all good things come from God. If you found this story good, give credit to God." An interesting way to think about what the Creator provides us.

Helga (near the end of the book): Ha! Here it is!

Snow White: Here what is?

Helga: "Helga and Danforth flew through the air—" (Reading further). Cinderella! Did you really say that?

Cinderella (smirking): I think I'll retire now and read Hero's newest book.

ABOUT THE AUTHOR

Jim Doran

Jim Doran is a genre writer who enjoys transporting his readers to unique destinations filled with wonder and spectacle. Within his novels, you will travel to fascinating places such as an invisible chalet built strictly for lovers or a swamp that grants wishes.

Jim has been published in multiple anthologies and online by Havok Online, Ye Olde Dragon Press, and Every Day Fiction.

PRAISE FOR AUTHOR

Kingdom Come
Hits all the right spots for a work in this genre.

- LAURA

On Earth, As It Is
This book is a great read for fans of the first story...sweeping high
fantasy plots, surprising urban fantasy influences, and multi POV.

- KRISTIANA SFIRLEA, AUTHOR OF THE AWARD-WINNING
STORMWATCH DIARY SERIES

Deliver Us
There's comic relief, peril, mystery, adventure, romance,
everything you could ask for in a good book. I didn't know how
I felt about an adult fantasy novel featuring fairytales, but this
world and story is so well told, I loved it.

- ASHLEY NICOLE, AUTHOR OF HAVEN

Kingdom's Advent

Kingdom's Advent is a great read for anyone who enjoys fantasy, fairytales, and fun.

- LISA CASKEY, AUTHOR OF THE FARMED TRILOGY

Kingdom's Acension
For the freshness of its tone and writing, the unexpected directions of the storytelling, and the vivid-in-small-packages character work, it should offer all-ages fans of the form much to enjoy.

- THEQISSILENT

BOOKS BY THIS AUTHOR

Kingdom Come: A Kingdom Fantasy Novel

When times are dim and full of woe / And devils threaten maidens low.

Harold Tray is haunted, not only by his past, but by a ghost as well. After he agrees to a request by the spirit, Harold is transported to the land of fairy tales called Kingdom. He partners with a pixie in search of a way home and discovers a prophetic scroll. The prophecy predicts the rise of five queens who will overthrow an illegitimate king. Harold, armed only with the knowledge of the stories he read as a child, encounters famous and obscure fairytale characters as he journeys around Kingdom. He is unaware of the villain who has set traps for the queens…someone who will grant Harold's fondest wishes if only he chooses to go home.

Kingdom Come is a fantasy drama that explores the potential of the human heart to live, grieve, and love.

On Earth, As It Is: A Kingdom Fantasy Novel

Three years after the events of Kingdom Come, Harold and Sondra are struggling to establish a lasting relationship. When a friend from Kingdom travels to Earth, she tells Harold that someone has abducted the realm's five queens. Harold assumes he will travel to the world of elves and dragons again, but the messenger has a different idea—one in which Earth itself will play a vital role.

In this whimsical fantasy tale, Harold, Sondra, and other characters, set out on a new adventure, spanning not only one, but two, worlds.

Deliver Us: A Kingdom Fantasy Novel

After Sondra and Harold Saturn bail the Little Match Girl and Alice of Wonderland out of jail on Earth, they learn the fairytale world of Kingdom is in peril once again. A trio of witches are killing and cursing the people of Kingdom, and the royals haven't been able to stop it.

In Deliver Us, curses, artifacts, murders, animated tattoos, and proper manners all combine toward a thrilling conclusion in which those who confront the evildoers must find a way to defeat the witches or lose their souls.

Kingdom's Advent: Kingdom Short Stories

Welcome to Kingdom, a fairytale world of grand fantasy consisting of endangered pixies as well as industrious giants, wishing wells and imprisoned towns, sorcery and swordship —and cursed corsets too. This collection offers up an ambitious young fairy who learns a secret that will change her life, a virtuous girl trying to make a living in a community harboring evil creatures, outcast dwarfs with loving hearts, and a princess who despises anyone who would save her life. The legends of triumphant heroes and foul villains are captured within these six short stories.

Kingdom's Ascension: Kingdom Short Stories

Being a queen in a fairytale world isn't a fairy tale. Just ask the sister queens who rule over the land of Kingdom. Cinderella wants to marry her sweetheart—but will true love cost him his life? Snow White desires to meet with her subjects though not all of them are admirers. For the Marsh King's Daughter, courtship rituals must be strictly obeyed, often to her displeasure. Kingdom's Ascension offers these and other tales of a fairytale world where happy, sad, and all endings in-between are possible.

Made in the USA
Columbia, SC
26 September 2023

23275014R00228